FIRST

"And what about you, kid'
voice, right next to him. "You've been awful quiet on
that phone."

Vic spun to his right, hard and fast, and brought
the phone receiver crashing across the jaw of the
man who'd been standing behind him. The blow
sent him reeling. His buddy was dragging a sidearm
from his waistband. Someone in the cafe screamed,
and several dived for the floor.

Vic leapt up onto the counter and lashed out with
his tongue. The muscle, slick with drool, darted half
the length of the cafe and knocked the pistol right
out of the man's grip.

In such a confined space, filled with civilians,
the odds weren't the worst but getting people out
without someone getting hurt looked impossible.
He had no more than a second to choose. Fight or
flight.

BY THE SAME AUTHOR

DESCENT: JOURNEYS IN THE DARK
The Doom of Fallowhearth

WARHAMMER 40,000: CARCHARODONS
Red Tithe
Outer Dark

WARHAMMER 40,000
Dawn of War III
The Last Hunt
Blood Of Iax

WARHAMMER: AGE OF SIGMAR
Scourge of Fate
The Bone Desert

WARHAMMER 40,000: WARZONE FENRIS
Legacy of Russ: The Wild King

NON-FICTION
British Light Infantry in the American Revolution
Battle Tactics of the American Revolution

MARVEL XAVIER'S INSTITUTE

FIRST TEAM

ROBBIE MacNIVEN

ACONYTE

FOR MARVEL PUBLISHING

VP Production & Special Projects: Jeff Youngquist
Associate Editor, Special Projects: Caitlin O'Connell
Manager, Licensed Publishing: Jeremy West
VP, Licensed Publishing: Sven Larsen
SVP Print, Sales & Marketing: David Gabriel
Editor in Chief: C B Cebulski

Special Thanks to Jordan D White & Jacque Porte

First published by Aconyte Books in 2021
ISBN 978 1 83908 062 3
Ebook ISBN 978 1 83908 063 0

Cover art by Anastasia Bulgakova

Distributed in North America by Simon & Schuster Inc, New York, USA
Printed in the United States of America
9 8 7 6 5 4 3 2 1

ACONYTE BOOKS

An imprint of Asmodee Entertainment Ltd
Mercury House, Shipstones Business Centre
North Gate, Nottingham NG7 7FN, UK
aconytebooks.com // twitter.com/aconytebooks

This book is dedicated to the memory of Grace Gaskell.

CHAPTER ONE

There was a fly beating itself to death against the window.

Victor Borkowski tried his best to ignore it. He stared down at his exam paper, struggling to drag the answer from the neat black lettering glaring back at him.

6) a. Write a short (500 word) essay on the primary causes of the Boston Massacre. Include references to secondary literature.

He was one hundred fifty words in. Well, one hundred fifty-three. He'd counted it five times. A little over one hundred fifty words was all he'd been able to wring from a very vague knowledge of Britain's "imperial crisis" in the 1760s. He remembered it mostly because the class had been interrupted mid-session by Glob throwing up. Seeing someone with translucent skin vomiting wasn't something Vic was ever going to forget, and the shock appeared to have seared the entire lesson onto his memory.

C'mon, Vic! Focus! Sam Adams. The Sons of Liberty. He'd watched the whole TV series over the last couple of days. That counted as studying, right? His other study plan – just talking to Graymalkin about the subject – hadn't worked as well as he'd hoped. It turned out that Gray's super-powers didn't include a flawless memory and being born in colonial America hadn't given him an omnipotent understanding of all events occurring in the year 1770. After Gray had started digressing about how the word "tricorn" was an inaccurate nineteenth-century invention, Vic had just let him talk, his own thoughts wandering to his acceptance speech for the student drama awards.

Would a tux be overdoing it? Would Striker be there this year? Would going chameleon halfway through be too showy?

No! Focus! He glanced back at the fly, still slamming relentlessly off the window, its every effort apparently bent towards escaping the stifling, drab examination hall. *You and me both, buddy*, he thought. He began to write, just for the sake of it. Any answer was better than none. Samuel Adams, brother of John Adams. He didn't like tea. No one in eighteenth-century Boston did. No stamps either. Damn, Glob's guts had looked weird when he'd thrown up. All squirming and twitching. Was that what everyone's insides looked like when they spewed? He'd never been happier about the fact that his own insides didn't show up when he needed to go invisible.

He stopped writing, sighed heavily, and scribbled an ugly, jagged black line through everything he'd just written. Back to one hundred fifty-three. How many words did that leave, three hundred forty-seven? Why was math so much easier than history? He'd aced that exam. Or fencing. Something exciting. Something he was good at.

Bzz-thunk! Bzz-thunk! Bzz-thunk! went the fly.

He looked up at it. The insect was resolutely attempting to headbutt its way through the reinforced glass of the large viewing window that lay between the exam hall and the war room. Its efforts were relentless, its head apparently unbreakable. At this rate it would be about as capable of sitting through an exam as he was.

As though sensing his thoughts, the fly abruptly buzzed upwards and began a frenzied orbit of one of the hall's cage lights, like a dog chasing its tail. Vic forced himself not to stare at it, letting his gaze sit neutrally on the rest of the room spread out before him.

Like much of the rest of the New Charles Xavier School for Mutants, the exam hall looked like a Cold War-era bunker that had decided to dress up as a high school for Halloween. It was a long, vaulted space of bleak and unyielding concrete, each pitted surface lit by the hard white illumination of the cage lamps overhead. To this austere, subterranean realm had been added a few half-hearted concessions to a bland North American school aesthetic. A large world map had been tacked to the wall, along with framed photos of previous graduations and a collection of rough-and-ready art class projects. Today the floorspace was also taken up by several dozen rickety desks and chairs, all of which bore enough graffiti to convince Vic that they'd come with the original base.

It wasn't somewhere that exactly inspired academic expression, and that was even before factoring in the infernal heat that materialized whenever more than a handful of warm, breathing bodies gathered in one of the school's many underground chambers. There was an AC system, of course, but it produced the most grating rattle imaginable, so it was turned off for exams. Vic found himself seriously considering raising his hand and claiming his coldblooded inability to self-regulate his body temperature counted as an exceptional exam circumstance. It wasn't often that he wished he could swap scales for skin that was capable of sweating, but this was one of those times.

Bzz-thunk! The fly was back at the window.

Sam Adams was definitely John Adams' brother, right? Paul Giamatti had been great in that role. He should have watched more of the *Adams* series instead of trying to coax the knowledge out of Graymalkin.

He glanced over at Gray, seated at the desk to his right. The lugubrious-looking youth was hunched forward awkwardly over his undersized desk, writing slow and steady, his expression one of tightly controlled focus. Apparently sensing Vic's attention, he paused and glanced up. Vic grinned broadly at him and gave him both thumbs up. *Come on Gray, give me something to work with.* Graymalkin simply held his gaze for a moment, then blinked and looked abruptly back at his writing. The sheet of his answer booklet was full of long, elegant cursive that Vic would've struggled to read even if he'd been trying to – not that he was, of course!

He looked away hastily, not wanting to catch the attention of Ms Pryde. She was stalking the aisles between the desks, air-walking with complete silence. Unlike the other examiners, you never heard her coming. Hell, she could even phase if she wanted to observe you without being noticed. Totally unfair. At least she was visible now, her back to Vic as she passed noiselessly between Pixie and Trance near the front-right of the hall.

He took the opportunity to glance across at his other neighbor, Cipher. She had been writing furiously, but had now paused and was staring straight ahead, expression blank, one hand teasing subconsciously at the strands of her long locs.

Vic felt a sense of undeserved gratification. It wasn't just him, Ci was stuck as well. The sharpest girl in the class, the de facto head of school security and the most mysterious student in the whole facility was struggling just as much with the history of colonial America as–

Cipher went back to writing, the renewed sound of her

scribbling crushing Vic's hopes utterly. He let out another sigh and slumped back in his chair, wincing slightly as it creaked.

The sound of his own disconsolance had drawn the attention of Ms Pryde. She gave him a hard look over the bowed heads of the dozen students seated between them. He smiled back at her and straightened up.

If he got through this, he would actually study next time. That was a promise. But now, he just had to put pen to paper and get it done. Gritting his teeth, he leant forward like everyone else and began to write. There had been disturbances between locals and soldiers just prior to the Boston Massacre. Street brawls, civil unrest. The tensions all contributed to the shootings. Keep expanding on that. You've got this. He paused to count up his word total again – two hundred twenty-one. Getting there. Practically halfway.

Bzz-thunk. Bzz-thu–

He blinked and realized abruptly that his fist was raised and clenched. The fly had been buzzing past, presumably with a splitting headache, and he'd just reflexively snatched it out of the air. He could feel it tickling his palm.

He looked up. At the end of the hall Ms Pryde was looking at him again, her expression cold. Slowly, almost imperceptibly, she shook her head. Equally slowly, Vic unclenched his fist. Freed from its abrupt prison, the fly zoomed back up towards the light.

As if on cue, there was a sharp buzzing sound at the end of the hall. Several students jumped. Ms Pryde held up her communicator – a small, circular flip-device – and killed the timed alarm.

"This examination session is ended," she announced. "Everyone, please remain seated while we collect your script books. And double-check your names are on the front, in capital. Real or alias, whichever you prefer."

Vic realized he'd even forgotten to do that. Giving up on the essay, he shut his answers booklet and printed his super hero name, ANOLE, on the front, along with the time and date. To hell with it. He didn't look at Ms Pryde as she she swept past and picked up the booklet.

CHAPTER TWO

"The second session begins in twenty minutes," Ms Pryde said as she returned to the end of the hall. "You're all permitted to use the bathrooms and the break room. Dismissed."

The hall resounded immediately with the harsh scraping of chairs on concrete. Vic joined the chattering crowd of students as they filed out, trying not to think about the past two hours. If he didn't ace the second exam session, he'd have to retake the course at the end of the summer.

"Cheer up, Borkowski," exclaimed a sing-song voice from amidst the crowd carrying him along. He looked up to see Megan Gwynn – Pixie – being her usual purple-haired, pointy-eared, grinning self. When Pixie smiled, it was hard not to smile back. Vic did his best though.

"Tough one, huh?" she pressed as she fell in alongside him, her slender wings buzzing faintly.

"We'll see," Vic said, not really wanting to talk about it.

"What did you put for question two? The date of the Quebec Act?"

"Tell me it was 1773?"

Pixie hissed between her teeth and shook her head. "I thought it was 1774?"

Vic groaned audibly and Pixie threw her arm over his shoulder, cutting through his misery with a short giggle.

"It could be 1773! I was basically just guessing!"

"You're just saying that to make me feel better."

"Perhaps," she smirked, removing her arm and giving him a nudge in the ribs. "Oh, Ben!" she continued, buzzing off to chat to the burning-haired Match before Vic could respond. He stepped into the break room after her, trying and failing not to look as miserable as he felt. He hated it when people knew he was down.

The "break room" was the war room's less aggressive title. When the underground labyrinth had served as the Weapons Plus Program's primary testing facility, it seemed the circular chamber had indeed been as some sort of command-and-control center. Smaller than the exam hall, though still fashioned from the same grim, unyielding blocks of concrete, its banks of computers now sat stripped out and inactive and its monitor screens dormant. Scrapes on the floor indicated where a heavy iron chart desk had once been bolted to the ground, while scuffed warning strips and hazard markings helped to demarcate an armored exit hatch and emergency lighting.

The military-industrial chic had been softened somewhat by the efforts of the students over the last few years. There were a few ratty old leather couches and chairs spread around, an old TV and a pair of chipped coffee tables, a row of prepacked cupboards and cabinets flanking a fridge and freezer that had been covered top-to-bottom with stickers – at some point it had become tradition for students to plaster them with images and cards from their travels. The space had assumed the status of an unofficial common room, especially for the students in the dorms on the west side of the cavernous danger room at the heart of the facility. It was soon loud with the chatter of the examinees as they swapped answers and commiserated with one another.

Vic found Cipher and Graymalkin on the edge of the semicircle of chairs and couches that occupied most of the middle of the room. The latter was standing stiffly, listening to Ci as she perched on the back of a chair currently occupied by Triage, who was sitting facing in the opposite direction. The pair looked up as Vic emerged from the crowd.

"Take it that went badly?" Cipher asked, her tone light.

Vic managed a shrug. "Well, if the Quebec Act was passed in 1773, then…"

"It was 1774."

"Then yeah, it went badly."

"You have my commiserations, Victor," Graymalkin said. After a second, in what seemed like an afterthought, he reached out and put a hand carefully on Vic's shoulder.

Despite himself, Vic laughed. "You know, they shouldn't really let someone who was alive at the time take the history exam," he told Gray. "Does it even count as history for you? You were growing up while George Washington was a Virginia legislator."

"Simply living through an event doesn't guarantee a nuanced understanding of it," Graymalkin pointed out in his stiff, archaic accent. "And do we not study modern history also? Were not all of these students alive for the last four presidential elections?"

Vic conceded the point with a wave of his hand.

"Well, that's my summer ruined, I guess," he said. "Looks like I won't get a chance to visit home after all. I'll have to stay in this sweltering dungeon, buried in textbooks until I have to re-take it."

"I will maintain your company," Graymalkin offered gallantly. "I have nowhere else to be."

"Yeah, welcome to the 'school-is-your-home' club, Vic," Cipher added.

"You guys really didn't have any summer plans?"

He caught Gray's glance at Cipher, the dark-skinned young woman far better at not giving anything away. He raised an eyebrow at them both.

"Well, there were some plans in consideration," Graymalkin admitted, looking almost sheepish. "We had thought we might... travel."

"A vacation," Cipher elaborated for the eighteenth-century kid. "We were thinking about going on a road trip. The three of us, after you'd been with your parents for a few weeks."

"Where to?" Vic asked, genuinely surprised. He'd never really considered either of his friends to be road trip types. Cipher disliked the unknown and was practically wedded to the school's security systems, while Graymalkin still seemed to struggle somewhat with the modern phenomenon of travelling for recreational purposes.

"We were thinking the Rockies," Cipher said. "Maybe drive north to south for a week or two. Gray wanted to see them, and I wanted to get a nice postcard for the common room fridge."

"The finest mountains on the continent," Graymalkin added with what amounted to an enthusiastic smile.

"You always say you don't really like living in the school," Cipher went on. "We thought it'd be good for all of us to get out for a bit. Change things up."

"Let's see if I've got this right," Vic said, shifting on the chair's back. "You two were planning a surprise road trip for the three of us to celebrate the end of exams? A trip that I've just ruined by bombing the history exam?"

"The examination is only halfway complete," Graymalkin consoled. "There is yet time for you to wrest it back."

"The second half is about emancipation and the civil rights movement," Cipher added. "And before you ask, the Emancipation

Proclamation was 1863. Same year as Gettysburg. You know the start of the Gettysburg Address, don't you? Four score and seven years. That's eighty-seven years since the Declaration of Independence. Easy way to remember it."

"Easy!" Vic exclaimed. "How was anything you just said there supposed to be easy to remember? What the heck's a score? How am I supposed to know how many that is?"

"A score is twenty, of course," Graymalkin said, as though it was the most obvious thing in the world.

"Vic, shut up," snapped Mark Sheppard. The raven-haired student was standing beside the old television that had been linked up to one of the room's many monitors. He was working the tuning dial, trying to resolve an image on a display dashed and distorted by digital static.

Vic abruptly realized that the idle chatter which had filled the break room had grown quiet. Everyone's attention was on the monitor, and the words now coming in over its speakers.

"Early reports indicate that there are a further five rallies planned across the Midwestern United States in the coming weeks. We can go live to our correspondent right now in Columbus, Ohio, where the self-styled Prophet Xodus is leading what he dubs 'a sermon for his congregation.'"

The screen resolved itself fully just as the camera switched from a CTV news anchor to a crowd in Columbus Commons. As the live reporter narrated the gathering behind her, Vic felt a chill run up his spine. He knew what this was. They all did.

The view changed again – now it was a wide shot of the head of the rally. A stage had been erected in front of the crowd, topped by a lectern that was draped in black cloth and emblazoned with a white cross-and-circle crest. A large timber rendering of the same emblem had been raised behind the lectern, framing it.

Nine figures occupied the stage. Four stood flanking the

lectern, clad in long black robes that had been embroidered with the same white cross-and-circle. They had cowls raised, and their faces were concealed by silver grotesque masks. The remaining figure stood between them. He too was dressed in black robes, though his grotesque was golden and fashioned differently to the leering harlequin faces of those flanking him. It was angelic, expressionless and serene. It gleamed brilliantly in the stage lights.

The audio cut from the reporter's voiceover to the words booming from the mics rigged up to the lectern. The words rebounded around the break room, the tone powerful, stentorian, and riven with a raw, tangible hatred.

"Make no mistake, my children! Be not in doubt! A reckoning is coming! A judgment long overdue! Your prophet is here to herald it, to give you fair warning! When the fires come, they will not only burn the mutant. The unrighteous will go up in the inferno with them!"

The large figure struck a palm flat against the lectern, then did so again, emphasizing each sentence with a fresh blow. "All who have aided them, all who have abetted them! Any who give shelter to their depravity or approval to their deformity! All are unclean, all with be remade in the fire! So says Prophet Xodus!"

A brazen cheer swelled furiously from the crowd just as the image cut back to the live reporter. Struggling to be heard over the uproar, she went on to describe how the rally was set to be repeated in states along the East Coast.

The report began to distort again as the static returned, chopping up and crazing the image of the rally. Sheppard tried to adjust it, before giving up and angrily hitting the off switch. The screen blinked to black.

The silence that followed seemed absolute. Nobody spoke. Vic found himself glancing back at Cipher and Graymalkin. The latter looked blank, an expression Vic had come to recognize as the mask Gray drew down whenever he was troubled. Cipher looked furious, and for a second Vic thought she was going to phase out.

He could understand why. This wasn't the first rally that had made the news. For the past two months the Purifier cult had been resurgent across the northern United States and southern Canada, carrying their quasi-religious anti-mutant vitriol to every town and city. And it wasn't just angry gatherings, burnt-out cars and cross-and-circle symbols daubed on doors and windows. The parents, friends and family of half a dozen of the students at the Institute had been attacked. There were even rumors of abductions. Vic had found himself worrying more and more about his parents, regretting how little he'd seen of them since he'd enrolled at the Institute. Now there was an added threat, the looming uncertainty of civil unrest, he found himself thinking about home almost every day.

Worst of all, it looked as though the authorities were powerless to stop the outpouring of hate. Arrested cultists seemed capable of affording the best legal counsel money could buy, and several police chiefs had spoken about their desire to avoid "riots in the streets" and "full-fledged civil unrest." As far as Vic was concerned, they may as well have just released a press statement saying, "go ahead and target that mutant minority, just try not to upset their neighbors while you're at it."

He looked at the rest of the class in the break room, seeing a bitter mix of anger and fear. Nobody met his eye. Somehow that made him feel even worse. The silence was unbearable. "Think Xodus would do well in our history exam," he said slowly. "He sounds like he belongs in the eighteenth century."

Nobody laughed, but then he hadn't expected them to. The words had the desired effect, breaking the silence that had taken hold of the room. Conversations restarted, though they stayed muted.

"How can we stay down here while those lunatics are taking over half of North America?" Vic muttered under his breath.

"Ms Frost and the rest of the X-Men are dealing with them," Graymalkin said without much conviction, his expression guarded once more. "They will do what is best."

"And when will it be our turn?" Vic said, trying not to let Gray's stoicism get to him. He found staying detached in situations like these almost impossible. "To hell with history exams. History's happening right now, and it's not going the way it should be. You want students like us to be reading about the successful Purifier uprising in fifty years' time? If there's even any mutants left, that is."

"There's nothing we can do right now," Cipher said, sounding exasperated. "I wish that wasn't the case, Vic. There'll be a reckoning, but right now that's not up to us."

"One day it will be," Vic said, standing up. He saw Graymalkin and Cipher exchange a look, but neither replied. They knew he was right. One day they'd all be X-Men, and things would start to go very different for Prophet Xodus.

There was a buzzing sound from the direction of the exam hall. The twenty-minute interval was up. Not speaking to anyone, Vic joined the flow of students leaving the break room, his thoughts turning over darkly.

The fly was gone. Vic knew he'd have been able to detect its maddening buzzing from the other end of the hall. Had it found an escape route through the AC, or had it finally pulverized itself to death against the exam room window?

He forced himself to look back down at the page, to read those unblinking, death-stare letters.

1) a. In what year did the signing of the Emancipation Proclamation take place?

Was it 1862? What had Ci said? Four score and seven years. A score was eighteen? No, twenty. Gray had said twenty. So twenty times four plus seven. That was eighty-seven. But eighty-seven from what? The Declaration of Independence? That was 1776. He'd seen the musical. So, 1776 plus eighty-seven was... 1863. That sounded right.

He scribbled it down. Next question.

1) b. Give a brief (200 word) description of the work of Frederick Douglass.

He knew that one too. Triage had played Frederick Douglass in a roleplaying exercise during class. Vic didn't think he could've done a better job himself, which was probably for the best as he suspected the real Frederick Douglass hadn't possessed a ridge of bony scalp nubs or a prehensile tongue.

1) c. Give the rough percentage of African-American soldiers in the Union Army by the year 1865.

He had no idea. Maybe the next question would be better? Nope. He didn't know the winner of the 1876 presidential election, let alone how it had impacted the Reconstruction era. He sat back, trying to think. *Don't let your mind wander. Focus and you'll get through this.*

He turned to look at Graymalkin. The pale, shaven-headed youth paused and looked back at him. Just as before, the fellow-mutant's face remained inscrutable. This time however – and clearly unsure about the gesture – Graymalkin slowly raised a single thumb.

Ordinarily Gray's tentative effort at something so recognizably modern would've left Vic battling laughter. This time though he just nodded and looked away. He felt sorry for Gray. Sorry for everyone. None of them deserved this. To live underground, hidden away in an old, derelict military facility, unable to do anything but watch as the world caved into hatred and discord. If they stayed here over the summer, what would they be emerging into after? What would be waiting for them once the fire and brimstone had died away? Would there be anything recognizable left? Anything not burnt or blemished by smoke and ash?

Snap!

The pen in Vic's hand shattered. He looked down at the black ink dripping slowly over his hand and down onto his answer sheet. He watched it drip and spread gradually, his expression blank. Then, abruptly, he dropped the shattered pen and stood up. The scrape of his chair echoed, cold and lonely, through the hall.

Heads turned. He ignored them as he signed and dated his ruined sheet and carried it to the front. Ms Pryde watched him approach. He held her gaze as he laid the sheet on the desk at the end of the hall.

She said nothing. Vic turned and left.

CHAPTER THREE

It was almost midnight when Vic heard a familiar knock at his door.

He'd been avoiding reality since leaving the exam hall, making a quick visit to the cafeteria to boil up some pasta before locking himself in his dorm room. Like all of the accommodation in the Institute, the space was cramped and overwhelmingly subterranean. A small window – which Vic had shuttered – looked out onto the corridor, presumably added in an attempt to lessen the claustrophobia. Thankfully, the confined nature of the room had never really bothered him. He'd made the space his own, even more so after his roommate had moved out last semester. Movie posters and autographed actor headshots adorned the walls, while an Xbox hummed softly in one corner beneath a TV screen. Since the start of exam season it also seemed as though a library had been upended inside the room. Books were stacked in teetering piles by the bed or spread in arcs across the floor, some lying open, pages stuffed with note tabs. Late nights studying – or, as often as not, procrastinating – had also ensured that there was a regular student detritus of stale clothing and even staler plates and ready-meal packets scattered around.

Clutter wasn't like him, but he'd been too deep in the stresses of studying to tackle the mounting mess. Now he was just too on edge. He tried to read for a bit after picking at his pasta, but it felt as though the history textbooks heaped across his desk were judging him. He fired up his Xbox and sank into the beanbag at the end of his bed, losing himself in button-mashing for the next few hours.

It didn't do much good. He tore through four or five levels of *Total Combat* – ones he'd completed dozens of times before – but it didn't banish the thoughts that had been with him since the break room. In the solitude of his cramped dorm, it was impossible to deny that there was more to his frustration than just news of the Purifier rampage.

It had brought back memories. The shadows of a time Vic thought he'd put behind him. He remembered his childhood: the struggles, so often unspoken, faced by his parents. How the hell did you go about raising a mutant kid in small-town Illinois? How did that turn out OK?

He knew the answer. It wasn't just that his parents had fought his corner from day one, though they certainly had, unflinchingly. They had come through because the town had been with them. Dan and Martha Borkowski were members of the community. They were known across Fairbury for their generosity, hard work and honesty. Dan had founded the town's electronics store and went out of his way to employ local kids struggling with their grades. Martha had worked as a receptionist in the hospital for the better part of thirty years, all the while juggling active memberships with the Fairbury Historical Society, the Illinois Alliance for the Protection of Animals, and the First Presbyterian Church. They worked hard, they lived honestly, and when Vic had come into their lives, they'd found they had far more friends in Fairbury than enemies.

There'd still been a few who didn't appreciate him, of course. Vic remembered one particular priest from an outlying neighborhood who'd preached against him on several occasions. He'd only found out years later, but he always remembered the man's unyielding, dead-eyed glare whenever he'd passed him in town. It had taken Vic the longest time to figure out why someone he'd never met, never spoken to, would feel that way about him.

The town had sheltered him. He'd been invited to barbeques, sat in church, played on the Little League baseball team. Any hint of bullying in school had been clamped down on by his teachers. His friends had seemed in perpetual awe of his ability to climb the sides of buildings, vanish into his surroundings, or catch flies with his tongue – an act he had disavowed as gross from the age of eight onwards.

It hadn't all been easy, but it had sure seemed that way to Vic growing up. After coming to the Institute he'd started to realize just how heavily he'd been shielded. He learned how rare a happy childhood was when he'd started meeting other mutants. Growing up free from trauma was a priceless blessing, something to be cherished. Graymalkin and Cipher were proof of that. Gray had been attacked by his own father when he'd tried to come out to him. He'd been buried alive, only discovering his mutant powers – his ability to endure in the dark – after being entombed. Cipher was even less forthcoming about her childhood, but Vic knew that she'd been abandoned by her parents. After a rare attempt by Gray to learn how to play Vic's console, he'd told him about the rumors that Jean Grey had found her after she'd infiltrated the school, using her invisibility and phasing powers to stay undetected. She'd never told Vic how long she'd actually been there before she'd been discovered. He got the impression it was a while.

All of them had been shaped by their upbringing. Vic was just thankful his had been so happy for so long. But now all of that was at risk.

GAME OVER.

He'd been stuck on level seven of *Total Combat* for almost an hour now. He needed to get a combo kill on Boss Red, but he was too distracted. He tossed the controller onto his bed, about to give up. That was when the thunderous knock came, making Vic leap to his feet.

For a brief second, he thought the Institute was under attack. The door to his dorm shuddered in its frame, enduring successive strikes, two, three, four. In the silence that followed he realized who it was. Nobody else in the school knocked like that.

He stood up, checked he hadn't spilled pasta down his tank top, and opened the door. Instead of the corridor outside he found himself face-to-face with a cliff. A mound of craggy, gray stone appeared to have collapsed outside his room, a mound that now looked down at him with pale and unblinking eyes.

"What's up, lizard boy?" said the rock.

"Not much," Vic answered.

Santo Vaccarro, better known around the school by his alias, Rockslide. His particular mutation was as obvious as it was impressive. Over six feet tall and seemingly almost as wide, his size alone was enough to attract attention, but that was before factoring in that his biological makeup consisted mostly of stone. He was all broad shoulders, rough-hewn pecs, and arms thicker than Vic's torso, cast in coarse, solid rock. It was as if a sculptor with a background in brutalist architecture had hewed a statue of a football lineman from the side of a mountain. His craggy head, perched like a boulder on the ridgeline of his shoulders, regarded Vic for a moment with all the inscrutability of a mountain peak.

"Can I come in?" he rumbled.

Vic stood aside, encompassing his room with a sweep of his arm. "I'm sure you know the way, Rocky."

Santo grunted and turned sideways – it was the only means for him to fit through the door without scraping it. Vic checked the outside to make sure the knocks hadn't left a dent, then closed it behind him.

"Welcome home," he said as he turned to face Santo again. The mutant seemed to fill the cramped room as he looked around, neck joints grinding slightly.

"Like what you've done with the place," he said in his grumbling, monotone voice. "Feels smaller though."

"I've spread out since you left," Vic joked, planting a foot on the end of the concrete slab that had once constituted Santo's bed. After he'd moved out Vic had started using the block as an extra book stand, the once-orderly stacks having long since degenerated to a jumbled mound. He shoved some aside so Santo could sit on the edge.

"*Total Combat*?" Rockslide wondered as he lowered himself down with a scrape. Vic hopped back onto his beanbag, legs crossed, and tossed him the secondary controller.

"You still remember how to play?" he asked with the slightest hint of a smirk.

"I still remember how to beat Boss Red," Santo replied. "Which looks to be more than you can claim."

"We'll see," Vic shot back and un-paused the game.

No further greeting was necessary. This was how the two of them had always been, after a little over two years sharing a dorm at the Institute. Vic would be angry after a botched stage rehearsal, or pining over a boy, or stressed from exams, or just missing home. Santo would always be there, watching TV for hours on end, acting as disinterested as an enduring mountaintop. They'd play Xbox in silence, and eventually Vic would open up, often all in a rush. Santo would let him vent, saying little, absorbing the heat of Vic's emotions.

Today it took a little longer than usual.

"I didn't know you were still around," Vic said as Boss Red hit the deck and blinked off the screen. "Thought maybe you'd already been assigned to one of the teams."

"You think I would leave without visiting?" Santo replied.

"Is that what this is?"

"No. I'm still waiting on my placement."

Vic lapsed back into silence as he skipped through the intro to level eight. Santo had graduated out of the Institute last semester. He'd been away on a couple of missions, he'd even been given staff accommodation while he was staying at the school, but he hadn't yet received a solo assignment. In all honesty, no matter how happy he was for him, Vic didn't look forward to the day Rockslide was gone for good. He'd hoped to get out in the field not long after him, but after bombing his test all his plans were up in the air.

"What was it like working with Ms Frost and the others out there?" he asked as a swarm of street goons assailed their characters on screen. He'd already heard all the stories – he'd been the first to ask about them – but he wanted a diversion. Level eight was too easy anyway.

Santo repeated the encounters of the last few months. The Hellions, most of them recent graduates, had been tracking down a global arms-smuggling ring that appeared to be in the thrall of an as-yet-unidentified mutant. No leads yet, but a lot of scrapes and close calls. Santo's geokinetic powers had already saved lives. Vic pretended not to be a bit jealous.

Level nine in no time at all. He was in the process of resurrecting Santo's avatar when he said it.

"I left the exam early today."

He hadn't really meant to speak, but it was out now. Already, it felt a bit better.

"I heard," was all Santo said, immediately attacking the cyber-hounds closing in on screen. Even after all this time, seeing him working the controller in his huge, gritty paws was faintly amusing.

"Did Ci and Gray tell you?" Vic asked.

"One of them," Santo responded, not taking his eyes off the display.

"They were planning a trip this summer," Vic admitted. "The three of us. I think I might have ruined it for them."

"You always do better than you think you will," Santo said without emotion. "It's annoying."

"Well, no one likes a bragger," Vic said with a small smile, his avatar dashing in to save Santo from the pixelated mechanical dogs.

"Why'd you leave?" Santo asked. Vic didn't reply immediately, grimacing as he battled through the right button combo to deactivate the hounds. He thought about lying, about saying it was just that the exam had been too difficult, but he knew Santo wouldn't buy it. Besides, his roommate hadn't come back to judge. That was why Vic felt comfortable telling him.

"There was a news report during the break. They were at one of the Purifier rallies. Prophet Xodus and his lunatics."

"They've been on the news a lot," Santo said levelly.

"Why does nobody stop them? The police, the authorities? They're totally out of control!"

"There's work being done. Part of the reason the Hellions have been struggling to trace this arms dealer is because everyone's focused on containing the Purifiers. Mutants are being attacked everywhere. It's like a sport to them."

"Someone needs to strike back."

For the first time since entering the dorm, Santo glanced at Vic.

"Someone will, when the time is right," he said.

"And when is that going to be? When they're burning mutants at the stake?"

Santo looked back at the screen, saying nothing. Level nine completed. One more to go.

"It reminded me of home," Vic went on as he skipped through the intro. "Growing up, there was only really one guy I knew who openly talked about not wanting me in Fairbury. He tried to get others to back him up, but he couldn't. And now that I look back, I see how rare that was. How eager people usually are to fall into line against anything they think is out of the ordinary."

"People are easily led," Santo said. Vic shook his head. The final level. The infamous Mechanoidian big boss rose from its scrap pit, its combat klaxon blaring over the speakers.

"I don't believe most people are like that," he said. "Maybe a lot find it easier to go whichever way the wind blows. But there are good people too. Plenty of them."

"And good things happen to good people," Santo said as he charged right into the Mechanoidian, raining blows on its rusty shell.

Vic wondered about that. It was true that he'd always believed goodness won out. Where it was contested, where it was challenged, it would endure and shine through. Wasn't that the whole point of him being here? The purpose behind the New Charles Xavier School, the "Institute," the reason he was striving to become an X-Man? The belief that good was a tangible force on the world, and that it needed to be championed and elevated? That was what his parents had always taught him.

Good certainly wasn't winning in *Total Combat* though. Santo's avatar was down, pulverized by a sweep of the

Mechanoidian's annihilation drill. Vic rushed to resurrect him while trying to fight off a respawned wave of the Demented, the Mechanoidian's cyber-implanted mind-slaves. He wrestled with the controller, his jaw clenched. Use the immobilize ability on the horde, cycle up the resurrection orb, dodge the annihilation drill and–

Too late. *Crunch!* The Mechanoidian struck home with a nasty burst of SFX. His avatar was flattened, and the screen turned a gory red.

GAME OVER.

Vic dropped the controller onto his beanbag and leant back against the edge of his bed with an exasperated hiss. Thirteen year-old him would have been less than impressed, not managing to dodge the drill like that. He was getting slow.

"You finishing this?" Santo asked.

Vic looked over and saw him holding up the half-eaten bowl of pasta he'd made earlier. He shook his head.

Santo began to dig in, fork held daintily between forefinger and thumb as Vic got up and switched off the Xbox. The screen switched to the regular TV setting, and Santo began cycling through the channels until he alighted on reruns of *The Million Dollar Question*. That would be him now, Vic knew, set in place for much of the rest of the night. Snacks and TV, the big guy's two favorite pastimes.

"I'm going to visit home," Vic said, sitting on the edge of his bed and looking at Rockslide.

"When?" the stony giant asked between mouthfuls, eyes still fixed on the gameshow.

"Like, tomorrow."

"Isn't it still the middle of exams?"

"Yeah. I don't care. This place isn't a prison, even if sometimes it feels like one and it always really, really looks like one."

Santo just grunted.

"I miss my family," Vic admitted. "And I can't stand staying buried here while everything seems to be going to hell in the real world. I haven't visited home since I moved out. I don't speak to my mom and dad as much as I should. I've started to realize recently what they went through when I was a kid. What they protected me from. Abandoning them to play super hero isn't right."

"You just want to go to that café you always talk about," Santo said.

Vic blinked. "Do I really talk about Roundaway's that much?" he asked, genuinely surprised.

"You said you miss it the way most students miss their dog while they're at college."

"That does sound like something I'd say," Vic shrugged. "Yes, Rocky, you've unmasked my entire scheme. I'm going to swap exam success and friend satisfaction for Miss Trimble's affogato with extra ice cream. You should tell the Hellions. They can come visit too."

Santo made a deep, rumbling sound that Vic recognized as laughter. He couldn't help but smile back. He hadn't heard that for a little while.

"Not going to try anything stupid, are you?" Santo asked, glancing over and catching his eye. "Like going after the Purifiers? Because that would be seriously stupid."

"I won't," Vic said earnestly. "The last thing I want is to bring trouble to Fairbury. Just a quiet week at home, catching up, chilling. I need it. I need some sun too. I'm a damn lizard!"

He flicked his tongue out for effect, dredging another sonorous chuckle from Santo.

"I'll tell Cyclops tomorrow morning," he went on. "Maybe he'll grant me an exam extension. Special circumstances."

"I'll be your reference if you need one," Santo said. "I'll make sure they know all the gory details about your Roundaway's coffee withdrawals. How you've started eating coffee beans raw and how you can't sleep at night without your fix."

"I'd expect nothing else from the best roommate in the Institute," Vic grinned. "Thanks, Santo."

CHAPTER FOUR

There was a hand on his shoulder, gripping him roughly.

Vic started awake. He twisted in his seat and found himself face-to-face with a stubbly, pox-scarred visage surmounted by a white-and-blue cap.

"You going to Fairbury, kid?" the man asked. His breath stank of tobacco and his uniform of axle grease.

"Yeah," Vic responded, trying not to act flustered as he realized the bus had come to a stop. The engine was grumbling, and people were shuffling past him with cases and backpacks. His hood had fallen down while he'd been asleep. He tugged it up reflexively.

"Well this is it," the driver said, turning back to his seat. Vic stood up and snatched his bag. He didn't remember nodding off. At the start of the two-day journey from southern Alberta to Illinois he'd been on edge, constantly alert for trouble. He'd seen the dirty looks some people had given him. Worse were the worried ones – he hated the idea that someone might be afraid of him without even knowing him, that they might expect trouble just from the fact that they were sharing a bus with him. No one had sat next to him in the twenty-three hours he'd been travelling, whether on the big cross-border transports or on the local commuter one he'd caught out from St Louis. He was surprised the driver had even woken him up.

He thanked the man as he passed him and stepped down into the sunlight. The familiar sight of West Street awaited him, rows of squat, red-brick buildings cooking off in the July sun. An optician's, a sweet shop, a Mexican restaurant, the Wayne County Press office, rows of small businesses that looked completely unchanged since Vic had last seen them. Across from the bus stop, dusty vehicles idled in rows at a gas station, while just past the next junction a truck driver was helping to unload apple crates into the back of Hassler's grocery store. A dog barked excitedly at him from outside a nearby dry cleaners, quickly shushed by its owner. Small-town Illinois, apparently just as he'd left it.

He slung his backpack over his shoulders and turned right. He could feel the stares of a few of the people waiting in line at the bus stop as he passed them. He ignored them, and others nearby, right up until a woman climbing into a car parked by the road called out to him.

"Hello, Victor! Good to have you back!"

He glanced back and was surprised to spot his former high school geography teacher smiling at him. She was carrying a laundry bag in both hands, still dressed as prim and proper as she had been when she'd been educating him about glacial erosion and the National Parks or welcoming his mother and father over for Sunday lunch.

"Hello, Mrs Templeton," he managed to call back to her just before she boarded the bus.

The encounter, however brief, left him smiling as he walked along East Locust Street. The sun was beating down, and the town was as busy as Vic had remembered it ever being on a Saturday afternoon. Familiar faces were everywhere. Most smiled and nodded, and he quickly grew accustomed to looks of surprise and recognition, repeated a dozen times.

A few didn't smile. They turned quickly away when they saw him. One, Tony the gym owner, offered him a tight smile then hurried across the street, his baseball cap pulled low. Vic tried to ignore that, tried not to let it sting.

He'd expected it. All the way down from the Institute he'd seen the influence of the Purifiers in more than just a few ugly looks. Their cross-and-circle symbol was everywhere. From the bus window he'd spotted it daubed in white paint at shelters, and sprayed onto the doors and the walls of derelict houses. He'd seen burnt-out vehicles marked with it, abandoned at the side of the road. Even out here in the country, passing through rolling fields of corn and hay, he'd spotted wooden crosses erected in pastures and at lonely road junctions. Every time he'd seen them, he'd felt a little angrier, and little more uncertain. He had started to wonder just what sort of home he was coming back to.

He turned off North 7th Street and took East Hickory Street to 10th Street, passing the small baseball park where he'd played as a kid. There was a class out, clustered around a coach he didn't recognize. He wondered what had happened to Coach Martin. How long had it been since he'd played Little League? Five years? Six? He followed the road on round the Indian Creek pond, then took the track north. The stores and diners that constituted Fairbury's center had rapidly given way to individual houses, small, white-painted timber structures with big yards in front and fields out back. The dwellings in turn became sparser, the fields larger, ripe with the oncoming harvest, spread out gold and green beneath a cloudless sky.

He followed the track as it meandered north-east, stepping onto the verge a couple of times to let several trucks clatter past. A forest stood off to his left, its dark, shaded boughs looking cool in the sun. The track split, one trunk turning off in amongst the trees. The last turn before home.

He'd phoned ahead the day he'd left the Institute to tell his parents he was coming. They'd been surprised. Wasn't it the middle of exam season? Was everything all right? He'd assured them that he'd been given a week's leave of absence by Mr Summers. He just needed a break. Cyclops had been understanding. He'd admitted to Vic that the Institute was considering curtailing the exams anyway. The growing violence was unsettling everyone. He wasn't the first to have been granted leave to be with friends and family. There were several crisis meetings with the Institute's staff scheduled.

Vic was just glad to be away from it all. The place had gotten claustrophobic, even more so than its usual, literal sense. The longed-for summer was slipping away while he was buried underground, stressing out over textbooks and the news. He needed out.

He'd had to work hard to convince his parents not to take time off from work to welcome him home. He wasn't sure he was ready for that sort of fuss, and besides, it would have been short notice. Dad was at the store overseeing the launch of a new smart TV while Mom was doing a grocery run for Mrs Keller. They'd left the key in the usual spot.

He could see his house through the trees now, one of a short row of nine homes set back along the leafy lane. It stood two stories tall, heavy brown timber walls and ochre roof tiles, as stout and unchanged as the day he'd left. He stopped at the wrought iron gate leading into the front yard, taking it in. The sun gleamed back from the upper windows facing him, the air heavy with the scents of the hostas and lavender that lined the path to the front porch. The trees rustled softly, adding a gentle undercurrent to the distant chatter of a woodpecker at work somewhere in the forest behind the house. It was a world removed from the bleak concrete, chilly corridors and harsh lights of the Institute. Vic breathed in, slowly, savoring it, before opening the gate and walking up to the front porch.

He paused just in front of it. The key should be in a crack under one of the floorboards. As he hesitated over which one it was, a scent reached him.

Meat. Cooking meat. He inhaled again and decided it couldn't be coming from the house. The windows were closed and shuttered from the inside, and his parents wouldn't be home for hours.

He glanced left and right, seeing no sign of activity at either Mr and Mrs Wilson's or Mr McTeal's – the neighboring houses were as quiet and tranquil as the Borkowski residence. Mystified, he stepped past the porch and walked around the side of the house, his senses on edge.

A fenced-off yard lay behind the back door, the forest stretching out beyond it, dappled in sunlight. Leaves whispered and rustled conspiratorially. The smell grew stronger. He unlatched the backyard gate and found it unlocked – another anomaly. It was usually locked from the inside when his parents were out. His heart rate beginning to climb, he eased it open and peered into the backyard.

The shout from the other side almost made him slam the gate back shut. There were dozens of people filling the yard, and it took a wide-eyed second for him to realize that he knew them all. If his biology had allowed it, he knew his face would have flushed red with embarrassment.

"Welcome home, son!" shouted Dan Borkowski, who snatched Vic into a bear hug. Martha followed close behind, beaming, turning the crushing embrace into a group effort.

"I thought you were at work," was all Vic could think to say, feeling like an idiot.

"You think we'd miss you coming home after all this time?" Dan demanded, releasing him before gripping firmly onto his shoulders. He looked him up and down, grinning broadly. "Well, you haven't grown at all, Vic!"

Vic rolled his eyes and broke free from his father's grasp, trying not to laugh. Relief washed over him. He didn't know why he hadn't anticipated something like this – his mood since sitting the exam combined with his experiences on the road seemed to have darkened the world around him. Yet here was his home, his family, an oasis of peace and joy unblemished by the dirty pyre smoke that seemed to be slowly befouling so much else.

And it wasn't just his family either. The yard was rammed with smiling, laughing faces, each from a time long before his current difficulties. Friends of his parents, neighbors, congregation members, employees from the electrics store, Dr Miller, old Mrs Keller, it seemed as though every person he'd known growing up had been packed into the space behind his house. They'd even gone in for a green and white banner, pinned up to the side of the house above the back door – "Welcome Home, to Fairbury's Very Own X-Man."

"How did you know I was coming?" he demanded, doing his best to mask his embarrassment. It wasn't as though he didn't appreciate the attention – you didn't win the Institute Award for Best Student Actor two years running without being comfortable at the center of things – but the surprise of it had left him feeling awkward. Dan smacked his shoulder and pointed past him, out the back gate.

"We had an informant on the outside," he said. Vic turned and saw Mrs Templeton coming around the side of the house looking decidedly pleased with herself.

"The driver wasn't exactly thrilled when I got straight back off the bus again after you," she said, winking at Vic and giving him a short, tender hug.

Vic threw his hands up, struggling to hide his own amusement. "Well, now you're all making me doubt whether or not I'm cut out to be an X-Man! Lured in, stalked, and trapped! I'm going to need to call in the first team if I'm going to get out of this one!"

There was laughter and a few cheers. Martha took him by the elbow and steered him in front of the banner for a photo. Arms around his parents' shoulders, he grinned and stuck his tongue out a whole foot, to gasps of amazement.

The faces descended on him, a swift and relentless barrage. Hugs, handshakes, air kisses, back pats. Smiles, laughter, jokes, questions. A voice called out through the press, firm and commanding.

"All right, all right, give the kid some space! He must be hungry!"

The crowd parted, and the source of the scent that had enticed him around the house was revealed. A grill was sizzling away in the center of the yard, overseen by his old baseball coach, Mike Martin. The big, apron-clad pitcher waved him over with a spatula, his voice as gruff as ever.

"How's my champion batter?" he demanded, delivering yet another firm pat to Vic's shoulder.

"He's glad to be home," Vic responded.

"Good," Mike declared before he could continue. "Then we can all get on and eat! I'm starving! Here, hand these out. And watch Sammy, he'll probably try and come back for seconds."

He indicated the row of fresh buns on the table beside the grill, ignoring the halfhearted protestations of Sam, the reserve coach. Vic busied himself preparing burgers and hotdogs, handing them out as quickly as Mike could grill them. As the coach had doubtless already realized, doing so provided a far more orderly means for Vic to see everyone than the initial mobbing. He spoke about the curriculum at the Institute with Mrs Templeton, his old batting injury with Dr Miller, the hikes he'd gone on in Alberta with Mr and Mrs Rasheed. He asked the Carter family about his two old schoolfriends, Jayce and Claire. The former had moved over to Evansville to be with his partner, the latter had gotten into MIT. Vic had already noticed that the barbeque had a gap the size of his own age group. His circle of high school friends had been small and close-knit, but it seemed they'd all moved on. They were at college or had moved for work, but either way they now seemed to be mostly out of town. Vic couldn't really blame any of them. After all, he'd done the same thing, even if the Institute wasn't exactly the same as hauling maize trucks or studying architectural engineering at MIT.

The younger kids were still around though. And while the adults were careful when asking him about the Institute or hinting at his abilities, their children were not so consciously polite. A dozen of the neighborhood's offspring – most of whom had been little tots when Vic had last seen them – were soon clustering around him, demanding his attention.

"How is it being an X-Man, Mr Borkowski?" the Jacksons' daughter, Julia, asked in between mouthfuls of hotdog.

"Can you fly, Mr Victor, sir?" asked Mrs Templeton's grandson before he could answer.

"Can we see your tongue again?" suggested the youngest of the gang, Charlie. The request was immediately backed up by a loud chorus of support.

"All right, but just this once," Vic said, swallowing the last of his hotdog and squatting down so that he was at the same height as the rest of the group. After the slightest dramatic pause, he opened his mouth and let his tongue extend. The sight of the prehensile muscle elicited a squall of screeches, laughs, and exclamations of disgust. One of the smaller kids in particular got a fit of the giggles and could hardly remain standing.

"You said Cyclops and Emma Frost are in charge of your school," Mari, one of the older children, asked earnestly. "Can you tell us about them?"

"I wanna know about Storm and Rogue," Templeton's grandson declared loudly.

"And Wolverine," Charlie practically shouted. Again, the gang delivered a storm of approval, shouting animatedly over one another. The kid who'd been giggling was now just squealing with excitement.

It was a struggle for Vic not to laugh at their raw eagerness. And of course they all wanted to know about Wolverine. It didn't seem to matter the age, any non-mutant he talked to about the X-Men wanted to know what it was like to be taught by "Weapon X."

"He's a pretty cool guy," he said, causing an immediate hush to fall over the children. "But I'll tell you one thing about him. He can't do this."

He took a step back so that he was almost up against the timber fence bordering the yard. Then he closed his eyes, relaxed his limbs, and shivered slightly.

A change crept rapidly over his skin, starting at his toes and fingertips and spreading like a rippling wave across his body. In just a few seconds every piece of flesh from his feet to his head spines had changed color to match the dark brown hue of the wood at his back. Keeping the fence as a mental picture in his head, he mottled parts of the tone to better blend with the grain of the timber. The result was an almost-perfect mimicry of his background, only ruined by the fact that he was still wearing jeans and a Chicago Cubs T-shirt that refused to blend in with the disguise.

While the tongue had mostly elicited disgust, the abrupt disappearing act drew out a universal shocked gasp. Even a few of the onlooking parents couldn't hide their surprise. Vic battled to keep his mouth shut when he smiled. The trick apparently never got old. His mom had told him that as a baby he'd done it instinctively, but it had taken years of practice before he was capable of doing it on command. He'd worked on it as vigorously in front of the mirror as he'd practiced his acting expressions. One day his mom had entered his room with an armful of laundry and not realized Vic was in there until he'd spoken to her. She'd yelped, dropped her laundry, and stormed out while demanding he put some clothes on.

"But we can still see what you're wearing," Julia pointed out sternly. Vic dropped the effect, the illusion of the varnished timber melting away in favor of his natural, pale green scales.

"That's very true," he acknowledged. "Normally if I'm practicing, or I'm going out on a secret mission, I have a special X-suit to wear. It can change like my skin, so I become almost completely invisible."

More exclamations of awe. Most of the kids were just staring at him open-mouthed.

"Did you bring the suit too?" one at the back blurted out. "Can we see it? Please!"

"I didn't bring it," Vic admitted. "I'm sorry. I didn't think I'd be doing much color-shifting while I was visiting home."

There were some exclamations of dismay. Briefly no one said anything as the gathering digested what it had witnessed. Then Charlie stuck his hand up, as though he was afraid of interrupting the class in the middle of a lesson.

"Yes?" Vic asked him.

"Is it true Wolverine taught you how to fight, Mr Borkowski?"

Vic couldn't help but laugh. It never did take long to get back onto Wolverine. He smiled and nodded, generating more awe from the assembly.

"He did, and a lot more besides. I don't suppose anyone wants to hear about that though?"

Outrage and indignation greeted his teasing, making a few of the onlooking parents laugh. Vic held his hands up hastily.

"OK, OK! But if you really want to hear all the good stuff, we could be here for some time. So, make sure you've all got your hotdogs, and sit down."

He led by example, taking a seat on the grass in front of the fence, cross-legged. The children scrambled to copy him, and in a few seconds he had a small semicircle of eager, serious faces ranged around him.

"So, first off," Vic began. "Can anyone tell me what Wolverine's claws are made of?"

CHAPTER FIVE

The shadows were getting long by the time the Borkowskis saw off the last of the welcoming party. Night looked as though it had already set in the forest beyond the backyard. A cool, fragrant darkness had spread slowly to envelop the houses ranged along the lane. Crickets began their chirring, and a trio of crimson cardinals were dancing in the air above the house, dashes of brilliance in the twilight.

Vic helped carry the used plates and napkins indoors while Dan took the banner down from the wall. It was the first chance he'd actually gotten to go inside since he'd arrived. Martha was already busy scrubbing down the grill rungs in the kitchen, dishwater threatening to overflow from the sink.

"They're too greasy for recycling," she said as she looked up and noticed Vic's armful of detritus. "Just dump them in the trash."

He did so, then moved to help with the drying up. Martha momentarily abandoned the grill to give him a ferociously tight, soapy hug.

"It's so good to have you back, sweetheart," she said, trying to hide the tear in her eye by fussily wiping off the suds she'd gotten on his shoulders and cheek. He grinned.

…o good to be back, I think. I haven't really had a chance to stop yet and take it all in."

"I've put fresh sheets on your bed," Martha said, giving up her struggle with the suds. "I'm sorry if all this was a bit much. You've been travelling for days."

"I loved it," Vic reassured her, giving her another quick hug before checking his dad didn't need help with the banner.

"I was thinking of giving it to little Charlie," Dan said as he finished folding it away. "He's obsessed with you. In fact, I think all the neighborhood kids are. The Willets twins have been demanding that their parents get them a pet chameleon since they heard you were coming back."

"I feel like the most famous man in Fairbury," Vic quipped. "Maybe I should hold a signing session in the town hall?"

"Don't tell your mother or she'll demand you do it," Dan joked. "It's about time this place was known for something more than country music and having the most fire outbreaks in the Midwest."

Vic opened the yard shed for Dan to put the banner away before heading back inside and upstairs to his room. A part of him had been putting it off. He didn't know how it would make him feel, being back among a childhood he was certain he'd outgrown. So little seemed to have changed, it had made him start to question just how much he himself had moved on.

The interior of the Borkowski home had always tended to oscillate between well-kept and overrun. Most of the time it was orderly and pristine – the kitchen bordered a living room hung with screed of family photos, including baby snaps of Vic that he had always insisted be taken down whenever his friends came over. Beside it was a hallway that led to the upstairs bedrooms and included a glass cabinet bearing Martha's prized crockery collection. This was the sort of sight usually presented to visitors, but when Dan's business was going through a period of expansion or a large sale, a clutter of boxed and wrapped electronic hardware soon filled every available space in the house.

Vic climbed the stairs to his room. The door had once been decorated with dinosaur stickers, but he'd angrily removed them about a year before heading to the Institute, caught up in a surge of teenage angst that wanted nothing to do with anything it perceived as childish. His name was still there though, printed off with help from his dad on his label maker when he'd been five. "Victor Borkowski." Underneath it a second label, this one crude and hand drawn. "Anole."

He grasped the door handle, hesitated, and turned it. Beyond the last of the day's light was shafting in through the half-drawn curtains. All was still and silent. Vic stood in the doorway, taking it all in.

It felt like stepping back in time. On one side of his room was his single bed, freshly made up with checkered sheets. Next to it was a desk with his old laptop and a stack of dogeared books – *The Greatest Actors of the Stage* by Anthony Mezers, *The Means Behind the Method* by Stephanie Grail, *101 Ways to Take on a Role* by Mark Deerfield. Across the room was his mirrored wardrobe, two bookshelves and a cabinet stand holding half a dozen trophies and medals, baseball and school drama prizes competing with one another for the top slot.

The curtains rippled gently in a light breeze blowing in through the open window. He stepped inside the room, carefully, as though entering some sacred space he dared not violate. Posters of actors and a huge chart following the development of dozens of species during the Jurassic period all gazed down upon him. Did his things still recognize him? Were they welcoming him home, or did they think he had abandoned them? Almost tentative, he walked over to the bed and sat down on it, slowly.

This was home. That's what he told himself. He was just experiencing the effects of a momentary dislocation. It was natural, having been gone for years, that being back would feel strange. Part alien, part familiar, uncertain yet comforting. The emotions certainly weren't complimentary, but he was sure they would subside. He just had to relax. The X-Men, the Purifiers, the Institute, it was all a world away now. Everything here was safe and undisturbed, a gateway to an unblemished past.

He plugged his phone in to charge by his desk and got up again, pacing over to the bookshelves to pick a volume at random. It was a picture book about different types of Triassic therapsids. Growing up he'd been obsessed with dinosaurs, convinced that he was their only remaining direct descendant. For a while he'd wanted to be a paleontologist, but that had fallen by the wayside somewhere around the time he'd discovered acting, baseball, boys, and the full extent of his own powers. He carried the book back to his bed and stretched out, leafing through pages that probably hadn't been turned in over a decade.

About half an hour later he heard a buzz and glanced over at where his phone was still charging. It was Cipher. She'd texted him a couple of times since he'd left the Institute. He knew she was checking in on him, and he suspected Graymalkin was asking for regular updates from her. Jonas still hadn't quite accepted the idea of phones, convinced that the Institute communicator given to all students was sufficient. As he liked to point out, he didn't have anyone to talk to outside of the school anyway.

"Back home OK?" Cipher's text read. "More Purifier crap on TV."

He was about to unlock the screen and respond when he heard a creak on the stairs outside his door. He could tell his parents apart based on the sound of their approach – these footsteps, a slow and steady ascent rather than a busy, swift bustle, belonged to his dad. Sure enough, a moment later there was a knock at his half-open door. Dan stuck his head around it before Vic could answer, a habit he had never managed to get him out of.

"Room service," Dan said with a smile, holding up one of the paper plates from the barbecue. It was heaped with more hot dogs and patties, slathered in mustard.

"This is all we've got left," he went on as he entered. "And I thought you should have dibs ahead of McTeal's dog. Angus is fat enough as it is."

"I'm stuffed," Vic said. His dad shrugged and sat on the chair by the desk. In the time Vic had been away he didn't seem to have changed much – the dark hair around his temples was more thoroughly edged with silver now, and the lines on his forehead were a little deeper, but really he was as untouched as the place he called home. He was a tall, lean man with a serious expression that could give way in the most unexpected moments to warmth and humor. Those who didn't know him might have had little time for a man whose most common attire was a short-sleeved shirt and a polyester tie, thinking him nothing more than a lifelong door-to-door salesman. Anyone with that opinion would find themselves badly mistaken. Dan Borkowski was a hard-working and conscientious father and husband, his judgments considered and his opinions honest.

"Sorry about all the fuss," he said, placing the overloaded plate on the desk beside him. "For the record, it was your mother's idea."

"I enjoyed it," Vic said diplomatically, swinging his legs over so he was sitting on the edge of the bed. "I'm amazed you managed to get everyone together at such short notice."

"Well, you know how your mother is when she puts her mind to something," Dan exclaimed. "The phone hasn't been back on the hook for the last forty-eight hours. She was ringing half the town."

"Only half?" Vic teased.

"I phoned the other half," Dan admitted. "So, what's it like being home? Is it all how you remember it?"

"Freakishly so," Vic said, looking around the room again. "Did you deliberately get all my old stuff out again? It looks like I haven't been away at all."

"We might have brought a few things down from the loft," Dan said. "Didn't want you to come home and find out we'd turned your old bedroom into another old electronics garage."

Vic wasn't quite sure if he was joking or not, but it made him smile. Martha waged a perpetual war with her husband over the amount of overspill from his store in town. Besides the clutter, what seemed to distress Martha most was the fact Dan didn't theme the placement of his products in the house – a trio of spare washing machines filling up the living room, big boxes of TV screens in the kitchen, plastic-wrapped spools of cabling scattered across the front hallway. Vic had noted the absence of electrical detritus when he'd entered the house, and he suspected Martha had used his return and the neighborhood BBQ as an excuse to mount a crusade on what she called "Dan's wiry stuff."

"It certainly makes a change from the Institute," Vic said, patting the side of his bed. "I'd almost gotten used to how uncomfortable the beds are there. This week away is going to ruin me."

"Is it really that bad?" Dan asked with a flash of concern. "I mean, I know you can't talk about it too much. Don't want Ms Frost turning up at my door accusing me of defamation. If your mother finds out she'd drive right up to Alberta today and break down the front door, then take the staff bed shopping."

They both laughed, Vic shaking his head.

"I don't mind any of it. I just… needed a break. Everything seemed to be piling up, you know?"

"I think so," Dan said carefully, looking closely at Vic. He had suspected his dad hadn't come upstairs just to try and offload spare BBQ.

"You know, we first sent you to the Institute for your own safety," Dan went on, his tone measured now. Vic put on a faux surprised expression.

"There was me thinking it was because I'm a talented young mutant with the capacity to do some good in the world," he replied, only half joking. Dan smiled, though his expression had grown more uncertain.

"Of course that's true. But the Institute offered you a lot that we couldn't, no matter how hard we tried. And that included protection. The world out there, it isn't always understanding, and it's very rarely fair."

"I know, Dad," Vic interrupted. "I've heard it all before. Some people don't like mutants. I get it. Anyone watching the news recently gets it too."

"This isn't anything new," Dan pointed out. "These zealots, the Purifiers, they're just the latest ones who can't accept that not everybody is like them. The last time something like this happened... well, that's when your mother and I agreed that the Institute was the best place for you."

"And that makes me one of the lucky ones," Vic replied. "I've discovered over the past few years that there's a lot of people like me who're less fortunate. Including a lot who don't have the good luck to get into the New Charles Xavier School for Mutants. What would you have done if I hadn't been accepted? How safe would I be if I still lived in Fairbury? I saw plenty of Purifier symbols on the way here."

"They haven't come here yet," Dan said. "And they won't be welcome if they do."

"Really? There's nobody in the town who doesn't sympathize with them?"

"No more than a couple."

"And I bet I know who they are. Seemed like more than a couple walking here from the bus stop though."

Dan gave him a sharp look.

"Did someone give you trouble?" he demanded. "Tell me who and I'll–"

"There was no trouble, Dad," Vic said, getting exasperated. "Just dirty looks. But that's how it always starts. When the Purifiers do come, you'll be surprised how many stand with them and not against them."

"Then they'll have your mother and me to contend with," Dan said firmly. "And a few more good people besides. This is your home, Vic, and that'll always be the case."

"I know," Vic said, quieter now. "Being away made me realize that."

"You came back because you were missing home?"

"I came back because I realized how much home meant. How much you'd both given me over the years, despite the challenges you must have faced. All your hard work and sacrifice, and I disappear off to the Institute one day and only see you for parents' evenings."

"That's just part of growing up," Dan said. "It's what every parent goes through. We've been doing OK. We're here for each other, and the neighborhood is always here for both of us. Martha's a church elder now and I've been looking to expand the business again."

"I'm sure Mom will be delighted with the extra stock," Vic said, deadpan.

Dan chuckled and shook his head. "It won't last more than a week, I've promised her! I promise!"

"What, you think I'll be taking it back to the Institute with me?"

They both laughed, though as the humor died the tension lingered. Dan spoke again after a short silence.

"If your time at the school is proving difficult, you can always talk to us. If it's your studies, or the other kids, or the teachers—"

"It's not," Vic said.

"But things were piling up," Dan pointed out.

"I mean, I don't know," Vic replied, doing his best to articulate the difficulties of the past few months. "Some of the exams were tough. Two of my friends were planning on a road trip after they were finished, but I'm worried I might have to stay behind to retake them."

"Which friends?" Dan asked. "That roommate of yours? The big rocky one?"

"Cipher and Graymalkin," Vic replied. "You met them both briefly last time you and Mom visited."

"I remember," Dan said. "The one who could turn invisible and the one whose powers come out in the dark?"

"You could say that," Vic said, the joke going straight over his dad's head.

"They seemed nice," Dan went on. "And if you have to retake the test, well, perhaps you can appeal the first outcome? They do that if the grade is close to passing, right?"

"Yeah," Vic admitted, lying back in his bed. He stared up at the ceiling for a while, struggling with his thoughts. He was worried about his exams, that much was true, but it wasn't the only thing. He'd been edging around it, not wanting to admit it. Afraid it would add another burden.

"I've been worried about home," he said eventually. "About you and Mom. What with everything that's going on, I was afraid Fairbury would get caught up in it all. The more I thought about that, the worse it got."

"You came home to protect us?" Dan asked with a look of

realization. "To check we're OK in all this?"

"I guess. I didn't really think of it like that, I just wanted to make sure everything was fine. And it really looks like it is. But how can I be sure it'll stay that way?"

Dan frowned, his expression growing stern. Vic knew that look. He was about to get a lecturing.

"Now listen to me, Victor," Dan said, leaning forward slightly in his chair. "I appreciate your concern. I understand that you're an adult now, and practically an X-Man as well. But your mother and I were looking after you in this very house from day one. We couldn't have done that if we didn't know how to protect ourselves as well."

Vic opened his mouth to interject, but Dan kept going.

"You don't need to worry about us. Your mother would be distraught if she thought your grades were suffering because you were concerned about how we were doing. I told you that these troubles aren't anything new, and I mean it. When you were born there were mobs out on the street. Sentinels hunting people like animals. The government was a lot less affirming about mutants than they are today. But we didn't let that change how we raised you. We did it openly. We weren't going to force you to deny what you were. And thank God, we were able to do so in peace. Maybe that was just because of where we live. Maybe you were overlooked out here in the country. But we never hid, and we won't now."

Vic was quiet, taking in his dad's words. They stung, because they confirmed in part what he'd been afraid of. Even unintentionally, he'd brought trouble to his parents and his neighborhood. He wondered how many nights they'd lost worrying about what was happening around them, the strain of having to stay constantly vigilant against the threats and prejudices of others.

"It must've been hard," he said. "Giving me a childhood so many other kids like me never had."

"It was nothing but a pleasure, son," Dan said, his smile returning. "We wouldn't do a thing differently."

He was quiet for a moment more before lifting up the plate and its contents.

"So, you're sure you don't want any of this?" he asked, performing that effortlessly awkward pivot only fathers seemed capable of. Vic laughed and shook his head.

"Throw it to Angus. It's probably better than the pizza slices Mr McTeal give him."

"Well, if you do need anything, you know where to find us," Dan said, rising and pausing at the door. "It's good to have you back, Vic."

"I know, Dad," Vic replied. "And it's good to be back."

CHAPTER SIX

That night, Vic slept soundly for the first time in months. He woke the next morning to the smell of pancakes and the sight of sunlight streaming in under the bedroom curtains.

For a second it was summer break, and he was twelve again, ready to race downstairs, grab a pancake and head out into the yard to play with the neighborhood kids or McTeal's puppy. He lay still and quiet, savoring the nostalgia. A sunny day with nowhere to go and nothing that needed to be done. It felt like a long time since he'd enjoyed one of those.

He got up, showered, and dressed in loose jeans and an old Cry Havoc hoodie he'd picked out of his wardrobe. Then, after opening the curtains to gaze out over the backyard, he headed downstairs to the kitchen.

Martha was preparing stacks of pancakes at the kitchen island, while Dan was sitting at the table with his newspaper, a mug of coffee and a few slices of toast his only concession to breakfast – the family had always taken polar opposite views on the first meal of the day, Vic's father preferring to eat light while his mother swore by something hearty to start out with. Vic had always erred towards Martha's preferences. Dan lowered his paper as Vic entered, feigning shock as he saw him.

"Didn't expect you to appear before I headed into town," he exclaimed. "Don't tell me you actually get out of bed before midday while you're at the Institute?"

"Only when someone makes it worth my while," Vic teased, sidling up to the kitchen island. "Someone like you, Mom."

"I thought you were a much better flatterer than that, Victor," she tsked, sliding a triple-stack over to him. She was a short woman, fair-haired and quick to laughter, with soft blue eyes that Vic counted as his luckiest inheritance. At college she had been the girl every guy on the football team had wanted to date, but she'd never had time for anyone other than the skinny, quiet kid she sat next to in her business lectures. They'd gotten married not long after graduating, taking on their dream to move further west together. Vic had come into their lives not long after.

"Syrup's in the cupboard," she said, shooing Vic and his plate away with a spatula. "And remember to wipe your fingers after! I don't want sticky paws all over my fresh tablecloth!"

"Lizards don't have paws," Vic said as he fetched the syrup and sat down opposite his dad. It was a little family in-joke, a phrase they'd been repeating since he'd first uttered it as kid. He'd totally forgotten about it until now, but the response had come naturally. He caught Dan smirking behind his newspaper.

"So, how was it sleeping in your old bed?" Martha asked as she bustled past with her own plate, doubling back to the sink to steep the frying pan.

"A lot better than sleeping in the Institute, that's for sure," Vic admitted as he began to drizzle syrup over his stack. "Just having a window and sunshine in the morning makes a difference."

"Isn't it strange not having a roommate?" Martha continued, taking her own seat at the table. Vic shrugged as he began to eat.

"I haven't shared my dorm since last semester. Rocky graduated, and they haven't found a replacement yet."

"Maybe one of your friends can move in," Martha said. "Like that nice, quiet boy we met at parents' night. Graymalkin?"

"He already has a room," Vic said. "And besides, he has to sleep alone. He's partly nocturnal, and when he does sleep he has nightmares."

"Oh, how terrible," Martha said, looking aghast.

Vic nodded. "He… had a tough upbringing. We all help him through it, though. He's come a long way in the time he's been at the Institute."

"Maybe your friends could come and visit us out here someday," Martha said, daintily beginning to carve up her pancake stack with her knife and fork. "I'm sure Dan wouldn't mind moving his office out of the spare room for a few days."

Dan shot her a look over the top of his newspaper, then cleared his throat in an effort to cover it up.

"I'm sure we could find the space," he said magnanimously. "Didn't you say yesterday you were thinking of going on a road trip with your friends this summer?"

"If I pass my exams," Vic said, busily wolfing down his stack. "We were thinking about going down the Rockies."

"Your father and I used to go on road trips every summer after we graduated," Martha said, smiling with reminiscent fondness. "Usually down to Colorado or through California. Those were some wonderful times."

"Why don't you go on one again?" Vic asked in between mouthfuls. Martha looked at Dan, who studiously avoided eye contact.

"Perhaps we will when work clears up," he said, still reading his paper.

"We've been saying that for, oh, half a decade?" Martha said with a knowing smile. "But maybe if you start doing it, Vic, we'll finally find the time. Can't stay in Fairbury forever."

Dan just grunted and took another sip of coffee, refusing to be drawn. Vic finished up his stack.

"I'm going to go out back for a while," he said, scraping back his chair and starting to rise.

"Fingers," Martha warned dangerously. Vic looked down at his hands and realized he had indeed got syrup on them. Huffing, he went over to the sink and washed them as Martha continued to speak.

"Are you going to visit your old treehouse?"

"That was the plan," Vic said, wringing his hands out. "Assuming it's still there!"

"As of last month, it was," Dan said. "And it better still be. Goodness knows how many hours I spent building that thing for you."

"I'll report back later today," Vic said, heading for the door without a backward glance. "Have a good day at work, Dad! See you later, Mom!"

Without waiting for his parents' replies, he strode into the backyard, unlatched the rear gate, and stepped out into the forest beyond.

It was like he had passed back to an arboreal existence, somewhere long before the coming of either man or mutant. Dense undergrowth and crooked, moss-dappled trees stretched away from him, denser and more knotted than he remembered. While the sun was climbing to its ascendancy, beneath the canopy the morning was still cool and fragrant, the last of the night's lazy dreams lingering between the roots and branches. All was quiet and still, not a breath of air disturbing the leafy paradise.

He took the track that had once led from the yard gate into the forest, now mostly overgrown. The forest floor was damp, the mulch soft beneath his feet. He went slowly and carefully, letting his senses attune to the new world he'd found himself in. It couldn't have felt further from life at the Institute. It was different to the warm, welcoming contrast presented by his home though, more mysterious, more unknowable. It had changed since he'd been gone, grown wild and dense. It made him feel like an explorer travelling in a strange land, an astronaut crashed on an alien world. There was a childlike thrill to it, a moment of excitement when he glanced back and found no sign of his home. The forest had swallowed him up.

This was where he'd spent most of his time growing up, playing with the rest of the neighborhood's families. They'd constructed huts in between the trees, chasing and scrapping with each other and trying to catch the occasional vole or rabbit. He remembered driving off a gang of older boys who'd been attempting to wreck a bird's nest up in an old sycamore. He'd "gone chameleon" and convinced them that the forest was haunted. Another time he and a few others had tried to dam up the creek that cut through the woodland further east. He'd gone home at the end of the day plastered in mud and endured the most furious telling-off Martha had ever given him, all while his dad pretended to be watching TV, struggling not to laugh.

The memories flowed as he picked his way along the path, in no hurry. The last few years before he'd left for the Institute had seen the activities of the neighborhood's children – now teens – shift from playfighting and forest huts to skipping school and late-night parties. Vic remembered sneaking out of class early to meet up with his first boyfriend, Sam. They'd talked for hours, exploring parts of the forest they'd never dared venture into as kids. He'd stolen his first kiss outside an old, rusting corrugated shack they'd discovered half buried in the undergrowth. He'd been sure that day that they'd be together forever. Of course, it had all fallen apart when Sam's parents had moved out of state. The first of many life lessons Vic had been required to learn.

He slipped between some foliage and stopped, looking up. His meandering progress had brought him to a mighty black oak, dominating a small clearing in the thicket. Its boughs stretched overhead like some ancient, primordial forest deity, imperious and grand. He approached it with a solemn tread, still gazing up into its foliage.

At the pinnacle of the trunk, where it split off into two great branches, a small wooden tree hut lay, lit by a ray of sunlight breaking through the canopy above. It looked almost a part of the tree itself now, its rough-hewn wooden walls and roof darkened by age, the green paint that had once coated it little more than flaking patches. The door, leading out onto a small wooden platform nestled between the tree's arms, lay crooked and ajar, the interior hidden by the branches overhanging part of it.

There was no obvious means of reaching the treehouse, no rope ladder or posts nailed into the trunk's bark. That was all part of the trick. Vic paused briefly amidst the tangle of roots at the tree's base, gazing up. How many times had he stood here down the years, contemplating his route up the craggy bark?

When his father had first built the treehouse, scaling his way up to it had seemed like a mammoth task, one that had filled him with equal parts anxiety and excitement. The oak had appeared fierce and towering, an unassailable fortress tower. Now it had a more venerable air to it, still imposing, but rugged and weighted down by the years spent overseeing the surrounding woodland. Its stout trunk no longer issued a challenge to him.

He extended a hand and placed it on the bark, resting it there for a moment before tensing it, feeling the microscopic setae which covered his hand bristle. It took a slight rotating motion to lock them with the rough surface. Once it was done though, his hand was stuck there, fixed in place until he rotated it back again.

He set his other palm on the trunk and did the same, starting to climb. It had once taken long minutes of poise and concentration – including battling with his locked-on hands and feet as he tried to detach them one at a time – before he'd been able to clamber all the way up to the treehouse. Now he was able to do it in seconds, scaling the oak's flank with a lithe, practiced ease. He alighted upon the board outside the treehouse door, crouched on his haunches, tongue flicking out to taste the air. He was alone. The treehouse stood long abandoned.

He peered inside, having to stoop to enter. The plyboard interior consisted of nothing more than a coiled rope ladder, which he tested briefly, discovering it to be still intact, as well as two small chairs and a cracked old leather trunk. There were drawn images and posters still pinned to the walls, though they were faded beyond recognition. At some point a bird had clearly decided to make its nest and raise a family inside – the floor was littered with twigs, broken eggshells, feathers and stale droppings. One of the chairs was on its side, and there was a gap in the corner of the room where one of the floorboards had sagged and fallen away, exposing the forest floor below.

He stepped fully inside, going slowly as the floorboards creaked underfoot. A part of him was surprised the little structure was still standing. It smelled damp and stale, and the plyboard was showing signs of decay. Still, it wasn't so far removed from how it had been in its prime. He still remembered his excitement when Dan had taken him out to see it for the first time, all freshly painted and clean. When Vic had initially asked for it to be built atop the old oak his father had claimed it was impossible, that it would be too precarious. That, Vic had learned, was just Dan's way of distracting him while his father undertook the arduous task of designing and building a treehouse that could sit safely amidst the old boughs. When Dan had revealed it to him months later, Vic had been unable to contain his delight, whooping and scrambling up the tree's flank. They'd decorated the floor with one of Martha's old rugs and filled the trunk with toys and the worthless woodland detritus children were wont to treasure – nuts, acorns, particularly large leaves, painted rocks, the tiny, fragile skull of a bird. The treehouse had been the gang hut and gathering place for Vic and half a dozen of his friends for years, the scene of endless amounts of childhood laughter, angst and drama. In his excitement he'd declared it his very own X-Mansion, the headquarters of a new school for mutant heroes and their human allies.

He moved over to the trunk, undoing its rusty latch and lifting it carefully. It was empty, bar a couple of spiders that fled at his sudden intrusion. He gazed down into the cobwebbed interior, wondering whether Dan had come and cleaned it out at some point. He suppressed an unexpected pang of sorrow at the idea of the junk he and his friends had once carefully hoarded being thrown away.

But maybe not all of it. He noticed something small lying in the trunk's corner, almost lost in a rip in the lining fabric. He picked it up, blowing off the cobwebs clinging to it – a little plastic toy, a nondescript dinosaur, probably a toymaker's approximation of a Tyrannosaurus rex. Vic remembered being distraught when he'd thought he had lost it years ago. Funny that it should turn up now, after so much time.

He put the toy in his hoodie pocket and half turned, having to balance precariously in order to not trip on the fallen chair. The discovery of the lone prehistoric reptile had awakened another memory. Crouching down, he gently swept aside the litter covering the floor, exposing the boards at the center of the hut. Sure enough, he found a small rectangle cut into the timber. Extending a claw, he hooked it in underneath the space and raised the concealed trapdoor. He smiled as he saw what lay beneath.

It was a little treasure hole, secreted under the floorboards and resting directly against the bark of the oak itself. Once hidden by the treehouse rug, it contained what Vic and the others had called the "emergency supplies." Cans of beans, fruits and vegetables, bags of nuts and jerky, chocolate and granola bars, a few empty water bottles, all scrounged from the neighborhood's kitchens over the space of a few years. Whoever had emptied the trunk had either forgotten about, or never discovered, the supplies, because the hole was still fully stocked. The sight of it made Vic smile. Just what catastrophe or prolonged siege they had been preparing for none of the gang had ever really considered, but they sure had been ready for it.

He lowered the trap door and stepped out of the treehouse, back onto the platform outside. The forest was spread out beneath him, beams of sunshine lancing down through the canopy in half a dozen places, driving out the last of the sultry morning. Insects danced and buzzed in the shafts of light, and he saw a rabbit scamper through the undergrowth near the oak's roots. The woodpecker he'd heard yesterday was back at work, its industrious chattering echoing faintly through the forest.

He sat down on the platform with his legs dangling into space, his thoughts lost in the moment. The shades of his past had been all around him ever since he had set foot back in Fairbury. They were happy memories, for the most part, but he couldn't help but view them differently now that he had a wider perspective. He'd come back partly to escape his troubles and partly to reassure himself that his family and his home were safe, untouched by the darkness that seemed to be rising up everywhere else.

What he'd found should have reassured him, but he'd realized it had left him with more uncertainties, more questions. People changed, even if sometimes the places they called home didn't. The fact that the world's troubles seemed to have fallen short of Fairbury didn't mean they weren't still happening. The combination of guilt and anger was still at the back of his mind, eating at him, suppressed but not banished by the tranquility of his surroundings.

He sat for what seemed like a long time, trying to set his emotions in order. Eventually a sound intruded, playing on his subconscious until it had pushed its way to the front of his busy thoughts. It echoed faintly through the greenery around him, distant but persistent. He cocked his head to one side, listening.

It sounded a lot like sirens.

A sense of foreboding began to creep over him. He darted back down the oak's trunk, dropping to the forest floor from halfway up and pausing to listen again. Down in the undergrowth it was even fainter, but it was definitely still there. If it had been an emergency vehicle just passing along the lane the sound would have faded by now. Whatever was emitting the noise, it was stationary.

Vic found the track leading back to the house. He began to run.

CHAPTER SEVEN

Vic raced through the undergrowth, his heart pounding. He didn't dare slow down to let his thoughts catch up. He needed to know that he'd been hearing things, or that he was just mistaken. He had to make sure that his imagination had been playing tricks on him, not that something terrible had happened. Not here, not now.

He burst through the undergrowth and reached the fence outside his backyard. The sound of sirens had cut off at some point while he'd been running, but he could now hear shouting coming from the front of the house.

He found the gate to the yard locked. For a second, he almost panicked. His parents knew he'd gone out into the forest. Why would they have locked the gate after him? He could've scaled the wall in a heartbeat, but he thought better of it.

Stay calm. Keep it together. He might have dazed out during a few history lessons, but he'd always been sharp in the combat bouts and situational training. A succession of teachers – Wolverine and Karma foremost among them – had commended him for a level head and an ability to solve problems under pressure. He wasn't going to forget all that now, when it counted.

He sprinted round the side of the yard, then carried on past Mr McTeal's before turning right onto the lane. If he'd gone immediately around his own home he would have emerged in the front yard and presumably come out right in the midst of whatever was going on there. That didn't seem wise.

He dashed past McTeal's to find the leafy street beyond packed full. Half a dozen vehicles, three of them trucks and three police cars, were parked up haphazardly at the side of the lane, while a small crowd had gathered outside the Borkowski front yard. There were people from the neighborhood – Vic recognized the Rasheeds, Mr McTeal, the Carters, and Mr Sloan – along with three police officers all outside the low front fence. Their attention was focused on the yard, where another eight figures had taken over the front lawn.

Dread filled Vic the moment he saw them. They were unmistakable in their black robes and ugly silver grotesques, the white cross-and-circle emblazoned on their breasts. Purifiers. Even worse, they were heavily armed. A few wore protective plates over their chests and shoulders, and six carried rifles, a mix of AR-15s and M16s, pointed at the sky but threatening all the same. The remaining two bore lit torches, the blazing tops giving off dirty black smoke.

They'd ranged themselves across the lawn. The front door to Vic's home had been kicked open. A police sergeant, undoubtedly more used to busting kids with dope than dealing with an impromptu cultist riot, was remonstrating loudly with the masked invaders, but none of them spoke or moved. Both his colleagues had their hands on their sidearms, but hadn't drawn them, clearly not wanting to risk an escalation. As Vic took in the scene, the sergeant turned his attention to the crowd, bellowing angrily at them to disperse. None of them moved.

Mrs Rasheed began to shout back at the officer. "Are you

insane! Are you just going to stand there while these madmen ransack our neighbors?"

This couldn't be happening. Why were the Purifiers here, in rural Illinois? How had they found him? Had he led them here? Had they picked him up on the road from the Institute, followed him ever since?

Vic stood, frozen between his desire to confront the people invading his home and the understanding that a head-on assault was rarely a wise strategy. He'd already considered stripping off and going full chameleon but didn't want to duck back up the sidetrack for fear of being spotted. Where were his parents? He cast a look around the lane, forcing himself to remember his tactical training. The Purifiers appeared to have arrived in a pair of rusty trucks painted with their uncompromising symbol, the third vehicle looked like an old prison transport. Its rear container was made of blocky steel and it had two small windows with bars covering them. The vehicles were being guarded on the roadside by several more armed Purifiers, with still more sitting behind the wheels, the engines idling – it looked as though they weren't intending to stay for long.

Vic couldn't back off now. He checked his pocket and cursed silently, remembering that he'd left his phone charging in his room the night before. He hadn't even answered Cipher's message before he'd fallen asleep. Not that it really mattered now – who was he going to call anyway? He looked to the police, but the sergeant seemed too busy taking instructions from his radio now to do anything. There were too few of them; a gunfight with these numbers and at this range would only end one way. There was no one from the Institute nearby either. Vic was on his own.

Don't panic, he told himself again. *Play this calmly and everything will be fine.* He pulled up his hood and carefully approached the crowd from the back, thankful that everyone's attention was on the Purifiers or the police in front of them. Perhaps his parents had heard them coming and already gotten away? Maybe they'd fled through the woods? But wouldn't he have run into them coming to the house? And how would they have locked the backyard gate from the outside? Perhaps, realizing that Vic was out without his phone, they'd left him the only message they could in haste – locking the gate so that he didn't stumble inside and run right into the cultists.

A commotion at the front door of the house caused Vic to pause. A figure emerged from within, stepping out onto the porch. He was clad in the same grim robes as his fellow Purifiers, but his grotesque was golden instead of silver, and he stood a good head taller than those around him. Vic recognized him immediately from the news reports.

Prophet Xodus.

He hadn't realized just how big the zealot was in person. The sight of him filled Vic with a potent mixture of hatred and revulsion, but it was quickly replaced by raw fury when he saw who was being dragged out after Xodus.

The Purifiers had his parents. Martha and Dan were manhandled out by three more of the masked fanatics and thrown onto their knees side-by-side on the lawn. Dan glared up at them, his left eye bruising, while Martha clasped her face in her hands and wept.

Vic was about to force his way through the crowd and into the Purifiers' midst, held back only by his training. He was shaking with rage, his body flushed with adrenaline, and his mind overwhelmed by the need to lash out in his parents' defense. One thing broke through his furious thoughts, one realization – the appearance of the Borkowskis in the clutches of the Purifiers seemed to have had the exact same effect on their neighbors.

A cry of outrage went up from the men and women who'd come out of their nearby homes to confront the invaders.

"That's Dan and Martha!" Mrs Rasheed shouted. "Who do you think you are? How can you do this? Let go of them both!" A dozen more voices joined hers as people began to push and shove the police, apparently intent on getting at the Purifiers. Despite being wholly unarmed and facing down automatic weaponry wielded by fanatics, Mr and Mrs Borkowski's neighbors clearly weren't going to let them be abused right in front of them.

The abrupt swelling of aggression caught the police by surprise, almost forcing them back against the yard fence. The sergeant, red-faced, was nearly thrown over and had to be dragged back by another officer. Even several of the Purifiers turned their masked faces in the direction of the towering Xodus, as though seeking instruction.

The crowd's anger also cut through Vic's haze. It made him hesitate before pushing his way to the front. What would that achieve? He was fast, yes, but not fast enough to take out a dozen Purifiers simultaneously. Not fast enough to dodge bullets. Maybe he could get in among them long enough for his parents to make a break for safety, especially if he went chameleon? But that ran the risk of the Purifiers opening up on the crowd. If they did, it would be a massacre. Vic couldn't risk the lives of his friends and neighbors, let alone his parents. It would be madness to try.

He forced himself to stand still and keep to the edge of the crowd, just a nondescript kid taking in the drama. He needed a plan. He needed a distraction. Most of all, he needed to remember what Rockslide had told him. *Don't do anything stupid.*

He looked again towards the line of Purifier vehicles ranked along the edge of the lane, currently ignored by both the crowd and the interlopers on the front lawn.

That was when the gunshot rang out.

A *crack*, startlingly loud, clapped back off the front of the Borkowski house. Someone in the crowd screamed. The two sounds combined to freeze time. The angry, forward motion of the residents ceased. The police had drawn their sidearms, but none of them fired. Vic felt as though his heart had stopped. He craned his neck to see his parents, still being held on the lawn. Both had been startled by the shot, but neither had been hit.

Xodus stood over them, a pistol in one hand. He'd discharged into the air. Now, in the shocked silence that followed, he spoke.

"Be silent, sinners!" the golden-faced giant roared. His voice came out booming and edged with static. Vic assumed he had some sort of speaker unit implanted into his leering mask.

"Stand and behold the judgment of the righteous!" he continued, his brazen words echoing up the leafy lane. "Long has this sentence been overdue! Long have you thought yourselves beyond the reach of the Purifiers! But no more! There is no place on this earth or the next that is not subject to our vigilance!"

It sounded like the same demented rambling that Vic had heard whenever the cult leader was on TV. What he said next though, wasn't, and it horrified Vic just as much as the sound of the gunshot had. As the police sergeant tried to shout him down, Xodus carried on over him.

"While the punishment that awaits each and every one of you should be severe, you may yet rejoice in our benevolent mercies. We have come for just one, a devious and deformed creature that you have suffered to live among you for too long. We are here seeking the Anole!"

A fresh surge of rage filled Vic. It was just what he'd been afraid of. This was all his fault. His parents, his neighborhood, were suffering because of him. Angry muttering and a few shouts issued from the crowd.

After pausing, Xodus continued. "Tell us where to find the mutant boy, or his punishment shall befall you instead!"

The crowd didn't answer, but Dan did. Glaring up at Xodus, he spat. "My son's name is *Victor*."

The Purifier standing over him struck him on the back of the head. Vic shivered. His hands clenched into fists. *Don't. Not yet. Don't, or good people will die.*

"If you wish your neighborhood to remain whole you will answer me," Xodus barked. "We know the mutant is here! Speak, or you shall never see these two again!"

He brandished his weapon at Dan and Martha.

"You can't bully us into submission, you lunatic," Martha said, looking up for the first time. Her face was streaked with tears, but her expression was filled with defiance. "You'll never take away my son!"

The crowd growled with agreement. Mrs Rasheed forced her way into the police cordon, gesturing at Xodus. "You speak about judgment, but your time is coming too, you mindless monster! You won't catch the kid, and if you hurt his parents, he'll hunt you to the ends of the earth!"

"I can only hope so," Xodus said. "The parents will be coming with us, but not before the filthy taint of this mutant-loving family is burnt from this sinful town!"

He gestured sharply at the two Purifiers carrying the torches. They moved inside the house while the rest continued to hold the crowd at bay.

It was now or never. Vic moved. He didn't head towards the yard though. He went in the opposite direction, slowly, glancing left and right to ensure he remained unnoticed. He had a plan, and he'd only get one shot at it.

Victor Borkowski had a number of unique abilities, but none of them were particularly suited to aggression. As of yet he'd never found himself to be notably strong or resilient. He had good reflexes, and his biology meant he tired at a slower rate than most humans. His finest attributes were his chameleon skin, his wall-climbing, and his wicked tongue, and all of those were best used covertly. So, Vic went covert. He slipped to the side of the lane, entering the undergrowth, and pulled his hoodie up over his head. Tying the sleeves around his waist, he took a deep, steadying breath, exhaled slowly, and let his skin change. His exposed upper half melded with the surrounding foliage, becoming nothing more recognizable than a moving distortion.

He crept through the brush, keeping low, almost invisible from the road. The crowd had started to shout again, though he couldn't see what the Purifiers were doing. His heart was racing and his palms had turned sticky, a sure sign of stress. He had to keep it together, just for a bit longer.

He passed the first of the Purifier trucks parked up at the side of the road. The small group of zealots guarding them were all on the opposite side, facing the crowd. If there was any trouble, surely it would come from there? Even if one of them had glanced back, they'd have seen nothing to raise suspicions – Vic was too deep in the undergrowth.

He came to the third vehicle in the Purifier convoy, the old prison truck. Its white-painted bodywork was rusting and dented, but the bars over its rear windows looked freshly soldered. He guessed the cult had salvaged it from a wrecking shop and done it up.

Vic crept up to its flank, going on all fours now. Like the other two vehicles, there was a Purifier sitting in the prison truck's cab. And like everyone else on the lane except Victor, the driver's attention appeared to be focused on the Borkowski front yard. Vic could still hear Xodus haranguing the crowd, presumably while his goons set fire to his home. He couldn't stop that now.

But he could still break his parents out. He reached the side of the truck and, after a slight pause, stood up and knocked once on the driver's window.

The Purifier turned sharply. As he did so Vic closed his eyes and held his breath. It was incredibly counter-intuitive, but he kept his nerve, trusting in the fact that the truck driver couldn't see his clothed lower half through the cab window.

There was the *thunk* of a lock disengaging, followed by the sound of the driver's door opening. Vic opened his eyes and lashed out, grabbing the edge of the door and hauling on it. With the driver holding it from the other side he was dragged out almost on top of Vic, letting out a muffled yelp as he lost his balance.

Vic sidestepped so that the Purifier fell into the undergrowth by the road. Immediately he dropped on top of him, pinning him as he tried to roll over.

This was when his reflexes counted. He ripped off the silver grotesque and slammed his fist down into the shocked, cringing face beneath. The man was rake-thin and balding, his skin a sallow, unhealthy color. He tried to cry out as Vic swung at him, as if he still couldn't make out what was attacking him. The next punch burst his nose in a flash of crimson.

Vic grabbed the edge of the Purifier's cowl and half-dragged him up onto his feet. The man lashed out in dazed desperation, catching Vic a glancing blow on the side of the head, but his bony skull carapace took the worst of it. Jaw clenched with rage and effort, Vic thrust the Purifier head-first into the trunk of a tree standing by the road.

There was a gristly thump. The Purifier went limp, slumping against the tree's roots. Vic knelt beside him and rolled him over to check he wasn't faking. The Purifier's breathing was still steady. Vic glanced quickly back toward the lane. A part of him expected to see a dozen Purifiers rushing him, weapons raised. Instead, he saw that the cultists guarding the truck still had their backs to him and their rifles trained on the crowd. The throaty grumble of the trucks' idling engines seemed to have covered the noise of the scuffle, and the sounds from the yard had helped. There were still raised voices, angry shouting, and Xodus's hateful diatribe continuing to boom out. The madman could talk, that was for sure.

Be quick. Don't hesitate. Vic reached down and hauled the black robes up and off the Purifier. It wasn't an easy task, manhandling the thick folds over the unconscious body, but Vic's frustration gave him a fevered determination. He managed to drag them over the man's head, leaving him in his undergarments – a worn set of combat pants and a stained vest that clung to his rangy body.

Vic hefted the robes over his own head. For a moment he was trapped in suffocating black folds that stank nauseatingly of stale sweat and body odor. He managed to battle his way to the hood, coming up gasping as the garment fell over his shoulders.

He found himself looking down at the white Purifier badge now stamped upon his chest. It filled him with skin-crawling revulsion, but there was no time for squeamishness. A series of gun shots echoed out across the lane. Vic looked over the hood of the truck in time to see one of the Purifiers letting off another burst of fire into the air. Xodus was advancing, the crowd and the police scattering. Cussing again, Vic cast about on the ground until he'd found the fallen Purifier's grotesque. He fitted the ugly thing over his head and immediately found his world constricting to its narrow eye slits, his own breathing quickly growing heavy in the stifling confines of the mask.

Almost as an afterthought, he heaved the unconscious body of the Purifier a few feet deeper into the undergrowth, before sprinting, head down, back to the prison truck. He had to hike up the ungainly skirt of the robes with both hands as he went. How did these idiots stand wearing this stuff full-time? They'd need more than divine intervention if any of them ever found themselves having to run somewhere.

He hit the side of the van and threw himself into the driver's seat, easing the door shut just as Xodus and his underlings crossed the street towards the parked-up vehicles. The crowd had been forced to scatter, the police begging the Borkowskis' neighbors to keep clear. Even with a phalanx of armed and aggressive zealots advancing through their midst, none of the residents backed off more than a few paces. There was booing and jeering as Xodus reached the first of the transport trucks.

They'd brought Dan and Martha with them. Both had been cuffed with zip wires and were being dragged along at gunpoint. Dan's expression was stony, his gaze unwavering as he stared straight ahead, but Martha couldn't resist looking back at the house as she was forced along. Black smoke had begun to billow from the bottom floor windows.

Vic forced himself to sit still and be silent. *Remember the training. Just a bit closer.* The robe and mask stank, and he was starting to get a headache, a sure sign that he was overheating. He needed to regulate his temperature, but he didn't even dare play around with the air con. He couldn't risk discovery, not now there were Purifiers actually passing the truck's cab. He experienced a flash of pure panic as he placed his hands on the steering wheel and remembered that they were still uncovered – the Purifier he'd taken out hadn't been wearing gloves. Green, scaly, clawed fingers might be a bit of a giveaway. He hastily triggered his chameleon effect on the visible skin and dropped his hands into his lap.

Xodus had mounted up in the front of the lead truck. More Purifiers were clambering into the open flatbed directly ahead of Vic, while several others led Dan and Martha past his own window, headed for the rear of the prison van. Vic fought the hardest battle of his life to ignore his parents while they were pulled past him. Still struggling to stay calm, he turned in his seat and looked back through the barred window between the truck cab and the containment trailer. A Purifier swung the rear doors open, and as he did so Vic put the gearstick into reverse, foot poised over the accelerator.

There were some barked commands, and Dan was thrust up by his captor into the back of the trailer. Martha followed immediately after. The second Vic saw her pushed up into the vehicle, he hit the gas. The engine roared to life with a violent jolt, sharp enough to fling both his parents from their feet and deeper into the trailer. It also flung off the Purifier who'd been about to clamber up after them, sending the rest scattering.

"Hang on!" was all Vic had time to shout. He slammed the shift into gear and dragged hard on the wheel. Tires shrieked and the engine protested as the truck made an ungainly turn in the lane, throwing aside more Purifiers like black-clad rag dolls.

The street descended into chaos. Residents fled in all directions, screaming as the police tried to get to their own cars. The Purifiers immediately ahead of Vic threw themselves out of the way, while those who'd mounted up in the other trucks leapt back onto the road, shouting and fumbling with their weapons. Vic urged the prison truck past the other cult vehicles and the police cars blocking the narrow lane. To do so he had to half drive on the verge – twigs and branches whipped at the cab as he wrestled the transport around and back onto the road, silently thankful that an evasive driving course was part of the Institute's educational program.

One of the Purifiers opened fire. A semiautomatic burst of shots perforated the cabin, clipping the hood and crunching through the glass of both doors, leaving them cracked and crazed.

Another cultist actually attempted to fling himself into the path of the careening truck. Vic clipped him with a thud, flinging the madman into the undergrowth.

He was past the police cars. The road ahead was clear. Vic accelerated.

"Hold on!" he shouted again, snatching a glance into the trailer compartment. He could only hope the desperate driving hadn't thrown his parents back out of the rear door. Dan had managed to catch hold of one of the window rungs, clutching onto them with his wrists still bound. Martha had in turn grabbed him to steady herself.

"What're you doing?" Dan shouted.

"Getting us out of here!" Vic replied. He pushed the grotesque back so it was on top of his head rather than over his face – handling a rusting old prison truck at speed was somewhat easier when he could both see and breathe.

He glanced in his wing mirrors and swore. They already had company. One of the Purifier vehicles was racing after them, coming up rapidly. He eased his foot down, taking the turn at the end of the lane as fast as he dared.

Downtown Fairbury lay ahead, its quiet Sunday afternoon about to be shattered. Vic shot through the red light at the first junction, hunched over the steering wheel, his concentration absolute. He could carry on straight through town, but he doubted he'd be able to lose their pursuers that way. He took a hard left at the next junction, teeth gritted as he battled the wheel once more, feeling gravity attempting to overturn the swerving truck. He could smell rubber burning as he took an immediate right, then left again, having to drag the vehicle around parked cars on a one-way street.

"You have to slow down, Vic!" Martha shouted. "You're going to hit something!"

Vic didn't have time to respond. Another red light, horns blaring at him furiously. Pedestrians and other vehicles just a blur. His attention was split entirely between the road directly ahead and the view in the mirrors. The Purifiers were sticking to him. They'd lost ground, but they were still in sight.

He didn't have a plan. Snatch the truck while his parents were in the back, that was as far as he'd gotten. He'd hoped the Purifiers would be slower to pursue, or that the police would at least impede them. They were relentless though. What should he do? Carry on out of town, pick up the highway? Dump the truck and head out on foot? Try and hide somewhere in town?

"Victor!" screamed his mother. He saw the danger in the same instant. An elderly couple had stepped out onto a pedestrian crossing directly ahead. They froze in terror as they saw the truck tearing towards them.

Vic wrenched the wheel to the left. Too late. The vehicle shrieked as it passed the couple, but in doing so Vic had lost control. Momentum carried it over. In that last instant, Vic realized he hadn't fastened his seatbelt.

The world went sideways. Vic was thrown across the driver compartment, his head crunching into the windshield. The impact was a visceral feeling, that hideous moment of force instantly followed by a lance of raw pain. Stars burst across his vision, and he tasted blood. He stopped thinking.

Glass rained down around him. Glass, and something else. Water. He didn't understand. Was it raining? His head hurt. A detached part of his mind realized that he was probably in shock, or stunned, or both. He blinked, wiping water from his eyes. Not water, blood. There was water too though, pattering down through the shattered windshield.

He groaned and tried to sit up, discovering as he did so that "up" had changed substantially. The cab was on its side, its right flank tipped in the air. After hitting the windshield Vic had been dumped down onto the crumpled remains of the driver's door, now crushed against the sidewalk.

He stretched out tentatively, expecting to find broken bones and torn muscles, but the only pain was in his scalp. He probed it delicately with one finger, finding it bloody and stinging. He'd taken worse knocks in the danger room though – his skull carapace had saved him from splitting his head open.

Water still fell from outside, running in through the shattered windshield. He realized where it was coming from. The truck had mounted the sidewalk as it overturned and had collided with a red fire hydrant. Water jetted vertically from the broken spout and rained back down, pattering steadily off the crumpled hood.

The distant shriek of tires reached him. He snapped fully back to the present, his dazed thoughts rallying. His parents. He had to get out. Now. He vaulted up through the shattered window of the right-hand cab door, landing on the sidewalk outside. It was slick from the burst hydrant. There were no pedestrians nearby. Everyone had scattered from the site of the crash including, he was relieved to notice, the elderly couple.

He found his parents around the back of the truck. Dan had crawled from the open rear doors, pulling Martha along with him. They were slumped side-by-side against the vehicle. Martha had a head gash not dissimilar to Vic's, and Dan was clutching his ankle, in obvious pain.

"Get your mother out," he said as Vic crouched beside them. "My ankle's gone. I'll only slow you down."

"No," Vic said, putting his arm around Martha's shoulder. She seemed dazed. Vic hoped she wasn't concussed. "We're all going. Come on."

"There's no time," Dan snapped. "I can barely stand, let alone run. I'm telling you, get her out! I'll be fine!"

Vic helped Martha to her feet. She looked at him un-comprehendingly, still clutching her bloody scalp, confused.

"Victor?" she mumbled. "What's happening?"

"Everything's going to be all right," he lied. "You've just got to walk with me, OK Mom?"

He could hear the sounds of running feet now. He glanced around the trailer's flank and saw that the Purifier truck, momentarily impeded by another vehicle, had mounted the pavement at the bottom of the street. Cultists were spilling from it, one still standing in the back gesticulating furiously towards him as another raised a rifle and let off a burst of shots. They whipped well overhead, the report chattering back from the surrounding walls.

Vic ducked back and looked down at Dan, horribly torn. Shouldn't he stay and fight? Maybe he could buy enough time for both of them to get away? Cause a distraction? But he could tell from the pain in his father's eyes that he wouldn't be able to get far.

There was no time to delay. Supporting Martha under one arm, he turned down the nearest side alley, looking back at his father. Dan caught his eye and simply nodded.

"I'll come back for you!" Vic shouted, before turning the corner.

CHAPTER EIGHT

The next few minutes were a blur. Vic half-carried, half-dragged Martha down the alleyway, his reptilian endurance helping to push him on. The immediate frenzy of the escape had given way to a colder, more calculating mindset. All that mattered was getting his mother to safety, and he now had an idea of how he could do that. He'd come up with it as the first police car had swept past, the sound of sirens spurring on his thoughts. He couldn't risk going to the station or a hospital, not with the Purifiers roaming the streets and the police apparently unable – or unwilling – to stop them. But he knew somewhere he trusted to hole up, at least for the night.

At the intersection with the next street Martha's senses came back to her, and she demanded that they turn around and go back for Dan.

"He can't walk," Vic said grimly as she forced him to a stop. "And they'll already have him by now."

"We can't just leave him," Martha cried out. "He's your father!"

"He told me to get you out," Vic said. "Do you think I wanted to leave him behind? We've got to keep going."

As though to emphasize his point, they heard shouting from the alleyway behind them. Vic hitched up the edge of his stolen robes and took his mother's hand, running with her across the street just as a police car tore past, sirens wailing. Another pulled up at the edge of the alley. Four armed officers piled out, aiming down the narrow space, their back to the pair. It seemed Fairbury's small police department had finally found the stomach and the numbers to confront the town's invaders.

"Maybe they'll be able to free your father," Martha said, a tremor in her voice.

"I wouldn't count on them, Mom," Vic said. "Come on. We've got to keep going."

"Where?" Martha asked, hurrying to catch up. "Do you even know where you're headed, Victor?"

"Yes," he answered. "Just stick close and don't look back."

They turned north after Danboro Street and took a right along Charles Avenue. People stopped and stared. Some called out. Vic ignored them. Right now, he didn't know who he could trust, and besides, they had to keep going. He knew the best place to stop, and it wasn't anywhere in town. He kept close to his mom, her hand still in his. She was frightened, he could tell. So was he. Showing it wouldn't help. It was up to him to get them both out. Once Martha was safe, he could double back for Dan.

Just as they stepped off Routledge Road, Vic heard a staccato burst, followed by a few individual pops from behind them. More gunfire, but distant. The police? The Purifiers? Maybe both. He picked up his pace, urging his mother to stay with him. She still seemed partially dazed, though he couldn't tell if that was because of the speed of events or because of the head wound. He'd need to get a closer look at it, and soon.

Keep going. They followed 38th Avenue north, then turned

east. At one point he thought they were being followed, though he wasn't sure. His every sense was on edge. His scalp still throbbed. He carried on along Franklin Lane and there, finally, were the trees.

"We're going in there?" Martha asked as Vic led her onto a forest track off the lane.

"We are," he said.

"But that will take us—"

"That's the idea."

Martha looked like she was going to argue but thought better of it.

"I've been trained by the X-Men, Mom," Vic said, trying to reassure her.

"I know," she admitted with a small shrug. "It's… difficult for me to accept that my little boy has been prepared to deal with emergencies like this. But I trust you. Always."

Vic gave her a short, firm hug, then carried on. The forest embraced them. It was warmer now, close and humid beneath the boughs. It made Vic's robes stink even worse than before. They passed a man they knew, Mr Seller, out walking his dog. He called out in concern after them, but Vic just shouted back, telling him to stay out of town. *Keep going*, he told himself. *Don't stop*. He knew that if he did, he might panic.

The trail led them further east, then north. He kept looking right, searching the forest for a marker, worried that what he sought might no longer exist. He sensed that his mother was flagging. She was damp with sweat, and her breath was labored. She stumbled over the uneven, root-cut track on several occasions, and only Vic's lightning reflexes saved her from falling.

"Not far now, Mom," he murmured, hoping he was right.

There it was. The sign he'd been looking for. An old red rag, now little more than a faded strip of cloth, nailed high up on a yew tree overhanging the path. One of the gang had pinned it up there years ago, standing on a stepladder stolen from their father's garage.

"It's this way," Vic said. He steered Martha off the path and past the tree with the old piece of cloth.

When they'd been kids, they had cut a different trail into the forest at the back of Vic's house, one that led into the foliage from the other side. The smaller streets and lanes he had taken out of Fairbury had carried them in an arc north-east, bringing them back round to the forest from the north. This was what the gang had called their "emergency exit." In all their childhood games playing X-Men, Vic had never imagined it would one day be put to real, urgent use.

There were more rags on the trees, nailed high up to the trunks or fastened around the boughs. Vic led Martha on through the undergrowth, following the hidden route. On several occasions he had to pause to get his bearings – a few of the markers were gone or faded beyond recognition. He would crouch, taste the air with his tongue, reorient his senses. Martha kept any doubts she had to herself.

After what felt like an age, they emerged into a point in the forest that Vic clearly recognized. Ahead was the black oak, its great branches standing resolute, untroubled by the desperate chaos that had befallen Fairbury. Vic led Martha around to the treehouse.

"This was your plan?" she asked as she gazed up at the weathered little hut.

"We need somewhere to stay until this all calms down," Vic said. "And if I'm going back for Dad I need to leave you somewhere I can be confident that you won't be found. We can't trust anyone in town. The treehouse has shelter and food. You can stay for a day or more if you have to."

"How am I supposed to get up there?" was all Martha asked.

Vic was already planting his hands on the bark. He scaled up to the platform and tossed the rope ladder down, testing that it was still capable of bearing weight with a few vicious tugs. He then clambered back down the side of the tree.

"One step at a time," he said to Martha as she gazed up at the ladder, a hand on her wounded scalp. "If you feel dizzy, I'll be right beside you."

She took a second to collect herself and grasped the rope. Vic scaled the trunk again at a gentler pace this time, keeping at the same level as his mother as she placed her feet on the first rung and began to climb. It was slow but steady going, Vic constantly on edge, ready to throw out an arm or, if necessary, his tongue to arrest a possible fall. Martha made it on her own, though, clambering over the edge and onto the platform outside the treehouse. It creaked but held as Vic hopped up onto it next to her.

"Welcome to the X-Mansion," he said with a tired smile. He showed Martha into the hut, helping her sit in one of the rickety old chairs.

"So, this is where you used to sneak off to," she said, looking around the dilapidated space. "If Dan had told me your gang hut was so squalid, I'd have thought twice about letting you come here after school."

"It wasn't always like this," Vic said, dragging off and gratefully discarding the stolen Purifier robes and mask. He pulled the hoodie that had been tied around his waist over his head before crouching in front of his mother. "And it'll do for now. Hold still."

He leant in close to inspect his mother's scalp. It had become badly crusted, caked brown with dried blood. He didn't want to touch it, not until he had something to clean it with.

"Does it hurt?" he asked. Martha gave him an are-you-serious look.

"Like an ache, or a sting?" he elaborated.

"An ache," she said. "All the way through."

"Do you feel dizzy? Light-headed?"

"I was," she admitted. "Less so now."

"You might be concussed. We need to get it looked at as soon as we can."

Martha sat quietly for a while, and softly began to cry. The sight almost overcame Vic. He embraced her gently, letting her weep into his shoulder. Until that moment he'd been operating on his training alone, treating everything as a problem to be overcome. Only now did the enormity of what had just happened begin to hit him.

"It was all so sudden," Martha mumbled. "I was just about to see Dan off to work and we heard the engines outside. They broke in, with their guns and their masks."

"I'm sorry," was all Vic could think to say, holding Martha close. "This is all my fault."

"No, it isn't," Martha sniffed, pulling away from him. Her face was ruddy and damp with tears, but her words were firm and earnest. "You're guilty of nothing, my son. Don't you forget that."

"But they came here for me," Vic said, his voice almost cracking as he was forced to acknowledge the truth. "They must have followed me. I brought all this to Fairbury. You heard the gunshots in town. What if people have been hurt? Killed? What about Dad?"

"You didn't do any of that," Martha reassured him. "That's the work of horrible, bitter people."

"I need to go back to town," Vic pressed. "I have to find Dad before they take him away. If they haven't already."

"Your father won't go quietly," Martha said. "Even unarmed, he fought them when they broke in."

"I've got to go get him. We've no idea what those madmen will do to him."

"That's probably exactly what they want," Martha pointed out.

"If you had the power to save him, would you?" Vic responded. "Don't ask me to not go back out there."

Martha said nothing, though her expression remained troubled, her lips pursed. Vic shifted across the floor and pulled up the trap door. "We've got food, for now. I'll need to go to the creek to fill these bottles."

"You had all this hoarded up here?" Martha asked as she peered into the treasure hole. "How old is it all? It can't still be good!"

"Nonperishables," Vic said. "Mostly. It'll be good for one day at least. You can rest up, and I can go back out safe in the knowledge that you're secure up here."

A part of him was still in operation mode, still thinking like a team leader in a training exercise. His mind was already on the next stage. His mother was safe for now, albeit in need of medical attention. He had to find out what had happened to his father. And to do that, he knew he'd need help.

Despite Martha's protests, he stole back down the tree with the supply hole's empty bottles and went east until he reached the creek. He returned and cleaned her wound, dressing it with a strip he tore off his hoodie sleeve with his claws. Then he went back out into the forest. He'd smelled something unmistakable while he'd been outside the hut, something he decided he had to see for himself.

He took the trail back home. It wasn't long before he smelled the burning again, this time accompanied by more sirens. The crackling, snarling fury of the blaze also became gradually audible. He realized that ash was falling softly, between the trees, adding a gray funeral pall to the summer's day.

As he cleared the last of the undergrowth before the backyard, his heart sank. Even though he'd expected it, been preparing for it, the sight of his home being consumed by flames tore at him. The fire was raging unchecked, firefighters withdrawing from the backyard, abandoning the house to its destruction. Flames were licking hungrily from the windows and from the partly collapsed roof. A pillar of gray-black smoke churned into the sky overhead, casting a cloud of ash that had already caked the forest at the edge of the yard in inches-thick gray desolation. Even standing well back amidst the foliage, the heat radiating off the blaze was intense. He found himself praying it didn't spread and ignite the rest of the woodland.

He crouched for a while and watched as his childhood was reduced to smoke and ash. He could see the fire flickering from his bedroom window. The curtains were long gone, and presumably everything inside wasn't far behind. His old trophies and awards, schoolwork, clothes, books, posters, his baseball bat, his DVD and music collections, his autographed actor headshots. Everything was gone.

Nearly everything. As he watched, entranced by the consuming work of the flames, he realized he was clutching something in his hoodie pocket. The little toy dinosaur. He pulled it out and looked at it, took in its snarling, ill-defined face and rubbery tail. The unwitting sole survivor of his past. It was at once miserable and fitting, like a savage joke. Two reptiles, outliving their extinctions.

A crash disturbed his bitterness. He pocketed the toy and looked up in time to see a section of the house – including his room – give way in a bout of flames and heat so intense it forced him back a few paces. Well, that was that, he decided. A cold sense of finality settled over him. He'd struggled to accept that his life had moved on from Fairbury, from his home, from his childhood. Well, the world had intervened, and now he didn't have a home or a childhood left to go back to. The only thing he could still save was the most important thing of all – his family. He turned his back on the pyre of his memories and headed into the forest.

CHAPTER NINE

It didn't take Vic long to realize that he wasn't alone any more. As he picked his way back along the trail back towards the treehouse, the crack of a twig and the overhead clatter of some disturbed woodland bird made him stop and crouch.

He caught movement seconds later, a shift at odds with the overarching stillness of the forest. Black and white, advancing furtively. Vic immediately shifted location, crouching and moving carefully off the path.

He tasted the air with his tongue, his other senses catching the hint of sweat and musty robes before his eyes picked up on them. Two Purifiers, perhaps fifteen paces apart, were picking their way through the undergrowth nearby. They were headed parallel to the lane, cutting across the track between the backyard and the black oak. They were carrying assault rifles.

Trepidation and anger gripped Vic simultaneously. He hadn't expected the cultists to comb through the woods. He hadn't even expected them to still be in the area. How many of them were there? Had the police really still not contained them?

He felt an overwhelming urge to attack the duo in front of him. They had hurt his mother and taken his father. These two looked isolated, vulnerable – while the sight of the sinister black robes, rifles and the grimacing silver masks all conjured up an almost primal fear, observing them unseen proved that they were just humans. Their robes made walking in the woodland difficult – several times one or the other would pause to disentangle himself from a bush or branch – and the fact that they kept having to look rapidly from side to side reminded Vic how poor the vision was through the masks. They had bad trigger discipline and didn't move with the confidence or purpose that he'd noted whenever he'd reviewed training videos or combat techniques at the Institute. They weren't soldiers, and while that didn't necessarily make them any less dangerous, it made Vic more confident that they weren't omnipotent, demonic beings. Just zealots sweating in heavy robes and bad Halloween masks.

He let the two pass, certain that the combination of the undergrowth and his chameleon skin would keep him concealed. He refused to give into the urge to stalk and bring them both down. It seemed as though wherever there were two there'd always be more. If something happened to him, who would help his mother? He felt his resolve harden further, decisions forming. He knew what he had to do.

Vic let them stumble on through the wood and continued back along the path to the treehouse.

"I think I saw one of them out there," Martha said when he'd climbed back up into the hut. "He walked through the clearing, but he didn't bother to look up."

"They were near the house too," Vic said. "I went to check on it."

"Is it..." Martha trailed off, catching herself. Vic just shook his head.

"Houses can be rebuilt," she said softly, sniffing.

"They can," Vic agreed. "But right now, the most important thing is getting help. I need to contact the Institute."

"How?" Martha asked.

"I need a phone. But for one of those I'll need to head back into town. And I don't trust many people in Fairbury right now."

"I'm sure anyone on our street would let us use their phone," Martha said.

"Perhaps, but what're the chances the Purifiers are still watching them? I don't want to put any of them in more danger. I won't be the reason for more home burnings in Fairbury."

"Then whose phone can you use?" Martha asked. "The one payphone on the main street hasn't been operating for months."

"I'll think about it," Vic said. "I can't risk going back into town just now anyway. If they're still in the forest they'll still be around the main street. It'll have to be tonight or tomorrow."

Martha didn't argue. Vic realized just how tired she looked. The rush of adrenaline had subsided, leaving in its wake a deep gulf of exhaustion. It was catching up with him too, despite the greater endurance offered by his unique biology. His skull still ached dully from the car crash. His limbs felt weak with fatigue. The strain was mental too, fear and pain crowding in on his thoughts, making him falter. He knew he had to keep his mind focused if he was going to get through it all, but right now all the training and experience he'd picked up at the Institute felt a million miles away.

He used his claws to open a can of dried fruit. Martha didn't want to eat, until he reminded her how she'd coaxed him to finish his greens as a child.

"Pretty ironic, don't you think?" Vic said, smiling slightly as he pointed out the role reversal. "We're going to need all our strength to get through this, so eat up, Mom."

Despite herself, Martha smiled too, and began to eat.

Outside, darkness started to fall. Vic sat watch as the shadows beneath the boughs deepened and lengthened, eating up the forest around him. He let it consume him too, closing his eyes. Were there still Purifiers out there, stalking between the trees, hunting him? Were they still in town? Had there been casualties from the day's events?

Thoughts continued to press in on him from all sides. How had the Purifiers found him? He was convinced someone in Fairbury had contacted them. But who? As much as his family talked about the town rallying behind them, he'd seen more than a few dirty looks after getting off the bus from the Institute. The likes of Tony crossing the street had seemed rude at the time, but now it had a more sinister tone. He had no idea how deep anti-mutant hatred had wormed its way into Fairbury as a whole since he'd been away. The actions of the Purifiers proved that those who supported his family were at great risk. Who else could he trust?

The answer seemed obvious. Until he could contact the Institute, he had to rely on himself. That wouldn't help him find a phone, though. For that he'd have to take a gamble.

Neither Vic nor Martha slept much that night. Vic stayed curled up on the platform outside the hut door while his mother remained in her chair, drifting in and out of wakefulness. He made sure she drank plenty and checked her head intermittently. They watched the sun rise over the canopy together. Ordinarily it would have been a quiet, peaceful moment, an opportunity for parent and child to share with one another. But Vic could hardly force himself to sit still. He'd made a decision during the night. He knew how he was going to reach the Institute.

"Are you sure?" Martha asked when he told her.

"It's the best I could come up with," he said. "It's on the other side of town. If the Purifiers still have a presence in the area, it'll surely be in this locale, not there. I just need to cut around Fairbury to the north and I'll make it."

Martha seemed too tired to argue. She promised to wait in the treehouse until he returned. In turn, he promised her she'd soon be safe, and when she was, he would find Dan.

He dropped back down to the forest and picked up the secondary trail leading north-west, away from the ashen ruins of his house. He was still in his hoodie and jeans, but he dropped into chameleon all the same and moved off to the side of the track rather than follow it directly. If there were still cultists in the forest, he was confident he could slip past them, but not if he ended up running directly into them.

The woodland was quiet and lush in the rising morning heat. At its edge, fields of ripe corn and maize stretched away towards a brightening blue horizon, swaying softly in the breeze. Vic darted across the road, jumped a rail fence, and was in amongst the crops.

It proved slower going than he had anticipated. Dirt dragged at his feet and pollen made his eyes water and sting. Twice he veered too far north rather than west, only realizing his mistake when he emerged onto a road and saw the signs to Fairbury. He dared to cut a little closer in towards town in an effort to save time. One field required a sharp detour as a distant farmer started shouting at him, his faint anger accompanied by the barking of his dogs. Vic gave that one a wide berth. He didn't get on too well with dogs.

Finally, he spotted the raised embankment of the north-western highway, Route 73, ahead of him. He scrambled up its flanks and made a dash across it, narrowly avoiding a collision with a silage hauler. On the other side he slid down and turned south, into town.

This was the moment of greatest danger. All he had was the possibility that the Purifiers were no longer in Fairbury and, if they were, that they weren't in this part of it. If they had sympathizers and they spotted him, his only hope was that he could get in and out again before the cordon closed. At least he could trust the person he was calling on.

A brisk summer shower had kicked up as he reached the edge of town, slicking the sidewalks and making the gutters drool. He was glad of it – it washed the worst of the dust off his clothes and gave him an excuse to pull his hood up. He stuffed his hands into the hoodie's deep pockets for good measure, trying to hide the fact he'd ripped his lower sleeve off to bind up his mother's wound. He felt the toy dino, still in his pocket. After all this he'd have to give it a name.

There were very few people out on the streets. Vic tried to keep his head down and walk quickly without seeming like he was hurrying – a near impossible task. He avoided eye contact with those he passed. He was convinced they were staring at him. If he'd had hair, he guessed it would be on end at this point. As it was, his palms were sticky again and his mouth full of spit – he kept having to swallow, trying to regulate his breathing and heart rate. Be calm. Be calm.

He glanced up and saw his destination. Roundaway's Cafe, a little red-bricked coffee house nestled in between Suzie's Pets and the West Fairbury Stationery Store. Its outside menu board and two small tables sat desolate in the downpour. In a moment of horror, Vic thought that the cafe was closed, but light spilled through the front windows. People sat inside, staring out blankly into the rain. Without lingering, Vic entered.

The bell over the door chimed. He kept his hood up. He could feel people looking, always looking. He stuck out. There was nothing he could do about it. He was committed now.

No more than seven or eight people were sat around the tables crammed into the little space. He didn't look directly at any of them – he knew he'd recognize them, and vice versa. He walked straight up to the counter and smiled.

Miss Trimble stared at him for a second, glanced past him over his shoulder, then smiled back. She was a tall, slender woman with large round spectacles, her mousy hair streaked with gray and her apron seemingly perpetually messy. She leant over the counter slightly, and while her tone remained neutral, Vic could see the mischievous recognition in her eyes. It filled him with an unspoken relief.

"Morning there! What can I get ya?"

"Iced Americano, please," Vic said, doing his best to sound unconcerned. "Also, if you've got a phone I could use, I'd be very much obliged."

"Right over there," Miss Trimble said, nodding to an old pay phone in the corner and sliding fifty cents from the tip jar across the counter. "Best make it quick."

Vic took the coins and walked to the phone, trying not to rush. There had to still be Purifiers in the area. Otherwise Miss T wouldn't have advised him to hurry. Heck, she was pretending not to recognize him! That spelt trouble.

He slotted the coins into the phone and punched in the Institute number. All students were given an emergency contact, a direct line to the school should they ever find themselves in a life-threatening situation. This absolutely qualified. As Vic entered it, he heard the bell over the cafe door chime. He didn't turn around.

CHAPTER TEN

"What can I get you fellas?" Vic heard Miss Trimble ask. The phone in Vic's hand was ringing through at the other end.

"Nothing," replied a man's voice. "We're just looking for some information."

Vic felt his heart rate spike. He didn't turn around. The cafe was deadly silent.

"Please identify," pipped an automated voice in his ear. The Institute's security setting – all it required from him was either his student number, or his name for voice recognition. He couldn't utter either though. He tried to shift so that the exposed hand holding the phone – clawed and green-scaled – was out of sight from the counter.

"Are you fine-lookin' fellas lost?" Trimble asked in her most chipper voice. "Needin' directions out of town?"

"No," growled a second male voice. While the first was deep and solid, this one had an unhealthy rasp to it, as though the speaker was suffering from some sort of deep-set chest infection. "We're looking for somebody. I think you know who."

"I've no idea, sweetheart," Miss Trimble said. "If it's the

manager you're after, you're speaking to her."

She'd raised her voice fractionally. The electronic tone on the other end of the line repeated its identification request in Vic's ear.

"Victor," he tried to hiss as Miss Trimble spoke.

"Please identify," the voice on the phone repeated.

He said nothing. He couldn't. Any louder and he was certain it would give him away. His hand trembled slightly. His grip on the phone was like a vise.

"Well, if you don't know who we're looking for, I'm sure some of your patrons will," said the first voice. It carried on in a louder tone, addressing the whole cafe. "Where's the lizard?"

Vic's skin crawled. He felt as though he had a target painted on his back, but he couldn't turn around. The urge to color-change was instinctive, almost overwhelming. The voice on the phone repeated its request. A few seconds more and it would automatically hang up.

"Someone in here knows where he is," rasped the second voice. "So, start talking."

"I suggest you two leave right now," Miss Trimble said, her own voice now riven with iron. "I hit the silent alarm as soon as you walked through the door. The cops are already on their way."

"We gave the cops the runaround yesterday," the rasper continued. "They've got no authority, and plenty of them sympathize with our cause. You don't intimidate the Purifiers."

"What about you?" the deeper voice demanded. Vic heard footsteps, before a different voice answered. He recognized it as Mr Parsons, the Fairbury Springs hotel owner.

"We don't know anything about any lizard. I'd suggest you do as Miss Trimble says and get the hell out of here."

"Hell's already here, old man," the rasping voice sneered. "Your salvation is in our hands. What about you, little missy?"

"Please, just leave us alone," said the trembling voice of Mrs Stevens, the bakery owner. "We don't know where he is!"

Vic heard more footsteps, moving closer now. He could smell rancid breath and stale sweat. The line to the Institute had terminated, leaving nothing but the dial tone droning in his ear.

"And what about you, kid?" rattled the chill, deathly voice, right next to him. "You've been awful quiet on that phone."

A split-second to act. That's all he had. Vic spun to his right, hard and fast, and brought the phone receiver crashing across the jaw of the man who'd been standing behind him.

He was a lot bigger than Vic had anticipated – tall, scarred and shaven-headed, with tattoos depicting blazing fire and wailing souls all up his bare arms. He also wasn't wearing Purifier robes – he was sporting frayed combat pants and a stained black T-shirt with a snarling wolf emblem. All this Vic took in in a heartbeat as he felt the phone shatter in his grip. Spittle and blood flew from the man's split lips.

The blow sent the Purifier reeling. His buddy was behind him, dressed in sweatpants and a vest that had been plastered to his torso by the rain. He was dragging a sidearm from his waistband, crying out. Someone in the café screamed, and several dived for the floor, chairs clattering.

Vic leapt up onto the café counter in a crouch and lashed out with his tongue. The muscle, slick with drool, darted half the length of the cafe and knocked the pistol right out of the Purifier's grip. Vic dragged his tongue back in and whipped out simultaneously with his foot, kicking the first man in the hip and dropping him to one knee.

In such a confined space, filled with civilians, the odds weren't the worst but getting people out without someone getting hurt looked impossible. He had no more than a second to choose. Fight or flight.

Turned out he wasn't getting a choice after all. The second cultist was winding up to charge him rather than scramble after his lost sidearm, but he never got the chance. There was an explosive crash of shattered glass as something – a body – came hurtling in through the cafe's window. It went right over the top of Mr and Mrs Ellis's table as the couple dove for cover, overturning their drinks and fruit cake slices to join the carnage. The head of the incoming figure struck the leg of the man going for Vic, bringing him down too.

CHAPTER ELEVEN

No one got a chance to move before the door came flying in as well, accompanied by its little clattering bell. Vic cringed away from more shattered glass, his eyes screwed shut. When he lowered his arm, expecting the worst, he found himself looking at the most welcoming sight he'd seen since reuniting with his parents. Over six feet of solid rock advanced implacably through the splintered doorway, crunching glass to powder underfoot.

"Having trouble, lizard boy?" Rockslide rumbled. All Vic could do was grin.

The man Santo had flung through the window – presumably a Purifier who'd been guarding the door – was unconscious. The one Vic had brought down had managed to find his gun in the chaos. Raising it, he fired. Somebody screamed, the discharge in the confined space threatening to burst Vic's ears.

The bullets had been aimed at Santo. Each ricocheted harmlessly off, one bouncing off the wall and the other two lodging in the ceiling. The impacts struck sparks off Rockslide's chest but left no further impression besides a trio of slight white scuffmarks.

"Good shot," Santo grunted, his craggy face looking even more displeased than usual. "Now get out, before I start crushing skulls."

Fanatics these three might have been, but clearly none of the Purifiers present were suicidal. The two who had first come into the cafe snatched the unconscious third between them and, with some difficulty, hauled him up and out of the broken window. Santo clearly had no intention of giving way to them so they could use the remnants of the door.

"I've never been gladder to see you, Rocky," Vic said, his voice heartfelt.

"We need to go, now," Santo replied. "I may have already been spotted, and even if I wasn't, those three will bring more of their kind."

"I'm so sorry for all this," Vic said, turning to Miss Trimble. To his surprise, he found her smiling.

"It's OK, Vic," she said. "Worth it to see someone stand up to those bastards. I've got property insurance. That's what this was, after all, even if it was the assailant's head being broken in through the window."

"Thank you," Vic said, looking at the rest of the customers. They seemed less delighted than Miss Trimble with the entire incident. Most were frozen at their tables, staring in fear and awe up at Santo or at the wreckage of the cafe front. Mr and Mrs Ellis were still on their knees amidst the debris of their own broken table, clearly in shock.

"Thank you, everyone," Vic repeated to them all. "You could have turned me in, but you didn't. If you had they might have taken me before Rocky even got here. I owe every one of you, and I won't forget it."

"Just get your father back, Vic," Mr Ellis said, finding his composure as he extended a hand to help his wife to her feet.

"We saw them take him in the street yesterday. Dragged him off into one of their trucks."

"Do you know where they went?" Vic asked.

"No. Last I saw they were headed east out of town."

"We must go," Santo urged, shifting his bulk out of the door with some difficulty.

"I'll find him," Vic carried on, nodding his thanks to Mr Ellis. "And that's a promise. Miss T, you better not be shut too long!"

"I'll have this place reopened as soon as I've swept up the glass," Miss Trimble called after Vic as he sprinted outside, grinning once more.

"How did you know I was in trouble?" he asked Santo as he caught up with him. The big mutant had begun to move at a sidewalk-jarring jog, heading north.

"I didn't," he grunted. "But your friends guessed."

Vic set off after him, having to move quicker to keep up. "Cipher? Graymalkin?"

"Cipher," Santo confirmed. "She told me she had not heard from you, and that she had seen reports of Purifier activity in the vicinity of your home."

"The text," Vic said, realization dawning. Cipher had sent him a text he hadn't responded to the night he'd arrived home. Any calls had likely gone unanswered while he'd been out in the woods. Not for the first time, he gave thanks for the caution of his friends.

"How did you get here?" he asked as they carried on. "And how are we getting out?"

"The SR-70," Rockslide said simply.

"They let you take the school's Blackbird?" Vic asked incredulously, shooting a disbelieving glance up at his big companion. "I guess you really have graduated then!"

"It was an emergency," Santo replied.

"Where did you even put her down?"

"Further north, in a corn field. The automated systems are engaged should anything threaten it."

"First a fanatical religious cult, now crop circles," Vic said. "The people of Fairbury really are going to think the world's coming to an end. How did you know where to find me anyway? At Roundaway's, I mean?"

"The school provided me with your address. I went there first, but it's toast. Your neighbors were good enough to speak to me. They said you'd last been seen making a break for it with your parents into town. I figured if you'd gone to ground it'd probably be somewhere near that café you never stopped talking about."

"Miss Trimble and Roundaway's have saved me yet again," Vic said. "Except this time without coffee. We're going to need to detour though. We have to pick up my mom."

"Is she nearby?"

"Near enough. And after that we need to go get my dad."

"He's been separated from your mother?"

"They took him," Vic said, an abrupt rush of frustration coloring his voice. "Xodus and his goons. I don't know where, but I have to get him back."

"The priority is clear," Santo responded. "Remove yourself and your mother from Fairbury to safety."

"I'll take you to my mom, but I'm not going without my dad."

"You've already admitted you don't know where he is. We will find him, but we cannot do that today."

"Your orders are to get me back to school, aren't they?" Vic demanded.

"You and your family, yes. I swear to you that we will find your father, but that's impossible while the Purifiers infest this town."

"I'll hold you to that promise, Rocky," Vic said as shouting broke out back along the street they'd just left. A crowd of figures had spilled around the corner, an unkempt collection of brutes in old fatigues or dirty shirts, some clutching rudimentary weapons like crowbars and clubs, others tooled up with firearms. A cry went up from their midst as they caught sight of Santo and Vic reaching the edge of town.

"I hope you can move faster than this, lizard boy," Santo grumbled.

"C'mon, Rocky," Vic said, flashing a smile up at his old roommate. "Don't you know me? Try and keep up."

Together, they began to run.

CHAPTER TWELVE

They managed to shake the Purifiers after crossing the highway, and doubled back to the edge of town. Vic led Santo into the forest north of his home, and then to the base of the treehouse.

"We have to leave, Mom," he told Martha after scaling his way to the treehouse's platform. She'd been asleep and looked exhausted.

"What's happened?" she asked, clearly confused. Vic crouched in front of her, trying to smile reassuringly while stressing the need for urgency.

"Help has arrived," he said, and steadied her as she rose to her feet before guiding her out onto the platform. "You remember my friend Santo, from the Institute?"

Rockslide stood at the base of the tree. He waved up at them both. Martha gasped at the sight of the hulking, stony figure.

"He's an X-Man," Vic reassured her. "A fully-fledged one. He's got transport out of town. We just have to get to it before the Purifiers catch up with us."

"What about your father?" Martha asked, looking at Vic.

"I'm going to find him," he told her, his voice firm. "But first I've got to make sure you're safe. The sooner we do that, the better."

He descended the tree alongside Martha as she clambered down the ladder. Once she stood on solid ground, she gazed up at Rockslide's intimidating bulk.

"A pleasure to meet you again, Mrs. Borkowski," Santo said with a smile, holding out one slab-like hand. "I'm afraid Vic's going to have to lead us out of here. I've never had a good head for directions in a forest. Cliffs and mountainsides are more like home for me."

Martha let out a little laugh, clearly not sure if he was joking or not, but took his hand anyway. Vic would've found the sight of the mismatched handshake endearingly funny, had time not been so pressing.

He guided them through the woodland, aiming for the Blackbird's location. If the Purifiers found the jet before they could reach it, the game would be up. He pushed Martha as hard as he dared, trying not to think about worst-case scenarios.

They emerged into the fields north of Fairbury. Santo then directed them, following his communicator. It was slower going than Vic would've liked, mainly due to the difficulty of forcing their way through the thick corn fields. Santo took the lead, his unyielding bulk snapping stalks and forging them a path.

"We're getting close," he said as they walked through an open gate into another field. They'd barely crossed the boundary before Vic heard a sound that made his blood run even colder than usual.

Dogs. He could make out the distant noise of barking.

"Many of the local farmers have dogs?" Rockslide asked, almost casually.

"How far's the Blackbird?" Vic responded.

"A few more fields over."

"Then we'd better run."

They took off again, Vic sticking beside Martha. She was

faltering, and Vic felt a rising panic threatening to overtake him. The snarls of the dogs grew louder, a reminder that they were now prey being hunted by an enemy that was both merciless and unrelenting.

"I'm just slowing you down," Martha panted as she struggled through the corn, red-faced. "Let them take me!"

"No," Vic said bluntly, glancing back over his shoulder. He could see the stalks on the edge of the field they'd just passed through twitching as though something pushed after them. The dogs' yapping was clearer now, making Vic's skin crawl.

"We're going to carry you, Mom," he told Martha, before calling ahead to Santo. "Rocky, can you give her a lift?"

The big X-Man obliged, scooping Martha easily up off her feet. Apparently uninhibited by his new charge, he set off across the field once more.

The Blackbird was now partially visible, its sleek, gleaming black shape incongruous amidst the expanse of gently nodding, golden corn husks. They kept going, scaling a wire fence. Vic glanced back again, catching dark shapes forging after them. They were gaining ground.

The Blackbird sat ahead now, the corn around it flattened in a near-perfect circle. Rockslide had already triggered the hatch ladder as they ran to it. He set Martha down beneath it. "Can you climb?" he asked.

"Yes," she managed to gasp.

Rockslide scaled the ladder up into the S-70. Martha followed, while Vic waited on the flattened corn and glanced back in desperation. He could discern the shouts of Purifiers now, as feral sounding as the racket of their hounds. A flat crack echoed out over the farmland, and he realized someone had discharged a weapon. It was followed by a few more, in rapid succession. He thought they were warning shots, until he heard a ping and realized a bullet had ricocheted off the nose of the Blackbird above him.

He crouched down instinctively, his heart racing with the sort of skin-crawling fear and adrenaline that only being shot at could produce. Martha had made it into the cockpit. Rockslide activated the flier's engines, a low whine beginning to build in the pollen-heavy air. Vic leapt onto the ladder and scaled it quickly as more gunfire rang out.

He emerged into the Blackbird's cockpit. Rockslide and Martha were already strapped in, the latter in the right-hand copilot's seat. Vic took the remaining space, buckling up as Rockslide's heavy hands manipulated a flurry of switches and controls.

"We're going up vertical," he said as Vic heard a series of small, clattering noises, and realized bullets were rebounding from the cockpit visor and the fuselage. A mob of Purifiers surged through the corn less than a hundred yards away now, their baying audible over the rising fury of the Blackbird's engines.

He forced himself to check his own flight display, motions mimicking Rockslide's as he tried to recall his training.

"You know how to fly one of these?" Martha asked him, her tone a mixture of shock and awe.

"Kinda," Vic responded. "I've passed my theory test. But if it makes you feel any better, Rocky definitely knows how to."

Santo merely grunted, easing up on the flight stick. The aircraft shuddered and began to rise.

"Hope you're both buckled up," he said as the speed of their ascent rapidly increased, the field beneath them dropping way. The farmland spread out beneath them in a patchwork of browns, greens and golds. It would've been an enjoyable vista if bullets hadn't been raking the S-70's underbelly.

"Punching it," Santo said, and opened the throttle. Sudden,

vicious acceleration pushed Vic back into his seat and made his stomach lurch. The sky beckoned out beyond Fairbury; the Purifiers left impotent far below. The last sight he caught before they arrowed across the town was gray smoke, still coiling lazily from among the trees where his home had once stood.

CHAPTER THIRTEEN

"Mr Summers will see you now."

Vic looked up at Miss Fullerton and nodded. He had been sitting on a bench in the hallway outside the principal's office for the past ten minutes. Rockslide had been next to him the whole time – standing, likely for fear of breaking the seating – but neither had spoken since getting there. Vic was trying to play it cool. He knew what was coming.

He stood and followed the school secretary into Mr Summers' office. Despite the school's militaristic past, the room felt as though its function had remained largely unchanged down the years. There were a few concessions to something more than the brute utility of the rest of the Institute – the lower halves of the wall were paneled with dark, varnished wood, and a nondescript, hard-wearing blue carpet covered the floor. Filing cabinets occupied the right-hand side of the space, while directly across from the door sat a hefty, imposing desk set beneath a large photo of the current school cohort.

Cyclops was sitting waiting beneath the image. He had presumably either just been, or was just going to, the Danger Room, as he was dressed in the stark black and yellow of his

X-uniform. He was in many ways the image of the all-American male – tall, handsome in a square-jawed sort of style, broad-shouldered without being too bulky. The only incongruence was, of course, the visor he was forced to wear to keep his powers in check. Vic knew it didn't bother the other students, but to him it felt as though the ruby quartz seemed to buzz a perpetual, angry shade of red, glaring down at him with the promise of total annihilation were it ever to be removed. It was the sort of power he was truly thankful he didn't possess.

"Welcome, gentlemen," Cyclops said, indicating the leather-backed chairs set before the desk. "Please, take a seat."

Vic did so, while Santo stood off to one side. Miss Fullerton exited with the silent grace of an experienced secretary, offering Vic a reassuring smile as she passed. As the door clicked quietly shut, Cyclops cleared his throat.

"Let me begin by saying that I'm extremely thankful to have you back, Victor," he said. "You, and your mother."

"All thanks to Rocky here," Vic said, nodding towards Santo. The words were earnest and genuine. They'd gotten back to the Institute the night before, piloted in by Rockslide in the Blackbird. Martha had been taken to the school infirmary, where she'd been treated for a minor concussion. Apparently after clashing with the police, Xodus had withdrawn from Fairbury but he'd left behind "covert" groups of Purifiers to continue the hunt. Vic had slept fitfully in the chair next to her after learning this, refusing to go back to his room. His parents had been to the Institute before on a few occasions to visit him, but Vic imagined it would still appear a grim and unfamiliar place to his mother, full of strange people.

The next morning Martha seemed more herself. She tersely ordered Vic to go and shower and demanded to know when he'd last eaten. Thoroughly chastised, he'd slunk off to the washing blocks and then the canteen. There, Rockslide had found him and told him the principal wanted to see him.

"Have you thought about your next steps, Victor?" Cyclops asked, his expression giving nothing away. The visor meant that Vic found it almost impossible to read him, especially when he was wearing his school principal persona. He shrugged. This was it, and they all knew it. He wasn't going to play games and attempt to deny anything.

"I'm going back out to find my father," he said.

"I suspected that would be the case," Cyclops replied, his tone measured. "And I hope you understand me when I say I can't allow that to happen."

Here were go, Vic thought. Don't get mad. Just tell him the truth.

"I can't stay," he said.

"The wellbeing of your father is of deep concern to everyone at the Institute," Cyclops said. "I assure you that we are considering every means of locating and rescuing him."

"You have no idea where he is," Vic said. "So just admit that for a start. And perhaps you can tell me what 'every means' is? Because that sounds like a throwaway phrase I'd use if I just wanted to placate somebody."

"I am in touch with my colleagues outside of the Institute," Cyclops said.

"You mean the X-Men?" Vic pushed. "From what I've heard, they don't exactly have the time to run around after one kid's missing dad. How soon do you think any of them will be able to divert from their current duties?"

"I'm still waiting for a response," Cyclops admitted. Vic felt his heart sink. As much as he'd been expecting the worst and acting accordingly, a part of him had hoped that there would be an instant reaction from the team beyond the Institute. It didn't look like that would be the case.

"Then you have to understand why I need to go," he said, meeting Cyclops' burning red glare. "Every minute we sit here is another minute my father is in the hands of those madmen. You expect me to stay in the Institute while I know he's out there somewhere? What's my mother supposed to do? You think she isn't worried sick as well?"

"Would your mother want you out there risking your life, alone, for your father?" Cyclops countered. "I understand this must be extremely difficult for you, Victor, but you don't have a choice. You have no leads and no backup. There's nothing you can realistically do."

"Only if you refuse to offer me any help," Vic snapped, his temper fraying despite his best efforts. "The Institute has systems with full access to the old X-Mansion's databases. You could tell me where the next Purifier rallies are being held, the probable identities of their leaders, the known locations of their safehouses and bases of operation. You could work it all out. Instead we're sitting here, having a pointless argument and wasting time!"

"I'll go," Santo said before Cyclops could respond. They both looked up at him.

"Assign me to find Victor's father, Principal Summers," the giant continued. "I will retrieve him from the Purifiers and bring him safely here. Immediately."

Cyclops was silent, pondering the suggestion. He looked back at Vic, that brilliant, unblinking visor burning into him. "I know what you're thinking," he said. "You can't go with him."

Vic started to protest, but Cyclops cut through.

"I'm not just doing this to spite you, Victor. Since you left the entire school has gone into lockdown. The attack on your home was the last straw. The Purifiers know of the Institute's existence, and they're deliberately targeting students. I have recent graduates currently escorting those classmates of yours who are still absent straight back here. We are at war, and with Miss Frost absent I am responsible for the safety and wellbeing of each and every one of you. I do not – cannot – take that duty lightly."

Vic glowered back at the ruby visor unflinchingly. He'd already been told about the lockdown by Santo. It didn't surprise him. The Purifier attacks were definitely targeted. Whether there was a purpose to them beyond their own bigotry though, Vic didn't know. It just made finding his father all the more vital.

"I made a promise," Santo said, looking at Vic. "A promise that I would find your father. I will fulfill it. Trust me on that."

"I trust you, Rocky," Vic admitted, not taking his eyes off Cyclops. "I just want to be the one to go with you."

"Not this time," Cyclops said, shaking his head. "You're not ready yet, Victor, and even if you were, I wouldn't permit you to go with Santo. You're too close to this. There's a drastic risk that your emotions will get people hurt."

"The only ones getting hurt will be Xodus and his cult," Vic said viciously.

"I'll leave immediately," Santo said, "and update you both via communicator whenever I have the opportunity."

"Which reminds me," Cyclops said, opening a desk drawer and removing a small package. "Santo tells me you lost your phone during the Purifier attack, Victor? I've had a reserve communicator rewired to full functionality. You can use it until you're able to get a replacement. It'll let you and Santo maintain contact, should either of you need it. It may well assist his search, and perhaps help ease your mind."

Vic took the package and unwrapped it, finding one of the glossy black, spherical X-communicators inside. A churlish part of him wanted to reject it, but he overcame the urge. If this was how it was going to be, he'd need a line of contact. He nodded.

"Santo, I will furnish you with what intelligence we've collated before you leave," Cyclops said. "Once you're out in the field, I expect regular updates. Consider this your first solo assignment."

Rockslide nodded, and Vic felt a surge of pride. Having Santo looking for his father was better than having any of the older X-Men on the case – the big guy knew what it meant to him. Vic had no doubt he'd go to the ends of the earth if he had to.

"Victor, you'll resume a light training regime for the time being," Cyclops said. "The remainder of your extended leave is terminated. I'll ensure that your mother has the best living quarters until your father is located and your family can be safely reunited."

"Thanks," Vic said, his voice riven with sarcasm. He knew that the "best" rooms in the Institute were still grim, claustrophobic cells, but right now there wasn't an alternative. At least he could be sure Martha was safe here. He stood up and faced Rockslide.

"I wouldn't have anyone else out there looking," he told him, placing a hand on his broad, stony chest. "I know you'll find him, Rocky."

"I won't let you down, lizard boy," Santo grunted. Vic cast another brief glance at Cyclops, lowering his hand.

"Permission to go back to my room, principal?"

"Granted," Cyclops said. "We'll speak again soon, Victor."

Vic returned to his dorm as soon as he left the principal's office. For a while he seethed, but his mood quickly gave way to the same cold acceptance he'd experienced watching his home be consumed by fire. He lay in the semi-dark on his bed, arms behind his head, staring up at the blank concrete ceiling. The only light crept in from under the corridor window shutters, the constant dull illumination of the emergency panels running the length of the dorms preferable to the harsh glow of his own room's bulbs.

His thoughts wandered, but they never strayed far from his father. He was genuinely glad Santo had been assigned to find his dad, and he hadn't been lying when he said he wouldn't have wanted anyone else out there. But that didn't mean he'd changed his mind about leaving. He'd made no promises.

At some point he dozed off. Tiredness had crept up on him since he'd made it back to the school. His dreams were dark and troubled, their exact shape and form remaining illusive until a knocking sound startled him awake.

He bolted upright, senses immediately on edge. It took him a moment to remember where he was. The knock came again at his door. He relaxed fractionally.

"Who is it?"

"It's Alisa," said a muffled voice. Vic frowned. Something was worrying indeed when Cipher used her real name rather than her adopted alias.

"What do you want, Ci?" he called out.

"Gray and I heard you were back this morning," Cipher replied. "We went looking for you at the infirmary, but we couldn't find you."

"Did you see my mom?" Vic asked. "Is she OK?"

"She's fine. She remembered us from the last time she visited you."

Vic remained silent. He knew he should go back and check on Martha himself, but a selfish part of him wanted to stay locked in his room, away from the questions and the pitying looks he was sure his classmates had saved up for him. His mind ran through possibilities, looking for a way out in every sense.

"Can I come in?" Ci asked.

"No."

"Can you at least open the door?"

"No, Ci. I don't want to talk to anyone. And don't even think about going invisible and phasing in here!"

There was another pause before Cipher spoke again. "We're worried about you, Vic. Not just me and Graymalkin, but a lot of the others too. We're all sorry about what happened to your father. And your home."

"Nobody needs to be sorry," Vic said, trying not to snap. He really didn't want to be having this conversation right now. "Rocky's going to get him back. Everything will be OK."

"Just, whenever you need to talk... we're all here, Vic."

"Yeah, sure," Vic said, rummaging in his bedside drawer until he found his old iPod and headphones. Anything else Cipher said was lost amidst the roar of some max volume *Dreadhaven*.

He stayed like that until evening with his songs on shuffle, stewing in his own anger and helplessness. He couldn't stay. He knew he wouldn't have a minute's peace if he did. He'd be checking the communicator constantly. He had no idea how Cyclops expected him to focus on lessons or training. All he could think about was his father, and the Purifiers. Where they might be holding him, what they might be doing with him. The visceral memories of the past few days were still fresh and intimate – the stink of the robes and the claustrophobia of the stolen mask, the smell of burning rubber in the prison truck, Xodus's great and terrible voice, the raw aura of hatred that pulsed from behind that beatific golden grotesque. He remembered the horrid crunch as he'd been flung forward during the crash, the moment of dislocation and pained confusion. His hand wandered up to his scalp, probing beneath the ridge of his carapace. Still tender.

He hunted around in his drawers for old food, not wanting to risk a trip to the canteen. He found a packet of still-sealed graham crackers under his bed, but that was as good as it got. Sucks. He ate a dozen, seeking distraction in his stack of vintage comics. He didn't want to turn on the TV. He was afraid of what he might see on it.

Eventually he glanced up at the clock. Decision time. Really, it was no decision at all. He cast the crackers aside and stood up, dusting off the crumbs. Then he picked his rucksack up from beside his bed and moved over to his clothing drawers.

Clean clothes, it seemed, were at a premium. Perhaps he'd give it a few more hours and steal down to the laundry rooms once everyone was asleep. He was sure he could avoid any late-nighters if he went chameleon. No matter. He was about to break far bigger rules anyway.

He stuffed a few items of casual clothing – a Crimson Fives T-shirt, a Chicago Cubs vest, a pair of tracksuit bottoms – into the bag as a starter and unzipped the utilities pocket. In went his wallet, the charger for the X-communicator, and his Institute dorm fob. He rummaged around in his torn Cry Havoc hoodie until he found the toy dino he'd rescued from the treehouse. He looked at it again for a minute. A lucky charm, or the cursed item that had brought all this down upon him? There was only one way to find out. He slipped the toy into the pocket and zipped it back up. A glance over at his bed made him hesitate before closing the main zipper too.

The Purifier robes lay across the end of the bed, the silver grotesque half stuffed beneath them, leering out at him in the half-dark. He'd still had them with him right up to his return to the Institute. When he'd dragged them off, his immediate instinct had been to toss them in the trash. They repulsed him. Even thinking about how he'd been forced to wear them made him shiver. But something had stopped him. A part of him – the dramatic part, he acknowledged – wanted to do something more than just chuck them out. Burning them felt right. Yet, there were other options. A set of Purifier gear, even grubby and torn, could come in handy. There was a certain degree of justice to that possibility. He forced himself to go over and fold the robes tightly, wrapping them around the mask before packing them away in his bag.

A *thunk* disturbed him. What the heck was that? He half turned towards the door and realized that it was standing ajar. He froze.

Nothing moved. The door remained open, the faintest sliver of light from the corridor spilling into the darkened room. He was absolutely certain he'd locked it, and now it was open. A deep sense of unease crept over him.

There was someone in the room with him.

He turned back around, whiplash fast, his claws out. What loomed out at him from the shadows was even more terrifying than he'd dared imagine. A gaunt, skull-like visage, pallid gray flesh, and pale, dead eyes. Vic threw himself back with a strangled cry, accidentally slamming the door shut and snuffing out all but the faintest sliver of light still spilling in from under the window shutters.

The apparition raised one bony hand and spoke. "Be not afraid."

"Oh my God," was all Victor could pant. He felt as though his heart was going to rupture in his chest, and his hands had instinctively locked onto the floor where he'd fallen. "Oh my actual God, Graymalkin. I thought we agreed you were going to stop doing this?"

"By 'this' I assume you mean visiting your room in the hours of darkness uninvited?" Graymalkin said, lowering his hand.

"I mean materializing behind me in the dark like some sort of blood-hungry vampire," Vic snapped, his fight-or-flight instincts still fizzing. "I could've killed you! No, you could've killed *me!*"

Graymalkin cast his eyes to the ground in shame, and Vic felt that usual rush of regret he experienced whenever he spoke angrily to him. He paused to unstick his palms from the floor and stood up, dusting himself down.

"Look, don't worry about it," he said, trying not to sound awkward. "I just didn't want to see anyone tonight, OK?"

"I am aware," Graymalkin said in his stilted voice, looking back up at Vic. "But I decided to disregard your wishes."

Vic sighed and slumped down in his beanbag, resisting the urge to flick on the lights as he did so. Graymalkin's peculiar mutant powers were triggered by the absence of illumination. They'd first manifested when his father, demented with rage, had attempted to bury him alive. Entombed in dirt, Graymalkin should have suffered one of the most hideous deaths imaginable, but the utter darkness had instead caused his powers to manifest. He'd survived in a semi-catatonic state for over two hundred years, until a group of mutant hunters had unearthed him. Unfortunately for them, they'd done so in the dead of night, when Jonas Graymalkin's powers were at their height.

"If you've come to be a shoulder for me to cry on, I'm afraid I'm past that point," Vic said. "If you've come to stop me, well, you shouldn't waste your time. I'm getting out of here. Tonight."

"This is as Cipher predicted," Graymalkin said. "May I sit down?"

"Go ahead," Vic grunted, making a point of not looking at his friend. Gray perched stiffly on the edge of Santo's old concrete slab, his posture upright. He'd have cut a terrifying figure to anyone who didn't know him, a white-eyed ghoul shrouded in the room's shadows. The weak light from the corridor made his features seem even more gaunt than usual.

"I regret that your visit home did not go as planned," he said, clasping his hands in his lap. Vic gave out a bitter laugh.

"Didn't go as planned is an understatement, Gray. My home was burnt down, my neighbors threatened, my parents beaten up and my dad kidnapped. It wasn't exactly what I had in mind when I said I needed a break from exams."

"And yet, that is what happened," Graymalkin stated. "These are the circumstances we must confront. I have come to dissuade you from doing anything rash."

Vic slumped deeper into the beanbag. "I've had enough lectures today, OK? Just go back to your dorm, Gray. I'll be gone in the morning."

"That is precisely why I cannot return to my dormitory," Graymalkin said. "To find you gone is… not something I am used to."

It took a moment for Vic to realize exactly what he meant. When they'd first met each other, Graymalkin hadn't long been free of the dirt grave his father had buried him in hundreds of years earlier. The young man had struggled to even speak, let alone interact with his fellow students. One day, tentatively, he had admitted to Cipher while she was phased and invisible that he struggled to sleep at night. The dorm rooms were too subterranean, too claustrophobic. They reminded him of the horror of his burial. His first roommate had moved out, unable to cope with Gray's night terrors.

For about six months Vic and Ci had taken turns staying with Gray. Vic had sat by his bed, headphones on and a book open, struggling to keep his eyes open. Sometimes he'd dozed off, but he didn't remain asleep for long once Gray's terrors woke him. At first the sheer force of the nightmares had been a horrifying thing to behold. Graymalkin would start from his bed slicked in sweat and howling, often bolting for the door before reality began to reassert itself. Vic had been advised by Gray himself to grab him, sometimes hug him, to try and speak slow and calm. They'd quickly learned that it was wise to leave the bedside lamp on – trying to stop Gray in the pitch black was not only impossible, it was dangerous.

It had been tough on Vic. His initial grades had been poor, and he'd struggled to attend class while trying to catch up on lost sleep. Eventually Ms Pryde discovered what was going on and made Gray see the school's therapist. To their credit, Summer and Frost hadn't demanded that Vic and Cipher stop helping Gray, understanding that he wasn't comfortable reaching out to anyone but them. Class timetables had been rearranged, and grades had improved notably. Cyclops had given them all a stern talking-to in his office, speaking in high ideals about how the Institute was more than just a school, that it was a family and it should be relied upon as such.

The terrors had slowly lessened over time, helped by the fact that Gray had been formally diagnosed with PTSD. He'd developed a routine to keep things in check. He'd learned his triggers and how best to avoid them. Miss Frost had permitted him to keep his dorm door open at night, and he knew he could reach Vic and Ci at any time using his communicator. Vic had no doubt that he still woke at night shuddering, his mind haunted by the memory of cloying, damp soil and the shovel's scrape, but he seemed to have made his peace with it. Graymalkin was a survivor, in every sense of the word.

"I'm not leaving you and Ci because I want to," Vic told him, trying not to sound too defensive. "I'm leaving because I have to. I'm doing this for my dad."

Gray seemed to think about that before speaking. "I have been wondering if I would do the same as you. If my parents were threatened, would I risk my own life to bring them out of harm's way?"

Vic frowned slightly. "How could anyone expect you to? Your father tried to murder you for being who you are, and your mother didn't try to stop him. Damned if I would risk my life for them after that."

"You say that as though it is an easy decision," Gray pointed out.

"Because it is?"

"Then it is clear you do not understand what it means to have a father who both hates and loves you. Do you imagine, perhaps, that a father's cruelty is a simple tale of morality? My father wishes for my death, so of course I must hate him? The same man who showed me how to sow seeds in the spring and harvest them in the fall? Who taught me my letters with his open Bible, and walked beside the horse with his hand upon the bridle as I learned to ride? The man who beat me when I refused to go to church one day, and would lock me away without any food for days at a time just to spite my mother? The same man who stood alone in the doorway of our homestead and guarded us from the frontier raids during one long winter? Such things are never simple. Surviving such an upbringing is never simple. Yes, I often think I hate my father. It is a strange thing to consider that he is long dead. Often in my nightmares, he is not. But would I save him if he were in danger? Did he not save me at times, even though he hated me? It is not simple."

Vic shook his head, feeling almost ashamed.

"I'm sorry, Gray," he said. "You're right. I can't understand what you went through. I can't make judgments about someone who had to overcome so much while he was still so young, not when my own upbringing was... well, it was a lot easier. Easier than everyone's, it seems."

"That is not something to be ashamed of," Gray said. "Be happy for it. Do not think I fail to value your opinions. I am better because of them. Our upbringing could not have been more divergent. That offers an opportunity for perspective, for both of us."

"Is that why you're here?" Vic asked. "To give me some perspective?"

"We are worried about you," Graymalkin admitted unabashedly, his expression earnest in the darkness. "It would be remiss of us not to see you, whether you desire it or not."

"We," Vic said, echoing the word Graymalkin had just spoken. He paused before continuing. "My door was locked from the inside," he said. "And while you're strong and fast in the dark, Gray, that doesn't mean you can pick locks or phase through walls. But we both know someone who can."

Graymalkin said nothing, an awkward expression creeping over his face as he realized the mistake he'd made. Vic gave him an exasperated look and cast about the room.

"Come on, Ci," he said loudly. "Drop the invisibility trick."

"Fine," said a voice right next to him, making him jump. Cipher materialized beside the TV, arms crossed, her expression defensive. "Took you long enough to work it out," she said.

"Maybe I'm just too trusting towards my friends," Vic responded, glaring at her. "I told you I didn't want to speak to either of you, yet here you both are, invading my privacy."

"I believe Cipher termed it 'an intervention,'" Graymalkin said, looking innocently at his partner-in-crime. Cipher planted her hands on her hips, unbowed before Vic's anger.

"You can't stop talking to us," she told him. "Not after what happened to you and your family. Did you really think we wouldn't guess you'd be leaving tonight? Did you think the principal wouldn't suspect it too?"

"Cyclops won't stop me," Vic said. "And neither will you."

"Do you even have a plan for getting out of the Institute?" Cipher pressed. "You know all the corridors and all the entrances and elevator shafts are being monitored continuously? You'll barely make it past the dorms."

"Won't I?" Vic demanded, raising a hand and letting it color-shift into near-invisibility.

"That's cute," Cipher said, raising her own hand and, in a mirror image, causing it to vanish into invisibility. "But don't tell me you're planning on sneaking out of here stark naked and not carrying anything?"

"My X-suit can shift too," Vic said defensively.

"I fear you miss the mark, Victor," Graymalkin interjected. "Whatever plan you hatch in order to depart from the Institute, the odds will be against you beyond its walls. You propose going into near-insurmountable danger."

"Standard X-Men stuff then," Vic said, refusing to entertain even a moment of their concern. "You'd do the same."

"Really?" Cipher asked, her voice turning bitter. "Two orphans abandoned by their parents would give up everything in a doomed attempt at saving their father?"

"It isn't doomed," Vic snarled. "My dad's going to be fine! I'm going to make sure of that!" He said that as much to stave off his own desperation as to reassure Ci. They'd all heard the rumors about what Purifiers did to "unbelievers." Stories about pyres and burnings, horrid tales of fanaticism and brutality.

"Does your mom want you to go?" Cipher demanded. "Have you thought about her? Or us, for that matter?"

"Drop the guilt act, Alisa," Vic snapped, rising to his feet. "Do you think for one second that I'm not worried about my mom as well? You think I want to go out there at a time like this? I've seen what's going on in the world, what they're doing to mutants on the outside. The stuff they cut out of the news reports you watch. I'm as scared as everyone, but I'm angry too. Angry as hell! And it's time I did something about it."

"And what do you intend to do about it?" Graymalkin asked. His calm and measured tone cut through Ci and Vic's rising voices

"Tell us what you intend," he elaborated as they both looked at him. "That we might at least be put at ease."

"So you can tell Cyclops and help stop me?"

"So we can help you get out," Cipher said, sounding exasperated now. Vic looked from her to Gray, surprised.

"What do you mean?" he asked.

"We had a lengthy discussion prior to this evening," Graymalkin said. "We agreed it would likely be difficult dissuading you from searching for your father. We agreed that, if all other attempts failed, it would be better to assist you in whatever way we can than allow you to struggle on alone. That, I believe, is what friends are for."

Vic felt his earlier anger burn up, leaving him with a sense of embarrassment. He'd been sick of the prospect of being harangued, so much so that he hadn't even considered asking them for their help.

"So again, Vic, tell us what you've got planned," Cipher said, moving to sit next to Gray on Santo's slab, her legs folded up under her. "Or we can't help you."

"Well," Vic said, collecting his thoughts. In truth he didn't have much of a plan beyond going chameleon and seeing how far he could get. But this changed things. "The big picture first. I've been thinking about the Purifiers, how well-equipped and coordinated they are. None of this was even on the radar four or five months ago. Why are they suddenly able to roam and attack people at will? I think the answer is they've got a backer."

"A patron?" Graymalkin wondered, putting the word in terms he understood.

"Someone well connected and wealthy," Vic went on. "That's the most obvious way to explain why the likes of Xodus have become so brazen of late. Someone's backing them. The questions then become who, and why?"

"Do they need a reason beyond hating our kind?" Cipher asked. "Anyone can be a Purifier. Anyone can hate mutants. I'm sure there's more than a few college graduates and wealthy businessmen beneath those black robes and masks. We don't even know Xodus's real identity. He could be anyone."

"True," Vic allowed. "But if it's just generic mutant hate, then where do I come into it?"

"Well... you're a mutant," Gray said without a hint of irony.

"Yes, but I'm one of thousands. So why target me specifically? And there's no doubt they did. Yes, there was a Purifier presence in my hometown, even though it's in the back end of nowhere. But for Xodus himself to rock up outside my house just a day after I got home? Someone either followed me there or contacted him the moment I got off the bus on East Locust. He practically confirmed he was only in town for me. He called out my neighbors, used my Anole alias, and now he's presumably intending to keep my dad as a hostage. So, why?"

"The Institute," Cipher wondered. "They're targeting the next generation of X-Men."

"Perhaps," Graymalkin said. "But there have been many rumors of disappearances and attacks on mutants who aren't members of the Institute."

"Maybe that's all a cover," Cipher continued. "Perhaps all the rallies and the mob rule are to disguise the more targeted attacks? Like the one on you and your family, Vic."

"That's what I'm assuming," Victor said. "And that's why I want to find out who's bankrolling it all. They've made it personal. Get to them and we may also be able to get it all to stop."

"So how do you intend to unmask them?" Graymalkin asked, apparently not realizing he'd made a joke about Purifiers and grotesques.

"Well, firstly, I won't be able to do it from inside the Institute," Vic said, a smile creeping across his face. "And since you're both here, I guess you might as well lend a hand. Here's what I'm thinking…"

CHAPTER FOURTEEN

Wilbur glanced up from his phone at the harsh glow of the monitor bank spread out before him. The dozen screens maintained their bright intensity, a patchwork display of the Institute's floors, corridors and chambers that sat seemingly frozen in time. The only movement was on Channel 18, the one covering the canteen's security cameras. A few night owls were busy making snacks.

Wilbur looked back down at his phone. He'd spent most of the evening trying to boost his score on *Farmyard Heist*. One of the game's AI farmers kept busting him before he could swipe his crop stocks. It was getting frustrating.

There was a bleeping noise, and the door to the security room opened. Eakin entered, accompanied by a blessed draught of cool air.

"Leave it open for a second," Wilbur pleaded, not looking up. His shirt was damp with sweat – there was something to be said for how quiet night shift in the security room was, but it did get unbearably hot in the cramped space, and protocol demanded they keep the door locked. In fairness the room was little more than a large cupboard that had been converted into the Institute's security center with the addition of the monitors, a desk and a few chairs. The base's original security control hub was now the Institute's main data vault.

Eakin obliged, standing by the door for a minute and letting the sticky air vent before returning to his own seat.

"All quiet?" Wilbur asked him, still on his phone.

"Yep," Eakin said, swiveling his chair to face the monitors. "Had to tell Sheppard to keep his music down in the dorms, but what's new?"

Wilbur grunted, not really listening. He'd managed to sneak a sack of beets and get out before the cartoonish farmyard hounds had caught him. Progress at last.

"Wilbur?" Eakin said.

"Hmm?" he murmured, refusing to look up. The sunrise timer was almost finished and he'd only half filled his crop sack. At this rate there was no way he'd be able to hold his place on the global rankings this week.

"You seeing this?"

Apparently not. Pausing the game with a sigh, Wilbur glanced at his fellow warden. Eakin, his freckled face set in consternation, was staring at the monitors. One in particular.

"What?" Wilbur demanded, following his gaze without noticing anything out of the ordinary. "Come on, I've only got six more bushels to steal before sunrise."

"Was that monitor on a minute ago?" Eakin asked, ignoring his friend's obsession with his game. For a second Wilbur was confused, thinking he meant the security screens, all of which were still functioning. Then he finally noticed what Eakin was staring at.

Channel 5, the bank of cams monitoring the data hub. The room was buried deep near the bottom of the Institute's labyrinth, cut into the rugged rock at the core of the former military base.

Its interior consisted of half a dozen large data stacks and a trio of display screens that provided access to the hundreds of thousands of files stored in the Institute's database. Access to the room was only permitted for school staff and security, so usually it was empty, and the display screens remained inactive. Tonight, however, one was lit up.

"Well, that's weird," Wilbur said.

"Was it like that earlier?" Eakin pressed.

Wilbur just shrugged.

"We should go check on it."

"I guess," Wilbur said. "It's probably just an automatic system reboot though."

"We're supposed to be in lockdown," Eakin pointed out tersely. "What do you think the principal will say if he finds out we skimp on half our patrol circuits and barely ever leave the control room?"

"Cyclops is too busy worrying about the kids to check up on us," Wilbur said confidently, looking back down at his phone. "Go check it out if you want. I'll hold the fort."

"He told us to remain extra vigilant tonight," Eakin went on. "Have you still got eyes on the Borkowski kid?"

Wilbur jabbed a finger at one of the screens. "He's right there, Eaks. In the infirmary with his mom. He's been there like half an hour, just sitting. Look!"

Eakin inspected the display. Victor Borkowski was indeed in a chair next to his mom in the otherwise empty infirmary ward. On the gray monitor screen, it looked as though they were both asleep. Poor kid, Wilbur thought. If the rumors were true, he'd been through a hell of a lot in the past few days.

"Go and check the monitor," Wilbur said. "I'll keep an eye on Vic. Doesn't look like he's going anywhere tonight."

•••

Cipher glanced at the monitor screen again. *Eighty-one percent.* She checked the communicator, wired into the data stack behind the desk. The connectivity was still good. There was nothing she could do but wait for it to finish.

She knew this was all part of what she did best, but the waiting aspect was the worst. At the moment she just had to hope that the communicator and its wire under the desk were out of sight of the data vault's cameras and that whoever was on shift in the control room tonight hadn't noticed that one of the displays was active. If someone came down to check she'd have to grab the device and get out, whether the transmission was done or not.

At least she didn't have to worry about getting caught, not immediately at any rate. Her invisibility was both flawless and effortless, and if she needed to escape, she could simply phase through the data vault's doors and up the elevator shaft. When combined with her ability to create a sound void around herself and the fact that she was unreadable on any telepathic spectrum, it was little wonder it had taken the staff so long to discover her very existence when she'd first decided to move into the school.

Eighty-five percent. As far as covert mutant abilities went, Ci knew her powers were exceptional. She took no pride in them though. What pride was there in hiding? That was the true sum of her skills. Sometimes she worried it was all she was good for. The fact that other mutants sometimes struggled to control their own abilities made her feel even guiltier. When her powers had first manifested as a child, right after her parents' death, she'd been afraid and confused. It hadn't taken her long to master them though once she realized how potent they could be.

Eighty-eight percent. Come on. She glanced at the elevator shaft.

This had been a bad idea, all of it. Why had they agreed to help Vic? As his friends, surely, they should have done the opposite and told Principal Summers he was planning on leaving. Or at least tried harder to persuade him not to go. What would a real friend have done? What was best for him?

She told herself that worrying was probably pointless. Vic would have gone no matter what either she or Graymalkin said, and the principal would have had to lock him up in the Institute's depths to stop him getting out. By helping him, Cipher knew that she was at least giving him a fighting chance once he was on the outside. Without it he'd have nowhere to even begin to look.

Ninety-two percent. Nearly there. She was going to catch hell for this, she knew. She and Graymalkin both. That didn't really bother her. Her grades were good enough to stand a points reduction, and there was no way the school could expel her. If it did, well, she'd had a life before she'd come here, and she would have one after. She was more concerned for Gray. The Institute was all he'd known since he'd been rescued. It was as close to an accepting home as he'd ever had. Still, she knew Gray better than anyone though, and she knew just how resilient he was. He wouldn't have survived if that weren't the case.

There was a small chime, almost lost in the perpetual background drone of the heavy data stacks. Cipher looked back at the elevator and saw that the downward arrow above the doors had pinged green. The number next to it was descending.

She cursed softly, looking back at the monitor screen, then the communicator. *Ninety-five percent.* Too slow. Whoever was in that elevator, they'd arrive before the full transfer was completed. She'd have to improvise.

She ghosted directly through the data bank towards the elevator, feeling the electrostatic buzz around her as she did so. Phasing through different objects brought with it different sensations. Particularly dense materials, like rock or concrete, sent a slight chill to her core. Passing through something with an electric current made her skin prickle and her hairs stand on end. Passing through another living being, well, that was exactly what she was about to experience.

She stopped outside the elevator, standing square at the entrance. There was another ping as it rumbled to a halt before the doors slid open. One of the security guards, the short redhead named Eakin, looked straight through her.

Cipher had long grown used to the more disconcerting aspects of hiding in literal plain sight. Eakin looked more exasperated than wary as he left the elevator, striding into the data vault. Instinct demanded that Cipher raise a hand, flinch or move in reaction to Eakin's advance right into her, but she did nothing. He walked through her.

A powerful bioelectric discharge flared within both their bodies. Eakin gasped and halted in his tracks, grasping his chest. Cipher floated back through him again for good measure. The shock occurred whenever she phased through another living being. It was harmless, but an unpleasant surprise for anyone not prepared for it. Eakin took a second to recover, his face tight with alarm. In Ci's experience, most people seemed to think they were in the early stages of a heart attack or a stroke. By the time Eakin had regained his composure, Cipher had ghosted back through to the other side of the data stack.

Ninety-nine percent. One hundred. She snatched up the communicator and killed the power switch on the monitor. Eakin was walking around the side of the data banks. She went the opposite way – it would be impossible to fully phase while she was carrying the communicator, but Eakin was out of sight anyway. She made it to the elevator and caught the open doors just as Eakin arrived at the now-dead monitor.

The elevator pinged. Cipher hit the button that would take her to Lower North, the Institute's smallest concealed entrance. Her last sight was of Eakin hurrying back round the data stack, mouth agape as the elevator doors rumbled shut in front of an X-communicator that was apparently hovering in midair.

Cipher had no doubt he'd hit the alarms now. That didn't matter. The first stage was complete.

CHAPTER FIFTEEN

Vic waited. His mother had been asleep since he'd arrived. The night nurse had told him to ring the silent buzzer if he needed anything before leaving him in peace.

He was nervous. After talking with Gray and Ci he'd been full of the same excited energy he experienced after a good scene reading. Now, though, he had the fright he always got seconds before curtain call.

He tried to rationalize his uncertainties. Would Mom be OK here on her own? She'd worry, he had no doubt. He couldn't help that, so he'd left her a small note, slipped beneath her pillow, reassuring her that she was safe here and telling her that he was going after Dad. She would understand. He had to believe that.

He did his best not to glance up at the security cam in the corner. He felt as though it was pointed straight at him. It felt like being locked in hostile rifle sights, making his flesh prickle, like he was going to color-shift. He quelled the urge. How long had he been sitting here, feigning quiet contemplation while his mind churned? Where were Cipher and Graymalkin? Would they be OK after he left? There was no way they'd avoid being caught. What would Cyclops do to them? Fail a grade, retake classes for a year? What if he got them expelled? Surely the school couldn't do that, not with everything that was happening on the outside? They wouldn't be left to fend for themselves.

He felt the communicator in his pocket pip. It made his heart quicken. That was it. Ci had completed the transfer. On to stage two. He waited a little longer, looking at his mother. She appeared peaceful and untroubled – were it not for the bandage around her scalp, it would be easy to imagine nothing had happened to her over the past few days. But that wasn't true. Everything had changed, in her life and in her son's. Victor forced away the pang of regret and stood up.

He had to do this. For his family.

No time left for hesitation. Ignoring the accusatory glare of the security camera, he pulled off his hoodie and removed his sweatpants. Beneath it, he wore the form-fitting black and yellow of his X-suit, bold colors that quickly began to ripple and shift.

In just a few heartbeats, Vic had melted from sight.

CHAPTER SIXTEEN

Graymalkin sat on the edge of his bed, his head bowed, hands clasped in his lap, waiting. The lights were off and his dorm window was shuttered, leaving the room in darkness. In the pitch black, his powers coiled within him, eager to be let loose. Strength, speed, his every sense honed and sharpened to the tenth degree, but only in the dark could he experience such vitality, rediscover the very essence of what had kept him alive. Ironic, then, that it was in the dark that he also felt the most afraid, the most alone.

He looked up, deliberately casting his eyes around his room. Now was not the time for introspection. He had no doubt that Alisa would have already completed the first stage of the plan. Stage two was where he came in. His curtain call, as Victor would have said.

He was ready for it, his powers idle but alert, waiting to be unleashed. He'd learned the value of calmness in the cold, crushing earth. That was one thing he could be thankful of. He took in his room as he waited, his eyes easily capable of piercing the dark.

Graymalkin had never been one for material possessions. In part he understood that was because he had been brought up in a simple household that cherished utility. It was difficult, however, to accept the sheer level of consumerism in the world he now inhabited. How many items did one need to own? How much happiness could be derived from so many individual objects? It seemed as though everyone he knew owned so much yet were no better for any of it. Graymalkin's only concessions to such luxury were his books. As a child the only text his family had owned had been the Bible. His mother had told him, though, that wealthy gentlemen sometimes collected entire libraries, covering all manner of different subjects. He'd dreamt of doing the same. Now he owned over eighteen books, stacked neatly on his shelf and desk. Most of them were historical or philosophical in nature. When he had first escaped from his early grave, he'd been hideously dislocated and confused. He'd begun to make sense of the world around him not with phones, apps and e-readers – all still alien and unnerving to him – but with those books, and a few magazines to accompany them. He was already planning his next purchase, the *Oxford Handbook of the Cold War*.

There was little else in the room. He preferred his clothing to be simple and comfortable, and his wardrobe was only half full. He had several framed pictures of himself and Victor, plus a few other Institute students. Alisa was in most of them too, albeit invisible. She didn't like having her photo taken. Gray could understand that.

The wait continued. His mind wandered to the task ahead of him. He felt no uncertainty regarding the plan they had hatched. It was well within his abilities. Less certain was the fate that awaited them once it was complete. There would be no hiding his involvement. What punishment would follow? Rule-breaking never came naturally to him. From a young age, his understanding of who he was had torn apart his conscience. How could his mere existence be a sin? Had God not made him this way? Had he been born merely for destruction?

Being confronted by authority filled him with dread. Memories of his father's rage, of the caning stick or the penance cupboard he'd been locked away in still haunted him when he tried to sleep. And no memories were as painful as the night when he had tried to explain to the furious old man just who he was. He'd been found with another boy in the family barn. His father wouldn't listen. The old man kept screaming at him, a litany of abuse. Graymalkin had forgotten much during the centuries of his imprisonment, but every single one of those words was still with him, ringing in his head.

Until finding the Institute, he had never known an authority that didn't hate him for who he was. He knew he would just have to trust the others. They would look out for him, and he would help whenever he could. Victor in particular was part of the reason he had found acceptance. To find someone that was at peace with themselves, who knew they had not been born a sinful creature... that had comforted Graymalkin, for the first time in his life.

Now Victor had to find his father. He couldn't possibly stay here. Gray accepted that, even if he couldn't entirely understand that familial bond, not in the same way. Victor's earlier words came back to him. Would his father have deserved the same? No, Graymalkin knew. But would he still do the same? He believed he would. Whether that was weakness or strength, he did not know.

When he was in his darkness, Gray could sense Alisa. It was the slightest of things, akin to a premonition or a sense of déjà vu, but he knew when she was there. He'd never told her – he was afraid it would undermine their friendship. He knew how important her powers were to her. She had never come across someone who could detect her when she didn't want them to. But there she was, just phased into his room.

"Are you ready?" she whispered gently.

"I am," he replied, not looking at the space he knew she currently occupied by the door. He had long ago come to associate her ethereal presence and soft voice as something akin to that of a guardian angel. Not, of course, that he would ever tell her that. He was not worthy to converse with angels, of that he was sure.

"Two more minutes," she said, and then was gone. Gray looked down at his hands, clenching and unclenching them, feeling the raw potency there. Then he stood.

Darkness was coming to the Institute, and he'd be right where he belonged. In the middle of it.

CHAPTER SEVENTEEN

One corn bushel and three minutes to go. He was totally going to do this. Another week in the premium tier of *Farmyard Heist*, the eighth-longest consecutive top one hundred of any player worldwide. Wilbur was about to grab the final sack when a loud bleep made him jump and nearly drop his phone.

It took him a second to realize it was the security radio sitting in its charging holster next to him. It blipped again, like it was laughing at him. Scowling, Wilbur snatched it and hit transmit. "Eaks, I was about to complete the final points challenge!"

"Just shut up and listen," Eakin snapped back, his voice chopped and distorted by static. "Did you see what just happened in the data vault?"

"The data vault?" Wilbur repeated, in no mood for these sorts of games. "Aren't you there right now?"

He looked up at the monitor showing the cam footage from the lower levels. Sure enough, there was Eakin next to the big data stacks, staring right up at him through the camera.

"Yes, but I don't think I'm alone," Eakin's voice crackled back. He sounded concerned. "I think ... someone was down here with me. They just took the elevator back up."

"What do you mean?" Wilbur demanded, confused. "Did you see them?"

"No. I just… I got this funny feeling when I first stepped out of the elevator. Then I swear I saw something weird in it when I was about to leave."

"What do you mean 'weird?' You're not making any sense!"

"Look, can you just check the student manifest and tell me how many in the current cohort have invisibility listed as one of their powers? And while you're at it, get eyes on Borkowski again. Something's up."

"Ah," Wilbur said as he glanced up at the infirmary screen. "Listen Eaks, about that–"

CHAPTER EIGHTEEN

Phase two.

Cipher bit her lower lip, a subconscious habit she'd only recently realized she fell into when she was under stress. This was the delicate part.

Another wire loosened and unwound. Flip the circuit breaker. After visiting Graymalkin she'd phased into the motherboard for the western wing of the Institute's electrical systems and set to work, isolating the Lower North exit. This was the sort of activity she'd done for as long as she could remember. It had started out as simple childhood pranks but had quickly developed as a survival necessity. Sabotage could be easy for one who could go anywhere unheard and unseen, but it still took practice and dedication. She'd kept those abilities hidden from the Institute, partly because she worried they would expel her if they discovered she'd spent months learning the school's layout, passcodes, alarm networks, camera grids, security failsafes and electrical systems before they were even aware she was inside. Those sorts of precautions came naturally to her. She was convinced they would come in handy some day and, lo and behold, here she was. The data she'd extracted was of a more particular nature where Victor was concerned, but it should make the difference between success and failure once he was out.

There was a dull thud, followed by a row of red LEDs flashing into existence on the motherboard. She allowed herself a smile. That had done it. The main corridor lights along the route to Lower North would be out. The emergency lighting had already kicked in, but there was nothing she could do about that, not from here anyway. This would have to do for now. On to phase three.

As she slipped out of the circuitry, she heard the faintest ticking noise, followed by an ear-aching, shuddering wail. It filled the corridors, ringing with deafening intensity through the Institute's depths.

Someone had finally triggered the primary alarm. It had taken them longer than she'd expected. It must have been Wilbur in the security room tonight.

Two more tasks to perform. She passed through a solid rockface, her body turning cold at the stone's density, and reached out with her consciousness, propelling her invisible form up through another elevator shaft and out onto the dormitory floor. A few students were spilling from their rooms, bleary-eyed and worried. One gasped as Cipher passed clean through her. No time for subtlety.

Graymalkin's door lay open. He'd already left. She carried on to Vic's room, passing inside before breaking her phase.

It was empty. She grabbed his rucksack and left via the door.

At some point the lighting system in the corridor leading to the Lower North hatch had failed. The cameras had gone with it, the monitor in the control room covering that section of the Institute reduced to a static fuzz.

Wilbur had gone to investigate while Eakin tripped the alarms and reported to the principal. The security guard tried not to panic. The night felt as though it had totally deteriorated before he'd even realized something was wrong.

And now Victor Borkowski was missing.

Wilbur had first hurried to the infirmary with Eakin's curses ringing at him over the radio. He'd found Mrs Borkowski still sound asleep in bed, the only incongruence the hoodie and sweatpants that had been left on the stool next to her. The night nurse hadn't seen Victor leave. That was when the circuit board had reported a systems failure in Lower North.

At least the emergency lighting had kicked in. That was what Wilbur had told himself as he'd hurried down the stairs to the reserve exit – the elevators automatically locked out once the alarms triggered. He quickly found himself less than reassured when he got down to the actual level itself. The backup illumination in this section of the Institute emanated from low-level red strips. They had cast the length of Lower North in a dark, deep crimson glow that seemed to Wilbur nothing if not sinister.

He stepped out of the stairwell and fully into the corridor. The alarms also appeared to have cut out down here, and while he didn't miss their ear-aching assault, it only added to the eerie sense of dislocation that permeated the scene. Alarms were still going off elsewhere in the Institute, but down here they were audible only as a distant, ululating clatter. Something about that seemed to further fray Wilbur's nerves.

He advanced down the corridor tentatively. The red-shot gloom hardly seemed better than the pitch black, and the sounds of his footsteps echoed weirdly back at him. He could just about make out the heavy hatch where the corridor terminated. Lower North was the smallest of all of the Institute's exits, little more than a service hatch that opened out onto the rocky slopes of the mountainside the school was buried in. Wilbur keyed his radio as he walked slowly towards it.

"I've got eyes on the hatch," he said, trying to sound unconcerned. Now he really did wish the *Farmyard Heist* top one hundred was the biggest of his concerns. "No sign of any movement."

He was about halfway between the stairwell and the entrance when he felt it. His first thought was that the hatchway was open – he sensed a sudden breeze stirring the still air of the corridor.

Then he realized that it hadn't come from the direction of the hatch. It had come from behind him.

He turned hastily, eyes straining in the crimson light. Had the stairwell doors just closed? Had what he felt been a breeze, or something passing by him? He spun again, stumbling, before coming to a complete halt.

There was something at the end of the corridor. Wilbur could have sworn it wasn't there the last time he looked, and yet there it was now – a figure stooped over next to the exit hatch, draped in shadows, the hellish red light giving it the appearance of some blood-drenched specter.

Wilbur stood rooted to the spot, unable to even raise his radio. He'd dealt with mutant kids with all kinds of abilities, but this, this was something different. The thing seemed to look at him, then shifted so it clutched the wheel lock on the rear of the hatch door. There was a heavy grating sound, and a reverberating thud as the wheel started to turn.

"Oh God…" Wilbur stammered, finally finding the strength to snatch up his radio.

"There's something down here," he whispered into it, voice hoarse. "There's something opening the Lower North hatch! From the inside!"

"Say again, Wilbur?" Eakin's voice came back at him,

accompanied by a harsh, static-edged blurt of alarms – they were clearly still ringing where the other security guard was on the upper levels. The abrupt noise made the thing in the red-dark look back at him again. He almost moaned with terror.

"Just get someone down here," he pleaded into the radio, eyes fixed on the thing as it went back to unlocking the hatch. "I need backup. Now!"

The corridor filled with the slow groan as the heavy door swung inward. The wheel lock disengaged, and the hatch was being hefted open by the thing. Beyond it was nothing but darkness.

"Give me your flashlight, Wilbur," said a voice from right behind the security guard. He leapt in fright, rounding to find Principal Summers looming over him. He'd entered the corridor from the stairwell without Wilbur even noticing, so focused had he been on the ghastly apparition. Wilbur felt a surge of relief as he saw the X-Man advance to his side, one hand on the edge of his visor. He was so thankful he missed what Summers had actually said to him.

"Your flashlight," Summers repeated, holding out his hand. Wilbur hurried to comply, pulling the flashlight from his security belt and giving it to the principal. He glanced back nervously at the specter, trying to find the right words to explain how it had simply appeared where it was. It seemed to be looking out of the hatch and into the night beyond, oblivious now to either Wilbur or the principal.

Summers strode further along the corridor, raising and switching on the flashlight as he went. The sudden beam of white light cut through the crimson gloom and framed the thing in a perfect circle. It turned, an arm raised to shield its eyes, cringing in the sphere of brilliance.

It was only then that Wilbur realized that it wasn't a specter at all. It was just a kid, dressing in jeans and a black T. Gray-skinned and gaunt, yes, but not a blood-dripping, fanged phantom. Wilbur hurried to catch up with Summers as he carried on along the corridor, beginning to feel thoroughly foolish.

"Relax, Wilbur," the principal told him as they went. "It's just Graymalkin. One of the students."

"It... He came out of nowhere though, principal," Wilbur tried to explain, still struggling to reconcile the terror he'd felt with the kid now frozen before him. "I couldn't really see him in the dark."

"Graymalkin's powers are their most potent in low light," Summers said, not looking at the red-faced security guard. "In the dark he is exceptionally quick, strong and resilient. But not in the light."

So it seemed. The student had lowered his arms but still squinted in the glare of the principal's advancing flashlight, looking decidedly uncomfortable. Summers stopped a few yards short of him and flicked the direction of the beam onto the half-open hatch. It lit up a section of the gravel path outside, and the rough rockfaces flanking it.

"I don't suppose you have a reasonable explanation for all this, Jonas?" Summers demanded. Wilbur stood beside him, feeling supremely awkward. Graymalkin faced them, his own posture stiff now that the light was no longer on him, his face set, unreadable.

"I would not presume to lie to you, Principal Summers," he said, slowly and carefully.

"Then you'd better tell me what's going on," Summers replied. "Where is Victor?"

Graymalkin glanced towards the open hatch but said nothing.

"I'm assuming Alisa is the one responsible for killing the lights," Summers went on. "Perhaps you can tell me where she is, if you're not going to give up Mr Borkowski?"

"She's still here, principal," Graymalkin said dutifully. "Within the Institute. Neither of us intend to leave."

"But you've helped Victor do just that?" Summers demanded. "I expected better from you, Jonas. Not only have you broken the Institute's rules and abused my trust, but you've embarked upon a scheme that is doomed to failure. How far do you think Victor will be able to get on foot before we catch up with him? His shifting abilities will not help him avoid the security team's scanners. I would have hoped for better from a trio of future X-Men."

"It was not my intention to deceive you or disrupt the school, sir," Graymalkin went on. "But I acted out of the necessity of friendship. Even if you do not approve of that, I'm sure you understand it."

Summers shook his head and turned towards Wilbur.

"Get on the radio and get Eakin, Sarah, Wyld, and Tamara down here right away," he said, his tone turning brusque. "Tell Eakin to bring the tracker and inform them they'll be doing a full external perimeter search beginning in Lower North. After that I think you'd best take yourself back to the control room. You look... flushed."

"Yes, principal," Wilbur said, wanting nothing more than to be released from the awkward conversation. "Right away."

He turned and keyed his radio, heading back along the red-shot corridor.

Cipher levitated gently eight feet off the ground, her face inches from the glassy black lens of the security camera. Despite the fact that she was staring straight into it, she knew the image it was recording back on the security room's monitors would be entirely unremarkable – grainy black-and-white feedback of the Institute's hangar bay, including the long, sleek length of the

Blackbird, the school's S-70 aerial training and rapid response aircraft.

The surveillance cam was Institute-standard – a 960H IC with a 4.6mm lens and thirty-six LEDs for night vision, protected from prying and tampering by an IP66 tempered metal housing and a non-stick glass cover. It was not, however, Alisa-proof.

She reached into it with an invisible hand, solidifying her fingertips and unplugging both the signal and the power cables within their protective coupling. The faint electric current playing through her fingers vanished. Another dead camera.

Phase four had now begun.

She willed herself through the hangar and up into the control blister overlooking the main floor. The systems room was locked, but she'd already phased in and activated the basic controls earlier. She checked the flight coordinator screen before looking down through the blister at the hangar spread out below her. The S-70 sat on its flight platform, sleek and angular, like a black-fledged bird of prey waiting to take flight.

The doors to the east stairwell opened. She triggered the speaker mic and spoke into it.

"The cameras are dead," she said, her voice ringing out through the hangar below. "I've input the remote coordinates you wanted."

Victor was a shadow, passing between the doors and the S-70. He was still color-shifted, though his rucksack was visible – during the confusion of the alarms Cipher had left it for him at the bottom of the east stairwell. He stopped at the S-70's cockpit ladder and waved up at her, dropping his chameleon trick. She stayed invisible.

"Hurry," she urged over the speakers.

Victor scaled the black flank of the aircraft, dropping in through the cockpit's rear hatch. Cipher saw instrumentation light up within, mirrored by the systems before her. A series of large thumps indicated the automatic activation of the illumination beams around the flight platform, lighting the Blackbird from beneath. The hangar was waking up.

She sat in the primary command chair and pulled on a set of headphones before tapping the transmission stud on the control panel, linking with the S-70's cockpit. "I'm reading engine capacity at just over thirty percent," she said into the mic. "Seems she wasn't recharged after Santo's trip."

"It'll be enough," Vic's voice crackled back at her. "Just give me a sec. Still familiarizing myself with the layout."

She could hear the nervousness in his voice. This was the part of the plan they'd been the most unsure about. Cipher had already completed her basic S-70 flight course, scoring an A+, but Victor had only passed his theory – he still had to take the final test. Back in the dorm he'd claimed he was more than comfortable using the Blackbird as a means of escape, but Cipher had picked up on his uncertainty. She suspected that without the driving imperative to make good his escape and find his father, undertaking a solo flying operation in the dead of night would have been the last thing he'd have agreed to.

"The air route between here and Eastville will be clear for the next hour," she said, doing her best to reassure him. "You'll have plenty of time. Just take it steady."

"Easy for you to say," Vic replied, his nerves beginning to show through. "Which one's the 'on' switch again?"

Cipher didn't reply. She assumed he was joking.

Wilbur sat down heavily in the control room chair and let out a long, slow breath. What a night. He looked down at his hands and realized they were both shaking. Grimacing, he planted them flat on the desk, forcing them to be still.

There was going to be hell to pay tomorrow, he could already tell. The principal would be furious, and God only knew how Miss Frost would react when she returned to the Institute. He had no doubt there'd be an inquiry, probably followed by a full security overhaul. The days of quiet nights in the control room ranking up his game scores would soon be a thing of the past.

As he contemplated the night's chaos and how best to work around his own part in it, he glanced up at the monitor screen. The cams in Lower North were still offline. Whatever that student had done to them, they'd presumably needed more than a system reboot to fix. They weren't the only displays that had gone blank though. With a horrible sinking feeling, Wilbur realized that another set of four panels – the ones covering the upper hangar bay – had also switched off at some point.

"Seriously?" he snapped and fumbled again for his radio.

"Opening hangar doors," Cipher said into her headset's mic, setting to work on the remote eVTOL takeoff protocols. With a steady hydraulic hum, the domed roof of the hangar began to lever back, gradually exposing a cloudless, starry night sky above.

"Automatic copilot is activated," Vic said. "All systems are go. I think."

"You'll be fine," Cipher reiterated as the dome finished retracting, a perfect sphere of silver-shot darkness yawning now above the Blackbird. She wasn't sure what else to say – she hated trying to give out this sort of motivation.

"I'll guide you out for as long as I can," she said. "You've flown to Eastville airfield before though."

"Once," Vic said. "OK. Engaging vertical thrust."

"Thrust engaged," Cipher confirmed as the monitoring lights on her dashboard lit up. Most of the Blackbird's systems shared remote links with the control blister's boards, allowing flight trainers to monitor their pupils. Cipher would be able to act as a virtual copilot, but only as long as she was still in the control blister.

Beneath her the Blackbird began to rise. The reinforced glass that separated her from the hangar thrummed, the pitch of the two F-4A hybrid engines rising to a piercing whine. The glossy, hard black carapace of the aircraft seemed to shimmer, melding with the darkening sky as it climbed vertically up out of the bay.

"Looking good," she said. Anything more was interrupted by a hard banging sound from the blister's rear door. She didn't turn. "Sounds like I've got company," she carried on into the mic. "Doubt I'll be able to copilot you for much longer. Take a bearing thirty degrees south-east."

"Open this door!" shouted a voice from beyond the blister's entrance. "Or we're breaking it down! You've got five seconds."

"I assume they'll be taking our communicators," Cipher said calmly, continuing to ignore the banging. "So don't worry if you don't hear from us. Just focus on the data I've transferred and go find your dad."

"Thanks, Ci," Vic's voice came back. "I owe you. Gray too. Look after him. Tell Cyclops if he goes too hard on you, he'll have me to answer to."

"Will do, lizard boy," Cipher said, as the control blister door came crashing in behind her.

CHAPTER NINETEEN

The Blackbird was coming in hard, and there wasn't a whole lot Vic could do about it.

He fought with the controls and tried his best not to worry about the nodes and messages lighting up the cockpit display. Ahead of him Eastville runway was a ladder of lights guiding him through the night and towards the ground.

He was going to overshoot it. That was partly accidental, but also partly by design. As he'd banked towards the small private airstrip, he'd spotted a gaggle of figures, illuminated by flashlights, spilling from the control tower and adjacent buildings towards the runway. Eastville belonged to the Institute and was used to help train students undergoing their flying courses. Vic had flown out of it once before and had hoped that at such a late hour there'd only be a couple of staff on security.

Apparently, that wasn't the case. Cyclops had clearly gotten the word out. Touch down on the runway and he'd be taken the moment he popped the cockpit hatch.

So Vic was going to overshoot. He'd dragged the flight stick back up, jaw clenched with effort and concentration. The S-70 complained fiercely, the cockpit's vectoring, altitude and stall warnings blinking and pinging. He didn't look at them, keeping his eyes fixed on those strip lights as they surged up to meet him with disconcerting speed.

Just a standard emergency landing, he told himself. Absolutely nothing to worry about.

The Blackbird's extended wheels hit the asphalt. The impact jarred Vic, bouncing him against his seat constraints. He battled to keep his grip on the flight stick. The engines screamed in his ears. The landing strip lights were on either side of him now, whipping past at a furious pace. Up ahead, they came to an end with the runway's finishing point marked by a timber X barrier. Beyond, it was nothing but darkness.

Vic had no time to savor the irony. He'd extended the flaps, hit the brakes and baffles, and could do nothing now bar hold on and try not to scream. The last landing lights darted past him, and the Blackbird's sleek nose ploughed into the timber barrier. Vic barely felt the impact as the wood exploded into pieces before he got a split-second impression of a high wire perimeter fence, looking out of the darkness beyond.

The Blackbird slammed into it. The second impact rattled Vic as badly as the initial touchdown. The fence crumpled, scouring the Blackbird's prow and cracking the cockpit's visor. The aircraft bounced and rolled as it passed out beyond the landing field's perimeter, and Vic was convinced it was going to capsize or dash itself to pieces against a boulder or some other immovable object. The Blackbird slowed, and the pitch of its engines dropped as it continued its unsteady deceleration. Vic saw nothing ahead, only the night. He didn't dare search the airfield through the rear cams.

Finally, the airplane came to a complete stop. Vic gripped the control stick with both hands so tight it hurt. He forced himself to let go, took a deep breath, and killed a flurry of control panel switches. He was down, and he was alive. The Blackbird was even pretty much in one piece. That had to count for something, right?

He unbuckled himself and checked the flight compass, orienting with the direction of the landing. Then he undid the cockpit latch and dropped down onto the ground below.

He landed in long grass, dry and brittle. If memory served open plains surrounded Eastville but the closest highway wasn't far, just due east.

He turned in the direction the flight compass had pointed and took a moment to steady himself. Since leaving his dorm room in the Institute he'd been operating on sharp wits and adrenaline. Until now he hadn't stopped to consider what might be waiting for him beyond the Institute, or what he was leaving behind. As far as he knew, no one had defied the principal to this degree before. What would Summers do to Cipher and Gray? Would he have them expelled? If so, how could Vic hope to pay them back for such a sacrifice? The future ahead was as dark and unknowable as the night-shrouded plains surrounding him.

Part of him felt even more determined now that he was out and committed to finding his dad. For the first time since getting back to the Institute he was taking positive action. He just had to hold onto his courage and keep going.

He slipped out from beneath the Blackbird, risking a glance in the direction of the airfield. The landing strip lights and the control tower backlit the crumpled remains of the fence and the ferocious furrows ploughed up by the Blackbird's landing. Shapes moved indistinctly towards the opening, the illumination of their flashlights oscillating in the dark. Vic caught the sound of shouting voices, growing louder.

It was time to go. He threw his backpack over his shoulders, turned and ran out into the night.

CHAPTER TWENTY

Absolution.

The thought of it brought him deep, mental agony. Why did it elude him? Why was everything he did never enough? Would he ever be worthy of it? Would he ever know peace?

Prophet Xodus attempted to quieten his mind by raising his head and cracking it back down on the cold stone floor. The stab of pain through his skull brought welcome clarity. How dare he demand absolution in this sacred space? One such as he, a worthless wretch, seeking divine forgiveness while the world was still overrun, tainted, *infested* by mutant filth? The thought made him shiver. He struck his head on the flagstones again.

The second blow brought peace. Something ran from his forehead down the side of his face. He lifted his head again and opened his eyes to find a few droplets of blood falling from his scalp and down to the white slabs beneath him. It looked so red, so vital against the flagstones.

Xodus had been lying spread-eagled on the cold floor since the early morning, letting the ache of the unyielding stone work its way into his bones. It did him good to be back in a consecrated space once more. It felt as though he had been on the road for months, locked in a perpetual crusade across the continent. He welcomed that work, but his soul craved sanctity. It needed absolution, like a man stranded in the desert heat needed water. He hated such weakness, but he could not deny it.

He tensed his outstretched arms, feeling the dull ache that had settled in them. He had lost track of time. His children knew better than to disturb him while he was before the altar. He permitted himself to look up at the graven stone, draped with the black-and-white Standards of Purification. This church, small but gothic, had been surrendered by its priest to the Purifiers several months earlier. Its congregation had been barred and the priest himself ejected – his parish would serve a higher purpose. Now its iconography bore alongside it the cross-and-circle and its arched, vaulted ceiling resounded with the purity oaths of the true faithful. It was one of a dozen such rallying places Xodus had established. In these sanctified houses of training, worship, and mental preparation could be used to further expand the hunt for the unclean.

The sight of the Purifier altar brought him some consolation. Progress had been made. The crusade was reaching farther, cutting deeper, than it had done for many years. And yet, Xodus remained troubled. Like everything, success came with a price. The holy work done by the faithful risked being sullied by their consorting with sin. He had prayed on this troubling matter night and day for weeks, but no answer had been forthcoming. The crusade's successes would have to be answer enough. The alliance of necessity he had subjected himself to was still the work of the divine, even if the allies in question were less than pure.

He looked back down from the altar. The blood beneath him had spread, running in small, crimson traces along the cracks between the flagstones. The side of his face was wet.

He heard the sound of hurried footsteps approaching down the church nave, echoing back from the stonework around them. He fought to suppress a pulse of anger. He had been expecting this.

The footsteps slowed, faltered and stopped at the edge of the chancel where Xodus lay. Silence returned to the church.

"Speak," he growled.

"My prophet," said a voice, breathy and nervous. "We have a visitor. I told him to await you in the sacristy."

Xodus grunted. He didn't ask who the visitor was. He had been awaiting him for several days now. He closed his eyes, mouthed a swift, silent prayer, and rose.

His body seemed to take a moment to obey him. Joints cracked as he stretched and flexed, working the dullness out of them. In his youth he had lain upon flagstones in penance for a day or more, and still sprung up at the end of it, filled with vigor. He was getting old.

He genuflected towards the altar and turned to glare down at the one who'd dared disturb him. The two white-robed Choristers attending him averted their black-masked faces, as did the lowly novitiate who had brought news of the visitor's arrival. Without taking his eyes off the youth, Xodus held out his hand for the Chorister on his left to pass him a square of white cloth. He raised and clutched it to his brow, catching the blood running down his scarred cheek. The motion brought a fresh pulse of pain to his scalp. He ignored it this time. The pain had nothing more to tell him today. He had duties to perform.

"Return to our visitor," he ordered the novitiate. "Bid him welcome and lead him to the confessional."

The Purifier bowed and hurried off. Xodus watched him go before handing the bloody cloth to the Chorister on his left and holding his hand out to the one on his right. The silent, white-clad figure carefully placed Xodus's golden mask into his fingers. Both attendants then took a step back as the prophet fastened it over his face.

"Clean this," he ordered them both, pointing at the bloodstain on the floor, before striding past it and down from the chancel.

The confessional boxes awaited, small stalls carved from ash wood, their flanks fashioned into the likeness of soaring cherubim. Xodus stepped into one and turned, having to stoop in the small space. He closed and latched the door before sitting down, waiting in silence.

The creak of the neighboring stall and the sound of a second latch announced the visitor's arrival. The head-height partition separating the two stalls was removed, leaving just a wooden latticework between Xodus and his guest.

He didn't look round, continuing to gaze straight ahead.

"You have taken the confessant's box, rather than the confessor's," the visitor said to him from behind the lattice. His voice was smooth like silk, soft as sin. "You wish to confide your wrongs to me, prophet?"

"I am not worthy enough to absolve wrongs," Xodus pointed out, his mask's vocalizer changing his voice to a low, electronic growl.

"But I am," the visitor answered. "So, tell me yours. I have heard… all manner of troubling reports in the past few days."

"The boy escaped," Xodus said simply. He was not a man to twist words or seek deflection.

"Apparently," said the visitor. "How?"

"He was aided by the Institute. We believe he has returned there."

"That is unfortunate. What of his parents?"

"His mother evaded us," Xodus said. "But we have his father."

"Your failure to take the boy despite the fact that I located and tracked him for you was less than ideal," the visitor said. "But his father will allow you to make amends. Make sure the boy finds him and bring them both to me."

"If the divine wills it," Xodus intoned. He could feel blood from the wound at his scalp beginning to drip down his face again, inside his mask.

"I will it," the visitor said, his honeyed words turning bitter. "And if you wish my funding to continue then you will see it done. Do not contact me until you have the chameleon."

CHAPTER TWENTY-ONE

At first Vic thought it was thunder that had woken him. It roared and clattered the stanchions around him, a great booming crash that triggered an instinctive desire in him to shiver and cringe. The metal he was perched upon shuddered beneath him, sending vibrations throbbing through his body.

He realized it wasn't thunder. It was a train.

He'd been perched in the metal-shod underbelly of the Hudson Yards Rail Bridge for the better part of a day, waiting. The tedium was killing him. Without meaning to, he'd dozed off, laid out and stuck to one of the support beams. The passage of the train overhead had startled him so much he'd have lost his balance without his reptilian grip.

He drew his feet up, changing his stance to a crouch and grimacing at the grime that covered the front of his X-uniform. He'd need to clean that. He could probably wash it by hanging it off the side of the bridge, though. It had been raining for the past three or four hours, a blustery summer's downpour that was cascading heavily from the edges of the great metal span and churning up the Hudson River ahead of him. He watched as a freighter from the docks opposite forged its way through the choppy waters, its laden prow framed by the soaring, clustered majesty of Manhattan Island.

It had been three days since he had made it to New York City, and a week since he'd escaped the Institute. After touching down at Eastville he'd managed to find the highway and catch a bus ride across the border, albeit with an excessive search and more than a few unpleasant looks at the checkpoint. Security seemed to be clamping down everywhere, though whether it was aimed at curtailing mutants or the Purifiers wasn't exactly clear. He'd stopped in Shelby, Montana, and drawn out almost all his savings in cash, then caught a series of trains and Greyhounds to Minneapolis, Chicago, and finally New York. He had a distant aunt on Long Island, but he hadn't seen her for years, and it seemed like a mistake to put more family members at risk. He'd spent the first night and much of the first day sleeping beside a log in Central Park, his rucksack stuffed inside it. He'd been woken by a curious golden retriever, and had melted away before its owners discovered him, much to the dog's confusion. In the past forty-eight hours he'd been living rough, running surveillance on the locations stored in his communicator.

Cipher had come up trumps, as usual. When she'd broken into the Institute's data vault she'd been able to pull information related to the rising Purifier campaign and transfer it to Vic's communicator. It turned out the files being kept by the X-Men on the latest vitriolic crusade were far from comprehensive, but they offered him a starting point. There was insider info on future rallies and possible targets, most of them mutants who were now enjoying the direct protection of the X-Men. There was also surveillance data from both known and suspected Purifier recruitment and meet-up points. The highest concentration of these, five in all, were in New York City. Vic had decided that would be the best place to start.

The dead ground beneath the Hudson Yard Rail Bridge was one of the locations believed to be a Purifier pickup spot. Just what was being picked up, Vic couldn't say. This was the second location he'd chosen from the list of five. He'd spent a day and the better part of two nights in an alley off West Park, perpetually chameleon except for when he slept concealed between two dumpsters. He'd seen nothing untoward, and he'd felt as though the monotony of surveillance was beginning to threaten his sanity. The space beneath the bridge, damp, dank and grimy though it was, had initially offered a change of perspective, but that was beginning to wear thin now as well.

He checked his communicator. It was a risk taking it. He suspected having it would potentially give the Institute the ability to track him. Yet at the same time, it was a risk he would have to take, especially if he was going to maintain any degree of contact with Gray or Ci. There was still no word from either of them. That was to be expected, but it didn't really make it any easier. He wondered what had happened to them both. How hard had Cyclops come down on them? Had they been suspended? Confined to their dorms? He didn't imagine the latter punishment troubling either too deeply.

Another train passed overhead, seeming to shake the whole world, the shriek of the rails piercing Vic's ears. Evening was settling in, and the distant, rain-shrouded spires of Manhattan became ten thousand tiny studs of twinkling light in the wet gloom. He sat back on the stanchion, dangled his legs over its edge and sighed. What the hell was he doing here? Hiding under a bridge in the rain and the dark, half the country away from home.

He didn't have a home any more, he told himself. That was why he was here. Every time he felt his resolve slip, he reminded himself of the sight of his father on his knees, or his home in flames, or his mother's tears. He thought of his father being taken, and how he might be somewhere in the city before him. It rekindled the anger inside him, gave him the fire to temper his resolve.

The growl of an engine interrupted his melancholy. He peered over the edge of his stanchion and down at the hard-packed dirt directly below, a span of about fifty yards. An unmarked black cargo van was rolling into view. It parked beside the bridge's support arch, the engine cutting out. Vic repositioned himself on the strut as he heard a sliding door open. He felt the boredom-induced evening gloom burn away.

Two men clambered out of the front of the van, another from the side. They were dressed in nondescript black suits and ties, wearing shades in defiance of the weather. Total government types. Vic's tongue flicked the air instinctively, tasting danger. He stayed still, watching.

One of the men paced around the space beneath the bridge, walking as far as the riverbank and back again. Vic heard him calling out to the others but couldn't make out what was said. One glanced up at him, idly. He didn't move a muscle. Even if he hadn't been using his color-changing abilities, he trusted the shadows of the upper struts to be dense enough to keep him concealed.

Was this a pickup? One thing was for sure, the trio below didn't look like Purifiers. He'd never known any that went about in suits and ties, even without their robes. These three were gunning so hard for anonymity it hurt.

The excitement Vic had felt at their arrival gradually began to give way. The three remained outside their vehicle, chatting in low voices. The minutes turned to an hour. More trains clattered by, shrieking and rattling.

What was in the vehicle? Vic shifted carefully along his perch so he could get a look at the registration plate. He ran the number over his communicator, but didn't get any solid returns.

Just over an hour had gone by before a second vehicle joined the first. This one was more familiar – a clapped-out old truck, its bodywork scratched and rusted, its hood sprayed with a crude white cross-and-circle. Vic tensed up again. Enter the Purifiers, stage right.

A pair of figures in black robes and silver masks dismounted from the battered truck and approached the black van across the mud. The three suits went to meet them. There were no handshakes, and whatever they were saying appeared to be terse. The lead suit gestured at the Purifier truck, then back at his own vehicle. One of the Purifiers responded by pointing across the river at Manhattan's glittering thicket of towers.

That appeared to settle it. Two of the suits returned to their van and opened the rear doors. One reemerged with a hefty-looking metal suitcase.

"Showtime," Vic murmured to himself, snapping a rapid succession of photos with his communicator. The suit with the case handed it over to one of the Purifiers. The pair retreated to the back of their own truck to open it. Vic slunk along the stanchion so he could get a view of it from above. The Purifier flipped the clasps and opened it – as Vic had expected, the interior of the suitcase was stacked with thick wads of cash. As one of the Purifiers leafed through it, the other turned back to the suits.

More words were exchanged. The suit who had climbed into the van reemerged with a duffel bag slung over his back and another carried in both arms. These were deposited on the trailer next to the suitcase. The second Purifier unzipped the bags and pulled something out – an assault rifle, which he appeared to turn over and check deftly.

More weapons followed, including sidearms. Several of the

weapons were particularly unusual-looking, short and bulky. They looked like some sort of energy rifle. That really was some serious hardware. Two of the suits ferried six more sacks out onto the trailer. The Purifiers checked every one. Vic felt a dangerous mix of fear and anger rising within him. There was enough gear down there to start a war. The Purifiers weren't a religious sect or a band of devoted, concerned citizens. They were a paramilitary cult.

All the bags appeared to have been deposited into the rear of the truck. One of the Purifiers secured a heavy tarpaulin over the trailer while the second spoke with the remaining spook. With the covering secured, the first Purifier got into the cab with the suitcase. Vic realized his time was up. He had to act, or it'd be too late.

He crawled across the stanchion and latched onto the flank of the concrete support pillar, following it round to the side so he could descend to the ground while staying out of sight of the exchange. As he went his colors shifted flawlessly, blending with the dirty, encroaching darkness.

He reached the ground and slunk back round the pillar just as the suits got back into their van. He had a few seconds to act. The question was, who to follow?

There was no real time to make his mind up. The Purifier truck was already pulling out of the underpass. He stayed still as they drove by barely a dozen paces to his left. The suits started up their engine. The vehicle was facing away from him. Go now, or all this would have been for nothing.

He sprinted for the back of the black van. It began to pull away and he managed to plant and twist his hands against the rear door, praying as he did so that those within didn't feel the thump of his impact.

He was on. He shifted up, got his feet above the bumper, and scaled onto the roof just in time to get hit by the deluge as the van passed out from under the bridge's protective awning.

The rain soaked him through. He shifted his grip so he was splayed on the roof as the van joined the road up onto the highway. As it did so, doubts harried him. Days spent preparing for something like this, and now that he had committed to it he realized he didn't have a plan that went beyond tracking the bad guys. What if he'd chosen wrong? Surely the Purifiers would be a better option than the goons arming them?

He readjusted his grip. He'd clung onto more daunting targets than a rain-slick vehicle picking up speed on the road, but it was still up there as a challenge. He had to keep re-sticking himself a limb at a time, and the rain and the wind in his face made it more difficult. He rode it out, trusting in himself.

The decision to stick with the suits had been a difficult one – his instincts cried out at him to chase down the Purifiers. He'd forced himself to use his head, and the strategic lessons taught to him by the Institute. It was clear enough that the Purifiers had to be operating with friends in high places. He was convinced that if he could locate a mysterious backer, he'd also find his father. Plus, there were practical considerations to following the supplier rather than the ones being supplied. If he'd ridden in the back of the Purifier truck, he could only assume he'd have arrived in the midst of a cult den, with a lot of fanatics looking to take hold of, and test, their newly acquired firearms. On the other hand, whoever the suits were, they must be thinking their job was done. Their guard would be down.

That's what he told himself as the vehicle took a left off the highway, then a right along increasingly crowded, narrow streets. Vic tried to follow where he was going and map it out in his head, but the elements forced him to keep his eyes closed, and much of his concentration was taken up trying to avoid sliding off the van roof. He got the impression that the buildings were crowding closer and looming taller in the encroaching night, streetlamps blinking on in the gloom, whipping past one after another in regimented rows. He felt as though he'd been stuck there for ages, his limbs beginning to burn with the effort of remaining tensed up and clamped to the vehicle.

At last, he felt the vicious forward motion begin to ease off. The van took another right turn, slowing. He managed to raise his head as the van eased to a complete stop and got a glimpse of their destination. What appeared to be an office block loomed overhead, while the shutters to an underground carpark slowly rose up in front of the van, exposing a steep concrete ramp beyond. He snatched a glance left and right, taking in a street of nondescript, shuttered shops and high-rise apartments weathering the evening's summer storm. He had no idea where he was any more, besides the fact he was sure they were still on the west bank of the river.

The van descended into the darkness of the carpark, bright industrial lighting blinking on automatically and making Vic cringe. The vehicle rolled along into an empty slot, the engine echoing around the space – the carpark must have taken up more than a whole block, but there didn't look to be more than half a dozen other vehicles sharing it. The sound of the van's brakes echoed through the deserted, man-made cavern.

Vic unfastened his limbs from the roof and rolled onto his side, clenching his knees up to his chest – he no longer had to worry about being spotted from above, and the vehicle had high enough sides for him to be confident they wouldn't see him if he kept central and away from the edges. He heard more doors bang open, the framework shivering under him. There was a jangle of keys, and a gruff voice spoke from just below him.

"Glad that's over. I swear one day those freakshows are going to turn the guns on us."

"Be thankful," grumbled a second voice. "I'd rather be dealing with the cult nutjobs than the guy the boss has to answer to. The Purifiers I can outsmart, but that corp guy? Gives me the shivers."

"First and last time you'll hear Rylan talk about outsmarting anyone," joked a voice Vic assumed belonged to the third spook. There was laughter, and a lot of cussing from the one he took to be Rylan.

He heard the sound of the van locking, and a trio of footsteps that began to ring away through the carpark as the group set off. Vic peered cautiously over the vehicle's edge to check the direction they were going, and slipped off after them, treading as lightly as possible for fear of setting off the van's alarms. He crouched on all fours on the concrete, his skin shimmering and changing flawlessly, his suit mirroring it. He became a faint distortion of blurred movement that vanished when still.

As he had hoped, the three suits were now leaving the empty van apparently without a care, two of them locked in a terse little argument while the third walked ahead. They were making for a stairwell next to an elevator shaft, stamped with exit signs. Vic quickened his pace as much as he dared, closing the gap behind them. Not for the first time he found himself thinking jealously about Cipher's ability to become both truly invisible and soundless.

The first spook had reached the stair doors. They were locked, but he punched something into an access code and held the doors open for the other two. Vic was forced to freeze as the man glanced back and ordered his companions to can it and hurry up. By the time they were both through there was still well over a dozen yards to cover. Slowly, the door began to close.

He flung himself forward and let fly with his tongue. This wasn't going to be pleasant. It lashed around the door handle and stuck there, wedging it open as Vic covered the distance with all the silence he could muster. The taste was metallic and cold, and he didn't dare give himself time to think about how disgusting it was licking a literal door handle. He did what he had to do.

He reached the door and placed a hand on it, as lightly as possible, carefully arresting his forward motion. It paused a hair's breadth from locking back in place. Shuddering slightly, he unlatched his tongue, the handle dripping with saliva, and slipped through the gap.

It was a pure gamble. The suits might have heard his oncoming footsteps or noticed that the door hadn't closed. They could be waiting on the other side, weapons drawn. But he hadn't been close enough to see the code they'd used on the stairwell, and spending a night locked in a parking garage wasn't ideal. Act now, worry later.

The gamble paid off. The trio had already made their way up the first flight of stairs, a complaint about the time it took to clock out echoing back down to Vic. He let out a slow, relieved breath and set off after them, his scales and suit shifting to mirror the interior of the dimly lit stairwell.

He passed the first landing, then the second. Each was signposted with a different company name and brand. Parker Insurance. Dwight and Hanlon Sales. Tomorrow Industries. Clearly, they'd passed from the parking lot up into the shared office block above.

The voices of the suits, which had been drifting steadily down to him as he followed, abruptly cut off. He realized they must have passed through a door on the next landing. He darted up to it, praying for the sake of his taste buds that it wasn't another self-locking one.

It seemed not. The entrance was as simple as the rest in the stairwell, the sign above it the only clue as to what lay beyond. Esson Electrical. Like the rest of the names he'd passed, it didn't exactly scream "sinister, arms-dealing billionaire." Vic glanced up the next flight, wondering if he'd missed the suits carrying on in silence, but there was no sign of them. They had to have gone through this door.

That meant Vic was going through too.

CHAPTER TWENTY-TWO

The sound of a hymn service spilled out onto the street from the church, filling the early evening with songs of praise. Rockslide listened for a while, crouched in the alley running along the side of the building. It felt incongruous, almost peaceful, far removed from the reality of what he knew was about to occur.

It had taken a week, and he'd had to call in several favors with the Hellions on top of the intel he had received from the Institute, but at last he'd found a good lead. Intercepted phone traffic suggested that a hostage was being held at a small church in western Newark. The identity remained a secret, but apparently, they were going to be put to use in tonight's sermon.

It was the best Santo had to go on. He'd attempted to track several Purifier leads in New York, but covert work wasn't exactly his forte, and he'd been forced to act faster after the Institute had contacted him to tell him that Victor had disappeared. It didn't surprise him. He'd hoped taking on the case personally would be enough to convince the kid to stay in school, but he knew what Vic was like when he got restless. He'd offered to switch his search from the father to the son, but Cyclops had refused – find Dan Borkowski and Vic would have no more reason to stay on the run.

He shifted his bulk, stretching out his arms and feeling the rock grind and scrape. He'd been in place for almost a full day, not wanting to break his cover and risk being detected. Mutants weren't exactly welcome around New York at the moment. He realized that the hostage the Purifiers were holding could well be another mutant or sympathizer they'd kidnapped over the past few months, but even if it wasn't Dan, they might know where more prisoners were being held.

The singing came to a stop, the final, long chord of the accompanying organ ringing away into silence. Santo shifted towards the church wall, crouching down and planting one large hand in the dirt. This was one of what the Purifiers called their "recruitment sermons." Similar services had started popping up across New England, steadily, and in the mid-Atlantic states too. At first glance they looked liked nothing more threatening than an unannounced guest lecturer in a random parish, but their true purpose was far more sinister. They were attempting to radicalize the faithful. The Purifier poison was spreading, its tendrils reaching out from soaring inner-city cathedrals to small, whitewashed-timber community churches like this one, drip-feeding people anti-mutant sentiment. Well, tonight's lesson in hatred was about to be rudely interrupted.

Santo heard a voice address the congregation within. It was time. He closed his eyes and delved deep into the earth with his consciousness, letting both body and mind commune with the bedrock below. The soil under his hand shuddered and shifted, slowly at first but with growing speed and purpose. Santo grasped the rocky roots he felt there with his mind, urging it on, stirring it up for the first time in eons. It would lie buried no more.

There was a low, grumbling crack. The tremors in the dirt spread. The lids of the trash cans lining the alleyway started to rattle, one clattering to the ground. The nearest streetlamp flickered. In the distance, a dog barked in a frenzy.

Santo heard the voice within the church falter. A crack began to run up one of the stained-glass windows. Teeth gritted and body shuddering, he let out a bellow of effort and surged upwards, the motion accompanied by an ear-splitting crash as the ground heaved before him. A pillar of jagged rock, caked in mud, slammed upwards like a spear tip punching through the earth's shield. The timber wall directly in front of Santo splintered and burst apart as the ground came slamming upwards with a cracking sound like the sundering of the world.

Splinters and shards of stone rained down on Santo as he relaxed, panting. With a spreading motion, he cracked the pillar of rock now set before him, sending an avalanche of split stone and dust cascading down the alleyway on either side. He advanced through the midst of it, untroubled by the torrent of grit, stepping right through the hole his geokinetic powers had torn in the church's flank and into the building.

A hundred faces turned towards him. The congregation sat in their pews, seemingly frozen in shock at the sudden invasion. To Santo's right was a simple altar table and pulpit, the latter occupied by a tall figure in black robes and a golden grotesque. Xodus himself.

"Hope you don't mind me rocking up at your sermon, prophet," Santo said, cracking his stony knuckles loudly. Without waiting for a response, he charged the pulpit.

CHAPTER TWENTY-THREE

"They were late again," DeFray complained, his expression sour. "Like, over an hour late."

His two accomplices nodded, looking equally unimpressed. They'd been summoned into their employer's office before clocking out and ordered to report on the handover. Mr Esson had been twitchy like that for weeks now, ever since the new contracts had come in.

"I don't give a damn if they kept you waiting all night," he responded angrily, leaning over his desk and glaring at the three men. "Did they take the goods?"

"Oh, they took them all right," Rylan said. "They were delighted. More toys for their little crusade."

"Good," Esson responded brusquely. "That's all that matters. I'll get on to the corporation and let them know the latest shipment's gone without a hitch."

"And what about us?" Dail, the last of the trio, demanded. "I don't know about you two, but I ain't dealing with those freaks any more. They're crazies, every last one. They're gonna turn the goods on us one of these days, I swear."

"You'll do whatever I tell you to do, numbskull," Esson barked, snatching a hefty brown envelope from his desk and flinging it at Dail, who caught it neatly. "Now take your pay and get the hell out! I'll phone you the next time the corporation sends another job through."

The three men in suits left the office. Esson slumped down in his chair, staring after them for a moment before snatching up the phone and dialing up the corp's number. As he did so, he thought he caught a half-glimpse of movement in the corner of his eye, in front of his filing cabinets. He looked around sharply.

Nothing stirred. He was about to rise and check that the files were still locked away when a voice spoke over the phone, startling him.

"You have reached the secure line. Please state your business and personal identification number."

Esson cleared his throat hurriedly and answered.

"Esson Electrical, five-eight-five-two-seven," he said. "Just tell him the latest shipment has been delivered." He hung up without waiting for a response and looked back at the cabinets.

There had been something... off about them. He'd thought his eyes were playing tricks on him – it was as if the metal boxes had been somehow distorted and misshapen. He stood up from behind his desk and approached them, shifting off to one side to get a different angle.

The cabinets were still cabinets. Nothing unusual. He avoided the urge to reach out and touch one. The stress of this job really was getting to him. Just keep thinking about the money, he told himself. The contracts he'd signed would make him a millionaire in a few short years. That made jumping at a few shadows all right, didn't it? A little longer and he'd cash in and be enjoying martinis on the beach somewhere in the Caribbean. Hired goons in suits and horrible, threat-laden phone calls would be a thing of the past.

He pulled his jacket off the coatrack, picked a folder up from his desk, and opened the office door. Before stepping out he glanced back one more time, though he wasn't really sure why. His office lay empty before him. The desk was undisturbed. The blinds behind it remained drawn. The ledgers on the shelves hadn't moved. The clock on the wall continued to tick away. Nothing else stirred. Shaking his head, Esson turned off the light and closed the door.

There was the sound of the lock turning, and footsteps quickly receding into silence. All that remained was the soft, regular ticking of the office clock. The space sat still and quiet, disturbed only by the occasional distant sound of traffic in the street below.

The blinds behind the office desk abruptly grew a set of eyes. Vic relaxed, daring to breathe again. He'd been sure the guy had caught sight of him when he'd been standing right in front of the filing cabinets, but the phone call had given him an opportunity to shift behind the desk. Going chameleon was one thing, but doing it in a confined office space with, at one point, four other people was asking for trouble. Thankfully they all seemed too angry and stressed to notice their unwelcome visitor.

Dropping his color-shift, Vic leant over the desk, careful not to touch anything. He didn't want to risk tripping any alarms, not that Esson Electrical looked like the money-laundering criminal lair that would be packing extra security. Their floor in the shared block appeared to consist of five or six half-empty offices, most of which were being vacuumed by evening cleaning staff. Had it not been for the strained, shady nature of the conversation between the suited spooks and the man he took to be Mr Esson, Vic would have very much doubted he was following the right lead.

He was in now though, and he might not get another opportunity like it. He had to make it count. He considered the cabinets, the desk drawers, and the small safe sitting in the corner of the room. Picking locks had never been his thing. He could try scanning with his communicator, but he wasn't sure what that would do. On an impulse he picked up the phone and hit the dial back button. As he'd expected, an automated voice answered him.

"You have reached the secure line. Please state your business and personal identification number."

"Esson Electrical, five-eight-five-two-seven," Vic said, hoping the line didn't use vocal as well as coded recognition. There was no response. He grimaced. What if it had already ID'd him? What if unauthorized use tripped an alarm somewhere? What if –

"You have one new message – from – Sublime Corporation," blipped the awkward, automatic voice. Vic didn't have time to feel relieved.

"Next time I want a proper report, Mr Esson," said a new voice, slick and nauseating. "You can expect new assignments presently, and I expect them to be done by the book. If not, I may have to reassess our business arrangements."

There was the crackle of a phone receiver being put down, followed by the return of the automated tone in Vic's ear.

"End of messages. To ring through to head office, please press 1. To hear the message again, please press 2. To delete the message, please press 3."

Vic put the phone down, hard. There was something deeply unsettling about that voice, something wicked and sick. It was like having a demon whispering in his ear, verbal barbs drizzled with honey.

The last thing Vic wanted was to meet whoever that voice belonged to, but he feared that was exactly what he was going to have to do. The important thing was that now he had a name, something that meant a bit more than Esson Electrical.

Sublime Corporation.

CHAPTER TWENTY-FOUR

Prophet Xodus's only response to the oncoming Rockslide avalanche was to spread his arms wide. In that messianic pose, he received Santo's fist to his stomach. The impact of the mutant's charge shattered the pulpit into a blizzard of splinters and sent both him and Xodus crashing backwards into the wall behind. Dust cascaded from the rafters and every window in the church shattered, raining shards of multi-hued glass down onto the congregation.

Santo arrested his rush by planting his other fist into the wall, almost punching right through it. He snatched up Xodus by the front of his robes and slammed him up against the woodwork.

"Where is Daniel Borkowski?" Santo snarled. The golden mask didn't reply. Grunting, he grasped it and tore it from the figure's face.

The man he had punched was unconscious, and blood ran from his lips – the impact had likely left him with more than a few internal injuries. He was big and shaven-headed, with tattoos of flames snaking up his broad neck from under his robes. He looked young though, probably his early twenties. Still holding the limp body by his robes, Santo rounded on the congregation behind him.

The rows of churchgoers had gone. The onlooking faithful had reached beneath their pews and pulled on beatific golden masks, identical to the one Santo had taken to be Xodus. The parish had transformed almost instantly into a Purifier gathering.

"The lizard's father is not here," droned a hundred speakers, each one a recording of Xodus's voice issuing from the array of unmoving golden lips. "Seek and ye shall find, sinner."

Santo now doubted very much the man still in his grip was Xodus. This had all been a mistake.

The door to the vestry burst open. Figures rushed out in full Purifier garb. These were different, though – their grotesques were black and their robes a pristine white. And unlike the so-called parishioners, they were armed.

Santo was outnumbered, but he wouldn't turn back now. He'd faced odds like these before, and Vic was counting on him. He flung the Purifier in his grip directly into the first of the oncoming cultists, tossing them both back into those behind, before slamming his fists into the floor. More woodwork splintered as he delved into the church foundations. The bedrock buried beneath answered his geokinetic pleas, and a lance of stone slammed up through the grounds in the midst of the white-robed Purifiers. Bodies were flung left and right, and there was a crunch as one of the cultists was run through on the tip of the exploding rock.

Santo dragged his hands free of the dirt and flexed his fingers, advancing on the momentarily scattered white robes. That was when the first energy bolt struck his chest.

He faltered, stung by the glancing blow. A second followed, a beam of crackling purple lightning that earthed itself into his shoulder. He grunted at the impact, feeling his craggy arm abruptly go numb.

He turned back towards the pews and realized his second mistake. It seemed as if some of the false parishioners had been armed as well. Half a dozen men and women had bulky energy rifles trained on him, their menace a disconcerting contrast to the pristine expressions on their masks.

Santo clenched a fist, once more seeking out the rock beneath, but this time it was too late. With a buzzing crack and an abrupt stink of ozone, the Purifiers opened fire.

CHAPTER TWENTY-FIVE

The Danger Room had been activated.

More than that, it was at Threat Level Alpha. The doors had been auto-locked and the heaviest defensive shielding both inside and out had come clattering down. The energy reroute was so intense it caused the lighting throughout the entire Institute to dim and flicker.

Cipher knew that the other students lived in awe of such moments. Threat Level Alpha wasn't something that even recent graduates were permitted to unlock. It transformed the Danger Room into a lethal chamber of destruction, one that would test the most skilled X-Men to their limits. The pupils of the New Charles Xavier School for Mutants would look up from their studies and marvel at the flickering lights or the tiny, barely perceptible tremors that ran through the subterranean base, and they would know that either a member of staff or a visiting guest was being put through the fight of their lives by the Institute's systems.

Even on its most lethal settings, though, the Danger Room had never impressed Cipher. Few of the students had even witnessed the chamber at its most lethal, but she had, on many occasions. Foot-thick steel, hardened concrete and energy baffles were no more a deterrent to her than red warning lights and "keep out" signs.

She'd turned it into a game not long after she'd first come to the Institute, entering the Danger Room when Emma Frost or Cyclops were using it and practicing the same course as them, dodging the same drone attacks and energy beams, invisible and undetectable by their side. It was supremely dangerous, but her injuries had only ever been minor, and not once had she been found out. No one knew of her extracurricular activities, not even Gray or Vic. That was how she liked it. They'd only worry.

She watched now from above the chamber's west entrance as the current engagement routine reached its climax. It had been initiated almost thirty minutes earlier, when the room had first gone into lockdown. Cipher had simply phased through the armored, reinforced door. Before her she'd found the fury of an X-Man unleashed.

Cyclops was running rampant through the deadliest drills the Danger Room had on record. When inactive, the chamber itself appeared to be nothing more than a great, metal-paneled cylinder buried right at the very core of the Institute. When triggered however it morphed to fit its required drill. Threat Level Alpha was the most extreme. The floor, normally composed of glossy, segmented panels, shifted on hydraulic pillars into over a dozen separate sections divided at different heights, some rising almost to the domed ceiling while others dropped away abruptly, all of them in constant vertical motion. The wall plates extended to act as obstacles, moving flawlessly with the shifting floor to block off routes or create new ones as the advanced combat AI that governed the room determined. The space, once cavernous and empty, became a maddening, constantly shifting chamber of stress and illusion. And that was without the smite drones, holographic projections and laser beams.

Cipher watched, maintaining a constant, phased hover above the closest floor plate, as Cyclops leapt across the space, battling his way through the maze crafted by the Institute's systems. Initial attack drones, malicious little fist-sized aerial bots, came at him in flocks or individually, wheeling and buzzing about the ceiling or bursting abruptly from their concealed charging banks behind the wall panels. They spat energy bolts at the Institute's principal, each one capable of a numbing sting. A whole volley of them could prove lethal.

They were the least of the room's combat capabilities though. Larger smite drones, complete with hefty, armored front prows, slammed towards Cyclops from almost every angle, seeking to shatter bones or pitch him from one floor panel to another. Their assault was further enhanced by the fact that not all were actually real – powerful projectors in the room's ceiling created holographic echoes, a convincing mimicry of the buzzing machines that could distract from the real ones as they swooped in to strike. And, to top it all, energy nodes at different heights in the wall occasionally emitted linked beams of crackling force at random intervals, searing across the space between them.

Cyclops battled them all at once. Cipher watched as he vaulted from one floor segment to another, higher section, rolling as he landed to duck beneath one of the energy bolts. A flurry of attack drone bolts rained down like a shower of stinging, crimson rain on the space the X-Man had occupied a split-second earlier, scorching it. He rose and turned in one motion, his visor searing the attacking flock from existence with a beam of red brilliance that left Cipher's eyes aching.

A smite drone swung in from the left, its rotors screeching.

Cyclops made no move to stop it, instead side-stepping another volley of shots from a second attack drone swarm holding station near the dome's roof. The smite drone slammed into his side, or it would have, had it been anything more tangible than a projection. It shimmered and blinked from existence as Cyclops dropped down to a lower floor section rising to meet him, using the higher one to momentarily block the angle of the real drones shooting at him.

Cipher shifted to avoid one of the energy node beams, not taking her eyes off Cyclops. This was a side of him the rest of the school almost never saw – swift and deadly, a near-flawless blend of focus, control and strength. He made tactical decisions in a heartbeat and moved with total conviction. It wasn't even that his fighting style was flawless. Nobody's was, and the scorch marks on his X-suit and the light graze across right thigh and shoulder evidenced where he'd taken hits. He always recovered though, always kept fighting and resisting. As Cipher watched, he unleashed another optic blast from his glowing visor, bouncing the beam from one of the angled wall plates and deflecting it up to knock out half of the drone swarm that had been seeking out a new angle on him.

She knew she was watching a demonstration of why, even among the most talented X-Men, Scott Summers was considered a leader. There was more to today's exercise than that though. She had witnessed him training before. She had never, however, seen him moving with such underlying fury. His efforts in this session seemed to possess a particular edge, a degree of viciousness that rarely showed through. Cyclops wasn't just running through the motions in an advanced training program. He was fighting something much larger.

Another beam, bounced between no less than four different surfaces, shattered the last remaining drone units. As charred scraps of metal and melted plastic rained down around him, Cyclops stood, head bowed, panting. There was a sonorous whirr of hydraulics and the whine of systems powering down as the floor panels slowly began to retract and the wall sections folded back on themselves.

"Session completed," intoned the automated female voice of the Danger Room. "Threat Level Alpha, rescinded. Beginning cooldown protocols."

"Twenty-eight minutes and nineteen seconds," Cipher said. "A new personal best."

Cyclops turned sharply, looking right at her. Momentarily, Cipher felt as though he was about to unleash that burning red glow. She didn't flinch.

"You don't have permission to be in here," Cyclops said as the segment he was standing on reached the rest of the floor, sliding home with a heavy *thunk*. "In fact, you don't have permission to be out of your dorm."

"I know," Cipher said, still invisible as she allowed herself to float to the decking plates as well. "But there isn't a security system in the Institute that can keep me there. And unlike Jonas, I'm less likely to follow instructions based solely on authority."

"I told you after the incident with Victor that you were on your final warning, Alisa," Cyclops said, his tone harsh. "You've left me with no choice other than to have you expelled."

"I know," Cipher repeated. "That's all right. I'm leaving anyway. Jonas too."

She walked towards Cyclops as she spoke, picking her way over the broken remnants of the drones. It would take months to restock the Danger Room's supply of self-automated units. As she went, she dropped her invisibility, the tall, dreadlocked girl materializing right in front of her principal.

"Jonas and I have been talking," she said. "And I've been

thinking. You know where Victor is. You know, but you haven't gone after him."

"And why would you think that?" Cyclops demanded, his red lens focusing on Cipher.

"I wouldn't want to reveal your secrets, principal," she said with the barest hint of a smile. "I know how important those can be. But I think you need to admit why you haven't gone looking for Vic when you could have. I think it's much the same reason you're in here tonight, wrecking the Danger Room."

Cyclops half turned away, his facial expression dark. He was clearly unused to being lectured by a student, but then few were as piercingly incisive as Alisa was.

"Go on," he said in a guarded tone.

"You don't have the resources to go after Vic," Cipher surmised. "You want to. You want to get his dad back too. But Santo was your last card. There are no senior staff with mutant abilities left at the Institute except for you. Everyone's out on operation, trying to hold back the tide of hate that's swelling up everywhere."

She paused to see if Cyclops had anything to add, anything to deny. He stayed silent. She continued.

"So, your first duty is to continue to oversee the Institute. Not only that, but to guard it. You don't want to. You want to be out there, with your colleagues, your friends, taking the fight to the ones causing all the harm. But you're a dutiful man, Principal Summers. And if duty means staying buried beneath a mountainside running endless Danger Room drills while making sure no more kids get hurt, then so be it. If Vic decided to ignore that and go off looking for his dad, well, the safety of the rest of the school has to come first. So you've got to leave him to it, and hope Santo comes through."

Cipher stood watching Cyclops after she finished, her arms crossed. The principal turned back towards her, and this time his expression held a bitterness that his visor couldn't conceal.

"I'm glad you're one of the sharpest students at the Institute, Miss Tager," he said. "If you weren't, I'd be deeply concerned that one of my pupils has discerned so much."

"I get to see and hear a lot more than most students, principal," Cipher said. "Luckily for everyone, I can keep a secret."

"You're a nightmare to try and confine. I hope you know that."

"It's what I'm all about. And it's partly why I'm here. As I said, Jonas and I have been talking."

"You want to go after Victor," Cyclops said. It wasn't a question.

"We do," Cipher said. "We can help him. We're both confident in our abilities. And responsible." She added the last word as though it was the sort of thing she thought a school principal would want to hear.

"You yourself said I was still here because I took my duty to protect the pupils at this school seriously," Cyclops said. "But you expect me to sanction two more of you to head out into grave danger without my assistance?"

"And you admitted I was a nightmare to confine," Cipher pointed out in turn. "You know you can't stop me. You might be able to stop Jonas, but I doubt you want to deal with him without either myself or Vic around."

"So, this is a courtesy call," Cyclops said, looking unimpressed. "You're happy to get yourself and your friends expelled into the bargain?"

"If it means making sure Vic is safe, then yes. You know you couldn't have forced him to stay here, even if it was for his own safety. The same applies to me. Out there the odds are against Vic and Santo. With Jonas and with me, they start to become a bit more even. I thought you'd appreciate that."

Cyclops stood looking down at her. There was a deep rumble, and the heavy blast shutters surrounding the chamber began to slide upwards, exposing the reinforced windows and the data nodes and security ports that dotted the Danger Room. Throughout the school, dim lights brightened once more.

"Cooldown protocols complete," said the automated voice. "Please exit at your convenience."

"Return to your dorm, Miss Tager," Cyclops said.

"You're not going to give me permission to leave, are you?" Cipher asked.

"You said it yourself," Cyclops responded. "I have a duty to my students. All of them."

Graymalkin remembered to not look up as he sensed Cipher enter. He sat at the desk in his dorm in the pitch black, reading. The text was a magazine he'd found abandoned in the canteen, entitled *Life Choice Premium*. It seemed to contain nothing but poorly sourced anecdotes about people he could only assume were what passed for "celebrities" in the modern sense. None of them seemed worthy of interest, but if there was a whole magazine full of them, he supposed he should at least make an effort to learn about some of them.

He waited for Cipher to speak, trying not to give away his anxiety. He knew she had the news he'd been waiting for.

"I spoke to the principal," she said, as unannounced as ever. "He said no."

Graymalkin sighed, closed *Life Choice Premium*, and slid it back on top of the pile of hot gossip mags he'd acquired over the past two years. It was as he'd feared.

"Did he threaten us with further punishment?" he asked his invisible friend.

"He did," she confirmed. "He said he'll expel us. I think that might just be me though. He wasn't pleased that I left the dorms and went in the Danger Room when it was live."

"It was bold of you," Graymalkin admitted. "But I would not see you suffer alone, my friend. The plan was conceived by both of us."

"You don't have to come," Cipher said. "It may be difficult getting you out, for starters. You don't deserve to be expelled. The school is your home. There's no shame in that."

"If so, then you and Victor are my family," Graymalkin said. "One is not much without the other."

A sharp rap at the door cut through the conversation. Graymalkin froze. He sensed Cipher looking at him. He had not expected the principal's reprisals to begin so soon.

He stood up from his desk and opened the door onto the dorm corridor. One of the Institute's paid security detail – Graymalkin believed his name was Wilbur – was standing across the corridor, as far as humanly possible away from the door he'd just knocked on. Graymalkin recalled him from the diversionary opening of the Lower North hatch on the night they'd gotten Victor out. He'd never seen someone look at him with quite as much abject horror as the poor man had on that occasion. It seemed he still hadn't fully recovered from the experience.

"Principal Summers would like to see you in his office," he said haltingly. "He also said... if Miss Tager is in there with you, to ask her to come too."

"Thank you, Wilbur," Graymalkin said with a polite smile and eased the door half shut.

"The principal wishes to see us," he said to the approximate location of Alisa. The words came out level, but the thought of being ordered before Summers made him nervous. He was, in a sense, the father of the Institute, and Graymalkin had more than enough memories of being ordered into the presence of his father.

"He's probably going to formally expel us," Cipher said with a dash of scorn, showing none of the apprehension Graymalkin couldn't help but feel. "I wonder how long he'll give us to pack our bags."

"We should still speak to him."

"I already tried."

"Then I will," Graymalkin said, mustering his courage. "And I will let him know that nothing shall dissuade us from finding our friend."

"Well, if you're going to see him, I'd better come too," Cipher said. "Otherwise he'll probably think you're just trying to distract him while I run another escape attempt."

By the time they reached the principal's office, Cyclops had changed from his battered X-suit into a shirt and tie. It was strange to see him dressed formally, the vision of a smart, professional young educator thrown off somewhat by the continued glower of the ever-present visor.

"Please, have a seat," he said, looking up from an open folder as Cipher and Graymalkin entered. They took the proffered chairs opposite the desk.

"Miss Tager, I'd appreciate if you remained visible throughout this exchange," he went on.

"Yes, principal," Cipher said quietly, phasing into view. Cyclops nodded his thanks and spoke to Gray in turn.

"I assume, Mr Graymalkin, that you are aware Miss Tager spoke to me recently in the Danger Room."

"Yes, principal," Gray answered with stiff formality.

"You know that following the incident with Victor I made it clear any further infractions would see you both expelled from the Institute," Cyclops said.

"Yes, principal," Graymalkin and Cipher repeated together.

"I had a discussion with all three of you in this very office some time ago, when you were all new to the Institute," Cyclops continued, setting down the folder he'd been holding. "Jonas was struggling, and Alisa and Victor were bearing that struggle without sharing it. Do you remember what I told you all when I found out?"

Cipher and Graymalkin were silent. Cyclops went on.

"I told you that no one in this school ever carries a burden alone. That is the very essence of the Institute. Could either of you explain to me the purpose of what we do here?"

"To prepare promising young mutants for inclusion within the ranks of the X-Men," Graymalkin said, like he was reading from a college prospectus. "To furnish them with both a higher education and the practical skills necessary for them to better both themselves and wider society upon graduation."

"Ostensibly you are correct, Jonas, as usual," Cyclops said. "These are indeed the outcomes of what we do here. But they are not the core reason for the school's existence. They are merely byproducts. You are both orphans, are you not?"

"We are," Graymalkin said. Cipher said nothing.

"You are probably aware that you're not the only ones here in similar circumstances," Cyclops said. "When I was still a child, I believed my parents had been killed in an airplane crash. I grew up in the State Home for Foundlings in Oklahoma. My powers were partly activated by the trauma of that initial incident, and the difficulties of the years that followed."

"I'm sorry to hear that, Principal Summers," Graymalkin said.

"It's all right, Jonas," he responded. "It turned out for the best, eventually. But that isn't the case for all of us. The number of mutant children worldwide who are orphaned, abandoned, even attacked by their parents is many times higher than that of the average human population. It is a terrible weight that thousands of innocent mutants are forced to live with, some for as long as they can recall. But there are people, and organizations, out there that try to make a difference. The Institute is one of them. We are not just a school. We are, whenever and wherever possible, a family."

Silence followed the principal's statement. Graymalkin bowed his head slightly. Cipher sensed he had been affected by the words, but they rang colder for her.

"Like any family, we aren't always perfect," Cyclops carried on. "We make mistakes. We have arguments. But we don't give up on each other. We're a safe home for everyone who hasn't had one before. And when it feels like no one will listen, and no one cares, my door is always open. That may not mean much, but you made the choice to come through my door today, Alisa. You didn't need to. You could have left and none of us would have been able to stop you. I know you don't care about my authority. But you showed the Institute respect. I've taken note of that."

"I didn't want you to punish Graymalkin," Cipher said. "I thought it would be worse for him if I left without saying."

"I would not have shirked any punishment," Gray said firmly, looking from one to the other.

"I know," Cyclops responded. "Which is to your credit. Between the two of you, you've reminded me why families exist. A family supports. Vic was trying to support his own. And it's our job to support him. Your job. He's a part of your family. For that reason, go after him, both of you, and make sure he finds his father."

Cipher and Gray stayed silent, and a small smile crept over Cyclops's face.

"Well, it's not often I get to see both of you looking surprised. I only have two conditions to allowing you out of the Institute to find Victor."

"What are they?" Cipher asked, finding her voice.

"Firstly, that you don't leave until tomorrow morning. Get a good night's sleep. I suspect you'll need it. Secondly, I'd like you to both visit Mrs Borkowski before you go. She's been moved from the infirmary to Miss Frost's old room. I've tried to reassure her about her son, but she's mentioned you both on several occasions, and I think you might do a better job than me. Let her know some of the Institute's finest will be looking for him."

"I'm sure that's the least we can do," Graymalkin said. "Are we to assume, also, that there will be no further punishment for our actions?"

"Consider that chapter now closed," Cyclops advised. "Just remember what I said. A family looks out for one another. If you need something, if you're struggling for any reason, if you think you're lost or alone or afraid, the Institute is here for you. Keep your communicators with you and keep me up to date."

"We will," Cipher promised. "And... thank you, principal."

"There's one more thing you should be aware of," Cyclops said before they both stood up. "You know that Santo has been out seeking Dan Borkowski too. I should tell you that he intended to strike a Purifier recruitment sermon being run by Prophet Xodus earlier this evening. Since then, I've not had any communication from him. It's possible that he's been taken prisoner by the Purifiers. Or worse."

Cipher and Graymalkin exchanged a look. Vic was one thing, but Rockslide was a fully-fledged X-Man now. What did the Purifiers have up their sleeves that enabled them to take down someone as unrelenting and powerful as Santo?

"I will continue to try and make contact," Cyclops said. "But if we do find ourselves facing a worst-case scenario, I may have to call upon you to keep an eye out for Santo as well."

"If they've taken him prisoner, it's likely they'll be holding him wherever Victor's father is," Gray hypothesized. "They can't have that many secret secure locations in the vicinity of New York."

"That's what I'm hoping," Cyclops said. "Track down one, and you might find them both. And speaking of tracking, I have something that you might find very useful."

CHAPTER TWENTY-SIX

Italian-based pizza with extra pepperoni and mushroom slices. Vic inhaled the fresh scents of baked dough and mozzarella before picking out a slice and setting the cardboard box aside. God, sometimes he really missed pizza. The closest takeout place to the Institute was still distant enough to mean they only did bulk orders for dorm parties.

He bit into the slice and closed his eyes for a few seconds, savoring it. New York pizzas really were a cut above. He'd always demanded one whenever his parents had taken him to the city. Every few years they'd spend about a week with his aunt on Long Island, and Vic would refuse to eat anything but Gabriello's pizza.

The abrupt memory of the family outing turned the slick taste in his mouth bitter. He set the slice aside on top of the box, wiped his fingers on the accompanying napkin, and picked up the binoculars he'd bought from the camera shop on West Broadway the previous morning.

Four days had passed since he had snuck into Esson Electrical. In that time, he'd shifted his base of operations – or, more accurately, his rucksack – to the top of an apartment stack on 18th and 7th, not far from the Brooklyn Bridge. Gabriello's Oven

Pizzas was only two blocks away, which meant pizza for dinner every day. It had also allowed him to renew an old friendship with Mr Gabriello himself. The old baker hadn't seen Vic since he was a kid. How were Mr and Mrs Borkowski? How was home? Was school still going well? Had he applied to college? Vic turned his acting up a notch and lied through his teeth. It hurt, somewhere deep down inside, but it was all necessity now. Hunter, hunted, he was both and he was just doing what he had to in order to survive. He told Mr Gabriello that his parents were fine, that he was in NYC visiting his aunt, and that they all still missed his pizza – that, at least, was no lie. The garrulous big Italian had laughed and whacked him on the shoulder but, when Vic casually asked him to text anytime he happened to see Purifiers out on the streets, his expression had turned dark.

"You don't wanna fall foul of those guys, Vic," he'd said. "They're causing trouble for your type all over."

"Sure," Vic had replied. "That's why I want to know if they're in town. Gotta make sure I give them a wide berth."

Mr Gabriello had agreed wholeheartedly and sworn his delivery boys would be on the lookout. The eyes and ears of a dozen busy delivery drivers thus enlisted, Vic had secured his new bolt hole and paid a trip to the New York City Central Library.

It was a risk, just like visiting Gabriello's was a risk, but he knew he couldn't last in New York indefinitely without continuing to throw the dice. He'd made progress at Esson Electrical, and he made progress in the library too. Using a guest pass on one of their computers, he'd hunted for anything on the Sublime Corporation. They were a mid-level New York trader, buying and selling stock to help fund small startup operations, of which Esson Electrical was apparently one. The trail began to go cold after that. Besides a bland website, he could find little evidence of Esson Electrical actually doing electrical work. The other startups were much the same. The Sublime Corp board were similarly opaque. There were only a few trustees listed on their website, and company shares and holding listings were threadbare. At least he had an address for the headquarters.

He'd checked into a grimy Long Island motel that night under a false name, mostly just for a shower. All the while he'd kept his skin tone "human" and his hood up to hide his skull's carapace. It was a deceptively simple trick, but one that could serve in a pinch. He'd passed himself off as a kid with a rough skin condition before. After spending a dreamless night in a real bed, he'd checked out and taken up his new residence along New York's skyline. Being close to Gabriello's was one benefit of his change of location, but the main one was that his vantage point – nestled between two fuse boxes and a mess of antennas and bird droppings – afforded him a half-decent view of the front of the Sublime Corporation headquarters. The towering skyscraper dominated the intersection at the end of the street, its seemingly endless ranks of windows reflecting back the sunlight throughout the warm early August afternoons.

Vic adjusted the folding chair he'd bought with the binoculars and settled back onto his elbows, peering over the edge of the rooftop ledge. The street stretched away, a corridor of tiny, churning people and vehicles framed by the vast blocks of glass, steel, and red brick that towered like cyclopean gods on either side. At times like these, he was thankful he had a head for heights. He trained in on the far corner of the street, adjusting the focus ring to bring the base of Sublime Corp's soaring headquarters into sharp relief.

There was the usually steady flow of suits and ties entering and leaving the building from its frontal glass façade, a sight he'd grown accustomed to in the last few days. He now regretted calling the time spent under the Hudson Yards bridge monotonous. It was practically scintillating compared to this. Still, he forced himself to focus. He had to stay sharp, for Dad. If he didn't, he might as well go back to the Institute and admit defeat.

He was looking for anything abnormal or out of the ordinary visitors, but for the most part he was trying to gauge a way in. He'd already passed by the front of the building twice, hood up, pretending to be looking for a cab as he checked out the security arrangements on the main door. There was at least one guard, usually two on at all times, and there looked to be scanners inside the foyer beyond the doors.

He'd checked out the side entrances as well. There was a loading bay and several fire exits, but none appeared particularly busy and he had no doubt they were alarmed. This place was the real deal, not Esson Electrical. The best he'd been able to come up with so far was hitching a ride in on one of the mail trucks he'd seen delivering to the building in the early mornings and evenings.

He kept watch for another hour, trying not to let his mind wander, sweltering in the afternoon heat. Eventually he was forced to retreat to the shade of the roof's access stairwell, needing to regulate his body temperature. Camping out on Manhattan roofs in summer was a dirty, stinking, heatstroke-inducing job. It was certainly a long way from how he'd imagined his first mission playing out.

He allowed himself to doze off, shutting out the bustle of the city rising up from far below. He awoke to the buzzing of the communicator in his X-suit's pocket. Sitting up sharply, he fumbled for it and flipped the screen.

"Hey, kid," Mr Gabriello's gruff voice said over the speakers. "You about or what?"

"Was just grabbing a nap," Vic admitted, trying not to sound tired. "What's up Mr G?"

"One of my boys was delivering to the GenWave offices along 7th and he said he saw a bunch of kooks in black robes heading along the street. You said you wanted to know if any of those sorts were in town?"

"I did," Vic said, scrambling back to his chair and almost knocking his binoculars off the ledge and onto the street below. "Thanks, Mr Gabriello. I owe you big!"

"Anytime, kid," came the response as Vic trained the binoculars back on the Sublime Corp tower. He got it lined up and focused just in time to see a hint of black and white being ushered through the front doors by security. Had that been Xodus? It looked as though at least one figure had been in fully white robes rather than black? Whoever it was, it had to be Purifiers. That meant it was finally showtime.

Vic hefted his rucksack up from where he'd concealed it beneath a ventilation cover and delved inside for the robes and mask he'd stolen in Fairbury. He'd been planning this since discovering the location of the Sublime building. Well, planning was a rather grandiose word. His first objective was to get inside the building and doing it while the Purifiers were in town seemed like his most certain bet. He'd worried that the covert handover of cash and weapons he'd seen under the rail bridge meant that cultists wouldn't be visiting Sublime Corp in person, but apparently not. This was his opportunity.

He pulled on the robes – foul and musky enough to make him retch as he plunged his head into the black folds – and settled the leering mask into place before heading for the fire escape. He descended, struggling somewhat in the robes, and stepped out onto the street. He felt ridiculous in the getup, and the horrible mask once again made it difficult to see anything, but he forced himself across the road and along to the front of the towering Sublime building. *Get in character*, he told himself. Would a

Purifier be feeling awkward and embarrassed? No, he'd be confident in his sacred robes, proud of the fearful glances passers-by gave him. He was above earthly, mortal concerns. All he cared about was saving humanity by purging it of the filthy mutants.

It wasn't an easy role to play, but nothing drove character acting quite like necessity. As he climbed the steps to the front doors of the building, having to hike up his robe skirts as he went, a security guard blocked his way.

"Late for the party?" the large, jowly man demanded. Now it was all just down to self-confidence and a sharp wit. Vic was fine with that.

"I have a vital message for my great prophet," he said, trying to sound gruff, aided somewhat by the muffled effects of the mask. He was already overheating again in the accursed garments.

"I'm going to need to see some ID," the guard said, his expression one of disgust – clearly even Sublime's staff didn't like dealing with the cultists.

"The only identification I require is my purity brand," Vic said, completely winging it now. He kept his hands clasped in front of him and concealed in the sleeves of his robes. If he had to take them out, he could color-shift to a human skin tone, but it was hardly ideal.

"I must see the prophet," he went on, pressing desperately. "The fires of damnation await all who would impede me!"

That was how they always talked, right? The guard looked unimpressed. He took a step back and turned to speak into a hand radio. "My colleague will escort you up," he told Vic a moment later, his tone dispassionate.

Vic considered telling him he was sure he could find his own way, but he didn't want to push his luck. He waited by the front doors before a second security staffer appeared and stared straight ahead to avoid the looks of the suits passing in and out of the building. He could never have been a cultist, he decided. Even playing the role, the secondhand awkwardness was just too much.

The second guard appeared, a shorter, goateed man with a suspicious, sneering expression. He gestured at Vic. "This way then," he said. "Stick close. Mr L doesn't like your kind wandering free at headquarters."

"As you wish," Vic said, wondering who "Mr L" was as he followed the guard through the glass front doors. A large, tiled foyer lay before them, sectioned off by security gates. The guard led Vic through an open, deactivated one and on to an elevator in the lobby beyond. Inside he punched up the thirty-fourth floor – the third from the top, apparently – and waited.

"So, busy week?" Vic asked in his gruffest of voices. He knew he shouldn't speak, that he should just stand in silence for the five minutes it took to reach their destination, but it was too painful. He cursed himself silently as the guard just looked at him, lip curling slightly. The man said nothing.

He stood sweltering in his stolen robes, wondering what he'd gotten himself into this time. He was in, yes, but at what cost? He'd hoped to break free at some point, get rid of the robes and go chameleon so he could start snooping around. Sublime Corp was clearly up to some seriously shady business, the sort of stuff that trips to the New York Central Library weren't going to expose. But now he was in it seemed he'd be getting ferried directly to the top office. It looked as though he was going to meet Mr L, whether he wanted to or not.

The elevator stopped half a dozen times on its way up. On every occasion the suited men and women who'd called it hesitated on the threshold when they saw who was currently occupying it. No one got in.

There was a chiming sound. The thirty-fourth floor. Vic steeled himself as the door rumbled open. He didn't know what he was expecting. Some sort of den of villainy, replete with weapons racks and torture implements. Instead, an overwhelmingly bland office corridor presented itself, complete with a tough, blue-gray carpet, white walls and foam ceiling squares. At the end of it sat a black door, slightly ajar.

The security guard stepped out, glancing back after Vic. He began to follow down the corridor. The only break in the corporate sterility was a few pieces of artwork hanging on the otherwise undecorated walls. They were modern, abstract-looking, just long stretches of white canvas smeared and splashed with red paint. They made Vic feel uncomfortable.

As they reached the black door, he realized he could hear raised voices from beyond. The security guard seemed to think better about going any further. He paused and eased the door further open, then nodded for Vic to step through.

"I was more than clear," barked someone from beyond the door. "Under no circumstances were you or any of your idiot fanatics to visit me here!"

Vic briefly contemplated trying to take the guard out, but even with the element of surprise he knew there was no way he could manage that without alerting whoever was in the room, even in the midst of an argument. Instead he pushed past the glaring man and passed through the doorway.

The space beyond was large, probably taking up the entire tower block floor. Rows of tinted windows offered a near-uninterrupted 270-degree view of the jagged Manhattan skyline, while the floor underfoot consisted of black tiling that had been polished to a reflective sheen. The room was largely empty, but for a few strange-looking, warped, black ornaments and more of the abstract art on the wall either side of Vic. That, and the large semi-circular desk that sat in the very center of the room. Like the floor and the sculptures, it was glossy black, like freshly spilt oil. A section of it had risen up to expose a monitor screen, but apart from that its surface was completely empty.

There were Purifiers already in the room. Xodus was one of them, standing off to one side of the desk, his serene golden mask a counterpoint to the anger that charged the air. Three others flanked him, one in black and two in white, the latter pair a sharp contrast to the black surfaces surrounding them. Vic experienced the usual jolt of revulsion at the sight of the cultists, but he didn't get a chance to stoke his anger – the other figure in the room, the man sitting behind the desk, had already noticed him.

He was a slight-looking figure with delicate, sharp features, tanned, and with a black goatee that was as impeccably groomed as his suit and red-and-black striped tie. At first glance he would have appeared little different from any of the hundreds of other sharply turned out, image-conscious CEOs within a five-mile radius of the center of New York City. But two things disrupted the look. The first was the top of the man's head – the flesh was bloated and distended, as though his brain had swollen and ruptured his skull, leaving the skin lumpen and taut. The second incongruence was the man's expression. It bore the rawest, most terrible anger Vic had ever seen.

It didn't seem to animate his face the way rage normally did. It didn't leave him with a throbbing vein in his temple, or ruddy cheeks, or a clenched jaw. But it was there, in his pale gray eyes. While the face remained as controlled and refined as Prophet Xodus's angelic mask, those eyes blazed with a deep, almost maniacal wrath. They were the eyes of a man who appeared so unused to being disobeyed that they were now almost crackling with displeasure. Vic was forced to endure their fury as they turned on him. He nearly did an about-face and left immediately. He was frozen though, trapped in that gaze as he watched the wrath turn to something just as bad – a chilling curiosity.

"I told you, our communications are compromised," Prophet Xodus said in his bass, mechanical-laced intonation. It seemed he hadn't yet noticed where the man behind the desk was looking. "The one who sprang our trap wasn't the one you were seeking, but he may still be useful."

It was clear the man behind the desk wasn't listening any more. He cut off Xodus, without taking his eyes off Vic. "Who… is that?"

There was a rustle of robes as the four Purifiers turned in unison to look at him. Vic remained rooted to the spot, lanced by the suited man's penetrating gaze, like a moth pinned to a lepidopterist's specimen board. He had to move, to say something, anything, but he couldn't.

"What are you doing here, you idiot?" Xodus buzzed, anger now coloring his own voice. "I told you to wait with the truck!"

"The truck…" Vic mumbled, forcing himself to look at the prophet and not the man who had just been haranguing him. "The truck was attacked, O holy one. Seized. The X-Men."

He knew he was coming across as a complete idiot, but he hoped that was what an average Purifier grunt sounded like. Perhaps his disheveled robes would lend credence to his on-the-spot invention? He wanted to know if the security guard was still behind him at the door, but he didn't dare turn around.

"Which of the X-Men was it?" Xodus barked, taking a step towards him. "Was it the boy, or one of the less valuable mutants? Were they searching for the boy's father?"

Vic caught himself. *Less valuable*? *Father*? They had to still have his dad. He suspected that part of the Purifiers' efforts were being targeted at him deliberately, but hearing it stated like that struck home. Why him? Why were they going out of their way to find him?

"You really are a fool, Xodus," said the man behind the desk. Vic realized with a sickening feeling that his voice was the same slick, horrible one he had heard over the phone at Esson Electrical.

"I've held off calling you one because I considered you to be at least a useful fool," he went on. "Until now. I know Sublime Corp doesn't bankroll any of you for your brains, but really? It surely doesn't take a savant to work out that our visitor here isn't one of your cultists."

Xodus hesitated, appearing not to understand. The man at the desk went on, now with a terrible smile on his lips.

"The only question is, just who is he? Judging by the fact that he appears to have stumbled in on us without any obvious premeditated plan, I suspect it's someone without experience. Certainly not a real X-Man. But someone with courage all the same. And, presumably, someone who has had a previous encounter with your underlings, Xodus, hence the robes and mask."

"Preposterous," Vic said, grasping desperately at a means to worm his way out of the situation. He backed up but butted into the security guard still at the door. "I am as faithful a child of the purification as any in this room!"

"Imposter," Xodus growled at Vic, finally catching on. "I will remove his mask, Lobe, and make his true identity known."

"Well?" the man behind the desk said, the words now directed at Vic. "This is what I assume you've been waiting for? Aren't you going to strike?"

In the tiny window of opportunity afforded to him, Vic did the cleverest thing he could think of. He snatched his robes up over his head – taking the grotesque with them – and flung it all in a bundle at the closest Purifier. Then he ran straight for the bank of windows nearest to the door.

The room exploded in violent motion. Both the Purifiers and the guard at the door rushed at him, shouting.

"It's the lizard," Xodus bellowed frantically. Vic danced past the first white-robe and ducked beneath the snatching arm of the second. The window was right ahead, and beyond it, Manhattan. Vic didn't contemplate what he was about to do. He just told himself it would all be fine and charged the glass pane.

He slammed into it head-first, his ridged, bony carapace doing its job. He felt the glass crunch and give, his X-suit and tough hide preventing him from being lacerated as his momentum carried him right through the window and out into nothingness.

Suddenly there was no floor, only the distant tarmac of thirty-four levels below. His stomach lurched and clenched up. His skin bristled, shifting instinctively. He would have cried out, but the wind of the sudden freefall tore his breath away.

In a few seconds he'd be a smear on the New York sidewalk, like one of those horrible pieces of artwork in the office corridor. He lashed out, blindly, panicking. His hand hit a surface with a shuddering impact.

Twist, hold. No. He'd struck one of the lower windows and halted his fall for a split second. It wasn't enough. He was plummeting too fast, and the surface was too smooth. He lashed out again, with both his hands and his tongue this time.

A jarring impact. Still not enough – he was still falling, his hands and tongue ripped painfully free from the surface by gravity. But his desperate stranglehold had been enough to decrease the speed of the plummet. Still, his head spun. He couldn't breathe. He struck out one last time and–

Suction. Grip. His body jolted as he was stopped, the windowpane beneath him juddering. He slammed his feet against it for good measure, desperate to banish that falling sensation. The window continued to quiver, but the glass held. His tongue had latched on too, smearing a great arc of saliva across the pristine surface.

As he clung there, his limbs locked and tense, he realized he looked through the window and into an office block beyond. Dozens of faces stared at him aghast from above monitor screens and work cubicles. Slowly, a thick wad of drool from further up the window dolloped down onto his head.

It wasn't the sort of display he liked to put on for an audience but needs must. Grimacing, he detached his tongue from the pane and, carefully, began to turn. He had to get to the base of the tower fast, just not freefall fast. The grip was precarious though, and even for someone who didn't suffer from vertigo, a head-first scurry down a sheer wall of glass to a concrete surface was somewhat daunting.

He worked his way carefully off the skyscraper's flank. As he did so he found himself – ridiculously – thinking about the fact that since he'd come to New York he'd licked both a car park door handle and an office window. He was definitely going to catch something.

He heard someone cry out from below. People started to gather around the spread of shattered glass that had preceded him. One woman was pointing. He'd have probably said something sassy-terrible like "take a pic, it lasts longer" if he hadn't been so focused on maintaining his ever-sliding grip on the building's flank and not receiving a broken neck once he reached the ground.

Three floors, two, one. He leapt the last length, landing in a crouch, head bowed, glass crunching beneath him. Flawless. No time to savor it though – he leapt back up and cast about, reorienting himself with the Sublime tower's front doors. The crowd that had initially gathered around him backed off with a gasp.

"Stop him!" shouted a voice. A section of onlookers parted hurriedly. The security guard from the front doors, accompanied by two others, rushed down the steps towards Vic. He was sure there'd be worse following.

Time to go. He slipped through the crowd, none of them daring stop him, and began to run.

The Purifiers came to a stumbling halt as they saw Victor disappear through the shattered glass and over the window ledge. Wind blowing in from the hole snatched at their robes. Xodus turned his masked face back to Lobe, apparently frozen in shock.

Lobe hadn't moved from behind his desk. He steepled his hands before him, his voice now filled with ice.

"The mutant can climb walls, my dear prophet. My people are already in pursuit. Get down there and bring that creature back to me, or not even divine protection will save you."

CHAPTER TWENTY-SEVEN

Victor ran for his life.

A spiky green lizard boy being chased through the streets of New York by bellowing security guards apparently wasn't a shocking sight for the locals, at least not enough to clear him an adequate path. People gasped and jostled out of his way, but the pressure of the mass of bodies occupying the sidewalk still slowed him down. His sharp senses allowed him to duck and weave between stumbling people while his pursuers were forced to elbow them out of the way, but Vic still didn't fancy his chances of making a clean escape. This had all gone very wrong very quickly, and right now he only wanted to put some clear space between him and everyone who wanted to kidnap or kill him.

It would have been nice to pause and trust in his chameleon abilities, but there was too much movement and shifting light around him. He'd only attract more attention. Instead, he took to the road. Traffic slowed to a crawl as the late afternoon rush hour approached. He used that to his advantage, running past stalled vehicles before diving back onto the sidewalk whenever the cars started moving again. At one clogged intersection he took to the center of the road, his head down and limbs pumping. Cars, at least half of them bright yellow taxis, stretched away from him seemingly endlessly on either side, while the skyscrapers and tower blocks appeared to loom over him, a thousandfold windows peering down at him like magnifying glasses assessing a fleeing insect. Everything became a blur as he pushed himself faster, harder, even his unique physiology beginning to hit its limits.

The moment of focused flight was broken when someone opened a car door directly in front of him. He had the barest chance to react. He directed his motion towards the car itself and, knowing he had no hope of slowing his momentum, leapt.

There was a thud as he landed on top of the taxi, rocking it on its tires. Someone screamed. He carried right on, rolling off the front hood, his skin momentarily flashing bright yellow in sympathy with the bodywork. He landed on all fours and was up and running again in a single motion, his mind buzzing.

Reflexes, reflexes. He didn't really know where he was going, except that it was away from Sublime Corp. He had to get back in control. Stop panicking.

He dared to slow his pace and wove back onto the sidewalk, throwing a glance behind him as he went. People stared after him and several vehicles he'd dashed past hit their horns in protest, but there was no sign of the Sublime Corp security. He dropped his pace further, feeling his heart rate beginning to ease off. There was no way they could have kept up with him.

The moment's reprieve didn't last long. He was quickly reminded that security weren't the only ones after him. At an intersection a truck tore past, ignoring a red light. The open trailer was packed with half a dozen masked Purifiers, all armed.

Vic hissed, a reptilian instinct, his tongue flicking the muggy air. Xodus had a whole team in town with him, and now they knew he was here. He didn't want to risk staying in Manhattan. He had to find a way to get out without drawing attention.

That was going to be easier said than done. Now that he'd slowed down, he was attracting more gasps and whispers. One kid being dragged along by his father even pointed at him and started shouting gleefully.

"X-Man! X-Man!"

Even without a powerful corporation's security guards and a gang of religious fanatics hunting him, a scaly green kid running about New York in an X-suit was a recipe for disaster. He shifted as best he could and headed back out onto the street while the traffic light was still red. With so much movement and so many reflective surfaces about, getting an even half-convincing color-shift on was almost impossible, but it would be a lot easier once he'd hitched a lift.

He grabbed onto the rear ladder of a hefty oil truck as it idled at the lights, getting a face full of exhaust fumes as he clung to it. His body melded with the rust-streaked white of the main tank section, glad to have something solid and stationary to mimic. He felt the metalwork beneath him thrum and vibrate as it began to move, the lights now green. The shouting, staring people were left behind.

The vehicle turned at the junction, the abrupt lurch forcing Vic to grab onto the vapor venting pipe to his right and lock on to avoid being tossed free.

He was moving, that much was positive. He focused on staying shifted, trying not to stare at the vehicles on either side. If the map in his head was correct, he was currently headed south-east. He just had to avoid being noticed by any Purifiers, and hope the truck carried him to Long Island.

He tried to collect his thoughts as he held on. At a glance, his plan to infiltrate Sublime Corp had nearly ended in disaster –

and it still might. Even if he escaped, the Purifiers knew he was in New York. That was the immediate negative. The positive was that he'd put a name and a face – well, a horrible, bloated head, anyway – to the position of Sublime Corp CEO. Lobe. What sort of a name was that anyway? It seemed as strange and unsettling as the man himself. Nobody had made Vic feel as uncomfortable in so short a space of time as he had, and that was saying something.

But all the big questions remained. Who was Lobe beyond his high-ranking business role, why was he supplying the Purifiers? Before Vic had crashed the party, it had sounded as though he was tearing into Xodus and the Prophet, himself so fiery, so intimidating, so full of strength and demented zeal, had been taking it. What sort of a man did that make Lobe? The obvious answer seemed to be "someone not to mess with." But Lobe knew where his father was. And that made Lobe his new number one priority.

The oil truck lurched heavily again, turning on itself as it took a short loop road. Vic grimaced, realizing that in his haste to grab onto the back earlier he'd loosened one of the fume vents next to him. The turn had caused something that looked clear and smelled very much like oil to begin leaking down the back of the main tank and onto the road behind.

"Wonderful," he muttered before pulling himself up the rear ladder and onto the roof of the tank, latching on hard. The last thing he needed was to get covered in exhaust fumes. He had no idea when he'd next get a chance to wash.

His new perch on the truck's top afforded him a view of where he was going, along with a welcome sense of relief. Ahead, rising up like the window supports of a great, red-bricked cathedral, were the two stone arches that marked the entrance to Brooklyn Bridge. The Stars and Stripes were fluttering hopefully over them, red, white and blue in the smoggy, late afternoon sun. They were his ticket out of Manhattan and out of the net he sensed closing around him. There was no way the Purifiers had the numbers to cordon off an area as large as Long Island as well. He just had to get there then he could regroup and reassess.

He kept clinging to the roof of the oil tank as it rolled up onto the crossing from the curve of the slip road. The bridge was split along its length by a raised pedestrian walkway, the timber boards to the left just slightly higher than the truck's roof. Vic could only hope the people crowding along it taking selfies didn't clock the lizard boy glued to the top of the passing truck.

They'd just reached the first of the two great, cyclopean brick arches that framed the bridge when he felt the truck slowing. He craned his neck so he could see over the front cabin, hunting for the reason the traffic on the bridge's three south-east bound lanes was decelerating. The answer wasn't what he'd been hoping for.

The middle of the bridge had been obstructed. One of the ubiquitous, scrapyard-style Purifier trucks had just slewed across the lanes, almost causing a pile-up. Masked and armed cultists were piling out of the back and bellowing angrily at the closest stalled vehicles. One had even lit up a torch.

This was just what Vic had feared most. The way ahead was blocked, and if more Purifiers were coming from Manhattan, the route back was about to be as well. He shouldn't have just gone for the closest bridge. He was supposed to be a good strategist. Stupid, stupid, stupid.

He glanced up at the pedestrian walkway running parallel alongside the road. No Purifiers up there yet, but it was now crowded with people taking pictures of the traffic jam and the sinister gang who'd caused it. Were there no cops? Nobody with the authority to make these zealots move? Vic knew it was pointless hoping for that. If the police were on their way, they wouldn't get here before the Purifiers reached the oil truck. And once they did, even if they didn't initially spot him on top of it, he was sure the crowd watching from the boardwalk just above and to his left would. There was no way there wouldn't be a commotion, and then he was done for.

What if he leapt to the boardwalk right now? But that would also cause a disturbance in the crowd. What about hiding among the thick, tan-colored struts that supported the pedestrian section? But if he jumped for that he'd definitely be seen. The Purifiers had reached the Ford Focus directly in front of the oil truck. He was taking too long! Make a decision!

Just go now, he told himself. *Get back along the bridge as far as possible, then get beneath the boardwalk.* He turned and bolted for the end of the oil tank, dropping off it onto the asphalt. As he did so he narrowly avoided the oil slick that was spreading from the rear of the truck. It was growing larger by the second, flushing from the now-ruptured valve. That was a real recipe for disaster.

Turned out he was in the middle of a disaster anyway. His twist to avoid the oil carried him almost to the side of the truck, and right into the path of a Purifier questioning the driver of the Ford in front. The terrible silver mask turned and caught Vic in its leer.

Vic ran in the opposite direction. This time though, he didn't get far. There were more black-robed bodies ahead, turning at the gasps and shouts that arose from the spectators on the boardwalk as they realized what was happening.

A gunshot rang out. The shouts became screams. Vic came to a full halt. Gunfire on a crowded bridge, and a rapidly spreading oil slick too – this had to stop, or a lot of people were going to die.

"Get back!" he yelled up at the boardwalk, then repeated it at the surrounding cars, rapping a fist on a windshield for emphasis. "Everyone get out and get off this bridge! Now!"

The people on the walkway weren't taking pictures and videos any more. Pushing and shoving had started as they tried to scatter, confined by the railings. Those in the cars were slower to react, only a few people beginning to exit their vehicles. A few others simply opened their doors and peered out or lowered their windows. The realization that this was a lot more than just a traffic jam had only just started to dawn on them.

Vic didn't know where to go. Up and onto the walkway? He wouldn't put it past the Purifiers to open fire and mow down half the crowd. Over the side and into the river? He didn't like the look of the fall, let alone the swim afterwards. Could he fight his way past them?

"Come on, move!" he tried to urge the people getting out of their cars. "This whole bridge could go up at any second!"

That got a better response. The oil truck driver had been hauled from his cabin by the Purifiers. They were letting people stream past them, but they were closing in. Some had firearms, including the same sort of energy weapons Vic had seen under the rail bridge.

The cars immediately around him were almost all abandoned now, and the cultists had let the truck driver go. Vic moved to the struts beneath the walkway, intending to bolt through them to the other side. That was when he saw the Purifier carrying the lit torch. The man was gibbering some sort of prayer or incantation, waving the naked flame towards his kindred, as though blessing them.

Time seemed to slow. He cried out in desperation, trying to get the fool to turn back. Too late. Far, far too late. The man, probably half-blind in his grotesque, stepped right into the slick that had spilled from the rear of the oil truck, passing through the fumes venting from the broken valve at the same time.

There was a rushing whoosh, and blue flame ignited and soared from the puddle at the Purifier's feet up to the loose valve. Vic flung himself behind the nearest vehicle.

The explosion seemed to tear the very heart out of the bridge. Vic felt the heat before the sound and fury of the blast hit him. Without his gnarly skin and his X-suit, he expected it would have seared the flesh from his bones. Even though the car took the worst of it, he was still picked up and flung back against the lower struts of the walkway, his cry of fear and pain stolen away in the whooshing rush of vaporizing moisture.

Then came the light and the sound, leaving him blind and deaf. He collapsed to the asphalt and rolled onto his back – it was scorching hot to the touch. He thought he was on fire, burning up, consigned to immolation. It was just like one of Xodus's sermons. He tried to scream but choked instead.

His eyesight returned, slowly and painfully. He wasn't on fire, but the heat remained. Flames surrounded him, a conflagration that had engulfed the western half of the bridge, slicking across the concrete and eating up the stanchions and struts with terrifying hunger. The car that had saved him was a blazing, melting wreck with black smoke broiling from it. Row after row of other vehicles also caught fire, leading to another tanker down the way. When it caught flame, a second explosion punched a shockwave out over the structure, making all of the ignited vehicles shudder.

Vic choked again and tried to summon some spit, raising an elbow to cover his mouth as he got up onto his knees. The exposed parts of his skin felt tender and sore, and his eyes stung from the smoke and heat, but he was still in one piece, and he wasn't on fire, yet. That was a start, he tried to tell himself. He crouched, searching desperately for a route out. He found none. His entire existence had been reduced to a few dozen paces of blazing metalwork and rapidly dissolving asphalt, walls of flame sealing off any path either forward or back.

That left only the sides. The river edge was several burning cars away, and he didn't want to negotiate a passage through the combusting substances spilling from them. The walkway was at his back. It hadn't yet caught light. It was his only hope.

He dragged himself onto his feet and jumped for the struts holding up the boardwalk. He met the metal, and agony exploded along his fingers and palms. The struts were scalding hot. He let out an agonized moan, but his reptilian grip ensured he didn't let go. He began climbing instead, hand over hand, scaling the scorching metal frame as quickly as possible. He didn't get far before he felt something clamp around his ankle.

He looked down and realized that one of the Purifiers had survived the initial blast. The man howled in rage, his robes ablaze from head to foot. Vic stared wide-eyed down into a silver mask that appeared to be melding with the face underneath. Fingers clawed at him, trying to drag him back down into the fires of hell.

He kicked out manically, dislodging the cultist's grip and sending him tumbling. Trying his best not to breathe in, he scrambled up the remaining struts and spilled up onto the timber boards above. Only then did he allow himself to drag in a desperate, choking gasp, one that was only half-free of the toxic smoke boiling up from below.

How much longer before the boardwalk burst into flames too? He had to keep moving. A hand covering his mouth, he stood and turned towards Manhattan. The route to Long Island was completely blanketed in black smoke, and it was right next to where the tanker had gone up. He couldn't risk pushing on that way. Before him the twin arches of the one hundred fifty-year-old bridge soared upwards, smoke coiling and rising from around their solid red bricks, the Stars and Stripes still fluttering above them. The flag looked small and forlorn, a little dash of color against the encroaching smog of fumes and ash.

The smoke directly ahead of Vic eddied, disturbed as a shape moved through it. His heart picked up its pace as he saw a golden gleam through the ruinous miasma, and a heavy, black-clad bulk that materialized with it.

Xodus had caught up with him. The Purifier advanced along the walkway towards Vic, emerging through the smoke like a demon summoned up from the infernal realms. The fanatic's mask, ironically so angelic, seemed to gleam and shimmer in the firelight, staring directly into Vic's soul.

The hulking zealot halted and extended one powerful-looking hand. "Surrender yourself," he intoned, his mask's vocalizer buzzing. "Even the mutant is not beyond salvation if he submits and confesses his sins. Come with me now, or you shall be consigned to the flames."

"What does your master want with me?" Vic demanded, taking a step back as he tried to assess his options. The vehicle section of the bridge to his left was a cauldron of fire and smoke now, and it had touched off stationary, abandoned vehicles on the right-hand lane now as well. The walkway remained a bridge over a lake of fire, but he feared it would be seconds, rather than minutes, before the wooden sections combusted or the struts began to give out. His only route was back, likely into more flames, or ahead, into Xodus.

"I answer only to the divine," the prophet declared, his hand still outstretched.

"Lobe didn't look divine to me," Vic shot back. The angelic mask offered no reaction, but the Purifier dropped his hand.

"He is just another instrument of the Great Will," he said. "Like all of us. Now, surrender. I will not offer you another chance."

Vic didn't have time for further retorts. He crouched and leapt, landing gracefully on the walkway's right-hand railing and attempting to spring past Xodus. The prophet responded with a savage, well-honed speed, and Vic caught the flash of steel just in time to launch himself from the railing and back onto the boardwalk.

Xodus brought the blade he had drawn from his robes down to the *en garde*, the tip gleaming. Vic recovered his balance, taking in the sight of the medieval-style arming sword.

"Seriously?" he demanded. "You're not a knight templar, big guy. The Middle Ages want their aesthetic back."

Xodus lunged. Vic was driven back three, four, five paces, on his tiptoes now. He'd taken fencing classes in the Institute – heck, only Striker and a couple of others scored higher with a sword than he did in training – but he currently had nothing to meet the oncoming Purifier with. Besides, rapier versus broadsword on a narrow walkway in the middle of a conflagration wasn't exactly a matchup he'd had much practice at.

He knew his fists better, and his speed. Xodus seemed fast for his size, but he wasn't Anole-fast. Vic kept retreating as far as he dared along the walkway, drawing him in before switching back to his front foot. He whipped in and snatched Xodus's wrist with one hand, pinning the blade to one side. He went in past his guard with a left hook, right to the angel's face. *Crack!*

He instantly regretted the strike as pain blossomed across his knuckles. He was committed now though. He let go of Xodus's wrist with his right hand and slammed that one home too, then back in with his left. *Crunch!*

The prophet reeled away, but got his blade back up before Vic could press his advantage any further.

"You're slow, prophet," he taunted, panting slightly, hoping the brute couldn't see the pain of his bruised knuckles in his face. "Shouldn't have brought a sword to a fist fight."

Xodus emitted a raw, static-cracked bellow and threw himself back onto the attack. Vic had been counting on riling him up, but the speed and aggression almost caught him off guard. He had to backpedal fast, razor-sharp steel parting the smoke inches from his face.

The Purifier paused his attack, appearing to collect himself after his momentary loss of control. Advantage Victor. He lunged in, again ignoring the tip of the sword, knowing that once he was past it, the Purifier was essentially defenseless. This time though, Xodus welcomed him.

The prophet didn't seem like the finest swordsman, but he had strength and size. Vic realized too late that he'd allowed him to bypass his blade, body-checking the mutant instead.

Vic grunted as he collided with him, getting a face full of stinking black robes. Xodus grappled with him, trying to fix an arm around his neck in a choke hold. Up this close, Vic could hear the buzzing of his breath wheezing through his mask's vocalizer, smell the stink of him, like stale sweat and brimstone, and feel the iron-hard potency of the muscles beneath the robes. The raw strength, the maniacal fervor there, left him in no doubt that he wouldn't win the contest like this. Luckily, he had other plans.

In fighting to keep down Vic's arms and get a grip on his throat, Xodus had neglected his own face. Vic planted his toes and slammed his head up and forward.

Xodus hadn't reckoned with the thick carapace and bony ridges that plated Vic's skull. There was a splitting, cracking noise as the center of his head met the Purifier's mask. The grip on Vic instantly vanished as Xodus stumbled back. He attempted to follow up again, but a desperate, seemingly blind slash of the sword kept him at bay.

Xodus recovered, standing firm, but there was a quiver in his blade now. His mask was cracked too – a fissure ran down from beneath its left eye. It looked as though the angel was weeping.

Vic was about to summon up another taunt, hoping to trigger a fresh attack, when a crashing sound behind him forced him to turn. A section of the boardwalk had collapsed, the empty space filled with a great surge of fire, smoke and sparks. The fresh blaze of heat almost drove Vic back into Xodus, coughing and flinching.

"Feel the fury of the fires of absolution, mutant scum!" Xodus declared, brandishing his sword triumphantly towards the rising flames.

Vic couldn't fight this. Smoke filled his lungs, making breathing difficult, and his body couldn't regulate the intense heat rising up around him. He was out of time. Flames started to run along the boards at his feet. In desperation he leapt once more onto the railing bars and from there threw himself onto one of the metal beams that ran from the walkway across the top of the vehicle lanes underneath. The space gaping below Victor was a cauldron of fire, the heat and smoke almost overwhelming. The beam itself seemed practically molten, and every step was agony. He fought on, though, somehow keeping his balance amidst it all, trusting his abilities to stop him from mis-stepping and plunging into the inferno.

To his horror, Xodus came after him. He had none of Vic's youth, poise or reptilian skills, yet he forged onto the beam in pursuit without even hesitating. He was madman, yet he kept his own footing, even as part of his hem caught fire. The material had to be flame-resistant, for it didn't spread further, but even stepping along the beam must have been like torture. Yet still he came, following Vic until he was standing on the very edge of the Brooklyn Bridge.

The waters of the East River surged far below him, dark and bitter. He turned his back on the sheer drop, confronting Xodus as the Purifier bore down on him once again. How the man still stood, let alone fought in the midst of the heat and smoke, Vic had no idea. He just knew he wasn't going to stop.

Xodus lowered his sword, the tip barely a foot from Vic's

breast. Fire and ash broiled around him hellishly, sparks dancing across the visage of the prophet's serene, cracked mask.

"I have you now," the broken angel snarled.

Vic lashed out, as much for support as to drive Xodus back. He snagged the collar of the black robes in the claws of his right hand. Xodus tried to disentangle him. For a few breathless, furious seconds they grappled on the precipice. Then, with a bellow of effort, Xodus raised his sword in his other hand and slashed down, once.

Pain the likes of which he had never known suffused Victor. He might have screamed. He didn't know. The pain was everything, right up until he felt his stomach lurching and his world turning end-over-end.

He was falling, he realized. Falling in agony, in despair. Falling to his death. He got a glimpse of the bridge soaring above him, engulfed in fire. The dark shape of Xodus stood, silhouetted against the inferno as he watched him fall. His world turned over again, and he stared down, down at the churning cold waters of the East River, rushing to meet him.

An impact. An icy, penetrating chill. Still, there was agony. Then darkness.

CHAPTER TWENTY-EIGHT

When Victor had been younger, his mother and father had bought him a pet lizard. It was an obvious attempt at helping him come to terms with his unique biology, and it succeeded. The creature was a knight anole, the largest species of the *Dactyloidae* family of reptiles. Vic had bonded with it instantly. He'd perceived himself in its rough green scales and climbing abilities and had been fascinated by its neck frills and unblinking intensity. It had lived in a light box on his desk, a constant, cold-blooded presence in his earliest memories. He'd named it "Sir Anole" and had insisted on being addressed as its squire. At some point, he'd begun to address himself as Anole too.

He dreamt of Sir Anole as he drowned, and afterwards too. It was a strange, listless dream. The creature was in pain, locked away in its little box, and he could not help it.

"You are wrong," the lizard croaked, for in this reality it could speak. "I am not in pain. You are."

"I'm fine," he reassured it, his face pressed up against the light box glass. The heat lamp within pulsed and stuttered, its power fading on and off. "I'm fine, really."

But he wasn't. None of them were. Mom, Dad, Gray, Ci, Santo,

Cyclops, the Institute. Any of them. And certainly not him. He lied about not being in pain, because he was an actor, and what was acting but lying to a knowing audience? But it hurt so bad that a part of him was sure he was dying.

Or already dead. Drowned.

Vic opened his eyes and sat up with a gasp. He immediately regretted the sudden motion. Pain flared through his body. It felt as though his skin was on fire.

Fire. He remembered that. Water too and just as unwelcome. Cold, dark waves that consumed him as greedily as the bright, scorching flames had. They all wanted to eat him up, until there was nothing left between them.

He fought to shake off the fever-dream. What had happened? Where was he?

He tried to take in his surroundings without moving too much. He appeared to be in a small, rectangular room composed of blue steel, the walls corrugated. It was stuffy and warm, partly because of the orange and black portable power generator and the two lamps and laptop it was rigged up to, set up on a foldout camp table in one corner. Much of the floor space was taken up by two inflatable mattresses and a foldout chair. There were several rucksacks stacked by what he took to be the door. He was lying on the only real bed, another foldout piece of camping kit. The mattress dug into his spine.

He looked down, tentatively. He was still in his X-suit. His head ached. He reached up to check his carapace, and as he did so a horrible realization dawned.

The arm he was reaching up with was no longer there.

He let out a cry of dismay. The pain across his body had been so general, and his confusion so total, that he'd only just spotted the fact that his right arm now ended just below his shoulder joint. The severed end was a semi-translucent mass of soft, tender-looking flesh. The sight of it made him feel sick and sent a shudder running up this back.

"Oh my God," Victor moaned, covering the numb shock he felt with vanity. "My acting career is finished."

"If you think you need both arms to be an actor then you really are an idiot," said a voice from nowhere. Vic yelped with surprise and twisted in his bed, once more regretting the movement – his rough skin was tender, the presumed aftereffects of recently being caught at the heart of a raging inferno.

"Ci?" he asked out loud. "Please tell me I'm not dead and this isn't some sort of weird afterlife?"

Cipher bled swiftly into existence, standing in front of the camp table and its laptop. She smiled, though Vic couldn't help but notice the tiredness and concern beneath the expression.

"Good to see you're awake," she said. "It's been almost a full day since we fished you out of the river. Jonas was getting worried."

"The river," Vic responded, his thinking still sluggish. He remembered falling, that terrible impact of icy cold. The East River. So, he'd survived it after all. Not fully intact though.

"My arm…" he began before trailing off, looking forlornly down at his stump. Now that he was fully conscious, he was aware of the pain – it was a deep, dull ache, separate from the soreness of his singed scales.

"I'm sorry about that," Cipher said. "We don't know how you lost it. There was no sign of it when we got to you."

"How?" Vic demanded, questions now beginning to jostle and compete with the misery of his missing limb. He fought the urge to reach out and touch her with his remaining hand, to check she was actually flesh and bone and not another dream or phantom. "How did you get me out of the river? How did you find me? And why are you here? Where's Gray?"

"Slow down," Cipher advised, moving from the laptop to sit

in the chair nearer Vic's bed. "Jonas is with us, but not just now. He's doing recon outside. It's the middle of the night, so he's in his element."

"Where's outside?" Vic asked cautiously, still not entirely convinced he hadn't perished in the East River and been consigned to some strange, cramped, stuffy afterlife with simulacrums of his best friends to keep him company for eternity.

"Red Hook docks," Cipher said. "Near the Atlantic basin, opposite Governors Island."

"So, Brooklyn," Vic surmised. "And… we're inside a shipping container, aren't we?"

"It's an Institute safehouse," Cipher said. "I told Jonas it was our safecrate, but he didn't really get it."

"I mean, I doubt the Institute could afford to keep an actual New York apartment on as a full-time safehouse," Vic said, managing a smile. "As long as we don't get hoisted onto any freighters, we should be OK."

"They'd be in for a nasty shock if we were," Ci said. Vic thought for a second before carrying on, piecing together what had happened.

"So, what's the deal?" he asked, his eyes dragged back down once more to his stump. He found the lumpen, jelly-like flesh at the end of it morbidly fascinating. "Don't tell me Cyclops expelled you both after you busted me out?"

"No," Cipher said. "Well, nearly. He tried confining us to our dorms. Didn't work."

"Who'd have thought," Vic said, forcing himself to stop staring at his wound and look back at Cipher. "You decided to break out too?"

"Not exactly," Cipher said, sounding almost uncomfortable. "I went and talked to Summers. I convinced him to let us come after you."

"What, seriously?" Vic asked. "And he just let you go?"

"Yep."

"What's the catch? Let me guess, you have to bring me right back to the Institute?"

"Nope. No catch. He made us sit through another speech about the Institute and the value of family. But I talked him around. I told him I could leave anytime I liked, but I was doing it by the book."

"Things really must be desperate then," Vic said. "You shouldn't have come. I told you not to follow. It's not worth the risk."

"If we hadn't, you'd be dead," Ci said firmly. Vic inclined his head, feeling chastened.

"I'm sorry," he said. "I owe you, big time. Gray too. But I still want to know how you found me."

"You think Summers gave you a new communicator just to replace your old phone?" Cipher asked. "He's cleverer than you give him credit for, Vic."

He frowned, reaching across with his left hand to find the X-communicator in his suit's pocket. It felt awkward using his opposite arm. Just thinking about the injury and remembering the pain caused by the Purifier's sword made his guts churn. He'd wondered before about the possibility of limb regeneration, given he'd witnessed it happening to an actual lizard once, but needless to say he'd never wanted to test the theory out. This was going to take more than a bit of getting used to.

"It's a tracker," Cipher said as Vic pulled out the circular device, speaking as though it was the most obvious thing in the world. Right then, it felt like it was. Vic was glad he was incapable of blushing.

"He put a tracker in my communicator," he said. "I wondered, but surely that is against school rules?"

"Don't act like you've ever read the policy documents," Cipher said. "You're just annoyed that he outsmarted you. He knew where you were this whole time."

"So why didn't he stop me?" Vic asked. "Surely he could have sent someone to pick me up? Even Rockslide, if one of the other X-Men wasn't available."

"Rockslide's still looking for your father, or he was when we last heard from him. And even if someone else was around to grab you and force you back to the Institute, what then? Summers was hardly going to lock you up in the basement. He knew as long as your dad was missing, you'd keep trying to get out."

"You make me sound like a stubborn ass," Vic said ruefully.

"I don't think I'm qualified to comment on that," Ci said with a hint of a smile. "Just be thankful the principal got one over on you. Once I convinced him letting us go would improve your survival odds, he wired our own communicators up so we could track yours. Lucky for you he did."

"Apparently I've got the whole Institute to thank for still being alive, sans one arm," Vic said, trying not to sound churlish. He hated falling for anything, even when it was a case of life or death.

"We managed to get to you just before you were washed out of the Upper Bay," Cipher said. "It was getting dark by the time we located you, so Jonas's powers were in effect too. It's a miracle you hadn't already drowned by then."

Vic grunted, trying not to think about the few memories he had of his time in New York's waters. He wondered just where his arm had ended up. That brought back images of Xodus, of fire, and of falling, wicked steel. He shivered.

"The Purifiers are in New York," he said, looking directly ahead now. "I tracked down the source of their funding. They have a powerful business backer. Sublime Corp."

"That's what you're doing in New York?" Ci asked. "You think they're the ones with your dad?"

"The Sublime boss is the one pulling all the strings," Vic said. "Some creepy dude by the name of Lobe. The Purifiers are practically just a front. It's Sublime who's taken my dad."

"But why?" Cipher asked.

"I still don't know, but it's definitely me they're after," Vic replied, wishing he had a better answer. "I've got to get at Lobe. Either expose him or make him talk."

"I doubt you'll be able to do either if we don't find out more about him and Sublime," Cipher said. "Why would some business CEO be after you? Are you saying he's stoked up the whole Purifier campaign just to try and lure you out?"

"No," Vic said with a defensive note. "I don't know. All I know is he recognized me, and he's got Xodus hunting me. They're both relentless."

"You don't think we should be prioritizing the Purifiers?" Cipher asked. "They're the ones who took your father, after all. We'll probably still have to go through them to get to this Lobe, even if he is the one now holding Dan."

There was a scraping sound and the *thunk* of a lock. Vic and Cipher both turned as the door to the shipping container squealed open.

The night beyond seemed to leak into the narrow space. The two lamps flickered, and for the tiniest moment Vic thought they were going to go out and leave the container in darkness.

The light recovered. Graymalkin stood in the doorway, the darkness at his back absolute. He smiled at Vic, a disarming expression for someone who had just appeared like Dracula returning to his castle.

"It does me well to see you conscious, Victor," he said, stepping fully inside and carefully closing and locking the container's door behind him. "I had started to become concerned."

"So I heard," Vic said. "I also hear you had a hand in saving my life. I'm going to have to think up new and creative ways of saying thank you to both of you."

"You would do the same for either of us," Graymalkin said, walking past Vic to type something in at the laptop. "Besides, much of the rescuing was Cipher's doing."

"How's it looking out there?" Ci asked, changing the subject rather than taking the compliment.

"The commotion is largely calmed," Graymalkin said, looking up at her from the laptop. "Bands of Purifiers are searching the riverbanks and the docks, but the NYPD appear to have them under control and are moving them on. I witnessed several arrests."

"For once," Vic said bitterly. Graymalkin continued.

"The bridge remains cordoned off. There was some structural damage, but it yet stands. The fires still smoke."

"Vic believes he's found a connection between the Purifiers and a New York businessman," Cipher said, looking at Vic to take over. He shrugged – the motion felt strange with only one arm.

"His name's Lobe. He's using his finances and influence to back the Purifiers and hunt for me. I don't know why."

"Then we will have to find out," Graymalkin said, gesturing to the laptop. "The principal has been good enough to provide us with remote access to much of the Institute's data archives."

"No more hardwiring into the vault," Cipher said. "Almost takes the fun out of it."

"Well, at least I won't have to sit in Central Library worrying about my skin accidentally shifting a few shades while I'm concentrating on the browser," Vic said. "We can start by looking for any mention of Sublime or Lobe in the digital records."

"I will do so," Gray affirmed, beginning to tap away at the laptop's keys – he'd more or less mastered such devices, though his typing was slow and conducted with forefingers alone.

"I take it you were snooping around Sublime's offices when you were caught?" Cipher asked Vic.

"Something like that," he replied. "I ended up having a one-to-one meeting with Lobe and Xodus."

"Sounds like you need someone more subtle for that kind of work," Cipher pointed out. "I'll pay them a visit tomorrow, see what I can learn. Any info on where your father is being held and it'll practically be mission accomplished."

"This is a mission now?" Vic asked doubtfully. "I don't think I'm much cut out for that sort of stuff any more." He looked down at his stump, feeling almost guilty now. Gray and Ci had come all this way, risked so much, and he was reduced to a single arm, no longer combat-effective. He didn't dare even think about how the injury was going to affect his balance or ability to climb. The absence felt wholly unnatural, freakish. It seemed as though he should still be able to reach out with it, still feel its physical presence. And yet, when he tried to move it, there was nothing there.

"Nonsense," Cipher said briskly. "I was going to bandage it, but I didn't want to disturb whatever your body's doing. You'll just need to get used to it."

"You know, certain genera such as the *Anolis carolinensis* are capable of regrowing severed tails," Gray said as he continued to slowly type, the world's most ponderous hacker. "Some reptilians can regenerate whole limbs, given time."

"You think I'm going to grow my arm back?" Vic exclaimed. "Come on, I'm not an actual, literal human-sized anole, Gray!"

"We'll give it some time and see," Cipher said. "You're not leaving the safecrate for at least the next twenty-four hours. Let us do the snooping. We're better at it than you."

"You want me to just fester here staring at my stump?" Vic complained.

"That's exactly what I want," Cipher said. "You know we're working round the clock to find your dad, so don't try and pull the restless and helpless card. You said it yourself, you're no use to us weak and injured. So, get your strength back."

"I brought some books you can read," Gray added brightly, moving from the laptop to his rucksack. "I thought they might help you study for your history retake."

Vic groaned and slumped back, laying his one remaining forearm over his face. Maybe he should've just drowned in the East River.

CHAPTER TWENTY-NINE

The drill emitted a piercing shriek, the pitch high enough to penetrate from the theater into the sealed observation room adjacent to it.

The sound didn't affect Lobe. He had simply deleted it from his consciousness – he'd long mastered the ability to compartmentalize and, if necessary, erase not only specific thoughts and feelings, but physical stimuli. When time allowed, he permitted himself to feel certain emotions, for some were conducive, and what was the point of success without satisfaction? But when he was working – as he was now – there could be no distractions.

The CEO of Sublime Corp stood in the semi-dark of the observation room, staring through at the brightly lit, pristine space that served as the facility's operating theater. The scene playing out before him had been fascinating at first, but it was rapidly becoming tedious. A trio of masked and gowned figures clustered around an upright operating slab, working with painstaking slowness on the figure bolted to it. The giant's body appeared to be composed entirely of a granite-like substance, craggy and incredibly dense. Initially Lobe had been intrigued by the prospect of capturing such a specimen – was the creature's entire body composed of rock, or did it have an organic core that merely bore a rock-like carapace? Was the ability to communicate with and craft nearby geology an innate or a learned process? Did it require conscious mental thought? The possibilities had almost caused him to forgive Xodus his failings. Alas, work on the subject had started to stall.

There was a crunch and a clatter as a segment of stone detached and fell from the creature's broad torso. The drill whirred as it retracted, one of the white-clad men waving the rock dust from the air. Lobe allowed himself a slight grimace.

The mutant had proven immensely resistant. After several days of effort with saws, drills and even, at one point, a sledgehammer, they'd managed to detach its left arm. Its remains were laid out on a gurney beside the operating slab, the limb reduced to half a dozen hunks of shattered stone. It appeared the thing was composed of granite through-and-through. That posed questions in its own right, but the answers were proving increasingly uninteresting to Lobe.

The operator with the drill stepped back, assessing the hole burrowed into the mutant's torso. Throughout the session it hadn't stirred once. As Lobe had calculated, a certain coagulant gel inserted into its rocky joints was sufficient not only to impede its limbs but also to stymie its mental processes. It was not completely unconscious, but it was too sluggish and confused to be able to formulate a coherent thought, much less unleash the geokinetic powers Lobe had heard it possessed. Delving into those particular abilities would require further, careful experimentation, but Lobe had no time for it. Test results had all come back negative. This mutant's DNA, such as it was, consisted of strands far too resilient and unyielding to be of use in the serum, and that meant it was of no immediate use to Sublime Corp.

As the drill began to shriek again Lobe detected a careful knock at the observation room door. He ignored his irritation and called for whoever it was to enter. One of the facility's suited guards stepped inside, not meeting Lobe's gaze. He was carrying a package.

"This was just delivered, sir," the man said, offering Lobe the wrapped parcel. "I was told it should be given to you immediately."

Lobe took the package and waved the man out. The paper didn't bear a sender name, but it had the Purifier cross-and-circle upon it. Just the sight of the symbol caused a flash of anger that took Lobe several seconds to control. He had endured a number of doubts before brokering an alliance between Sublime Corp and the Purifiers, not least of which involved the competence of what appeared to be nothing more than a cult of militant religious fanatics. Xodus had succeeded in ticking a number of boxes however – he was single-minded and physically capable, and had one of the few things that Sublime Corp was lacking, namely a small army of demented followers who could be harnessed across a swath of North America. They gave Lobe a reach beyond the boardrooms, banks, and businesses he'd spent his life subverting and controlling, an ability to conduct direct action on the streets, provided he occasionally stoked up the fires of their fanaticism. He was also discovering, however, that the prophet and his cult were a blunt instrument. Indiscriminate hounding of the mutant population was one thing, but they appeared incapable of targeted operations, especially when it came to the lizard. Somehow the boy had found his way right to the heart of Lobe's empire. He was practically taunting him. The rage it had all induced was almost more than he could control.

He busied himself meticulously unwrapping the package, trying to ease his frustrations. The capture of the rock mutant –

Rockslide was his moniker, apparently – was a kind of progress. The boy also couldn't have gotten far, despite Xodus's failure to find him in the river. He was outside of the Institute and isolated. It was only a matter of time.

The wrapping paper came away in Lobe's manicured hands, and he experienced a rare moment of surprise. There was no note, but the contents of the package said enough. He held a limp, green-scaled, severed arm.

He smiled. Progress indeed.

CHAPTER THIRTY

Vic slammed his fist against the inside of the shipment container's door. He ignored both the pain shooting up his arm and the slight dent that appeared in the blue metal surface. It made him feel better.

He had yet to find a more ideal way of venting his frustrations since he'd been pulled from the river. Today had been a particular low. He'd almost been caught while trying to scale a wall into a warehouse compound. He'd lost his balance and upended a row of trash cans. Although he'd managed to fully shift to avoid security when they'd come to check on the disturbance, they'd still almost rumbled him. Backup had arrived, and he'd barely shaken them before making it back to the dockyards.

He felt incapable. Worse, he felt like a liability. Two weeks and Gray and Ci had been out every night, scouring the city for leads. Cipher had spent almost five days in the Sublime Corp headquarters undetected, and Gray had been tracking the subsidiary company holdings and the movements of their employees, much of which appeared to occur after dark.

In that time, Vic had achieved nothing. He had tried to follow up on a few of the leads Gray had unearthed, infiltrating various warehouses and office spaces, but he'd come up with nothing useful, and on each occasion he'd nearly blundered into disaster. He welcomed Ci and Gray's arrival, was reassured that they were there for him, but their presence had thrown him all the same. Perhaps he was relying on them too much? He cared about them, and that added an extra layer of concern. All this was happening because of him, after all. Mainly though, he couldn't get used to working with just one arm.

At least that wouldn't be the case forever. It turned out Gray was correct – his arm really was growing back. Not only that, it was doing so at a fearsome rate. The translucent gloop that had initially covered the wound was developing into an entire limb. The flesh was slowly growing scales, but much of it was partially see-through, so Vic was treated to the sight of knots of vein and muscle developing over a steadily increasing length of bone. It ached like crazy, but he swore that if he sat and looked hard enough, he could actually see the growth.

It was also giving him a fearsome appetite. He was perpetually hungry, and ate four or five times a day. He swore Gray and Ci spent about a third of their time outside the container getting food for him, everything from hotdog stands to half an aisle of Walmart nutri-bars. He'd almost eaten Gabriello's out of business. He supposed it was a natural side-effect of his regeneration, but between that and growing aches so bad he could barely sleep, it was maddening.

He stepped away from the door and flexed the fingers of his left fist, cracking the knuckles. He had to stay in control, for Dad's sake. The weeks were ticking by and he felt as though he was getting further away from him, not closer. Every time any of them went out looking for answers they seemed to find more questions. What was the real purpose behind Sublime Corp's existence? Most of their money appeared to be earned off the books, but where was it coming from? What was behind Lobe's desire to persecute mutants? To capture him in particular? He felt as though he was caught in a web that he was only just becoming aware existed.

The news about Rockslide had only worsened that. Cipher had admitted to him that his old roommate had failed to report in after hitting a Purifier church in Newark before Cyclops had allowed them to leave the Institute. There'd been no news either from or of him since. Vic had paid a covert visit to the church in question, but he'd found it boarded up. There were signs of battle damage, but no further evidence. It only added to the sense of guilt he felt. Who was going to have to suffer next for his failings? Was he going to lose Ci and Gray too? Would he eventually find himself completely alone, fighting to rescue – or worse, avenge – all the people he cared about?

He stepped over a small mountain of greasy, empty pizza boxes and slumped down on his bed. Despite Cipher's level-headed advice about taking shifts to work, none of them were getting much sleep. Vic found himself gazing down at his right arm. The hand had only just started to form, vestigial fingers detaching from a gelatinous lump that he assumed would become his fist. There appeared to be five of them, so that was good news. He wasn't able to move any of them yet, but when he squeezed one, he could feel a pain beyond the deep, hideous ache. He guessed that was good too.

He heard the scrape of the lock, and looked up as the crate door eased open and darkness bled in. Graymalkin, back from the hunt. The dawn was faintly visible behind him as he stepped inside. He looked as tired as Vic felt – his gaunt face was even more drawn than usual, his eyes ringed with darkness. He'd had a few night terrors while trying to sleep. It seemed he hadn't yet settled into the claustrophobia of the shipping crate. Ci and Vic had calmed him as best they could.

"I did not expect to find you awake," he said as he turned to close the door.

"I'm just back too," Vic said, trying to keep the weariness from his voice. "The Zeng Foundation warehouses. No luck."

"I have been a little more fortunate," Graymalkin began to say, then hesitated when he noticed the dent in the door caused by Vic's one good fist. There were two others like it further along, an ongoing reminder of his repeated failures.

"Sometimes I worry for your hand, my friend," Gray said, going to sit down on his mattress. Vic grunted, laying back on his own bed.

"Hitting stuff takes my mind off things," he lied, trying to mask the constant strain he'd been under now for weeks. "Kinda."

"I doubt that," Gray replied.

"I feel like I'm failing at everything right now," Vic carried on, raising his new right arm with a little difficulty and looking at it. He was convinced it was going to end up larger and thicker than his other arm.

"I often feel as though I am failing," Gray confided, almost conspiratorially. Vic scoffed.

"You've got some of the highest grades in our year and some of the most impressive powers, when the circumstances are right. Have you ever failed anything in your life?"

"Failure has different meanings for different people," Gray pointed out. "There is more to either of our existences than examination results or our peculiar abilities. I fail at a great many other things."

"Like what?" Vic asked, genuinely curious now, lowering his aching arm and looking over at his friend.

"Being a good companion," Gray said, not returning his eye

contact. "Being a… normal member of society. Being accepted in the company of my peers. I worry that my intonation is abnormal. Despite having lived in the current period for several years, there are still many mannerisms and turns of phrase that I do not comprehend. I rarely admit to this discomfort, yet I feel it on an almost daily basis. I do not fit in."

"That's crazy," Vic said, before checking the instinctive impulse to dismiss his friend's worries out of hand. He sat up again, moving to sit on the edge of the bed facing Graymalkin. "I mean, none of that in itself is abnormal. In fact, I think pretty much everyone feels the way you do from time to time."

"I believe that may be easy for you to say," Gray said, now meeting his gaze. "You have always been comfortable around others. You are popular in the Institute. You have no reason to feel ostracized."

"But sometimes that feeling doesn't need a reason, right?" Vic asked. Gray seemed to consider his words before offering a nod.

"I suppose that is so," he said. "Each of us has their own struggles."

"But that doesn't mean we can't understand each other's," Vic pointed out. "It might surprise you how much you have in common with other people. How much they're not admitting. Do you remember the time we spent in California, not long after we both joined the Institute?"

"The night I… admitted who I am to you?" Gray wondered hesitantly.

"You came out to me," Vic said. "The only person you'd ever done that to before was your father, and that was only because he'd caught you with someone else. We sat beneath the stars in San Francisco Bay, looking out towards the Golden Gate Bridge, and you told me you were gay."

"I knew you were as well," Gray said. "Just seeing you living a life without struggling against it, by accepting it, being at peace with it. It helped me to talk about it."

"I'm glad I was the one who could help you," Vic said. "It's one of the greatest privileges of my entire life. I was lucky enough to have parents who loved and supported me every day. If I can pay that forward somehow, then I will. Being at the Institute has made me realize how few of us have a family to fall back on."

"It's what Cyclops has always been telling us," said Cipher's voice from the ether. "The Institute is the family now."

"How long have you been listening in?" Vic demanded, though without venom. Cipher appeared just inside the door, brushing a dreadlock from her face.

"Not long," she admitted. "Sorry, don't let me interrupt your boy chats."

"Family chats, apparently," Vic corrected. "The principal would be proud of us."

"In all honesty, without the Institute I'm not sure I'd understand how much getting your dad back means to you, Vic," Cipher said. "But I think I'm starting to get it, thanks to both of you."

"Glad I could be of assistance," Vic said, lying back down again. "But don't you ever stop and think that maybe all this is a bit dangerous for a bonding session?"

"You're just feeling guilty about us helping you," Ci surmised. "Don't. Only an idiot would think that way. We're not leaving."

"Consider our perspective," Gray added before Vic could respond. "Do you think we would have been content to stay at the Institute for any length of time while knowing you were beyond its walls, risking your life?"

"So, what you're saying is that we're all unbearably stubborn and self-centered," Vic said with a sarcastic smile, "and we can't help but dive into danger for one another as it gives us all peace of mind?"

"What are families for?" Cipher said. "The more I learn about them, the crazier they seem. Speaking of, Vic, stop punching the container door."

"I'll stop if you go and get me more pizza?" he asked hopefully, poking a discarded box with a leg draped over the end of the bed.

"This'll literally be your third one since yesterday afternoon," Ci said with faux disapproval. "Where are you putting it all?"

"His arm," Gray said, then caught himself as he realized it was a joke.

"I'll get you one more," Cipher said. "But you're going to have to wait until the afternoon. I need to sleep. In fact, I suspect we all do."

"Woe my aching stomach," Vic said. "Did you manage to find anything at the depot?"

"No," Cipher said, passing between Vic and Gray to reach the laptop table. "But I did manage to hitch a ride with a Purifier trailer leaving it. They took me up to Clinton Hill."

"Lucky lady," Vic said. "Hope you tipped them."

"They tipped me, actually," she said. "Tipped me off about activity in an old church up near the expressway. There's Purifiers gathering there from all over."

"What're they up to?" Vic wondered. "Is it another recruitment sermon like the one Rocky busted?"

"Don't know, but they don't look like they'll be leaving anytime soon. I'll swing by again tomorrow. I'm guessing they'll be more active during the day. The church is rundown, looks like it was abandoned before they arrived."

"They're probably setting up a new base of operations this side of the river," Vic said. "They're closing the net. I almost got caught earlier."

"You need to be careful," Cipher admonished. "For all our sakes."

"I know," Vic answered, trying not to let his frustration get the better of him. "It just … feels like Dad's slipping away. Day by day, and we're no closer. Sometimes it feels like he's further away than ever. What have they been doing with him? Does he know he's being used to lure me out? What … what if I never see him again?"

"Don't think like that," Cipher advised. "We spoke to your mom before we left the Institute. She told us to tell you she loves you and that she knows you'll get your father back. I've never seen anyone more confident. Plus, I know she's right."

Vic smiled. He could very well imagine his mother's conviction.

"I'll be back at that church as soon as I've caught a few hours' sleep." Cipher continued. "Gray, didn't you have a new lead to check tomorrow as well?"

"Rikers Island," Graymalkin said with a nod. "I've identified several transports with Sublime Corp subsidiary markings travelling to and from it in the past forty-eight hours."

"I think we're closer than you imagine," Ci told Vic. "Get some rest, and try to ignore your stomach. At this rate your new arm will be twice the length of the other."

CHAPTER THIRTY-ONE

"Careful with that, ingrates," Prophet Xodus barked, gesturing at the dozen masked men struggling to erect a twelve-foot timber pole near the center of the cleared nave. "If you can't manage that, how will we be able to raise the metal one?"

There were mumbled, cringing apologies as several more Purifiers hurried over from the front doors of the church to help their brethren with the pole. Xodus glared at them until they had it upright and stable.

He'd been in a dark mood since the incident on the Brooklyn Bridge, and no amount of self-flagellation or snapping at novitiates seemed able to improve it. Even being in the echoing, lofty space of the Church of the Seven Virtues, newly consecrated to the Purifier faith, offered him no respite.

The crusade had reached a crossroads. Such a truth had become undeniable. The faithful in his charge had reached a fever-pitch of devotion, while the man – or devil, Xodus was coming to believe – who had made all the Purifiers' victories possible was almost beyond appeasement.

Despite their best efforts, none of Xodus's devoted followers had been able to locate the lizard creature. He had excommunicated five of his most senior deacons and several Choristers for their repeated failures. Others had been flogged. Only the prospect of the coming confrontation eased the prophet's wrath.

He stalked along the floor of the nave towards the stairwell that led to the bell tower, scattering underlings in his wake. This was what it had come to, a final gamble. At least the setting was agreeable – he had coveted the Church of the Seven Virtues for some time. It lay in the dense urban sprawl between Brooklyn and Queens, a neo-Romanesque structure of thick sandstone walls and rounded arches and towers, its curving barrel-vault nave supported by vast pillars of stone. Anywhere else it might have acquired the status of cathedral, but its former overseers had squandered their money and their influence, and its parish had dwindled into insignificance. When the Purifiers had arrived, its windows had been boarded up and its great oaken doors firmly locked. But now, praise be, the children of the prophet were to bring light and salvation back to its draughty, echoing stone spaces once more.

Xodus stepped from the bell tower stairs onto the balcony cloisters that ran the full length of the church interior. Like much of the derelict structure, the upper reaches were in dire need of repair. Masonry had fallen away, lying in scattered heaps across cracked flagstones whose crevices had been invaded by weeds. Xodus reached out and brushed a hand against one of the pillars, seeing how the sandstone gave way beneath his fingers.

This church needed to be revitalized, and Xodus knew just the sort of sermon it required. He paused halfway along the western wing of the cloisters, looking down at where the nave broadened out before the apse and the new altar his devoted children had erected.

Almost a hundred Purifiers worked below him. Some were collecting the smaller shards of dislodged masonry scattered across the nave and stuffing them into hessian sacking before beating them with hammers, turning them to powder within the cloth. That done, the bags were being stacked close to the apse, creating a heap of sacking that Xodus anticipated would prove vital when the time came. Most of the faithful, however, were hauling bundles of sticks along the shattered flagstones, collecting and binding them into two great clusters at the heart of the church. The first of the two poles that accompanied them had now been raised, while the second was still being lifted up. Unlike the first, this one was made from metal, and included heavy steel bolts. Such precautions were necessary, if their mutant guest was to be kept docile. Xodus was particularly looking forward to seeing how much heat its body could endure before it split and cracked. The thought almost brought back his good mood.

He let his gaze wander up from the industrious work of the faithful, to where the church's dome had once arched away overhead. Now it was a jagged hole, early evening sunlight streaming through to illuminate the efforts of the faithful. The sight of the ceiling's ruination brought a pang of sorrow to the prophet, but it would be put to good use, and soon. They would need the ventilation.

He watched the construction efforts of the faithful for a while longer, occasionally barking orders down at those battling to erect the second, larger metal pole. Everything had to be perfect. This was the reckoning they had been working towards, the moment of divine inspiration that would accelerate the faith into a new, bright future. The crusade thus far had only been a beginning. The Church of the Seven Virtues, worn with age and bowed and stooped in neglect, would bear witness to the dawn of true purity.

His mind somewhat eased, Xodus took the bell tower stairs

back down to the nave. As he went, he experienced a sudden, slight shock that checked his descent. He shivered, wondering if some angelic deity had just passed through him. Further divine inspiration.

Murmuring a catechism, he went to oversee the final preparation of the pyres personally.

CHAPTER THIRTY-TWO

"Hurry up," Melissa urged, tearing a fresh strip of tape from the roll she held and using it to seal up the top of another heavy box. "He wanted us done by this evening. I don't want to end up on one of these racks, and neither should you."

Her lab partner, Michael, didn't answer – he was too busy trying not to slash his fingers on the surgical blades he was attempting to pack away into their leather cases. This kind of work didn't go well with being told to hurry, but he understood Melissa's need for urgency. He didn't want to be left in the lab after dark either.

None of them had been told anything other than the fact that the boss wanted the facility cleared. By "cleared" he apparently meant "completely stripped out and abandoned" – everything was going, from test samples and research records to bulky scanning kits and life monitors. The tiled floors, the burnished metal gurneys, and the operating slabs had all been hosed down and thoroughly disinfected. The clear-out should have been finished by late afternoon, but completely evacuating a high-end medical research facility at such short notice was easier said than done.

There was a clatter as Michael accidentally dropped a long, slender bone saw. He cursed, reaching down to retrieve it. None of this was his kit anyway. Neither of them had seen the surgeons since yesterday afternoon. He and Melissa had been working in the lab next door for the past four months, overseeing the genetics results. They'd tried to avoid mixing with the surgeons and other, less readily identifiable medical professionals who operated in the theater as much as possible. In fact, they'd made a private pact, just the two of them, to not even discuss the ethics of what they were working on together. That was on top of the folders-worth of non-disclosure forms they'd signed in an official capacity when they'd joined Revitalize Incorporated, Sublime Corp's primary pharmaceutical enterprise. The forms reassured them that letting slip a single detail of the work they'd been undertaking would see them locked away for the rest of their lives, but that wasn't even the main deterrent. They'd both met the boss on several occasions, and seen the sorts of people he had dealings with. If one of them let slip about what was happening on Rikers Island, Michael doubted either of them would get as far as a court room, let alone a jail.

"Help me with this one," Melissa demanded, struggling to heft the box she'd just sealed onto the gurney they were using to transport the last of the theater kit. The facility appeared wholly deserted now, bar the foul-tempered delivery driver who'd been hired to shift the last of the place's contents, and the security team who manned the bridge from the island to Brooklyn. Michael stacked the medical case he'd been packing on top of the box and hefted it onto the metal frame.

"Just two more to go," he said, glancing back at the final pair of boxes and the stack of files next to them. So much for the promising career in medicine he'd looked forward to in college, he thought bitterly. Here he was, lugging gear around like a student nurse on an assignment. He could do without adding a physical burden to the literal one he'd been carrying for some time. It wasn't that he cared about mutants – his father had made sure he instilled a fear of them from a young age – but sometimes the screams from the theater were loud enough to reach the lab, and it made working difficult. Usually they just sounded too human. They'd even started giving him nightmares. He knew that Melissa was the same. She'd confided as much once over after-work drinks, prior to their "no talking about what goes on at work" pact. If Melissa was being made uncomfortable by the nature of their research, he knew he wasn't overreacting. Six months ago, Michael would have called some of the experiments he'd been ordered to undertake insane. But that was before he'd seen the results.

"Remember those files," he said, glancing back at Melissa as she hefted one of the two remaining boxes. The stack of documents next to them on the operating slab was all that remained to pack away.

He maneuvered the gurney towards the lab doors, before realizing that the brake was still on. He looked down to flip it with his foot, and as he did so his world went dark.

He froze. Melissa's swearing reassured him that he hadn't just blacked out.

"Power's gone," his lab partner hissed. He heard her fumbling around near one of the operating slabs behind her. There was a clatter, cold steel on a polished floor, as she knocked one of the remaining instruments out of its box.

"Careful," Michael hissed back. The last thing he wanted was to step on an uncapped scalpel. "Just hold still. I'll get the door to the corridor. The emergency lighting might still be working there."

"Why isn't it working in here?" Melissa replied testily. "Isn't that the whole point of 'emergency lighting'?"

Michael didn't answer, too focused on feeling his way around the gurney without upending it. He heard the sound of footsteps nearby on the tiled flooring.

"I said stop moving," he demanded.

"Mike," Melissa said, the tremor in her voice giving him pause. "I'm not moving."

Michael went very still. His skin prickled, and a chill ran down his spine.

Someone else was in the lab with them.

He didn't dare breathe. Slowly, he reached out and placed a hand on one of the boxes on the gurney, orienting himself in the pitch black. A part of him wanted to believe it was the delivery guy, come to check on them. But why hadn't he said anything to them yet?

The sound of footsteps came again, more rapid this time. Behind him. Michael spun around just as he heard his lab partner cry out.

"Melissa!" he shouted.

"Something went by me," she exclaimed, almost shrieking. "Mike, there's someone else in here!"

"Just hold still and keep quiet," Michael urged in a strained tone, his heart pounding. He swore he could hear movement all around him now, as though multiple figures were shifting through the lab, the feet passing right by him in one direction, then another, their breath on the nape of his neck. In a blind panic, he lashed out and gripped onto something.

The something screamed. He realized it was Melissa, and he grabbed hold of her fully.

"It's me," he snapped, desperate to shut her up. "Be quiet! Please, just stop!"

She stopped, but Michael didn't think it was his demanding that did it. With an abruptness that left them both dazed, the lights blinked back on, searing the scrubbed white tiles into their retinas.

"What the…" Michael swore, letting go of Melissa and

shielding his aching eyes while desperately attempting to take in the lab around them. He half expected to find the two of them surrounded, though by what he didn't even dare to imagine. Instead, there was just a single other figure present, standing in the doorway, his hand on the light switch.

"What the heck are you two doing in here?" the delivery driver demanded, looking decidedly unimpressed as he took in the sight of the pair of terrified lab workers

"That wasn't funny," Melissa all but screamed at the man. "Why would you do that to us?"

"Maybe you two should leave the fooling around until after the job's done," the sallow-faced man responded.

"Were you just in here with us?" Michael demanded before Melissa could launch into a fully-fledged tirade. "In the lab, moving around?"

"In the lab?" the man repeated, expression oscillating between angry and confused. "Son, I came by to check what the heck's keeping you both. I was supposed to finish my shift three hours ago. My wife's had to put the dinner on the stove."

"There was someone in here," Michael said with more certainty than he felt. "Maybe more than one. They switched the lights off."

"Then they must still be in here," the driver said. "Because there's only two doors in and out of this room. One's locked, and I just walked through the other and didn't see a thing."

"The papers," Melissa said abruptly. Michael glanced around to see what she meant, and realized she was staring at a spot on the operating slab next to the medical boxes. The space that, just before the lights had gone out, had been occupied by a stack of the lab's test results.

"The files are gone," Melissa said.

CHAPTER THIRTY-THREE

Graymalkin placed the last remaining sheet down on the stack of papers he'd piled neatly next to the laptop and turned to face Vic and Cipher.

"I will need to make a more comprehensive reading over the next few days," he said, his tone precise. "But based on my initial observations, I'm certain of two things; a number of Sublime Corp subsidiaries are currently conducting highly illegal experimentation into mutant genomes and DNA sequencing, and our friend Santo was recently being held prisoner at a facility on Rikers Island listed at Companies House as Revitalize Incorporated."

"They've got Rocky!" Vic exclaimed over a mouthful of pizza – had the rest not still been in his lap, Graymalkin was sure he'd have surged to his feet.

"I believe so," he confirmed. "Though he is no longer on Rikers. I suspect he's been moved within the last twenty-four hours, though to where I do not yet know. A more detailed reading of the files I recovered from the facility may yield possible locations."

"You said this facility was being cleared out when you arrived?"

Cipher asked from where she was sitting in the safecrate's only chair.

"Yes," Graymalkin said. "I was not able to gain access when I first visited it several days ago. I now regret that. It appears the vast majority of useful information has already been stripped from the site." Frustration filled him at failing to get the files faster. Graymalkin felt a personal burden building – he was horrified at the thought of not only Victor's father, but now a fellow compatriot, being held by fanatics who reminded him all too clearly of his own father.

"I should have gone," Cipher said, sounding exasperated. "I was too busy following up the leads in Brooklyn."

"But Santo was there, in the facility?" Vic pressed.

"It appears so," Gray answered as he quickly masked his feelings. While less free with expressing himself than the likes of Victor, he didn't want to futher agitate his friends by indulging in what-ifs. He stuck to the facts. "His description shows up a number of times in the files."

"What were they doing to him?"

"That remains unclear. As I said, these matters relate to mutant DNA, but I'm afraid I'm supremely unqualified to understand it exactly. Whatever form the experiments took, they appear to have already moved him."

"I should go there," Cipher said. "See if I can pick up anything they might have left behind."

"I'm coming too," Vic said immediately, setting aside his pizza box. Graymalkin suppressed a sigh.

"I'm better suited for it," Cipher responded. "I can be in and out of there without them even knowing."

"It'll be better if all three of us search," Vic said. "We need to go now. If they're moving stuff, we might catch them before they finish. We could tail them to their new facilities too."

"I might already know where that is," Cipher said. "The Purifiers are all over the Church of the Seven Virtues. Xodus is there too. It looks like they're building something."

"Something?" Graymalkin queried, unused to Cipher being evasive.

"They looked like pyres," she said, glancing away as she spoke. "Pyres for burning people."

Silence followed her words. Graymalkin felt a plummeting sickness that left him devoid of words.

Victor spoke first. "Was there any sign of Rocky there, or my dad?"

"I'm afraid not," Cipher said. "I searched the whole building from the spire to the crypts. As of this afternoon it was just Purifiers setting up. No Sublime Corp, no one matching Lobe's description. But I did see Xodus. Had to go right through him."

"It could be a distraction," Gray pointed out. "After all, they know Victor is in New York, and they must surely suspect he now has assistance. Maybe they're trying to draw our attention away while they change their primary facilities?"

"But why would they change them in the first place?" Vic wondered. "We won't know unless we investigate it."

"You're sure you're ready to come?" Cipher asked, not quite able to keep the concern out of her voice. "It would be a lot quicker if it was just me."

"I've got to step up at some point," Vic replied. "I'll go insane if I spend another night in here. Besides, look how shredded I am now."

Putting on a grin, he extended his right arm. It had continued to grow at an aggressive rate and was now visibly larger than its counterpart. He flexed his fingers and jagged spines formed along his upper biceps and shoulder, the jelly-like nubs beginning to acquire a hardened, carapace-like skin.

"You look like you're a quarter ape," Cipher said unenthusiastically. "Have you even got full feeling in it yet?"

"It's fine." Vic clenched and unclenched his fist, but Graymalkin noticed his wince. "I'll need to break it in anyway."

"The facility may still be guarded," Graymalkin said. "The bridge to Rikers Island certainly will be. I can gain entry in the dark, and Cipher can go whenever she pleases, but how do you intend to get inside?"

"Don't worry about that," Vic said. "There are these three guys I know."

CHAPTER THIRTY-FOUR

It was raining hard as the black vehicle crossed the long, desolate length of the bridge to Rikers Island. Rain thundered on the asphalt and flurried through the harsh security lights at the entrance to the complex, drenching the security guard the moment he stepped out of his post. His partner – wisely sheltering inside – had already run the van's registration plate as it approached the checkpoint. It passed the clearance. Apparently, it was one of the unmarked ones used by Esson Electrical.

The guard on the gate had heard something about a power outage the day before. It was a strange time to visit, but he'd long stopped questioning the odd hours kept by many of the people working at the facilities he was paid to protect. His mood tonight was as miserable as Rikers Island itself, a bleak spit of land in the East River that had long borne an equally bleak purpose. Since the nineteenth century it had been used to house New York's criminals, and had acquired the reputation to match. In the past few decades, the prison population had dwindled as public opinion turned against the idea of the island and its massed incarceration, so that now a little over half of it was privately owned and the Correctional and Detention Center was confined to a nest of razor wire and searchlights on the west side of the island. On the surface, it appeared Rikers' new population consisted of a disparate collection of animal testing facilities, recycling centers and pharmaceutical labs owned by half a dozen different companies. All, however, had links to Sublime Corp.

"Let's see your papers," the guard demanded as he stepped up to the driver's window. He peered through the rain-slick glass before he realized that there was, in fact, no driver. The cab was empty.

He called out to his partner at the same time as he heard a muffled grunt, followed by a splash. He spun, fumbling for his sidearm as his shift buddy was thrown from the guardhouse and out into a puddle by the gate, groaning.

Something was in the now-dark cabin, a suggestion of a shadow, pale and ill-looking. The guard tried to bring his weapon to bear, fingers slipping, torn between the need to keep the thing in his sights and the desire to call for backup on the radio. The monsters were all supposed to be locked up inside the island. They weren't supposed to be outside.

The terrified man heard a soft hum behind him and spun around. The window in the driver's door lowered, exposing the inside of the cab. Still, though there was no one there.

He hadn't believed in ghosts before tonight. He certainly hadn't believed they could knock him out with a single, invisible punch. That, however, was exactly what happened. There was a crack. The last thing he remembered was hitting the asphalt.

CHAPTER THIRTY-FIVE

Vic found the sight of Graymalkin with a fully grown man slung over each shoulder like twin sacks of potatoes vaguely funny. If the situation hadn't been as tense as it was, he'd have probably been able to come up with something side-splitting to say. As it was, he just watched from the back of the Esson van as his friend tied the two unconscious men back-to-back inside the guardhouse.

"All clear," he said, before raising the shutters on the security gate. Cipher, sitting in the cab, gunned the engine as Gray rejoined Vic in the back.

"Halloween is in two months," Vic said as his drenched companion closed the van door carefully behind him. "Please tell me you're going to go as Nosferatu?"

"I do not... understand," Gray said slowly, wiping rainwater out of his eyes and off his slick skull.

"Like a vampire?" Vic said. "You know, Dracula and stuff."

"Ah, the work of Bram Stoker," Gray said, catching on. "Yes, I have read that. Diverting enough, but somewhat unbelievable. Why would anyone be that afraid of the dark?"

"I don't know Gray, why did that security guard freak so bad when he saw you throwing his buddy out into the rain?" Vic quipped.

"Can it, you two," Ci called through from the front. "We're here."

Vic felt the van rock to a halt and opened the back door, hopping out. The rain pelted down with vehement ferocity, hard enough to make the tender, fresh skin of his exposed right arm sting. Before him, across an empty carpark, sat a squat, solid-looking concrete building, its windows like dark, dead eyes, its front doors shut. A sign over them – the only thing lit up – read "Revitalize Incorporated."

"This is it," Gray said. "This is where I tracked a removal truck contracted to Sublime Corp. There's a laboratory inside and an operating theater."

The words caused an icy anger to settle over Vic. He'd been trying to avoid thinking too much about what they may have been doing with Rockslide in the time since he had disappeared. It would only lead to him worrying more about his dad. He knew he had to try and stay level-headed, or he'd be putting Ci and Gray in danger, not to mention himself.

"How did you get inside?" Vic asked Gray as he glared across at the building. He found himself unable to imagine it in any setting other than a miserable, rain-slashed night.

"I cut the external fuse box," he said. "Then entered through a side door, on the north face of the building. Security was light at that point. Most of the removal work appeared to be complete. I would be surprised if anyone still remains now."

"There's an easy way to find out," Ci said. Vic hadn't heard her get out of the van, but here she was, standing next to them as the rain drenched her dreadlocks. She vanished without another word. Vic and Gray waited for a minute and, sure enough, she reappeared ahead of them, phasing back through the facility's front doors.

"All clear, and I've unlocked the doors and deactivated the alarm from the inside," she said.

"Flawless," Vic replied, moving with Gray to join her. She huffed.

"Like I said, I could have done all this without you."

"But you'd miss our wit," Vic pointed out, and pushed the doors to the Revitalize Incorporated laboratories open.

The corridor beyond was dark but for some low-lying illumination strips. Vic passed warily along it, trying to relax and let his senses attune themselves to the building. It was difficult, knowing that both his companions were so much more adept at these kinds of stealth operations. Ci had gone completely invisible again, and Gray practically thrummed with pent-up energy next to him, his eyes gleaming a deathly, spectral white in the gloom. He really had to get Gray to go as Nosferatu this Halloween. Find some old armor plates for Ci and she'd make a great spectral knight. As for him… He glanced down briefly at his right arm, looking so bulky and lopsided now. Frankenstein's lizard. That worked.

Focus. They'd reached the end of the corridor. Vic opened the next door to find Cipher, now visible, once more ahead of them.

She stood in the middle of what appeared to have once been a laboratory. Several work islands complete with Bunsen burner nodes occupied the center of a swept tile floor, while the walls were covered in shelves and included several sinks and equipment racks. All of them appeared empty. There were no windows, but there was what looked like either an observation room or an isolation unit off to the left-hand side, complete with a glass panel. The floor tiles were scuffed around several empty wall sockets, where it looked like heavier lab equipment had been unplugged and shipped out.

"Doesn't look like there's much left to work with," Vic murmured, a sinking feeling settling in the pit of his stomach. He'd hoped the hurried evacuation described by Gray would still be in progress, but it looked as though the entire space had been thoroughly cleared and scrubbed within the last twenty-four hours.

"The operating theater is through those doors," Gray said, indicating the exit opposite them. Cipher vanished once more, scouting ahead.

The next room was similar to the first, but instead of the workstations there were two operating slabs, one notably larger than the other. The observation room was also a more separate affair, with no door directly into the theater and a large, opaque window, set beneath a blank monitor screen. The whole place gave Victor the chills. He was convinced somebody was watching them from behind that window, or over the security cameras that sat, seemingly deactivated, in the room's corners.

"What were they doing here?" he wondered aloud.

"Nothing good," Cipher answered darkly.

Vic sniffed. There was a strange smell in the theater, one he hadn't noticed elsewhere in the facility. It was almost like peppermint, albeit with a bitter aftertaste that caught in the back of his throat. It was somehow vaguely familiar, but he couldn't quite place it. He'd caught it in the Institute before.

"Can you smell that?" he asked the others.

"No," Ci replied. "What does it smell like?"

"I'm not sure," Vic said, wondering if his senses were playing up. Scenting something that was invisible to others was hardly unusual for him.

"The communicators might be able to pick up something we've missed," Graymalkin suggested, pulling out his device. "Given the haste of the evacuation, I consider it highly unlikely that they will have been able to completely purge the entire facility of evidence."

"I'll see if I can hack the security footage," Cipher said. "There might be a way of extracting deleted files."

Vic knelt beside one of the abandoned gurneys, his tongue flicking the air as he sought out the source of the strange smell and tried not to dwell on the abandoned theater's grim ramifications. The sight of the operating slabs in particular made him feel sick. Had Santo been strapped to one of those? Had he been tortured, experimented on? He forced himself to concentrate. Where had he sensed that smell before? Last Christmas? Sometime around then. The end of term combat trials. He'd been fighting, hadn't he?

"That's strange," came Ci's voice from up beside one of the cameras. "The surveillance systems in here are still operating. They weren't next door."

"The scan is picking up structural anomalies," Gray added, frowning as he held up his communicator and rotated slowly on the spot. "Perhaps a security failsafe in case one of the theater subjects becomes compromised. It looks as if..."

"It's a trap," Vic said, standing up sharply. "We need to get out. Now."

He'd recognized the smell. It was a byproduct of selenium 5, a component in a nerve gas sometimes used in Danger Room exercises. Non-lethal, but debilitating. And at some point, it had started leaking into the operating theater.

Vic turned towards the doors leading back into the laboratory, but a thumping impact shook the room before he could move. Steel plates, branded with the Revitalize logo, slammed down over both entrances to the theater. Somewhere, an alarm began to clatter.

"It's gas," Vic said, looking around desperately and spotting several sets of vents ranged high up along the wall above the observation room. "Nerve gas. We've got to get out!"

"I'll try and cut it off," Ci said, already phased.

"No," Graymalkin urged. "I can use my powers to break out if you kill the lights."

"I can't do both at the same time," Cipher snapped. Vic began to cough. He could feel the selenium now, burning in his sinuses, making his eyes water.

"There are multiple vents," Gray said, a hint of panic in his normally clipped, precise tone. "You can't cut them all off."

"There are multiple lights too," Ci pointed out. "They're powered by a backup circuit somewhere, I can't just flick the switch!"

Gray tried punching the plating that had clattered down over the door to the lab. It barely left a dent.

"Stop arguing," Vic snapped, attempting to cover his face with his elbow as he spoke. "We're meant to be a trained team. Ci, get into the wiring of those shutters and see if you can retract them. Gray, go for the wall, not the door. It's probably thinner."

He had no idea if Ci was doing as suggested – she was still invisible – but Gray joined him at the wall that partitioned the theater from the lab. Vic hit it with his left fist, twice, cringing at the pain. A crack appeared in the plaster, though. Gray took over hitting the same spot.

"I wondered how many would find their way into the web tonight," said an abrupt voice. Vic recognized it immediately. Lobe. He spun round, ready to lash out. Instead he found himself looking at the now-active display of the monitor above the observation room.

"You seem surprised to see me, Anole," Lobe said, his face set in a chilling smirk. "I thought you came here looking for me. Or maybe your friend?"

Lobe moved to one side, an arm extended as the camera refocused on the scene behind him. He appeared to be standing in a section of a ruinous church, jury-rigged industrial lamps lighting up the nave behind him. The space was dominated by two stacks of timber, bundled around two poles. A figure was bound to each – Santo and Dan.

"No," Vic barked, the word descending into a racking fit of coughing that felt as though it was never going to end.

"Consider yourself invited to the party," Lobe continued, his face once more dominating the lens. "Tomorrow afternoon. Bring your plus twos, if you'd like. I wouldn't want anyone to miss what dear Xodus has in store. That is, of course, if you don't find yourself permanently incapacitated by the hard work of Revitalize Incorporated."

Vic doubled over, choking, every breath a desperate effort. He was half aware of Gray stumbling away from the wall, clutching his throat, his pale eyes bulging. He could hear Cipher choking too, though from where he didn't know. She alone could already have left, but she still fought to free them. He lunged desperately at the wall, blinded by tears as he began to strike it with both fists. He couldn't stop. He couldn't give up. Otherwise nobody would ever find his father.

Something gave way beneath his right hand. It hurt to use the new limb, but just then it was nothing compared to his throat closing up and his eyes feeling as though they were being seared from his skull by boiling water. He punched again, putting his all into his new arm. There was a crack, and white plaster cascaded down before him. Still the wall endured. He slammed his fist in once more, feeling more of the structure give way. He felt as though he'd broken every new-formed bone in his hand, but he didn't care, because with the next punch his fist met only air. He was through.

He felt a hand clutching at his shoulder – Gray. He couldn't turn to see him. In fact, he couldn't see anything. His eyes were screwed tight shut, overwhelmed by the seeping agony of the nerve agent. The wall was breaking though, crumbling before his new-found strength. He shoulder-charged it, spines-first, and burst through the damaged section with Graymalkin trailing blindly behind him.

He tripped and fell, in a total panic. He still couldn't breathe. Was the whole facility flooded? He rolled, questing about in the broken plaster, still blind, trying wildly to inhale.

Finally, air filled his lungs. His chest burned. His right hand was in agony. He cuffed tears from his eyes with his left, blinking furiously, trying to see again. The air in the lab appeared to be clear, though it wouldn't stay that way for long with a hole now punched through to the adjoining room.

Did I just break right through a wall? Vic thought. First time for everything.

That was as much as he was able to take in before he heard a mechanical rattle. He managed to open one eye as he got up onto his hands and knees, and realized for the first time that they weren't alone. Ten or more men in black fatigues and combat kit, replete with rubbery, bug-eyed respiration masks, levelled a plethora of firearms at where the two of them were sprawled.

"Oh, hey guys," Vic managed to gasp.

CHAPTER THIRTY-SIX

Vic tried to react, but the aftereffects of the gas made him feel as though his eyes had been scrubbed with a stiff brush and his lungs filled with tar. He saw the closest muzzle aimed at him, before it jerked abruptly backwards, cracking off the masked face of its wielder. He scrambled to his feet as the men on either side turned, but too slowly. One was sent reeling into the other by an invisible force, slamming them both to the tiled floor. Vic grinned.

Cipher was in among them. Shouts went up, and someone discharged their weapon, the report ear-shatteringly loud in the confined space. There was a scream. A snap – Vic got the impression someone had just received a broken arm – and another gunshot. It burst plaster from the remains of the wall behind Vic.

He rose, struggling to find the breath to shout, swinging his left fist at the nearest man. Vic caught the briefest glimpse of eyes wide with shock behind the glassy lenses of his respirator. His fist caught the man's throat and doubled him over.

Gray was up now too. Though the lights in the lab were bright enough to negate his powers, he was still quick and strong. He kicked in the ankle of one man with a gristly crunch and slapped aside the pistol of a second who was attempting to bring it to bear on him, the sidearm discharging and hitting the first man in the arm. The unfortunate figure went down screaming, trying to clutch his wounded arm and ankle simultaneously. Graymalkin punched the man with the pistol hard enough to splinter his mask's lenses.

For a few seconds Vic's blood sang with the adrenaline high of close quarter combat. This was the real deal, not a Danger Room test or a scrap with fellow students. All of them had trained for this for over two years, week in, week out, and suddenly it was happening. He didn't have time to think, and that was just fine. He spun into a low crouch, lashing out with his tongue and snagging the barrel of a rifle being pointed at Gray. He yanked it aside as he kicked out with one foot, toppling the prospective shooter. The man dropped his weapon and drew a short, wicked-looking dagger from a vambrace over his forearm, punching it towards Vic. The move caught him by surprise, and he wasn't able to stop the blade digging into his ribs. It didn't pierce his X-suit though, deflecting into the floor. Vic's left arm was pinned under him, so he slammed his right into the man's chest. Something crunched. This man was tough though. Despite the blow he still managed to raise his knife, aiming now at Vic's exposed face.

The blow fell short, quivering a few inches from Vic's right eye. There was a crack, and the knife fell to the floor with a clatter. An invisible force had caught and twisted the man's wrist. He writhed on the tiles as Vic scrambled back to his feet.

Cipher seemed to be everywhere. She was the difference between life and death, invisible and avenging, seemingly impervious to their attackers. Vic ducked as one of the men was flung bodily over him, crashing into one of the laboratory's work islands. Graymalkin had brought down another assailant, slamming his head into a shelf and crumpling the door.

Vic looked around, ready to lash out, convinced they were still surrounded. Instead all he found were black-clad bodies, some moving sluggishly and groaning, others lying still. He realized the fight had probably taken perhaps a minute. His throat, nose and eyes were already starting to burn again. Gas still poured into the room. He spat a wad of phlegm and helped Gray stay on his feet as he was hit by a fresh bout of coughing.

"There's no shutter over the lab doors," Vic said as Graymalkin recovered. "Got to keep going."

Graymalkin clutched at him and held him back.

"Ci," he managed to gasp. Vic realized why. There was blood on the floor, blood that didn't belong to any of the goons who'd tried to jump them. It was running seemingly from thin air next to one of the work islands.

Cipher blinked into existence, flickering for a moment, as though not wholly in control of her abilities any more. At some point in the melee she'd been shot. She clutched her left arm, blood welling between her fingers.

"Ci," Vic exclaimed before another fit of coughing hit him.

"It's just a graze," Cipher said. She looked angry rather than pained. "Come on, we need to get out of here."

Gray struggled to even stand any more, overcome once more by the nerve agent. Vic hauled them both toward the doors. They burst through together, and Vic finally caught an aching lungful of clear, untainted air.

Behind him, faint but audible from the operating theater, he could hear the video link of Lobe laughing.

CHAPTER THIRTY-SEVEN

"You shouldn't have come." It was the first thing Cipher said when they'd made it back to the safecrate. She sat on her mattress with the upper part of her left arm tightly bound with white dressings.

Vic resisted the urge to bite back, saying nothing instead. It had been a little over an hour since they'd arrived back at the docks. The struggle to get off Rikers had been hardly any less intense than the fight to get out of the Revitalize facility. There'd been more thugs with firearms waiting at the bridge. Unfortunately for them, they didn't have any bright laboratory lights to protect them from Graymalkin. He'd been angry too, a rare and dangerous thing indeed, infuriated at Cipher's injury. They hadn't lasted long.

"The venture was not wholly without success," Gray said now from where he was sitting by the laptop. He'd been even more taciturn than usual since escaping the island. Vic wondered if he was ashamed of how he'd unleashed his powers in front of them. "We know the location of both Santo and Mr Borkowski. They are being held at the church."

"Yeah," Vic said bitterly. "Strapped to the top of a bonfire and probably surrounded by Purifiers."

"It will be another trap," Cipher said. "Guaranteed."

"Oh, that's fine then," Vic said, failing this time at keeping his tone in check. "We'll just let my best friend and my dad burn to death in some ruined old church. It's not worth the risk."

"I didn't say that," Ci replied, equally sharp. "What I'm saying is you should let me go alone."

"That is impractical," Graymalkin cut in. "You are injured, and none of us are yet fully recovered from the nerve agent at the laboratory."

"Are we really going to do this?" Vic asked, exasperated. "Are we really going to argue over who's going to that church today? Because none of you can stop me from going, and in all honesty, I think I stand a better chance having both of you with me."

"We'll be walking right into Lobe's clutches," Cipher said with the slightest of smiles. "He knows the three of us now, probably knows most of our abilities too."

"That's true, but he's picked the wrong setup to snare us," Vic said. "We're the ones with the initiative now. And tell me who was always in the top five of our year's covert and infiltration exercises back at the Institute?"

He let the question dangle rhetorically before answering it.

"We're the ones best placed for this, and we're not going to get another chance."

"Fine," Cipher said. "But we're not going right now. None of us are in a fit state."

"And give Lobe more time to prepare?" Vic asked.

"You think he isn't already ready for us?" Cipher pointed out. "We need food and rest, and I need to wash the rest of that nerve agent out of my eyes."

"Cipher is right," Graymalkin added. "My sight is still somewhat impaired. If we strike now my powers will not be optimal, and our chances will be greatly reduced."

"Fine," Vic conceded. "Six hours, then it'll be midafternoon. I'm going then, whether you're ready or not."

He looked down at his right arm. The fist ached like crazy, and discolored blotches had appeared across his knuckles. Had he broken them punching his way out of the theater? Would they heal if they were damaged this early on? If the arm was cut off a second time would it still grow back?

He picked up a half-empty pizza box, trying not to think about any of it. His dad was out there with Rocky, both of them tied up and at the mercy of a cabal of madmen. Only the knowledge that they were about to attempt to free them gave him any kind of solace. Without Ci and Gray, he knew he'd already be back out there.

No, he corrected himself. Without Ci and Gray he knew he'd already be dead.

He settled back on his mattress, slowly chewing on the pizza slice while he clenched and unclenched his right fist, waiting for the dawn.

There was going to be a reckoning.

None of them slept much. Vic dozed for a while, and when he came to, he looked up to see Cipher sitting cross-legged on her mattress, unbinding the bloodstained dressing from her arm.

"What are you doing?" he asked her as she exposed the raw wound.

"This won't phase with me," she said. "I'll have to go without it."

"It'll reopen."

"I'll deal with that when it happens."

Vic stretched and rolled off the bed. His eyes still ached, and his throat felt raw. He picked a water bottle from the crate Cipher had bought when they'd first moved in and carefully opened the door. The strip of concrete between the row of shipping containers and the East River was deserted. Sunlight broke through the low somber gray clouds to pick out Governors Island across the bay from the docks. Vic upended the water bottle over his head, scrubbing at his eyes, then drank the remainder. It made him feel fractionally more alive. Shaking water from his carapace, he stepped back inside and refastened the door.

Gray now sat at the laptop. It didn't seem as though he'd slept at all. The harsh glare of the screen gave his sharp features a skull-like appearance. Vic peered over his shoulder and found him scanning a map of Clinton Hill.

"Do we have a plan?" he asked him.

"Not especially," Gray responded unhappily. "It is certain that Lobe will have the streets surrounding the church under surveillance. The question is how far does that surveillance extend? We cannot walk from here to the location without attracting considerable attention, but it is certain Lobe will be aware of the identity of our stolen vehicle."

Vic leant further over Gray's shoulder, assessing the map.

"Here," he suggested, pointing past him. "Jaffers Street. That's about halfway between us and the church. This lane here, then this one, will almost take us to the back of the block overlooking its front doors."

"That might work," Gray conceded.

"I'll head out first," Cipher said, standing up. "And scour the route. Stay on your communicators."

She made for the door, but on an impulse Vic took her wrist and pulled her back. "Thank you for being here Ci," he told her, his earlier frustrations evaporating as the moment of action loomed. "Thank you for... just for being on my team."

"It's my first team," she said simply and then, without warning, embraced Victor. He was so startled he didn't immediately react.

Gray watched them for a second then, tentatively, moved in to hug them both as well.

"We're in this as one," Cipher told them both. "To the very end, whatever that may be."

They broke it up. Gray, so rarely prone to physical displays of affection, carefully patted Vic's back after drawing away from him.

"I wished to say thank you too," he said, almost apologetically, as though offering an explanation.

"What for?" Vic asked. "You're only out here risking everything because of me. I'm meant to be thanking you."

"There is more to say thank you for than the last few weeks," Gray said earnestly. "You've been a source of strength since the day I woke, Victor. Thank you for being there every night when the nightmares came. For being there to talk when I was afraid to talk to anyone else."

"Any time," Vic said, tapping Graymalkin's chest for emphasis and smiling at Ci before she departed. "It's what families are for."

CHAPTER THIRTY-EIGHT

The Church of the Seven Virtues had fallen far from the grace intended for it when it had first been built almost two centuries before. The misdeeds of its benefactors and the slow but seemingly inevitable shrinking of its congregation had left it bereft. Eventually the spirit of the building had passed away, alone and uncared for – now its body remained where it had fallen, brittle sandstone walls and the dead eyes of boarded-up windows and doorways, overshadowed by a steeple that was due for demolition following local concerns about an imminent collapse.

There were, of course, online petitions to save it and occasional requests filed at City Hall calling for it to be listed as a site of historical significance. In the current climate, though, nobody had the money or the genuine desire to throw their weight behind a renovation project, and so the church lay steadily rotting in the midst of an equally dilapidated and forgotten corner of the city.

The decay appeared to be accelerating too. At some point, seemingly quite recently, part of the west transept wall had collapsed on itself, exposing a direct route into the nave and onto the balcony cloisters, albeit a direct route that was strewn with rubble and weeds.

"It's too obvious," Ci's voice clicked over the communicator.

"Are there Purifiers watching it?" Vic responded. He crouched on the ledge of an apartment rooftop he'd scaled almost opposite the church, his skin tone shifted. Graymalkin was in the darkness of the alley below. They'd been observing the broken old church for about fifteen minutes, but Ci had been inside for almost an hour.

"It doesn't seem like there are any in the immediate area. They're mostly at the far end of the nave, where the pyres are. But I'm not omnipotent. Xodus is at the altar, but I can't find any sign of Lobe."

"Maybe he's not here," Graymalkin hypothesized over the link. "He does not seem like an individual who would desire to become embroiled in physical exertions."

"What about Rocky and Dad?" Vic asked Ci.

"Still tied to the stakes. Your dad is awake but he's been gagged. Santo looks unconscious. I think they're drip-feeding him something to help keep him docile, it's fixed up to the pole he's tied to."

"Don't suppose you can free them without anyone noticing?"

"No," Ci said bluntly. "There's well over two dozen of Xodus's stooges all around the stakes. They've started to chant too."

"We need to get in there," Vic said. "We've delayed long enough as it is. I'm coming down."

"Like I said, if that gap in the wall is unguarded that's exactly where they want us," Cipher repeated.

"Relax, they can't even see me," Vic said before pocketing the communicator. As he did so his hand brushed against a small, rubbery shape. He'd brought the toy dinosaur, recovered along with the rest of his rucksack by Gray from the rooftop where he'd left it. He didn't really know why he'd decided to take it with him today, other than the fact that he thought it might bring him luck. He'd take anything he could get just now.

He headed for the wall and began to descend carefully. His arm appeared to have recovered from the brutalities of the night before. In fact, it felt stronger than ever, and he seemed to have gotten a good deal of his balance back. He no longer felt as though he was a misplaced fingertip away from losing his purchase whenever he tried to climb something. The arm twinged, but it was a sure sight preferable to not having one.

He reached the ground, ghosting along the sidewalk to the ruined flank of the church. The area in the vicinity of the former place of worship seemed just as run down as the building itself. Old discolored trash littered the gutters, crude graffiti was scrawled across every surface, and there seemed to be more broken or boarded-up windows than whole ones facing onto the streets. Vic doubted there would have been much foot traffic in an area like this on a busy day, but now that the Purifiers had moved in, people knew to stay away. He'd already spotted their symbol daubed on doors and walls, and passed a trio of their rickety transports parked up in nearby side streets.

Vic passed into the shadow of the Church of the Seven Virtues, the sudden cold making him shiver. He could hear the chanting from within now, echoing sonorously. It made his skin crawl. There was nothing holy about the Purifier cult, nothing actually pure. He had no doubt that they were the embodiment of the evil they claimed to be rooting out. He had to get Rocky and his dad free from their clutches or die trying.

The opening in the wall was ahead of him now, a slope of rubble leading to a ragged gap in the stonework. Beyond it was darkness, and the unsettling chanting. Vic climbed the slope, forcing himself to go slow and careful, his senses on edge. As much as he'd refused to admit it to Cipher, she was absolutely correct – there was no way this wasn't some sort of trap. And Vic was determined to spring it.

He reached the gap in the wall without incident and slunk inside, on all fours now, skin rippling slightly to match the change in lighting around him. He was in an aisle that seemed to run around the length of the nave, between the exterior wall and the great pillars that supported the vaults. The nave itself stretched out ahead and on either side, littered with rubble, expanding where it met the crossing of the east and west transepts. That space, right before the apse and altar, had once sat beneath a great, soaring dome, but much of the roof there appeared to have caved in at some point. Sunlight beamed down through the hole, leaving the rest of the church in smoky, gentle darkness as it beamed down upon the church's new, blasphemous congregation.

Cipher had been right. There were Purifiers everywhere. Vic counted over two dozen, most clustered around two large bundles of timber and kindling. The stakes had been erected there, one timber and one metal. Vic's heart quickened as he saw his dad and Rocky, the latter missing an arm. His stomach knotted up with tension, his whole body flushed with the need to act. He couldn't stand to see his dad and his best friend bound and helpless in the midst of these zealots.

Xodus was present too. The prophet stood beyond the pyres in front of the altar, his back to it. He was flanked on either side by six figures in white robes and black masks. Choristers, Cipher had called them, though just how she knew the specifics of Purifier ranks, he had no idea. Ci tended to know a lot of things. None of them appeared to be joining in the slow, swaying chant that was swelling from the cultists around the pyres. They were just watching. As he assessed their position, Vic noticed a mound of sacks near their feet, midway between the pyres and the apse.

He had no idea what they contained. Explosive charges? A final doomsday device should the Purifiers lose the upper hand?

He crouched beside one of the great support pillars and keyed his communicator, trusting in the echoing reverberations of the dark plainsong to mask his speech.

"Ci, where you at?" he hissed.

"West cloister balcony," she replied softly. "You?"

"Just came in through the gap," he said, glancing briefly up at the second level of the church that ran around the upper walls on either side. Unsurprisingly, he caught no sign of Ci.

"I am outside," Gray's voice added. "The light levels are not yet conducive to my work."

"It's darker inside the church," Vic said, attempting to reassure him.

"Regardless, it would be optimal if we could wait until evening before making our play."

"Don't think that's going to be possible, Gray," Vic murmured. A new procession of Purifiers emerged from the transepts, marching with echoing footsteps towards the pyres from left and right. The lead cultist in each group was carrying a lit torch.

"We've got to hit them, now," Vic said, tensing up, looking for the shortest open route to the transept crossing.

"A second longer," Cipher urged. "I'm coming down."

"I'm at the demolished section of the wall," Gray said. "Like we planned it?"

"Yes," Vic said, then checked himself. "No, wait."

The torch-bearing Purifiers had halted and turned towards the altar. It wasn't their pause that had caught Vic though. It was the figure who had just emerged from the stairs to the bell tower, on the eastern transept.

Lobe. The man was attired as Vic had last seen him in his office in Manhattan, suited and booted. His stride was almost leisurely, as though he had wandered into the old church as part of a tourist trail featuring New York's least-known run-down historic buildings. He walked unhurriedly through the midst of the Purifiers assembled around the pyres, looking entirely out of place. As he came to stand between the two stakes, facing out towards the rest of the church, Xodus – still behind him at the altar – raised both arms sharply. The chanting came to an abrupt stop, and all those within the church were treated to the unsettling echoes of the throaty words fading slowly away into the dark, crooked corners of the fallen place of worship.

"Quite something," Lobe said, calling out as though to an invisible congregation seated in the pews that would once have occupied the long nave before him. "I really must commend Xodus for unearthing this gem. It adds a real touch of the theatrical to proceedings. Don't you agree, Victor?"

Vic stayed frozen, convinced Lobe was about to look directly at him. He didn't though, instead casting his gaze up at the cloisters, the motion somewhat exaggerated, like a showman before a conjuring trick.

"What's this I hear?" he carried on. "Nothing? Silence? Don't tell me the brave students of the Xavier Institute didn't have the courage to show up after all? I can only apologize, Mr Borkowski."

He turned towards Victor's father, bound and gagged on the smaller of the two pyres, and offered a mocking bow.

"It seems your son values his own life over yours. He's not willing to risk his neck fetching his old man out of the fire. Pity. Still, at least it should please our masked guests. I promised them quite the blaze today!"

Vic's every instinct screamed at him to tear into his smug tormentor. He checked himself at the last instant. *He can't see you,* he told himself. *You've got to keep calm. Stick to the plan.*

"Maybe you expected that?" Lobe went on, looking from Dan over to Santo. "He's probably a regular disappointment, isn't he? It must cut deep though, knowing in your heart that your son, your friend, is such a coward. Not worthy of being an X-Man, certainly. Not worthy of any mutant powers at all. Such a shame. Such wasted potential. Still, no matter. We are making progress every day. Soon the work will be complete. Unfortunately, neither of you will live to see it."

Lobe raised a hand and clicked his fingers. Xodus nodded down at the torch-bearing Purifiers, who turned towards the pyres.

"Vic, wait," Cipher said over the communicator, but Vic wasn't listening, not any more. He charged, out from behind the pillar, skin rippling as he vaulted the rubble littering the nave and went straight for Lobe and the pyre stacks framing him.

They saw him coming. Lobe smiled broadly and spread his arms wide, welcoming him even as Purifiers closed in from left and right, barring Vic's route. They were armed, too. The echoing space filled with the vibration of charged energy weapons.

Vic turned his headlong rush into a diving roll. He thumped into a block of fallen sandstone masonry just as the air around him went electric. The stone at his back shook, and dust filled the air, lit by actinic bolts as stray shots whipped overhead. He snatched up his communicator.

"Ci, you going?" he asked breathlessly.

He got no direct response, but the shout of dismay ringing over the *crack* of gunfire was enough. He risked a glance around the side of his cover, just in time to see one of the torches being torn from the fingers of an advancing Purifier by an invisible entity. While Vic had been rushing forward, Cipher had gotten down amongst them without being detected. The first torch went arcing into the east transept, its flame doused as it clattered over the flagstones. The second soon followed, the Purifiers casting about in dismay. A great wail rose up from them, and Vic wondered if they believed some devious, invisible spirit had come to confound their dark worship.

The fire being directed at where he sheltered slackened off almost as quickly as it had started, and it wasn't because of the sudden attack on the torchbearers. There was a blur of activity, in amongst the shadows beyond the pillars off to the right. Graymalkin was in the building.

Sensing the imminent attack, the nearest Purifiers turned their weaponry on the encroaching darkness, but Gray drew enough strength from the half-shadows to tear behind the final pillar on the east side of the nave. More energy blasts lacerated the stone, filling the air with fresh bursts of dust.

Vic shifted and moved. The ripple of motion directed more bolts back his way, but too slow. He managed to get down behind a second fallen wedge of masonry, his heart hammering, thoughts racing. Thanks to Ci, they had them torn and confused, but he doubted it would stay that way for long. Regardless, the plan was now underway. And that involved Vic shutting Lobe out of the game, even if it meant ignoring the instincts crying out at him to reach his father and get him to safety.

He broke again, right this time, making for the nearest pillar in the same moment that Graymalkin shifted from behind his. The air was alive with the discharge of the energy rifles and swirling clouds of shattered stonework that eddied as Vic surged through it. One bolt passed right by his shoulder, causing a jolt to stab through him, but not slow him. He reached safety again, coughing out dust.

He tried to get a view of the back of the church without exposing himself, managing to get an angle on the entrance to the stairwell leading up to the bell tower. That was where Lobe was headed. As the transept crossing had descended into chaos he'd retreated, beginning to climb the stone steps up, either to the belfry or the second-tier cloisters. The change in position had removed him from the center of the action, but it had left no more Purifiers between him and Vic.

Charged with the need for vengeance, Vic rose and followed.

CHAPTER THIRTY-NINE

The Purifier's mask crumpled beneath Cipher's fist, the silver turning red around the leering mouth and hooked nose. The cultist went down.

She threw herself left, phasing hard through another pair of Xodus's minions. Both cried out as they were riven with bioelectric shock, and one fired his energy rifle wildly, sending a trio of bolts lashing into the upper section of the apse. Ci lashed back with both elbows, solidifying her form and catching one on the back of the neck and one in the head, sending them sprawling in their black robes.

The crossing between the transepts was a scene of carnage. There were Purifiers scattering left and right, thrown into confusion by Cipher's unseen assault. She'd been forced to adjust her plan in order to take out the torch-bearing cultists before they'd been able to light the pyres, but knew she was running out of time. In their frantic state, it was only a matter of time before a Purifier landed a lucky blow or shot on her. She needed backup.

She willed herself up, leaving the flagstones behind. Dan

and Santo were both still bound to their stakes, the former struggling against his bonds as the battle unfolded around him. The latter, though, hadn't moved since Ci had set eyes on him. At some point Rockslide had lost his left arm, a sight that sent rage coursing through her. What had they done to him? What were they still doing to him? It was obvious that the metal pole holding him upright amidst the great pile of kindling was more than a simple restraint. Wires in protective flexi-tubing extended from an armored box near the top of the pole, their ends thrust into the craggy splits in Santo's joints. Ci assumed some sort of electrical charge or neural-inhibiting gel was keeping him in a docile state, unable to activate his powers. And that was going to make the difference between winning and losing this fight.

Precautions had clearly been taken to protect the inhibitor from tampering, but those wouldn't stop Cipher. She phased through the box at the top of the stake and starting tearing leads off from the inside. A clear, viscous liquid began to spray free, stinging her hands and forcing her to twist so that it didn't hit her wounded arm too. She phased out as the severed leads went slack, still dangling and gushing liquid from Rockslide's knees, waist, shoulders and elbow.

"Come on, Santo," Cipher pleaded, moving round to the front of the hulking figure, laying an invisible hand on his broad chest. "Wake up."

Santo's eyes, half-lidded, flickered, and more clear liquid oozed from his slack jaw. He didn't move.

The nearest Purifiers had been focused on pinning Vic, but some realized that an invisible presence was doing damage to the stake and its couplings. One shouted, gesticulating up at the pyre and squeezing off a semi-automatic burst that by happenstance just missed Cipher. Several more cultists started to try to clamber up the bundles kindling, while another opened fire alongside the first with an energy rifle. The first bolt was so close to Cipher it sent a jarring pulse through her body, but the second struck Santo in the chest. Power lashed and sparked across him. His eyes snapped open.

With a roar, Santo Vaccarro returned to consciousness. He tore his right arm free of the bolts securing him to the stake, then ripped several of the leads still attached to his body away, spraying more clear liquid.

The Purifiers directly below froze. Ci was forced to fully phase as Santo lunged right through her at the nearest one, perched on the edge of the pyre stack. The sound of rock meeting meat clapped back from the shattered dome overhead. The cultist was sent flying like a broken rag doll, sailing right over the heads of the ones underneath.

Santo wasn't done. He turned and tore the metal stake from its fixings, securing it beneath the elbow and shoulder of his one arm like a lance, then swung it at the remaining Purifiers who had been clambering up the pyre, swatting them off like flies. He turned the same swing into a throw, flattening another trio beneath the now-bent pole.

"Santo!" Cipher shouted from behind Rockslide. She phased through him, hoping the brief shock would cut through his frenzy. She risked materializing in front of him. She saw his eyes focus on her; his raging motions momentarily stilled.

"Vic and Gray are here," she said. "We've got to get Vic's dad to safety."

She directed Santo's attention towards the neighboring pyre. Dan Borkowski was still bound there, gagged and struggling against the cords pinning him to the stake. In the carnage it looked as though he'd been totally forgotten, but Cipher doubted that would last for long.

Santo took in the sight, then looked at Cipher and said one thing.

"Get back."

Cipher phased and withdrew as Santo raised his one great fist and, with a bellow, brought it crashing down into the timber and kindling around him. The pilings went flying, a shockwave of splinters and split wood exploding from what had once been the pyre stack. It collapsed, taking Rockslide down with it.

In the midst of the debris, he kept punching. Bundles of sticks were shattered and mulched. The flagstones beneath soon followed, tremors running through the church as Santo plunged his hand into the very foundations of the old structure.

The rock answered him. Sediment burst up, splitting the flagstones apart. The mass of stone struck Santo's left shoulder, fusing and melding with it, grinding and grating as it reformed his missing arm. He raised the new appendage, flexed freshly formed fingers of rock, then slammed both hands down together.

This time the church really did shake. Dust and small particles of masonry fell from the barrel vault. The gap in the broken dome above widened, larger chunks of stone cascading down upon the crossing.

Tremors preceded a titanic upsurge of rock. Santo's grating shout became a drawn-out roar of effort as a dozen spikes of stone and soil ploughed up through the church's undercroft and foundations, sundering the flagstones around the pyre holding Dan Borkowski. The nearest Purifiers were flung away or pulverized, no match for the tectonic surge Santo had unleashed. When his shout finally echoed away into nothing, a parapet of jagged stone shards over a dozen feet high had been erected around much of the pyre, shielding it from the apse, Xodus, and most of the cultists.

Santo stood slowly, drawing his fists from the rubble beneath him. His panting breaths clattered like a stone bouncing down a mountainside. He looked up at his approximation of where Cipher had phased to.

"Untie Victor's father," he said. "I will keep the rest at bay."

CHAPTER FORTY

More shots scorched past the pillar Graymalkin was crouched behind. It wasn't just energy weapons either, but hard rounds now too. Bullets cracked and chipped off the stonework around him. The battering reports of gunfire echoed back like a crazed, booming drumbeat off the church's interior, filling his senses with the fury of combat.

He was not afraid, he realized. Only purposeful. They had reached the conclusion of their quest. The next few minutes would be decisive.

A terrible series of great tremors had shaken the whole church moments earlier, and he had recognized a familiar bellowing from somewhere close to the apse. That meant Alisa had succeeded in freeing Santo. The plan was working, despite Vic going early. The only problem, right now, was that he was pinned, and it wasn't necessarily because of the projectiles whipping past.

The long space between the support pillars and the external walls of the church was shrouded in shadows, but the nave wasn't as dark. The crossing before the apse and altar was still drenched in light coming through the broken dome overhead. It was too bright, too powerful. As long as he stayed in the shadows of the pillars, Graymalkin's abilities were potent, but if he went beyond them he'd be bereft. He hadn't yet been able to marshal enough of the darkness within himself to fully access his powers.

That was deeply frustrating. He'd seen Vic make a break towards the east transept and reach the stairway to the cloisters and the bell tower. He'd considered following – the route was open between his position and the transept – but he knew he was needed down here. Even with Santo now at her side, it was likely the Purifiers would overwhelm Alisa. As long as he had a breath left in his body, Graymalkin wouldn't let that happen, but providing assistance right now in the fight before the apse was impossible.

So Gray stayed, crouched on his haunches, and tried to gauge the movements of the nearest Purifiers based on the direction of the projectiles that passed him by, rather than those that struck the pillar at his back. He was sure they were attempting a crude, untrained form of fire-and-maneuver, splitting off into separate groups and attempting to work their way to his left and right so they could find an angle past the pillar. Given he had no ranged weaponry to oppose them, that in itself should have been easy enough. There was just one problem, as far as they were concerned.

Flanking the pillar would bring them into the shadows.

The first one had placed a single foot in the darkness creeping along the church's east wall when Graymalkin struck. He was a blur, a livid burst of force that dragged the darkness after him. There was a crack, a crunch, a scream. The scream ended. The Purifiers who had been about to follow the rush of their first comrade thought better about advancing any further. They tried to hit Graymalkin as he darted back between the pillars, but their shots struck only sandstone.

He returned to his crouch, forcing himself to be patient. Little by little, the sun was lowering as the evening approached, and as it did so the circle of light bathing the heart of the church became an ever more slender, tenuous crescent. Soon, inevitably, it would be gone entirely.

CHAPTER FORTY-ONE

Prophet Xodus's blood sang with the joy of purification. At long last, the time of reckoning had come. The hour was at hand, the promised moment of confrontation between the wicked and the divine, the righteous and the corrupt, the pristine human and the devolved mutant. He almost shook in ecstasy as the Church of the Seven Virtues resounded with screams and gunfire and the deep grating of rock and broken flagstones.

He knew he had to stay in control, just for a little longer. One last directive and he could lose himself to the fire, could draw his blessed sword and wade into the midst of the struggle. It had tasted mutant blood when it had cleaved the lizard thing's arm off on Brooklyn Bridge. Now it wanted more, and so did Xodus.

The rock beast had broken free, wrecking his pyre and half of the church in the process, but that did not concern him. If anything, he rejoiced even more. Now he could slay it in the midst of glorious battle. The divine would not allow him to be defeated, not this day. The salvation he craved could be earned not just in fire, but in blood as well. Lobe was no longer his concern either – he had gone from the nave, and the lizard had followed. Neither of them could halt the great purification, not now that it had begun in earnest.

Just one more order, and he could join the fray. It was time. He motioned to the white-robed Choristers standing on either side of him, one clutching a detonator, the other a power node with a series of switches.

"In the name of all that is holy," he snarled. "Do it."

The final part of the plan was activated. At the flick of the node's dials, a series of heavy industrial lamps rigged up around the dome of the apse thudded on, spearing a dozen beams of brilliant light across the nave and transepts, bathing the interior of the church in stark illumination. In the same instant, the detonator triggered the pile of burlap sacking that had been heaped before Xodus, set almost between the two pyres. The explosion was not large, but it had the desired effect. The sacking, stuffed full of powdered sandstone, burst upwards. A huge cloud of dust blossomed from the center of the crossing, instantly shrouding it, the brilliance of the spotlights making the space look like an old television screen marred by swirling, eddying grains of static.

"There," Xodus barked after peering into the cloud for a few moments, thankful for his mask's filtrations. "There it is, my good children!"

He pointed into the air above the second pyre, the one that had recently been surrounded by the stones summoned by the rock monster's sorcery. The dust there didn't churn as it did everywhere else. Rather, it seemed to have taken on the suggestion of a human form, caught in the spotlights as it surged down to help the pathetic heretic struggling against the stake.

Xodus smiled and drew his sword. The demonic night mutant and the invisible phantom mutant – neither of their powers would be much use to them now.

CHAPTER FORTY-TWO

Vic bounded up the stone stairs to the cloisters, his every thought bent towards catching Lobe. He'd find out why Lobe was tormenting him, and he'd make the man answer for the pain he had caused. That was all that mattered – so much so that Vic didn't even pause to consider the fact that the fleeing CEO appeared to have discarded his suit and shoes on the landing leading out onto the cloisters.

Vic stepped over them and through the narrow, arched opening, slipping into the pillared corridor that ran along the east wall of the church. He felt a savage thrill of triumph. He had Lobe cornered.

As he entered the cloisters a great tremor ran through the stone around him, shaking off dust and rattling loose masonry around his feet. At first, he'd thought the raised walkway was in the process of collapsing, but as he stepped out onto it, he got a view from its open right-hand side of the main section of the church beneath. He almost punched the air with delight at what he saw. Ci had gotten Rocky free, and the big guy was tearing it up, hammering pillars of stone up into scattering Purifiers and creating a defensive ring around the pyre where his dad was still being held. He fought the urge to watch over his father from above or, worse, double back down to the ground level to help free him. He trusted Cipher and Rocky completely. He had to stick to the plan.

He refocused on the cloisters, beginning to advance along them. Light from the broken dome streamed past to illuminate the ground floor, but it didn't reach the pillared corridor. Here was just darkness and old stonework, and the unblinking, graven eyes of status set into alcoves on the left-hand side, every ten or so paces.

Vic continued carefully, aware of the debris that littered the floor. His heart was beating a furious tattoo and his senses seemed to have gone into overdrive. He tasted the air with a flick of his tongue, catching the acrid tang of dust and weapons discharges, but not a whole lot else. What had happened to Lobe? Didn't that big, bulging head contain a big, bulging brain? The cloisters were a dead end, so why would he enter them in the first place?

"You seem to be growing more hesitant, Victor," said the sickening voice. It echoed from up ahead – presumably Lobe was in one of the statue alcoves. But which one?

"I'm surprised you followed me, instead of running to help your father," the voice went on. "It showed some mettle. Perhaps I underestimated you."

"You've underestimated us all," Vic snapped, in no mood for verbal sparring but knowing that if he kept Lobe talking it would be easier to find him. "You're going to pay for that. I'm going to put a stop to whatever you're planning."

"Oh, poor, foolish Anole," sang out Lobe's rich, ugly voice from just up ahead. "All this effort and you don't even know what you're fighting for."

"I'm fighting for my family," Vic declared, eyeing each statue he passed. They were as broken down and faded as the rest of the church, a parade of forgotten saints and divine beings whose luster had long been lost. There didn't look to be much room to hide behind any of them though.

"How short-sighted," taunted the voice. "I'm fighting for the betterment of all humanity. I wonder whose cause is more worthy?"

"Why do you want me?" Vic demanded, giving in to the question that had been plaguing him for so long. "Why are you doing all this? The Purifiers, the attacks on mutants, kidnapping my family? What sort of business do you think you're running?"

There was no immediate reply. Vic had almost reached the end of the cloisters. Just two more alcoves to go. He was tense, his skin shifted, expecting the trapped businessman to make a break at any moment.

"I'm running the best sort of business. One that expects massive profits. If you'd stop trying to evade me, Victor, I could look forward to a very healthy balance sheet indeed."

"I'm not evading you," Vic said, his skin crawling. "I'm right here."

"So am I."

The voice had come from just behind him. He spun wildly. Lobe stood before him, close enough to touch, with a smug look on his face. He'd completely shed his business attire, his lean frame now clad in a form-fitting black and red flexi-garment that looked like a dark parody of Vic's own yellow and black X-suit. The veins in the man's distended head appeared to be pulsing.

"Surprised to see me?" he asked. "Oh, don't worry. I can change that."

With a ripple, Lobe's form shifted, and he disappeared. Vic was still trying to make sense of what had just happened when the first fist struck him square on the side of the jaw.

CHAPTER FORTY-THREE

Cipher made it to Dan's pyre just before she was hit. The worst of the energy blast dissipated across her X-suit, but it still lashed at her hard enough to make her cry out and drop back off the side of the timber stacks. She halted her fall in midair, energy fizzing across her torso.

What had once been a fight in the most open space in the church now resembled a battle in some collapsing subterranean cavern. The detonation of the sacking had completely choked the air with dust, and the spotlights the Purifiers had triggered had served to turn that dust into a near-impenetrable wall, shifting but too dense to see more than a dozen or so paces in any direction. Cipher's world had been reduced to the pyre stack and the jagged rocks that Santo had driven up around it. Dan struggled desperately against his bonds, trying to shout something to her.

Purifiers had started to scramble over Santo's rocks. One hastily recharged an energy rifle from a perch atop a newly formed crag. That had to be the one who'd shot her.

They could see her. Cipher realized that as soon as the sacks had blown. It was a simple enough trick, but effective. Dust coated her body, highlighting her despite being nominally invisible. If she phased fully, she could lose the particles, but then she would merely become a negative imprint in the swirling clouds, picked out by the very absence of a presence.

In a training exercise she'd probably have withdrawn and reassessed, but this was all far from a training exercise. Shrugging off the last of the dissipated energy, she willed herself back onto the pyre. Dan Borkowski stared at her, eyes wide above his gag. She wasn't sure he was aware of what was happening around him, but she trusted he knew he was being rescued. Judging by his frantic efforts to free himself, he was as eager to help her as she was to help him.

Another energy shot passed her by, followed by a *whip-crack* she recognized as the close passage of a hard round. If the Purifiers had been trying to take them alive before, they certainly weren't any more. Cultists swarmed over the rocky barricade on all sides now, firing as they came. She saw impacts in the timber around Dan, one striking splinters off the stake above him. She realized she wasn't going to be able to get him untied without drawing fire down on them both, not while she was even partially visible. Cursing, she launched up into the air once more and away, energy bolts darting through the surrounding dust cloud like bright fish through murky waters. She had to draw them away until the dust settled.

Below her Santo was engaged in his own struggle. The hulking X-Man was the focus of much of the Purifiers' ire. Energy blasts sizzled around him and hard rounds cracked chips and sparks off his stony frame. Cipher saw him lash out with his mind once more, tearing free a fresh spike of geological stratum from underneath the church and slamming it up into the midst of a knot of cultists. The golden-masked one, Xodus, was among those thrown aside by the fresh upheaval. The whole church shook again. As she swooped down to Santo's side, Cipher found herself wondering how much longer the aged building could endure.

Xodus was slammed sideways into one of his Choristers as a pillar of rock burst forth to his right, tearing part of his robes and making him lose his grip on his sword. The weapon clattered across the flagstones as the prophet struggled to right himself, impeded by his robes. A second Chorister helped him to his feet.

"My blade," Xodus snapped at the black-masked devotee, ignoring the Purifiers who had been injured in the rock burst. The Chorister hurried to retrieve the sword and knelt before his prophet, offering it up to him hilt-first, head bowed. Xodus snatched it and waved him away, looking beyond him at where the infernal rock monster had just pulverized two more Purifiers as they charged him, their weapons chattering.

Closing with these filthy mutants was proving more difficult than he had hoped. Still, preparations had been made. He raised his sword, the blade catching the beams of the floodlights above the apse, shining brilliantly in the swirling dust.

"Strike them down, my Choristers," he bellowed, his mask's amplifiers making his voice boom through the embattled space. "Shatter that horror into a thousand blasted shards!"

The Choristers obeyed. While a trio had accompanied Xodus down from the apse, the others had remained there. At the prophet's command they turned and drew back the black and white banners covering the makeshift altar. It was revealed to be a heavy crate, newly installed by the faithful. Its contents were just what Xodus needed – a brace of rocket-propelled grenade launchers and the corresponding ammunition. The Choristers loaded them with practiced ease. Xodus dropped his sword so that its bright tip pointed squarely at the rampaging rock beast. As he did so he roared a single word, voice riven with raw fanaticism.

"Purify!"

Cipher realized the danger too late. The dust was too thick, and the attacks on both her and Santo were too continuous. The first thing she knew of the Chorister assault was the *whump* of air displacement, and a streak of white contrails billowing by. The RPG corkscrewed wide of Rockslide and impacted in the center of the main doors to the church, right across the nave. They blew out in a blizzard of shattered oak.

"Santo, watch out," she screamed. Rockslide had spotted the threat too, but before he could plant his fist or summon up his geokinetics, the second and third grenades had been loosed. Neither of these missed.

There was a hideous double *crack*, and smoke and flame engulfed the X-Man. Cipher threw herself down towards him as it dissipated, oblivious now to the small arms fire still slicing through the air around her. She dreaded what she might find.

Santo was shattered. One of the rocket grenades had taken out his right leg. The second had split much of his torso and dislodged one shoulder. He was on his side, smoke rising from scorched stone, parts of him reduced to rubble.

"You've got to get up, Santo," Cipher urged, kneeling by his head. She fully materialized so he could see her, forcing his glazed eyes to focus on her. "Vic still needs you. I still need you."

It was hopeless. She knew that, if she wanted, she could still simply phase and vanish. She didn't entertain the idea, even for a second. Not this time.

Santo didn't reply. Cipher looked up as a shout rang out. A pair of Purifiers charged through the dust and smoke, their rifles levelled. Their hellish masks had lost the silver luster and their black robes were caked gray with dust. Their weapons flashed and barked in the gloom, bullets striking and ricocheting off Santo's back as they rushed in.

Cipher met them with a roar. She phased completely as she did so, passing right through Rockslide and the bullets tearing into him. She dropped the ability the moment she reached the two Purifiers, blinking into existence between them and slamming her forearms into their heads. Her momentum scythed them both down onto their backs, masks as broken as the faces underneath.

More Purifiers emerged through the smog ahead, backlit by the unyielding light of the lamps rigged up to the apse. She glanced back at Santo. He'd managed to drag himself up onto one elbow. She didn't know how great his powers of regeneration were, but she knew she had to give him a chance to get back onto his feet. If not, they were finished.

The sound of shattered glass turned her attention back to the apse. She didn't realize it immediately, but the brilliant beams of the floodlights were beginning to go out one by one. The reports of the individual gunshots were almost lost amidst the wider firing, but someone was shooting out the lights in the apse, slowly and accurately.

As the last of the beams blinked out, Cipher smiled. Trust Graymalkin to work out a solution to that particular problem.

CHAPTER FORTY-FOUR

Graymalkin centered the rifle's open sights and took the last shot, squeezing off two rounds for good measure. The shots blew out the final light above the apse with a crash and a hail of fragmented glass. The weapon clicked empty.

He had been more than impressed by the precautions taken by the Purifiers thus far. They did, however, seem to be laboring under the misapprehension that none of the Institute's students knew what a firearm was. Graymalkin wondered what effect half a dozen such weapons would have had if they'd existed around the time he was born. Nothing good, he imagined. Still, he'd managed to find a use for the one that had been carried by the Purifier who'd tried to outflank him earlier on, and it was certainly a sure sight more accurate and more rapid-firing than the old flintlock fowling piece his father had forced him to learn to use when he'd been a child.

The floodlights bathing the center of the church with illumination were now gone. Sunlight still gleamed through the broken dome, but the huge amount of dust and smoke unleashed had diffused it. Graymalkin's power built within him, something akin to a rising vibration that made his heart tremor and his limbs quiver. It was all he could do to contain it, and it was still a long way from its peak.

He could have waited for longer, marshalling his strength in the shadows, but his friends could not. He tensed and unleashed the darkness.

Xodus advanced through the dust-choked shadows, holding his sword aloft.

"Rally," he bellowed at the faithful around him. "Rally and strike them down, my children! They are there for the taking!"

The lights had failed, but there was still enough illumination coming through the shattered dome overhead. Xodus strove to make out the two pyres on either side, directing the Choristers flanking him to open fire.

Before they could, the dust before him swirled. He swung his sword at the shade materializing before him, driven by instinct to lash out. The blessed steel hit home, just as Xodus caught an impression of deathly-pale skin and terrible eyes.

Exultation filled him, followed by a horrifying realization. He had not cut down one of the vile mutants, as he had supposed. The blade of his sword quivered. Somehow, the mutant had blocked Xodus's razor-sharp blade with one hand. Xodus cried out and tried to wrench the sword out of the horror's grasp. It held on with almighty unnatural strength, like death incarnate in the gloom.

Then, the horrifying creature struck – not him, but Xodus's sword – by hitting the flat of the blade with the palm of its other hand. A dull clang rang out, followed by the clatter of falling steel. Xodus's shattered weapon fell to the flagstones, leaving only one remaining shard of metal sticking out of the prophet's grip. The demon wasn't even cut or bleeding.

Xodus remained frozen, struggling to find the words of a

prayer for protection. The creature was a true demon from the depths of some infernal realm. It showed no hesitation though and slammed its palm against Xodus's chest. Xodus was pitched backwards into several Purifiers behind him.

By the time he'd recovered and gotten to his feet, struggling for breath, the Choristers had finally opened fire. The thunder of gunfire assaulted the prophet's ears, but the demon was already gone, vanishing as quickly as it had appeared into the swirling dust and shadow.

"The pyres, you fools," Xodus managed to grunt as one of the white-robed fanatics helped steady him. "We have to secure them, before they free the prisoners!"

CHAPTER FORTY-FIVE

Vic slammed back into the cloister pillar behind him, feeling loose masonry crack and tumble as his vision flashed with pain. He wasn't able to recover in time to avoid the second blow, or the third. The fourth put him down on his knees, blood from his nose and lips messing his face.

"So fast," Lobe said, becoming visible once more as he stood over him and cracked his knuckles. "I really could get used to this. Get up."

Vic spat blood onto the flagstones, shook the stars from his eyes, and slammed his head upwards. The same blow that had sent Prophet Xodus reeling almost caught the CEO of Sublime Corp as well, but Lobe's apparently new-found reflexes allowed him to dodge the worst of it. Vic's spiny skull caught him in the side, driving him back with a grunt and giving Vic time to regain his feet, but no more.

Lobe came in with another flurry of punches, their positions now reversed – Vic was being driven back along the cloisters towards the stairwell, his footing uncertain on the debris-littered floor. He managed to block Lobe's blows this time, but the supposed businessman was far faster than he should have been.

Lobe paused, still smiling, clearly relishing the confrontation.

"What are you?" Vic demanded, taking another step back and cuffing the blood from his nose.

"I'm you," Lobe answered. "Why, just look…"

He held an arm out, and it changed. With a ripple it shifted color, becoming a near-flawless mimicry of the dark sandstone behind it. He moved and flexed it, the limb now little more than a distortion of its background.

"Blink and you'll miss me," Lobe said. "Almost as much fun as the wall-crawling, or the tongue!"

Lobe dropped his jaw with the final syllable and lashed out with the muscle – it was forked, and it snared and wrapped around Vic's left wrist, whipcord fast. Vic let out an exclamation of disgust and ripped his arm free, but not before it had left him off balance and allowed Lobe to close the distance again. He was forced to parry another pair of stinging punches, giving ground again.

"You've stolen my abilities," he snapped, equal parts outraged and horrified. "How? Why?"

"Oh, I doubt a country kid like you would understand much of the how," Lobe mocked. "Suffice to say it took a great deal of financial investment, and a particular breakthrough in the form of one severed arm."

"You used my arm?" Vic asked, the memory of Graymalkin's findings in the Revitalize facility flashing through his thoughts. "You've done something with my DNA. My genetics. You've… cloned my powers."

"Isolated and replicated specific strands of your personal mutant gene," Lobe said with relish. "The first fully successful experiment of such a nature in the history of the world! And as is only right and proper, I'm the first benefactor. Behold the future, Victor Borkowski. Mutant powers, just a serum away!"

"But why me?" Vic asked. He was desperately trying to keep the egotistical maniac talking while he backed off towards the cloister stairwell. He had to get word to the others. What if he'd done something to enhance the Purifiers as well?

"I'll admit, I thought I could do better for the first trial run," Lobe said, stalking after him. "I wanted real powers, not some reptilian gimmick. But the clever people I pay a great deal of money to were insistent. Mutants with particularly malleable physiology are by far the best test subjects. Your genetics are some of the most pliable, the most adaptable. I needed you, and mutants like you."

"That's why you hired the Purifiers?" Vic asked, taking another careful backwards step.

"Something like that," Lobe smiled, and attacked again. Vic avoided his punches, but this time the crazed CEO was pressing him forcefully, getting inside his guard. Lobe managed to grab Vic's left arm and flung him with brutal force into one of the alcove statues. The worn idol collapsed. Vic grunted with the impact and felt broken stone shatter and bounce off his head carapace. He sprawled, trying desperately to get to his feet as Lobe pressed his advantage. Another fist cracked against his cheek, more striking his raised forearms and shoulders. He kicked out, thumping a foot into Lobe's thigh and doing enough to drive him back.

"Why do you hate us?" Vic panted, managing to get up again before Lobe came in for another round. The words had the desired effect, checking Lobe.

"Oh, I don't hate your kind, Vic," he exclaimed, laughing. "On the contrary! I want to be you! Everyone wants to be you! The X-Men, brilliant heroes with fantastical abilities! And everyone *will* be you, once I'm finished. For a price, of course."

"That's what this is all about? Money?"

"Money and power," Lobe clarified. "The power to beat the X-Men at their own game."

Vic had dropped back again. There was only one more alcove left between him and the stairwell. With all the speed he could muster, he snatched the head of the statue and dragged it down, splitting it across the cloister corridor. Then, skin rippling and shifting, he turned and bounded into the stairwell.

He didn't get far. Purifiers scrambled up from the ground floor like gray phantoms, caked in dust. It looked like he wasn't going down then.

He ran up instead, towards the belfry. As he went, he heard Lobe snapping at the oncoming cultists.

"Leave him! He's mine."

CHAPTER FORTY-SIX

Santo was up, but Cipher didn't know how much longer that would be the case. He'd managed to reform enough rock to bind a new limb, but his injuries were telling – a latticework of cracks was steadily spreading across his body as he fought, driving back a fresh wave of cultists with another burst of stone shards.

The crossing at the heart of the church was now a shattered, uneven mess of dust, jagged rock and scattered bodies, but still the cultists came, seemingly endless in number and driven into a frenzy. This was their hour of reckoning, and none wished to be found wanting. Cipher was tackled as she rounded the broken remains of Santo's pyre, the impact of the robed figure almost throwing her over. She grappled with him before phasing, leaving him clutching nothing but air. A strike to the back of the neck felled him.

She winced. The wound in her arm had reopened – her bicep to her wrist was red with blood, a dark contrast to the dust caking her. She was starting to lose feeling in the limb too. There was no time to dress it, though. She turned just in time to see a Purifier, lowering his rifle at her, thwacked from existence by a vibrating blur of inky blackness. Graymalkin darted to her side, his expression grim.

"They are numerous," he said as he looked towards where Rockslide threw off a cultist who had leapt onto his back and was trying to wedge a knife into a crack between his shoulder blades.

"Where's Vic?" Cipher asked. "He must've caught Lobe by now? We need him if we're going to call these lunatics off."

"I don't know," Gray admitted. "I last saw him pursuing Lobe up the spire stairs."

"What about Xodus?"

"I fought him a moment ago. His sword is now broken, but his white-robe servants saved him."

"We need to help Santo," Cipher urged, "and try and reach Vic's dad. We can't keep this up for much longer."

"That may not be possible," Gray said.

Cipher could already see what he meant. The worst of the dust from the sacking explosion was beginning to settle, and she could almost see across to the opposite transept now. Dan's pyre lay ahead, the rocks that Santo had thrust up to shield it partly toppled and collapsed. Purifiers were all over them, setting up defensive positions, pausing their assault to center their resistance on the mound of sticks and kindling. They knew the mutants were going after their captive. They had them just where they wanted them.

"We need to regroup as well," Cipher said to Graymalkin.

"If my powers were at their height I could likely free Victor's father, even in the midst of the cult's defense," Gray said. Cipher looked up at the broken dome overhead, through the remnants of the swirling dust and smoke. Sunlight still beamed through, albeit weak and slender.

"It isn't nightfall yet," she said doubtfully. "We don't have time for you to build your power."

"There may be another way," Graymalkin said. "But you're going to have to trust me."

CHAPTER FORTY-SEVEN

Vic had a plan. It wasn't his best, but it was all he had. None of them had predicted this. Vic had feared, at worst, that Lobe shared the fanatical views of the Purifiers, and was using his wealth and power to develop some sort of strain that would target mutants in an attempt to wipe them out. Never had he imagined the madman would be trying to replicate mutant genes, let alone bottle and sell them.

He bounded up the steps. He knew he would hit a dead end when he emerged at the tower's belfry. That couldn't be helped. He'd have to face Lobe at some point. It may as well be atop the spire of an old, crumbling church in east-side Brooklyn.

He burst up onto the timber boards of the bell platform. New York stretched out beneath him, Manhattan visible in the distance, the sun behind it sunk into the midst of a jagged nest of spires and towers. He turned, finding two great cast-iron bells at his back, suspended along with their ropes above a sheer drop that appeared to plummet away down to the east transept of the church's interior. The sounds of gunfire and shouting from the still-raging battle echoed up through the opening, a constant, stress-inducing reminder to Vic that he had to hurry.

Trying to stay away from both the interior and exterior edges, Vic snatched his communicator free from his suit and keyed it. "Lobe's got my mutant powers," he said, hoping that any of his companions could hear him. "He's been gene-splicing–"

He got no further. With a scrabble of claws on stone, Lobe burst up onto the tower, going from all fours to an upright posture. He grinned manically.

"Going somewhere, Victor?" he demanded, and lunged. Vic had no more room to retreat and could only take the blow on his right side, a flurry of punches striking his larger arm. He cried out, dropping the X-communicator. It rolled across the floorboards, stopping at Lobe's feet.

"I wondered when I'd get my hands on one of these," the head of Sublime Corp said, pausing to scoop up the device. Vic tried to lash out at him as he did so, but he darted back with the sort of speed Vic just couldn't match.

"You're going to have to be quicker than that," he said, killing the communicator's transmission. "Sublime Corp found your special suits easy enough to replicate, but the communication hardware… We've been looking for a device like this to reverse engineer for quite some time. Perhaps it'll even let us hack the Xavier Institute's database. You really are invaluable to me, Anole."

"What do you want with me?" Vic pleaded as Lobe pocketed the communicator. "You've already taken my arm. You've got your powers. Just let my dad go and leave us in peace."

"You're so petulant," Lobe snapped, his dark humor abruptly vanishing. "I've taken one of your arms, yes. But I see that you've replaced that. It's intriguing, I didn't realize you possessed that level of regenerative ability. You and me both, now. But I'm going to need everything you've got, I'm afraid. I wish I could claim it's going to be a quick, painless process, but it absolutely won't be."

The attacks resumed, relentless now. Vic tried to color-shift, almost instinctively, but he had nowhere to hide. Laughing madly, Lobe changed too, becoming a blur as he drove Vic almost right around the bell tower. Vic favored his right arm in his defense, crying out whenever it was hit. His side already hurt from the clash in the cloisters, and trying to match his own powers was exhausting. Lobe seemed as adept at using them as he was – there was a viciousness to his speed, and a freshness to him that Vic, burnt out, couldn't match.

"Hurts, does it?" Lobe demanded, still shifted, panting slightly. "Not fully formed then. Tender. Practically useless. I almost feel bad, beating up a kid. Almost."

He grabbed Vic, but as he did so the arm that seized Vic's shoulder rippled and became visible again. They both stared down at it, before Lobe snarled and slammed Vic into one of the pillars supporting the bell tower's spire. Sandstone crumbled and gave way behind him. Vic struck Lobe with his left fist, catching him across the jaw, but it seemed to only enrage him more. He hauled Vic in the opposite direction and cracked his head off one of the mighty bells. There was a shuddering *clang*, and Victor went limp in his grip.

"Pathetic," Lobe growled, tossing him down onto the floorboards. Vic groaned and rolled onto his back, looking up at him.

"You're losing your powers," Vic said, managing to smile. "The serum is only temporary. That's why you need me to finish your experiments. To find a permanent solution."

"And we'll find one," Lobe said, the rage in his eyes no longer masked by mockery. He kicked Vic's left arm, then reached down and hauled him back onto his feet, pinning him against the barrier that separated them from the sheer drop down into the transept. Vic tried to fight back with his left arm, his right hanging bruised and useless, but Lobe clearly still had enough of the serum left in his veins to hold him in place. He pinned the left arm by the wrist. An icy calm filled Vic.

"You were born with your abilities," Lobe snarled in Vic's face. "I've earned mine through hard work, through merit."

"Through money," Vic managed to say, his lips bloody. Lobe backhanded him.

"Silence, boy! I'm a genius," he barked.

Vic, his head turned to one side by the blow, looked slowly back at Lobe, and this time his pink-stained teeth bared in a grin.

"Not much of a genius if you still haven't realized there's actually nothing wrong with my new arm."

He paused, taking in and relishing the understanding, the horror, in Lobe's eyes. Then, jaw clenched with the effort, Vic swung his arm – his right arm. The full force of the heavy, gorilla-like limb thundered into the Sublime CEO's abdomen, slamming him backwards with such power that he crashed through the belfry's external barrier and plummeted out over the edge of the tower. There was no scream – Vic doubted Lobe had any air in his lungs for that – but eventually there was a small crunching sound from far below.

Vic turned away and wrung out his right hand, trying to work the pain from his fist. The urge to revel in vengeance was a strong one, but he didn't give in to it. He peered over the edge of the belfry, down at the street below.

Lobe was sprawled across the sidewalk. Vic couldn't make out if he was still alive, but the CEO wasn't moving. Vic readied to scale down the outside of the tower, when he realized something.

The gunfire he'd heard earlier seemed to have died down. Was that a bad sign? Had the Purifiers overwhelmed the others? He battled with the need to ensure Lobe was finished over concern for his friends. The latter won out. If Lobe still lived, Vic doubted he was going anywhere fast. He had to get to the others, and to his father.

He knew he didn't have time to rush back down the stairwell. He clambered onto the edge of the barrier between the belfry and the drop into the transept and reached out, tugging one of the hefty ropes dangling from the bells. It creaked ominously but held. Cuffing the blood from his mouth and nose and wiping his palms on his X-suit, Vic launched out and caught onto the rope fully.

The bell tolled, a great, sonorous peal that rang through the broken church and out over east Brooklyn. Vic shimmied down the rope, trying not to go too fast so he didn't scorch his palms. As he went, he got a view down into the transept and the wider church beyond.

The air was full of dust and smoke, but Vic could see that Santo's pyre had been wrecked and that his father's was still standing. Worse, his dad was still bound to the stake, and there were Purifiers in the shattered rocks and rubble all around him. He spotted Rocky almost directly below, sheltering behind one of the transept pillars. Ci was with him, and Gray was behind one of the supports further along, wreathed in shadow.

Vic's descent brought him down right into the middle of the transept, squarely in the sights of the Purifiers defending the pyre. While dust still hung heavy in the air, the bell's tolling alerted them all to his presence. The roar of gunfire competed with the unheeded call to worship, and in seconds the air around Vic was alive with whizzing, cracking death. He swung perilously and let go, thumping down on all fours onto the flagstones like a feline. He immediately scrambled for the pillar Ci and Rocky sheltered behind, bullets and energy bolts chewing up the sandstone around him. One grazed his shoulder but didn't pierce his X-suit, and he felt the passage of another lash right past his face. Then he was behind the pillar, panting. He hugged Rocky. The big guy looked in a bad way, his stony skin scorched and scarred, large chunks missing. Ci's arm was bleeding too, and she looked bruised and worn. He supposed he didn't look much better.

"It's good to see you, big guy," he told Santo as he eased out of the hug. "Everybody still alive?"

"We are," Santo grumbled. "Can't speak for the Purifiers."

"Where's Lobe?" Cipher cut in. Vic shrugged, wincing at the pain the motion caused. He was pretty sure he'd broken something when he'd been flung into the cloister statue, and the jump from the bell rope had aggravated it.

"Lobe took a fall," he told Ci.

"You couldn't catch him?"

"I'd have had to have been at the bottom of the bell tower for that, not the top. If he's still alive, I doubt he's going anywhere fast. I was worried about you down here. Xodus still has my dad, I see.

"Jonas has an idea," Cipher said, raising and keying her communicator. "But you're not going to like it."

"If it involves none of us dying while we get Dad out safely then I'm going to absolutely love it," Vic quipped.

"That's the ideal outcome," Gray's voice clicked over Ci's communicator. "But there are… many potential variables."

"What is it then?" Vic demanded, frustrated, not understanding why they were hesitating. It was Cipher who spoke up.

"Jonas wants us to collapse this part of the church. On top of ourselves."

CHAPTER FORTY-EIGHT

Xodus ordered the last of the faithful to cease fire. A silence, great and terrible following the thunder of battle, settled over the church's brutalized remains. He took a torch from the Chorister who'd just lit it, advancing through the ranks of his children with the burning light held aloft.

"Behold your end, mutant," he bellowed, his voice filling the void left in the wake of the Purifiers' gunfire. "You can no longer deny the inevitable! Step forth and die with dignity, or watch your own misguided father burn!"

He brandished the torch at the intact pyre and the old fool still tied atop it. This was what he'd been brought here for, to draw out these unclean monsters like rats to dead flesh.

There was no answer from the east transept. Xodus growled and thrust the torch in amidst the base of the kindling. So be it, this conflagration was long overdue. He would have his pyre, and nothing would now stop him.

Xodus hadn't heard from Lobe since the mutants had first attacked. He didn't care either. One swollen-headed fool and his money didn't concern the prophet, not any more. He had what he wanted – a holy battle, a confrontation with creatures of horror and darkness. Lobe was hardly better than the mutant filth anyway. Xodus would deal with him as well, after he'd purified the ones before him. Fire and smoke and burning flesh, that was what he had craved for so long and that was what he would have.

The flames took quickly. The prisoner tried to fight and cried out, but Xodus had bound and gagged him personally – he wasn't going to escape, not that way. The sight of the rising fire beginning to gnaw at the lower bundles of the stack had the desired effect. Movement at the end of the transept caught his attention. The great rock mutant bounded from his cover behind one of the pillars, its smaller kindred scuttling behind it. Xodus briefly thought they were making for the center of the transept, apparently happy to be gunned down right in front of the Purifiers, but he realized they were instead heading for the narrow set of stairs in the far wall that led down to the church's crypt.

"Kill them," Xodus screamed, brandishing the hilt of his shattered sword towards the deformed creatures. "Kill them all!"

The thunderous roar of the gunfire was so loud Xodus thought his eardrums were about to burst. Individual shots and the many echoes of their reports melded together into one continuous din. The east transept seemed to disintegrate beneath the fusillade. Sandstone burst and shattered, statues toppled, carvings broke apart. An RPG streaked past the fleeing figures, impacting in the far wall and blowing a hole clean through to the outside. Xodus took in the destruction with the intensity of a zealot, eyes locked onto the mutant band, willing them to be struck down before him. The rock brute was hit multiple times, but carried on through the storm, shielding the others. They reached the entrance to the crypts, though the rock didn't descend. Instead it hunched over, still defending the shadow one.

Xodus snarled with frustration. He had fought that terrible creature earlier. It was a true demon of the darkness, and it had broken his holy sword. He'd sworn to plunge the remnants of the blade through its black heart.

"Advance," he bellowed over the barrage, gesticulating furiously at the Purifiers around them. "There's no way out of those crypts! They're trapped! Advance and finish them!"

CHAPTER FORTY-NINE

Graymalkin placed both hands on Rockslide's shoulders, looking up into the giant's eyes. He was hunched over Graymalkin, turned away from the pyre and the Purifiers. There were audible cracks and clacking sounds, like pebbles bouncing down a craggy slope, as bullets flattened and rebounded off his scarred back.

"I'm sorry, Santo," Graymalkin told him. "I'm sorry for what you've had to endure through all this."

"I can take it," Santo grunted. "You ready?"

"I am," Graymalkin confirmed, letting go and taking a step back. "Let us bring an end to this."

Santo nodded once and, with a roar, pounded his fists down into the flagstones one last time. Stone split and shattered as he delved down, reaching out both mentally and physical, communing with the stratum beneath the church. He'd already asked so much of it, but now he called for something more, something final. The rock answered.

It began slowly, an almost imperceptible tremor that Graymalkin sensed through the soles of his feet. It increased rapidly, making the stones scattered across the broken floor rattle, then spreading its tremors up the walls. Soon the whole church trembled. Santo's voice rose with the power of the quake, going from low and grating to a powerful, drawn-out roar.

Cracks ran up the wall, splitting it, arcing along like lightning to the vaulted ceiling. Graymalkin noticed with alarm that the splits formed in Santo's own body over the course of the battle had started to worsen as well, as though in sympathy with the church. His friend was close to shattering.

The trembling built to a roar, becoming one with Santo's own bellow. A section of the transept roof close to the bell tower stairs gave way with a monumental crash, a weight of brickwork slamming down into the floor not far to Graymalkin's right. He tried not to flinch. Suddenly his plan seemed altogether more desperate and dangerous than he had hoped.

Rock punched up from the flagstones around where he and Santo stood, showering them both in dirt and grit. More of the roof caved, an ever-widening collapse now that spread inevitably over the transept. The bell tower started to go with it. One of the bells came crashing down with a reverberation that shook Gray to his core. His senses had become filled with dust and broken stone. It seemed as though his very bones ached at the seismic discord around him, as though just the sound and fury alone would tear him to pieces.

He forced himself not to look up as the collapse in the ceiling reached them, locking his eyes onto Santo instead. The giant's roar burnt out – he was silent now, his rough features set, his whole body trembling and shivering, on the cusp of splitting into pieces.

Graymalkin placed a hand back on his crumbling shoulder. The rocks around them surged, and the roof came down, and the worst of Graymalkin's night terrors returned.

CHAPTER FIFTY

More than ever before, Vic was convinced he was about to die. He stood with Cipher as, around them, the crypts of the Church of the Seven Virtues shook and groaned, like a man caught in his final frenzied death-throes.

The crypts themselves were a low, dank space beneath the east transept, a collection of old stone tombs laced with cobwebs and heavy with dust. There was nothing down here but old bones and spiders, and no light except for the thin illumination coming down through a barred grate in one corner that Vic assumed looked out at street level. It was too small to fit through, so Vic just stood with Cipher in the tiny strip of daylight and waited for the crypt's ceiling to come crashing down on them both.

Ci looked exhausted. The wound in her arm was bad, and her eyes unfocused. Vic hugged her tightly.

"You should get out of here," he told her over the thunder of grinding, shifting stone above. "There's no reason for you to stay now."

"No," she said simply.

"Then at least phase. Then you won't be crushed."

"No," she repeated.

"Why not? There's no purpose in all of us dying."

"Because I always get out," Cipher said, her voice dull. "I always survive when others don't, and I'm tired of it. I want to stay with you. No more hiding this time."

Vic didn't know what to say, so he simply clung on as the Church of the Seven Virtues collapsed around them. Something dug into his side where he was hugging Ci. He delved into the pocket and found the little rubber dinosaur.

"Oh look," he said, holding it up in front of Cipher as part of the ceiling across the crypt collapsed, crushing a tomb slab beneath it. "My lucky dino."

Cipher burst out laughing, though there were tears in her eyes.

"You have a lucky toy dinosaur," she said. "Of course you do."

"I used to think I was one," Vic said. "I was devastated when I found out they were extinct. I was scared I was the last one."

Ci laughed again, the sound strangely pure and carefree in the trembling depths.

Gradually, the thunder quieted. The tremors eased. Vic held his breath, looking up at the crypt's brick arches, still expecting an abrupt cave-in to end their existence in an instant. It seemed impossible that they'd survived.

"Is it over?" he dared whisper, looking wide-eyed at Cipher. Her response was just as pressing.

"Did Santo and Jonas survive?"

CHAPTER FIFTY-ONE

Graymalkin remembered his father. In life he had not been a large man, neither tall nor broad, but he had possessed the fearsome, rangy strength of someone who had labored hard with his hands all his life. In Graymalkin's nightmares however, he always appeared huge, his frame almost as vast as his hatred. He would strike Graymalkin, his pox-scarred face riven with a wild and unreasoning fury.

"Devil," he had screamed at him, stinking breath and spittle hitting his face. "You're not my son! You're a devil!"

Graymalkin cried out, bringing his arms up to shield himself. Mercifully, the blows ceased. Darkness enclosed him. For a while he thought he could hear the dull scrape and thud of a shovel, beating the earth above him. Then silence, more profound and lasting than any he had ever known, or ever would know again.

He reached out, trembling. His fingers met something cold and firm. It shifted. At first the motion alarmed him, but it also brought back a memory. Rock. Sandstone. The church, coming down around him, a scene of total annihilation. He had survived though, shielded by Santo, protected by that living rock.

And there, buried beneath the rubble of the east transept, he was in complete and utter darkness.

He felt his powers surge. He was no longer afraid. For a few brief, precious seconds, he couldn't even remember his father's face.

He became the darkness, melding with it, raw energy cast in the form of inky blackness. The stone around him started to vibrate and shift. The blackness bled over and around the rock, rising up out of that stone tomb.

Darkness was coming, and now its power was absolute.

Xodus swore as he struggled to right himself, flinging the hem of his torn and dusty robes to one side.

Briefly, he had thought he was about to meet the divine. He'd been advancing in the midst of the faithful, preparing to finally cut down the mutant scum who still, somehow, refused to accept their fate. Then the whole church had started to shake, and the east transept had begun to collapse.

He'd barely gotten clear of the cascading masonry, scrambling back to where the walls still stood. The pyre which he had lit had been extinguished by the blizzard of dust and stone that had exploded from the collapse. Many of the faithful had been crushed with it.

Xodus hauled himself up, struggling to breathe or see in his mask. Around him the surviving faithful were doing likewise, moaning and dazed in the grim silence following the collapse. Where once the east transept stood, only a wall of rubble remained, sealing it off from the rest of the church. As Xodus struggled to focus, the stones seemed to stir. It took him a while to realize that it wasn't the masonry itself that was moving. Something oozed out of the wall of debris, a strange, inky blackness that appeared to be coalescing in the gloom of the dust-shrouded crossing.

With a jolt, Xodus recognized what it was. The shadow demon was returning.

"Fire," Xodus shouted, grasping around for support from the faithful. "I need fire! Light!"

He looked desperately over at the pyre. Part of the kindling stack had collapsed, the fire extinguished, but the central stake remained standing, the prisoner still lashed to it. He turned his gaze up to the dome overhead. Sunlight shone there, like the promise of salvation, a final, slender ray that pierced the gloom and fell just before the apse and altar. Xodus stumbled towards it, but even as he did so it grew thinner and weaker. Then it was gone, blinking from existence just before he could get to it, plunging the interior of the church into darkness.

"No," he shouted. "No! Do not abandon me!"

He heard the sound of rocks tumbling as something burst free from the east transept. It was coming. The screams started.

The darkness lived. It shifted around Xodus, wrapping him up in its suffocating folds. He lashed out blindly, staggering. Where was his sword? He'd dropped the broken hilt. He needed a weapon. No, he needed to get out. He tried to pray, but he could not.

The prisoner. That was the key. They would not risk harming the man they had captured, Borkowski. If he had him, he could escape. He just had to get to the pyre.

He fumbled his way through the all-consuming blackness. Several of the faithful strayed into his path and were thrust aside. They wailed. A few who still had their weapons fired, the little bursts of light swiftly snuffed out as the sound of the gunfire rolled aimlessly around what remained of the church's interior. Xodus snarled, his heart racing, body slicked with sweat. The demon would not take him. It could not.

He reached the flank of the pyre, feeling brittle charred wood beneath his fingers. Panting, he began to climb, struggling onto the wooden platform where the stake still stood. He fumbled around it, breath wheezing through his golden mask's filters. He found the ends of the cords used to tie the prisoner. They were loose. Cut. Borkowski was gone.

Xodus moaned in fear and dismay. A splitting sound disturbed the church, a heavy, laden crack. It sounded like more stonework giving way. It continued to spread and grow, rising once more to the furious thunder of falling masonry and splitting stone. The whole church began to come down now, unable to support its aged weight any longer.

He tried to clamber back down from the pyre, but the cords snagged him, and he tripped, sending him sprawling across the wooden board. He made it back up onto his knees just in time to hear the splitting noise coming from directly overhead. He looked up.

As the remains of the dome caved in and crushed him, Prophet Xodus screamed. After a lifetime of judging and punishing others, he'd only just realized that he was about to face a judgment of his own.

CHAPTER FIFTY-TWO

All was dust and silence. Vic approached the entrance to the crypt tentatively, as though one wrong foot might bring the whole structure tumbling down. He peered up the narrow stairway that led up to the church interior. His eyes strained in the dark. As he'd feared, it was completely walled off with debris. They were trapped.

"You should go," Vic said to Ci, returning to her beneath the grate that led out onto the street. "Find out if there's still anyone up there."

Before she could reply a second round of tremors shook the crypt. They both froze, Vic convinced the whole ceiling was about to come down. Gradually, though, everything faded back into the silence. Vic dared to breathe again and realized how thirsty he was. Everything ached. He just wanted to lie down and sleep.

"I won't be long," Cipher said, but again she was interrupted. Both of them looked up as a fist materialized at the grate facing out onto the street. It tore open the iron bars, then punched the gap wider with a few, shuddering blows. A voice followed, one that Vic recognized.

"Come out, lizard boy."

Vic surged to his feet, his pain and exhaustion evaporating. Cipher phased and flew straight up through the wall as Vic leapt and grasped onto the sides of the broken grate with his heavy right arm, heaving himself up and through it.

He blinked in the last of the evening's sunlight. He was out on the street next to the church. What would once have been a wall next to him was now rubble – where the church had stood, only ruins remained, a great pile of broken stone and debris, still shifting and settling. Dust from the collapse coated everything in the street, and cracks decorated the walls of the neighboring buildings. People were visible at the far end of the street, hanging back and staring. More were gathering.

Vic barely took in any of it – his attention was on the figures in front of him. Santo smiled down at him. His former roommate was battered and broken, but he was still standing, unbowed. Next to him was Graymalkin, looking relieved and covered head-to-toe in dust. As Vic got to his feet he stepped aside, revealing the third member of the group.

"Hello, son," Dan Borkowski said with a smile.

Vic flung himself at his father, latching onto him and almost carrying them both over onto the ground. Dan laughed as he returned the embrace.

"Thank you," Vic said, crying into his dad's shoulder. He didn't know why those were the words that came to him, but he found himself saying them again and again as he clutched him, his grip shaking. "Thank you. Thank you."

"It's OK, Vic," Dan hushed him, patting his back. "I've got you, kid."

Vic eventually let go, sniffing, feeling abruptly self-conscious. He wiped away tears and took a step back, looking his dad up and down. He was as dusty as the rest of them, scratched in a few places, and his shirt and jeans were torn, but he looked otherwise unharmed.

"Gray got you out in one piece then?" Vic asked him.

"I don't remember much," Dan admitted. "I think I was carried out. There was darkness and a lot of screaming."

"Sounds about right," Vic laughed. "I'm only sorry it took us so long."

"In Fairbury you said you'd come back for me," Dan replied. "I never once doubted you would."

Vic hugged him again, feeling every second of pain, uncertainty and torment from the past few weeks drain away. He closed his eyes and let the newfound sense of peace settle within him, before letting go once more and looking at his friends.

Cipher materialized next to Gray. Vic had never seen her smiling so broadly. He approached Graymalkin and gave him a huge hug. "Thank you for getting him out," he said. "Thank you to all of you. I'd have never managed this on my own. You've all given me so much. I don't deserve it."

"What're friends for?" Santo rumbled.

"What's family for?" Graymalkin corrected as Vic finally let go of him.

"We're glad we could help," Cipher said. "More than that. It felt right. It felt like… finally I've done some good in my life. Something really worthwhile."

"I am experiencing similar feelings," Graymalkin said. "Though I cannot help but wonder why this struggle was necessary in the first place? What did the businessman Lobe wish to achieve by capturing you and tormenting us?"

"He wanted to replicate mutant powers with a serum he could mass-market," Vic said darkly. "And my DNA is apparently ideal for production. I think perhaps we should ask him a bit more in person."

"He used your own powers against you?" Cipher wondered, a look of horror crossing her face. Vic understood why – he wouldn't like to imagine what the maniac could've achieved if he'd been able to replicate Ci's abilities.

"This explains why they were kidnapping mutants," Rockslide said, a note of disgust in his voice. "They must have tested and tortured dozens, maybe hundreds."

"You defeated him in the belfry?" Graymalkin asked.

"Punched him right out of it. He still had a good amount of my power though, so I suspect he survived."

"If so, he could have gone anywhere," Cipher said. "Even if he was badly injured, he's had time to make his escape. We'd have to search every street in a two-mile radius, at least, and it's getting dark."

"Actually, I can take you straight to him," Vic said with a satisfied smirk.

"How?" Cipher asked. Vic's smirk became a grin.

"You were able to use your communicator to track mine, weren't you Ci?"

CHAPTER FIFTY-THREE

Lobe gritted his teeth and paused, leaning against the wall of the grocery shop by the intersection. His ankle, chest and back were in agony. He looked down at his broken leg, drew in a breath, and staggered a few more paces along the street, wincing as his fractured ribs grated.

Blast, it hurt. He would make that little green reptilian pay! He would give back every ounce of pain a hundredfold! Just as soon as he had more serum. He'd hoped the injection would last longer. Without it, admittedly, he wouldn't have survived the fall from the bell tower. There were still side-effects that he guessed would continue for a few hours yet – his tongue was still flexible, and parts of his body would occasionally ripple and shift, unbidden. Neither were particularly useful right now. He needed a ride out of this miserable sinkhole corner of Brooklyn, and then he needed to see a good Sublime Corp doctor.

He paused to check his phone, fighting the pain suffusing his body. He'd already demanded extraction. Where the hell was it? He should've had at least one vehicle standing by, he now realized. Maybe even a helicopter. In all honesty, it had never occurred to him that he'd need one. None of this was supposed to be happening.

He put the phone away and carried on, limping heavily. He tried to shut out the pain. In truth it was secondary to the shame of failure. It wasn't over, though. He'd gotten out, that was what mattered. All this was just a long, agonizing learning curve. He'd get the boy yet, and if not him, some other mutant. There were others on the list, less optimal, but viable all the same.

He stopped once more, leaning against a lamp post as a single vehicle rounded the corner and slowed down in the gathering gloom. *Finally*, he thought as he took in the glossy black van, one of the unmarked transports used by Sublime Corp subsidiaries for dirty work. He waved angrily at the driver behind his tinted window as the vehicle pulled up beside him, the headlights making him squint.

"Unlock the backdoor, you idiot," he snapped. There was a whine as the window rolled down, revealing the driver. He wasn't one of the suited spooks Lobe had been expecting. He looked to be in his forties, with ruffled hair and a ragged shirt, covered in fine grit.

"Think you've got the wrong vehicle, mister," the man said. Lobe had long enough to recognize him – Dan Borkowski – before a blow struck him on the side of his distended skull, flinging him down onto the sidewalk. He cried out in pain trying to roll away from his attacker.

"Going somewhere, Lobe?" Vic asked, crouching over him with a boyish grin.

"Get away," Lobe hissed. "Leave me be!"

"We already asked you for the same courtesy," Vic answered, wagging a finger at him. "Rude, Mr Lobe, rude. Do to others as you would have done to you."

Lobe lashed out with his tongue, grunting as he wrapped it around Vic's left wrist. The kid's eyes widened for a moment.

"Ew," he exclaimed, taking hold of the slimy length with his thick right fist and holding it firmly in place, not allowing Lobe to draw it back. "Someone really needs to teach you when it's appropriate to use that thing."

Lobe tried to answer but couldn't, wincing as Vic kept a hold of his tongue. Tears filled his eyes as he heard the slam of car doors, and more figures loomed over him – the rock creature, the shadow thing and the invisible girl, that horrible little team of pretend X-Men.

Vic began to laugh, his friends grinning. He was still laughing as the first sirens became audible in the distance.

EPILOGUE

Vic woke up slowly and found himself looking at sunlight beaming through his curtains. He yawned and stretched, feeling the soft sheets around him, the deep pillow underneath. The urge to sink back into it and doze off again was almost too much. He could smell pancakes cooking downstairs though. The enticing scent triggered a memory. He twisted in the bed to check the calendar on the wall and let out an exclamation of dismay.

Today was the day. He'd gotten his dates all wrong. Since moving into Mrs Templeton's house the days had all seemed to blur together, as they always did when it was the holidays and the tyranny of work schedules, class times, and essay deadlines fell away for a time. He scrambled out of bed and got dressed, struggling to find the right clothes in the unfamiliar bedroom.

It had been two weeks since the Borkowskis had accepted Mrs Templeton's invitation to live in her home while they got their new place sorted. Vic's old teacher had been insistent – her husband had passed away, her children were grown, so she could use the company. Vic, Dan, and Martha were more than happy to oblige. After what had happened to them, the Templeton household, with its shaggy rugs, pristine bathroom, and quilt blankets, had felt like a familiar slice of heaven.

Vic hurried downstairs. Dan was at the table, drinking his coffee and reading his paper. He'd refused to take more than a couple of days off work. Quite aside from almost being burnt alive then crushed, sitting around was apparently driving him crazy. Martha was standing flipping pancakes behind her husband, looking radiant in the bright morning sunshine beaming in through the kitchen windows. Mrs Templeton tended to rise late, so her guests had the run of the kitchen for much of the morning.

"You look like you're in a rush," Dan said over the edge of his coffee mug as Vic raced by. He doubled back to give him a firm slap on the back, followed by a hug and a peck on the cheek for his mom.

"Today's the day," he said, snatching a white envelope from where it was sitting propped up on the kitchen counter. He slipped it into his back pocket and headed for the door.

"Already?" Martha exclaimed. "I didn't think it was until this weekend!"

"Nope," Vic replied, stepping out into a fresh September morning.

"Won't you have any breakfast?" Martha called after him.

"Just save me a couple of pancakes," he shouted back over his shoulder, and then he was out and onto the street, hurrying.

He got to the stop on West Main just as the bus was pulling up. He waited, equal parts excited and nervous. The letter felt heavy in his back pocket.

A few people got off the bus, none of them giving him a second glance. Then the whole vehicle seemed to tip slightly, the suspension groaning. A heavy shape stepped awkwardly onto the street, struggling to exit down the front door steps.

"Rocky," Victor beamed.

"Lizard boy," Santo said.

"We were wondering if this was the right stop," said another voice behind Vic's old roommate. "Jonas has been insisting on using a paper map instead of our phones."

Santo stepped aside, and there stood Graymalkin and Cipher, the former in a plain black T-shirt, shades, and jeans, the latter in a gray hoodie, yellow bandanna, and lean black sweatpants.

"Welcome to Fairbury, kids," Vic said, greeting each in turn. "It's so awesome that you're finally getting to visit."

"I mean, it's not quite a road trip through the Rockies," Ci said with a sarcastic smile. "But hey, who doesn't want to spend the last few days of their summer vacation in rural Illinois?"

"And we have so many sights to show you," Vic said, beckoning the gang to follow as he set off along East Locust Street. "How was your trip?"

"Quiet," Graymalkin said. "Which, given our recent occupation, has been a blessing."

"Summers didn't give you any trouble?"

"Summers is way too busy with the Institute's internal review to care about where the students are headed for break," Cipher said. "And after what we did, I think he'd rather not have us around at the start of school anyway."

"We're going to have to retell all this so many times next semester, aren't we?" Vic said with a smile.

"Just wait until I have to tell the X-Men about it," Santo added.

They swapped news as they walked. After the incident in Brooklyn they'd returned to the Institute with Victor's dad, where there'd been a rather tear-streaked reunion between Dan and Martha. Cyclops had permitted the Borkowskis to leave with their son while Cipher and Graymalkin provided him with a detailed debriefing on their first successful assignment. Any remaining talk of being expelled had been put to bed. Santo had been granted leave from his own operations with the Hellions in order to rest and reknit his shattered frame. He admitted to Vic that he was secretly glad of the respite – he missed their dorm back at the Institute.

As they walked Vic asked cautiously about Sublime Corp, and Lobe. He'd been avoiding the news ever since that day in New York, refusing to let those desperate weeks take up a second more of the life they had almost ruined. Santo told him that apparently Lobe was being held at a secure location by the X-Men, and the Institute was handling his, Ci's, and Gray's side of things. There was no doubt that the eventual trial would be drawn out and fraught, but Sublime Corp's stock had already nosedived, and its board of directors had closed up. The subsidiary companies were vanishing as quickly as they had appeared, and the facility on Rikers Island was now a federal crime scene. Whatever fate awaited Lobe, it would no longer be that of a so-called genius businessman.

"And what about the Purifiers?" Vic asked as they turned onto the shady lane he'd once called home.

"Xodus's remains were recovered from the ruins of the Church of the Seven Virtues," Cipher said matter-of-factly. "Almost all rallies appear to have been cancelled. It seems like local law enforcement and the state governments have found the guts to crack down on the cult."

"Better late than never," Vic said, and came to a halt near the end of the lane. Once upon a time he'd have been looking up the front yard at his home. He supposed that was still the case, though the home in question was currently only partially finished. Work on the new Borkowski residence, built over the bones of the old, had continued for the past two weeks, funded in part by donations from across Fairbury. Vic had successfully encouraged his parents to look at it as a fresh start. There'd be a huge underground garage where Dan could store his electronics surplus, and a trio of expensive glass cases in the living room to show off all of the new crockery Martha was already in the process of ordering online. It would never be their old home – it would be even better.

Vic greeted the builders in passing and stepped into the hallway, joking about Santo having to tread lightly. Most of the rooms were in the process of having their wiring installed and were still stripped bare. The living area was starting to take shape though, with a fireplace and a freshly laid carpet. Vic had already added the house's first decorative item – his toy dinosaur was standing proud on the mantelpiece overlooking the otherwise empty space. He took up position in front of it, facing the other three as they came in and looked around.

"It seems nice," Cipher said.

"Looks solid enough," Santo rumbled.

"A pleasant abode indeed," Graymalkin said with a smile.

"It'll be fine," Vic said. "Even better once we've got some more stuff to go inside. I didn't just bring you up here to check out my new home though. I've got an announcement to make."

He cleared his throat, drew the envelope from his back pocket and opened it. He paused after drawing out the sheaf of papers inside, clearly looking for a reaction from his audience.

"What is it?" Ci asked.

"Wouldn't be very dramatic of me to just tell you, would it?" Vic said, flashing her a smile before beginning to read off the headed letter.

"The General Assembly of the State of Illinois hereby ratifies and makes note of the successful application of Mr D Borkowski and Mrs M Borkowski for the adoption of the underscored, Mr S Vaccarro, Mr J Graymalkin, and Miss A Tager. The Board of Adoption now awaits the formal response of those listed, and the binding agreement thereof. For more details, please see the enclosed documents, sections B1 through F7."

He lowered the paper and looked up at his friends, suddenly nervous. They stared at him.

"Is this a joke?" Cipher asked slowly.

Vic shook his head. "I spoke to my parents not long after we got back to Fairbury. We thought, I mean, I thought, that this might be a nice way of paying you back for saving our lives. Even if it's just symbolic… I reckoned that maybe we'd make it more than just friends. I thought we'd turn our first team into a family."

Santo and Cipher stared, but Graymalkin rushed forward with a speed that belied the fact he was standing in a sun-drenched living room. He hugged Vic, and when he finally let go there were tears in his eyes.

"I do not know what to say," he murmured.

"It's going to make for some crazy family reunions down the years, that's for sure," Cipher said, smiling as she tried to hide her own tears. Santo just grinned.

"Guess it's lizard bro from now on, huh?" he said. Vic laughed and gave him a bump with his thick right fist.

"I wasn't sure how you guys would take it," he admitted. "I didn't want to be too forward. But after everything that's been said, everything we've done and been through, it just felt like it was the right thing to do. If you want, you can sign your names and I'll send these forms back. If not, it doesn't really matter."

He took in the three of them as he continued.

"The important thing is we all know we've got each other's backs. First team or family, it's all the same thing."

ACKNOWLEDGMENTS

I would like to thank and pay tribute to my publisher or, more accurately, to the many personalities that constitute it – Anjuli, Gwen, Lottie, Marc, Ness, Nick and Vincent. You have all made my work as an author more than enjoyable. A thank you also goes out to the Marvel team making this book possible, and to the original writers who first came up with the wonderful characters that feature in the pages of *First Team*. On the shoulders of giants.

ABOUT THE AUTHOR

ROBBIE MACNIVEN is a Highlands-native History graduate from the University of Edinburgh. He is the author of several novels and many short stories for the *New York Times*-bestselling *Warhammer 40,000 Age of Sigmar* universe, and the narrative for HiRez Studio's *Smite Blitz* RPG. Outside of writing his hobbies include historical re-enacting and making eight-hour round trips every second weekend to watch Rangers FC.

robbiemacniven.wordpress.com
twitter.com/robbiemacniven

MARVEL

Two exceptional students face their ultimate test when they answer a call for help, in this action-packed Xavier's Institute novel of mutant heroes.

Sharp-witted, luck-wrangling mercenary Domino takes on both a dangerous cult and her own dark past, in this explosive introduction to a new series of Marvel adventures.

MARVEL

In a realm beyond Earth, mighty heroes do battle with monsters of myth and undertake quests to restore peace and honor to the legendary halls of Asgard and the Ten Realms.

The young Heimdall must undertake a mighty quest to save Odin – and all of Asgard – in the time before he became guardian of the Rainbow Bridge.

The God of War must explore a terrifying realm of eternal fire to reclaim his glory, in this epic fantasy novel of one of Odin's greatest heroes.